THE VINES OF DE GRESSIER

The Vines of de Gressier

1921 - 1958

Charles Bunker

YOUCAXTON
PUBLICATIONS

ISBN: 978-1-913425-82-1
Published by YouCaxton Publications 2021
YCBN: 01

YouCaxton Publications
www.youcaxton.co.uk

Cover art by: Timiarts Design
Typeset and cover design by Ella Knight Designs

Books in the de Gressier Series

The Vines of de Gressier - Family Tree

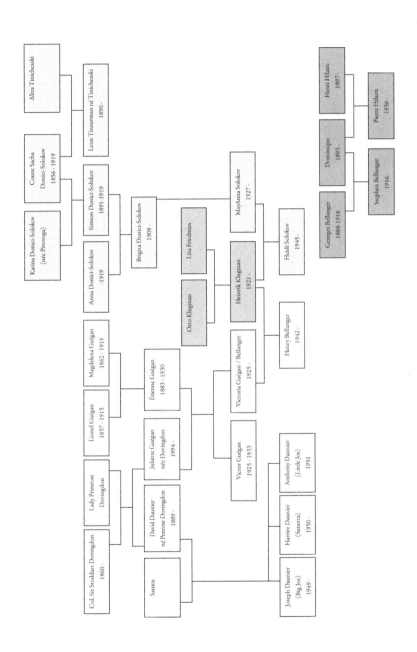

The Vines of de Gressier

This is a story which only the grandchildren can tell for they are not the secret keepers.

Prologue

Welborough Green, Sussex, England, May 1918

Dearest Penrose,

I trust you are safe and well.

Thank you for your letter. I am so pleased with your answer on Mills[1]. I worried about your reply, as I couldn't possibly have married a man who didn't agree that men and women are equal; and yet I wasn't too anxious because I knew I would find satisfaction in your answer.

Things are much quieter here now the men, who were camped all around, have gone. We don't know where, and we aren't allowed to ask, but I suspect they've been sent to France. Rationing is all people talk about. It wasn't too bad when they rationed just sugar, but the limits on meat, flour, cheese, butter, and milk have caused great difficulty. It means Papa's pubs are much quieter. But we don't grumble because we know it's far worse for you. I just hope it's far, far worse for the Germans.

I am ploughing through Juliette's reading list which she sent me. Half of what I have read is quite ridiculous. I am told it is to make us think. The only thing I think is what a waste of time it all is. I

---

[1] In earlier correspondence, Drew had written to Penrose asking whether he agreed with John Stuart Mills, as set out in his book The Subjection of Women, that there should be perfect equality between men and women.

don't think anyone at Cambridge has considered the syllabus for over 100 years. I had hoped that I had left Latin and Greek behind but thankfully it's coming back to me. Why I must read Aristotle in the original Greek text, when there are lots of good translations, is odd. However, there is a strange satisfaction about getting a translation right and doing a job properly which I did only half-heartedly at school.

I was wondering where we might live after the war, for I am sure it will be won now the United States has joined in. They are so big that the Germans don't have a chance. Of course, we will have to live in Cambridge for a while, but after that, will you come to Sussex? I don't think I could abandon its beloved countryside. Kent is horrible, particularly in winter, but Sussex is delightful all the year round.

I enclose a photograph of me as you asked. I wasn't sure whether I should send it, for I didn't want a man who wasn't going to marry me to have a picture of me in his wallet. Think of the problems it would cause if he were to marry someone else. It would mean my picture torn in pieces or kept as a secret, neither of which is acceptable to me.

Nothing is formal between us. My brain tells me, in these uncertain times, we should be satisfied with our understanding, but my heart is in turmoil as it challenges my logic, for our arrangement does not say enough about how I feel. I worry constantly that you might still see me as too young. I have so much to learn.

In this confusion, I have decided you can only have a photograph of me on two conditions – that you send me a picture of you, and you promise that, if you ever decide to marry someone else, you will return my picture to me.

You might recognise what I am wearing. It is what I wore when we had afternoon tea in Brighton. It was such a special occasion.

With enormous fondness and affection.

Drew

Chapter 1

South Africa February 1921

DAVID DAUNIER, NÉ David Victor Penrose Dovingdon, arrived in South Africa in February 1921. He was thirty years old but looked much, much older. There was not a mark on his body, but he was a man broken, both physically and mentally, by war. All he wanted was to be left alone to lead a quiet and simple life. When he walked down the gangplank at Port Victoria in Cape Town he had a number of objectives in mind: to buy a small farm so he could plant a vineyard with the vines he had cultivated when convalescing at Château de Gressier, to earn a modest living, to keep a very low profile, but above all to find peace.

His departure from Château de Gressier, and the care of his sister Juliette Guégan and her husband, Étienne, was carefully planned. If they had known he was leaving they would have tried to stop him, but then they had no idea how his circumstances made him feel a prisoner in the freedom and protection they gave him.

David left Bordeaux with a small valise packed with one change of clothes, his washing and shaving kit, his father's officers' cane with its silver head embossed with the emblem of the Hampshire Regiment, and the last letter he had received from Drew Stubman which contained her photograph. He had read her letter a thousand times and stared at her picture more often than that. In his mind's eye, the photograph changed so he could see the thickness of her hair, the colour of her eyes and her beaming smile as she waved him an anxious goodbye. It was the last time he would see her, and this was the last letter from her he would ever receive. David had experienced a lot of death during the war, but none had affected him as deeply as his loss of Drew. Would he have run away if she had lived? It was a question which would plague him for the rest of his life.

The first boat leaving Marseilles was going to South Africa and not Egypt as he had hoped. It meant that his longed-for trip through the Suez Canal and to see the pyramids was not to be. It was also quite fortuitous for his precious de Gressier vines would never have survived in the Kenyan climate, where he first planned to make his home. Instead, David crossed the equator on 1st January 1921 and thought how auspicious it was that with the New Year, and a new decade, came a new hemisphere.

Cape Town was again in the grip of the fear of the influenza virus when David's boat docked. On disembarkation, he was instructed to go straight to the Mount Nelson Hotel, which had been declared a 'plague free zone'. He found this most unsatisfactory. Unlike his ship, where his fellow passengers were small in number but were an eclectic international group as could be assembled, The Mount Nelson Hotel was a fiefdom of Englishness where each visitor sought to establish the credentials of the other and their ranking in society. It worried David for, in such a place, his secret could easily have been revealed.

Feeling very conspicuous, David kept himself to himself by reading books from the hotel library and writing down everything he could remember about unbreakable cyphers and codes. This had been his hobby since a schoolboy. Every night, just before he climbed into bed, David would look at Drew's photograph and read her letter. He took comfort from her words for he had always doubted whether she would marry him, but her answer was there on the paper. It was not in plain back and white, not in a yes or no, but in code which was as transparent as could ever be written. If only things had been so very different.

David broke out of The Mount Nelson Hotel after two weeks and well before the quarantine was lifted. He could take the claustrophobia no more. He hired a car to go in search of land to plant his vines and headed off in no particular direction. In one of those serendipitous, life-changing moments, he found a fruit farm which was for sale, ten miles outside Paarl. A husband and wife team wanted to retire and return to Wales. As a result of their ages the farm was run down so David was able to buy it quite cheaply with the cash he had brought from France.

David knew nothing about fruit farming or how difficult it could be. It turned out to be much harder than he thought, but unlike the owners before him, David worked the fields himself. Instinctively, he considered every plum not as a commodity but as actual cash, worth real money. It was this philosophy which saw his trees yield more fruit year on year, and with a strong market for plums in England, David started to make a good living; that was until 1929.

Chapter 2

Munich 1920

IT WAS A silly game. She knew it was, but she couldn't help herself. In her old age she would look back and wonder why she did it, but at that moment, Lisa Friedman didn't care. Much later, when, as part of her training to be a doctor, she was forced to study her own personality, she discovered it was about her need to win, however small the victory. Through self-analysis, she had learnt that winning was an important part of her make-up. It was deep within her psyche. The question was whether it was nature or nurture that made her this way. She thought it was primarily nurture for, as the only girl in a family with three elder brothers, she always felt she was in a fight for survival. It was something which had not served her brothers well.

Her elder brother was one of the very few Germans who fought in the Gallipoli Campaign[2]. He was a Festungs Offizer with the Pioniere whose unit volunteered to advise and supervise the Turks in mining the ANZAC beachhead. She never knew how, when or exactly where he died and always wondered whether his grave was marked with his name on a headstone. Her second brother was a young Lieutenant on SMS Frauenlob. She knew exactly where he lay buried, for his ship was sunk during the Battle of Jutland[3]. Her youngest brother had been so severely injured in the first few days of the Battle of Verdun[4] that his war was over before it had even begun.

---

[2] The Gallipoli Campaign ran from 17th February 1915 to 9th of January 1916.

[3] The Battle of Jutland was a naval battle fought between 31st May and 1st June 1916. Over 320 died when SMS Frauenlob sank. Only 9 of her crew survived.

[4] The Battle of Verdun was fought between 21st February 1916 and 18th December 1916.

Lisa Friedman got into Munich University Medical School because of one thing: her determination to win. Now, for her brothers, she wanted to be the best doctor she could possibly be.

"I am told you have Schumters Anatomy," said Otto Klugman addressing Lisa in the same stage whisper in which all discussions in libraries are held.

Lisa looked up and smiled victoriously. She had seen him come in, as he had done for the last four days. She had deliberately kept her head down, as though she were studying the book in front of her, but her thoughts were only on one thing: willing him to come across and talk.

"Yes," she replied looking back down at her study book as she spoke.

"I was wondering whether you were using it?" asked Otto.

"Yes," she lied, trying hard not to look up.

"Do you think I could borrow it for a minute?"

"Yes," she said again, taking a book from the middle of the pile she had placed by her side on the library table. She held it out for him. "One minute," she repeated quizzically, clearly seeking his confirmation.

Otto paused for he needed the book much longer than that. In his hesitation, Lisa snatched it back, winning yet again.

"Perhaps a little longer," he said, disappointed at the loss of his prize. "Perhaps thirty to forty minutes."

"Thirty minutes," said Lisa. The look on her face told him there was no room for negotiation.

Ten minutes later, Otto handed back the book. The look on his face showed he had failed in his task. As he did so, Lisa smiled the most delicate and delicious smile, and with it, she captured his heart. There was something about that smile which told him that this was just a game, which is exactly what it had been.

Lisa had no need for a book on maxillofacial surgery. She was light-years away from studying that medical specialism, if at all. All that had happened was that, when she heard Otto ask for the book when it was already lent out, she guessed he would be back. So, the next day, as soon as the library was open, she borrowed the book and waited. Two days in a row Otto sought the book only to find it was out. In her eyes, Lisa had won, and he had been defeated. Now, on the fourth day, and desperate to resolve a debate with a couple of his classmates, Otto presented himself in front of her, tongue-tied and flushed with embarrassment. Before him was a girl who had already taken his eye for she was a mix of plain and pretty at the same time. Plain because she took little care about the way she looked, other than making sure everything was neat, clean, practical. There was no time in her life for anything else, including makeup. She was pretty because her face was balanced and delicate, dominated by bright eyes, framed by thick wavy blonde hair cut in the bob fashion of the times.

There was no obvious reason why Otto Klugman should have been in the medical library for he was studying at the Clinic of Veterinary Surgery. It was common knowledge amongst every veterinary student that pigs, like humans, develop two generations of teeth. This fact alone made Otto argue that the jaws of humans and pigs had a common muscle structure, even though he had no basis for his argument other than instinct. It was an argument which Schumters Anatomy should have helped him win. It did not.

"Was it helpful?" asked Lisa as Otto returned the book.

"I'm afraid not. I was looking for a simple diagram or drawing of the muscle structure of a human's jaw to show how it works. I need to compare it to a pig's," he said.

"That's easy," said Lisa. Over the next few seconds, with her pencil skipping across the page of her notebook, she sketched the human jaw, labelling the bones, muscles, and ligaments. So intense were her thoughts that she no longer noticed the man sitting before her. Not Otto, he was studying the finesse of her hands and the dexterity of her long fingers as they moved rapidly.

"Where is yours?" asked Lisa when she looked up.

Otto looked confused.

"Your drawing of a pig's jaw."

Otto didn't have one, so he clumsily drew one from memory. He badly lacked Lisa's deftness of touch. In Lisa's world, where there was always a winner and a loser, she had won the sketching competition too.

Very quickly, they identified enough commonality for Otto to claim a win in his argument with his colleagues.

"May I keep this and buy you a coffee to say thank you?" he asked, pointing to her drawing. His initial nervousness was gone. If he had been asking her out on a date it would have been different. Otto had already rated her highly in the beauty stakes, well beyond his league. His fear of humiliation, merely from the thought of her rejection, meant that, in all probability, he would never have had the courage to ask her.

Otto should not have feared, for in Lisa's eyes, he was one of the more eligible men she had seen in her days at university. The sad fact for Lisa, and all her women colleagues, was that the male stock had been badly depleted by four years of war. The pickings were not good. Through her time at medical school, there had been far fewer male students on her course than in past years, as all full-bodied men had been doing their duty, fighting at the front. Lisa dismissed her contemporary male students as likely suitors, for in her mind, they should have been in the army, serving their country.

It was obvious to Lisa, from his age and demeanour, that Otto was a *recurrit*. The name used by the university for those who had returned to finish their studies after an interlude forced by war. Her evidence was his face which had the leathery look of a man who had spent years outdoors baking in the sun, beaten by rain, and cracking in the freeze of winter. There was something else. Otto gave out the aura of a man who had never been defeated. His army might have lost, but not him. He held himself as erect and tall as he did on the day he was commissioned as an officer.

The invitation was music to Lisa's ears. It was what she wanted him to ask. There was no doubting in her mind that she had won again. She had been invited out by someone comfortably older than her and by one of the better-looking men.

"Yes, at lunchtime, that would be nice, thank you," she replied confidently.

Otto couldn't help but notice the aristocratic tone in her voice and the crispness with which she spoke. He was supposed to be at lectures later that morning but, after hearing her speak, he was not prepared to mess up on the chance of having a cup of coffee with the lady in front of him, so he took a seat at her table, reached into his satchel, withdrew the books he needed for that day's lectures and tutorials and started to study.

They sat diagonally opposite each other in complete silence, only looking up occasionally to examine the person in front of them. When their eyes touched, they each smiled and, with embarrassment, turned quickly away. Neither noticed the commonality: their Aryan blonde hair and blue eyes.

It was past lunchtime when Lisa started to pack up. Otto followed quickly. It was only then that he noticed how slim and petite she was. His eyes could see over the top of her.

Within the cocoon of the university library, it was as though World War I had never taken place. As Otto and Lisa walked out on to the streets of Munich, their lives were taken back to reality. A life where there was real hardship. Inflation had started to get out of control. What you could afford yesterday, you could no longer afford today. A loaf of bread, which cost one Deutschmark in 1914 was now costing ten times as much. This uncertainty, coupled with the survivors of war learning that there might be no tomorrow, meant that everyone lived for today. As a result, there was a new carefree attitude in the coffee bars and nightclubs of Munich. They came alive to the sound of Jazz, the Blues and Ragtime.

Over coffee and sugary Berliner Pfannkuchen[5] the two shared their stories. Otto was in the last year of veterinary school; his final year had been deferred for the duration of the war. Lisa was in her fourth year at medical school with two more years to go before she qualified. As they spoke, both realised they came from the same kind of middle-class family. It meant that they always had more than enough money. This gave them a feeling of confidence in their place in society.

Lisa asked Otto about his war. He answered vaguely for, like many of his contemporaries in the veterinary corps, he started the war looking after the armies' animals. But as the casualty rate increased, someone in high command decided that veterinary skills were interchangeable, and so Otto was transferred to the medical corps to look after injured soldiers. In this role, he saw sights he would like to have forgotten. With a badly injured animal, you put it down and used its meat to feed the troops. However, a man with the same

---

[5] Doughnuts

horrendous injuries needed to be operated on and somehow put back together. Sometimes the wounds were so bad that Otto didn't know where to start. Now, like every German, he was pleased to be getting his life back to normal, but with the advantage that, at vet school, he was in his element. He found the decision making with animals easier. It was less emotional than dealing with the lives of humans.

Later, over schnapps, Otto and Lisa shared their desire to learn the new flapper style dance which had just come over from the United States. So that evening, in a fit of giggles and laughter, they went dancing at one of the new culture clubs which had opened all around Berlin and were quickly being copied in Munich.

The next day, Otto made several unsuccessful trips to the library to find her. It was on his last trip, when he saw Lisa sitting there, that he went and asked to borrow a book she had in her pile. He needed no such thing, but it started a teasing game that they would play with each other every day until the last day of the summer term.

Lisa came as Otto's guest to his graduation ceremony, after which they danced until the sun started to rise the next morning. She knew she shouldn't invite him into her college room but their passion, started on the dance floor, had to be consummated. It was impossible for the two lovers to imagine such a wonderful night never being repeated. By the time the trams started to rattle outside her bedroom window, carrying the early morning workers to their tasks, Lisa was pregnant.

Otto was thrilled when he learnt he was to be a father. Lisa was furious with him. In her world, it was entirely his job to make sure she was safe and didn't get pregnant. Angrily, she told him so. The fact that he was a medical student meant he should have known better. In her opinion, this made his neglect of her body doubly unforgivable.

The news of a baby started a whirlwind of activity. They had to get married. Otto had to find a training job and they had to find a home, and all of this had to be somewhere close to where Lisa could finish her training as a doctor. Under no circumstances was Otto's carelessness going to stop Lisa achieving her ambition.

Otto and Lisa's wedding was quickly arranged without either of their parents being told the reason for the rush, although both guessed. Otto's parents objected quietly amongst themselves, disapproving of their son marrying a Friedman, assuming that, with her surname, Lisa was Jewish. But, when they saw her blond hair and blue eyes, their objections were transformed into obvious delight.

Chapter 3

Bamberg 1921 - 1926

IT WAS WORK which took Otto and Lisa to Bamberg, much to Lisa's disapproval as it meant that, for a time, her medical studies were suspended. For how long she didn't know.

As war reparations hit the German economy hard it became nigh on impossible for any veterinary graduate to find a vet's practice that would employ them. Every graduate had to complete two years of practical training before they could get fully qualified. The realisation that, after fighting and training so hard, no one wanted to employ him was a body blow to Otto's self-esteem. It was Otto's father who concluded that the only way Otto was going to get the practical experience he needed was through the purchase of a veterinary practice from someone who would like to retire. Such an opportunity was found in Bamberg.

It was Otto's father who, because he was paying, led the negotiations. The house in which the vet lived and had his surgery was bought outright, although it was agreed that the owner would not move out for two years, until after Otto had qualified. Once Otto had his licence to practise as a vet there would be a payment for goodwill of one year's profits with further payments based on the next three years' sales. Otto would get paid during his two years of training, but it was only a token amount; far from a living wage. Going to his father for an allowance to maintain both himself and his family was a humiliation which Otto found unbearable. It created a tension between them which would never end; not even after Otto had repaid every penny to his father.

The allowance from his father, and his stipend from the vets' practice, was not enough to enable Otto and Lisa to afford the rent of an apartment in Bamberg. It meant that they started their married life in a tiny, rented cottage. It was set in a large nursery garden with an orchard and grazing fields. Running through the land was a river which could be crossed via a small make-shift wooden bridge to go into pine woods on the other side. It was ten kilometres south of the centre of Bamberg but only seven kilometres from his vets' practice. This meant that, on a good day, Otto could cycle there in less than twenty minutes.

It was during his training period that Otto Klugman began to despise his job. While he was good at dealing with domestic pets, as he empathised with their owners, it was in the unforgiving world of large animals where his views on their right to a quality of life was at odds with the economics of the farm. Either way, he felt he was permanently administering death. While putting an animal to sleep and out of its misery was sometimes the best thing to do, he found that too often the judgement of his client was influenced by their resources, or lack of them, and he hated it. Some people could deal with it. Many saw it as the right thing to do. The moral thing to do. Otto found he could not think so clinically. Too often he came back from his days work upset rather than feeling fulfilled.

The birth of their son Heinrik allowed Otto to find respite from his daily work travails, but three miscarriages over the next two years strained Otto and Lisa's marriage to its core. Each time Lisa got pregnant she got very cross with her husband, accusing him of playing Russian roulette with her life. She would then blame him for her failure to carry their child to its full term. Eventually, their relationship became too damaged to ever be repaired.

It was when the retiring vet moved out of the house with the surgery in it, that Otto and Lisa's relationship finally broke. It was a few months off Heinrik's fourth birthday. She locked their bedroom door to him and refused to move out of the cottage. Otto moved into the large vet's house on his own. The cause of their marriage breakdown was simple to explain. Lisa needed to be with winners. Otto's depression, created by a job he hated, meant he was no longer a winner.

Otto's early salvation came in the care he paid to the administration of his vets' practice. One evening, sitting alone in his surgery with a bottle of brandy by his side, it slowly dawned on him that the practice he had acquired was taking far more money than the previous owner had ever reported; over one third more and yet nothing had changed. Otto carefully went back through the books to discover that, in the past, none of the cash takings had been included in the accounts, only the money from those customers who paid by cheque was accounted for. The cash had simply gone into the back-pocket of the previous owner, tax unpaid.

This discovery presented Otto with a conundrum. Should he continue with the same accounting practice or should he be honest? More importantly, on what figure should he calculate the deferred consideration payment due to the previous owner. Should it be based on only those who paid by cheque or the full amount?

Otto would like to think that it was his higher moral standards which caused him to do the honest thing, but morality didn't come into his decision making. It was a letter from his last tutor at the Veterinary School which helped him make up his mind. 'Now he was in practice on his own account could Otto offer one of their best students a training place?' he was asked. Otto decided that, if he included in the accounts the cash takings, then this extra money would help pay for a trainee. He would be no worse off financially and better off personally, for he would not have to put down animals day after day.

It was when Otto gave the previous owner of his practice the first deferred payment that the opportunity to buy another veterinary practice was created. It was common practice amongst all vets that the cash takings were exclusively theirs and not shared with the taxman. A man who understood this, and was prepared to include this income in the amount calculated to be paid as goodwill, was a recommended buyer for other veterinary businesses when their owner wanted to retire.

Thanks to the honesty of his accounts, which created a trust in him by his bank, Otto was able to borrow the money needed to buy another veterinary surgery practice, together with its premises, on exactly the same terms as his father had negotiated for him;

then a third and a fourth and then a fifth. In each case he bought the premises, kept the name of the practice unchanged, hired newly qualified vets and trainees, whom he demanded should live above, or next door to, the surgery. He introduced strict operating protocols and kept tight control of the finances himself.

Otto quickly discovered the commercial joy of buying up competitor surgeries and becoming a monopoly supplier. Firstly, it allowed him to increase his prices, which he did substantially. Secondly, if one farmer decided to leave one of his practices because he didn't like the vet, the service, or the charges, then that farmer could only transfer to another one of his businesses. This way the work was always retained by him, and if a debt was outstanding to the former practice, then the work could only be transferred to the new one with a hefty payment upfront.

For all his commercial success Otto was unable to recover from the breakdown of his marriage. He could not pick himself up with enough energy and confidence to move on. Instead, he turned in on himself. He became negative, nasty, and uncaring, attracting amongst his so-called friends only those who were mean and gossipy. Lisa saw all these traits come to the fore in Otto's character, and she hated him for them, not least because he was not providing her with the money she needed for Heinrik and herself, although he could afford it.

Lisa found her freedom just after Heinrik started school when she gained a place at Ergland-Nuremburg University to finish her medical degree. It was not as straightforward as she would have hoped. Although she got excellent references from Munich University, Lisa was made to sit Ergland's second and third-year final exams to assess her competence. She revised hard and was disappointed to be told that her place was conditional on her having to repeat her third year. It was not what she wanted to hear.

Lisa would always say, in retrospect, that getting back into medical school was the easy part. Finding the money to go was almost impossibly hard. She knew Otto would not help her financially and her pride would not allow her to ask. The fact that Lisa's husband could afford to pay, but would not, ruled her out of any bursary which the university might have offered. At the outset Lisa had hoped that her family might fund her course, as they had done at Munich University. However, when French and Belgian troops marched into the Ruhr district in January 1923 to seize coal, in place of the gold bullion war reparation payments which had not been made, Lisa's family finances were all but destroyed. It was when the workers in the region went on general strike, and the German government printed money to pay for their resistance, that hyperinflation raced into the German economy. Lisa's family, along with millions of others, lost everything.

The Bund Deutscher Frauenvereine[6], the umbrella organisation of the German women's rights movement, introduced Lisa to a huge number of its affiliated groups. It was through an extensive letter-writing campaign that Lisa found the loans, grants, and gifts she needed to pay for her tuition and travel. There was nothing in the budget for her own subsistence.

Otto knew of Lisa's plans, but he was convinced that, even if she got a place, she would not be able to find the money to go to medical school. He learnt of her success on the first day of the new academic year. His response was both immediate and vicious. It was made in the form of a letter from his lawyer explaining that Lisa had no rights over his son. He demanded that, as a result of her neglect of Heinrik during her studies, his son should come and live with his father immediately. It was a fight which was to last two years. Finally, the court ruled that, on his seventh birthday, Heinrik was to move to live with his father. A few months later Lisa finished at medical school.

It was with enormous pride that she had her medical certificate recorded in her maiden name of Dr. Lisa Friedman. It was with even greater delight that she took up a junior doctors' job in Bamberg's hospital. For the first time, Lisa had money of her own. She might now have her freedom, but it came at a huge cost - the pangs of guilt for her son, who she missed dreadfully.

Otto didn't really want his son with him. He just didn't want Lisa to have him. Further, the antagonism that Lisa had against Otto had rubbed off on to Heinrik which added to an already complicated situation. Consequently, when he was not at school or at his studies,

---

[6] Federation of German Women's Association

Heinrik was either left with the vets in the surgery where he lived or was carted around by his father from surgery to surgery, and farm to farm. Wherever he was, Heinrik was expected to help, whether it be at lambing time, mending the bones of a cat or dog broken in an accident or cutting out a malignant tumour. By the age of ten, Heinrik was as competent at giving injections, administering anaesthetics, and sewing up an animal patient after an operation as any qualified vet. The only thing his father refused to let him see was an animal being put down.

Instead of Heinrik's presence being a joy to Otto, it had the opposite effect by adding to his anguish and misery. At every sight, his son reminded him of Lisa and his obsessional wanting of her. To ease his pain, Otto drank more and more. It was not unusual for him to drink a bottle of brandy in the evening before falling into a comatose sleep. As his hangovers became more aggressive and persistent Otto started drinking in the morning too and then injecting himself with heroin so he felt just a little bit better. Thus, started an addiction to alcohol and heroin which outwardly no one noticed as Otto worked hard to keep it well hidden.

It was in the haze of a cocktail of drugs that Otto's character changed to create a Gemini in character, both Mr Jekyll and Mr Hyde in one person. This not only made him vile to work for, as no one could tell what mood he would be in, but in his newfound megalomania he was driven to acquire more veterinary practices. Because most vets were bad businessmen, and unable to deal with the aftermath of hyperinflation, selling to Otto Klugman and working for him became their least worst option.

Driving around Bavaria to visit his practices and to see his vets at work, not only in the surgery but on the farms, was a relentless task causing Otto to spend many hours at the wheel of a car when he was in no condition to do so. It was the skills of a good salesman who, recognising a drunkard acting sober, persuaded Otto that he needed an aeroplane. Much better to fly directly from one farm to another than fight the roads, he was told.

After one flight, on a warm summer's day when the world from the sky looked magical and everything seemed possible, Otto contracted to buy a second hand Albatros D.III biplane. This was a former German fighter plane with the machine guns removed. It was only after the plane had been paid for that Otto was made to think about where it could be hangered. It was in a moment of pique that he decided that the plane would be stored at Lisa's smallholding; after all he was still paying its rent. The salesman, making the best of the opportunity, sold Otto a hangar and took a commission on the groundworks needed to turn Lisa's small holding into a grass runway. Lisa protested loudly but to no avail. As far as Otto was concerned, the lease was in his name and he was going to do what he liked with the land.

Of course, owning an aeroplane was a bad idea. Otto's senses, numbed by alcohol and drugs, meant he found learning to fly impossibly hard. The weather was never ideal and the idea of landing in a farmers' field was considerably less attractive than had been suggested, not least because farmers didn't want his flying machine disturbing their cows or ruining their crops. Just three trips after his first take-off as a trainee pilot, Otto abandoned the plane in its hangar to the schadenfreude of everyone who worked for him. In Otto's eyes he had failed again. This time publicly and he did not take failure well.

Chapter 4

South Africa 1929

DAVID COULD SMELL the Great Depression coming long before it came. Having worked in the British Treasury, he had an instinct that the US and UK economies were over-heating. When everything crashed, he worried for his future. Economic history had taught him that it was always the farmers who came off worse at times of recession. He cursed himself for not having remembered this when it came to buying a farm.

The biggest problem for all South African fruit farmers was that there was only one major buyer for their apples, pears, peaches, and plums. This was a large UK fruit-tinning business based in Liverpool. They set the buying price for the fruit, which they shipped in from both the Southern and Eastern Capes and then sold on at a huge profit as tinned products in the UK and around the world. As a result of the depression, they were insisting on lowering their buying price. Their buyer continuously argued he was doing the South African farmers a favour by buying their fruit at all, claiming that it could always be bought in the United States more cheaply. None of the South African farmers were brave enough to form a union to challenge the price reduction; not even finding out if the claim of cheaper US fruit was true.

David wanted to dispute this perceived wisdom, for he knew that their tinning factory was a large, expensive beast which they had to keep running to reach break-even, let alone be profitable. Without South African fruit as their input, they would have no output and thus no income. The trouble for David was that he could not lead the challenge and become the centre of attention. His life depended upon not being noticed.

For months David worried about what he was going to do when chance took him to the docks area of Cape Town to buy a stock of wooden pallets to better store his crop of plums. It was the overpowering smell of oily fish cooking which drew his attention to a small, scruffy factory with a newly painted sign which read 'Tinnerman Fish Tinning'. David walked nosily up to the factory entrance where he was met by the owner, Leon Tinnerman, whose Jewish religion was confirmed by him wearing a kippah on the back of his head.

Leon Tinnerman was one of five children born to his father, Count Sacha Donici-Solokov, and his mother, Aliza Tinicheaski. His parents were never married. The Count was an Orthodox Christian and Aliza was Jewish, and the religious dogmas of the time made their wedding almost impossible. To make matters more complex, the Count had another five children with his lawful wife. And so it was that the Count lived, time-in-and-time-out, with his *wives* as he called them, moving from one household to the other when one became disgreeable, and to the family's Woodman's Hut when they both did so.

The 1903 Kishinev[7] pogroms saw Leon's maternal grandfather's house and their workshop fire bombed and destroyed in antisemetic rioting. Leon's family escaped with their lives and just a few bars of precious metals which they recovered from their burnt out house the next day. The Count arranged for all of the Tinicheaski family, including Leon, his mother Aliza, his maternal grand-mother and grand-father, and his two brothers and two sisters, to emigrate to Kraków. His father promised to follow, but he never did. Leon never saw him again.

In Kraków, Leon's grandfather once again opened his gates as a blacksmith and all the family were put to work in the forge. When

---

[7] Kishinev is now known by its original name of Chişinău. After Bessarabia was ceded to Russia by the Turks in 1812, Chişinău became known by its Russian name of Kishinyou albeit that the country remained under the Romanian Government for administration purposes. After World War II, when Moldova became part of the USSR, the English language spelling of its name changed slightly to Kishinev. In 1991, with the collapsed of the Soviet Union, when Moldova became an independent country, the former Romanian language spelling of its name was formally re-adopted.

World War 1 came, and the Austrian government needed tinned meat and vegetables to feed its widely dispersed army, the Tinicheaski family entered the tinning business. As a result of this large, captive and demanding customer, and the fact that Kraków was never invaded, the Tinicheaski family's war was significantly better than most – no one died and no one went hungry.

After the war to end all wars, Leon's grandfather Mendel Tinicheaski thought it was time for his family to get back into the jewellery business. Mendel, like his father before him, had trained as a lapidarist, before economic need forced both of them to retrain as goldsmiths (a profession into which every male member of his family would follow) and then into the rougher, but more reliable, trade of a blacksmith.

It was in memory of a known wish of Leon's great-grandfather, Zechariah, that his grandfather instructed him to travel from Kraków to South Africa to source uncut diamonds for their newly planned jewellery business. It was on no more than a rumour that there were 'diamonds as big as rocks in them there hills' that the decision was made.

It was the immigration officer at Cape Town's port who changed Leon's surname to Tinnerman. The reason was simple. Neither being able to speak the other's language, he found Tinicheaski too complex a word to write on Leon's 1919 entry visa.

Yes, there were diamonds, but they were deep underground and not accessible to a man without a fortune. So Leon went back to making his living, doing what he knew how, firstly as an employed blacksmith and then as a skilled tin maker.

David and Leon chattered cautiously at first, but after a little while they found empathy for their business plights were the same. Over two hours spent together and drinking many cups of tea in a local but rather scruffy café, they created, on that day, a business relationship between the two of them which was to last over twenty years, with never a cross word spoken.

On one piece of paper, which was never signed and looked at again, they wrote down the key elements of a joint venture to can and sell tinned prunes. David would sell his prunes into their joint venture at the local market price. Leon would do the cooking, tinning, and shipping at cost. David would be responsible for selling the finished product. They would share the profits from their joint venture equally.

Leon thought little more of this meeting. In the meantime, David set himself to work, inspired by a conversation he'd had with the economist John Maynard Keynes, with whom he had worked in the British Treasury before the war. Keynes complained bitterly of the inefficiency of dried plums being shipped from around the world to Liverpool where they were canned, sold to the army, and then shipped to India. David knew that by canning locally and shipping directly to India there would be a huge saving in transport costs which would enable him to offer a much lower price.

The following week David arrived back at Leon's factory with a sack of dried plums which he asked Leon to wash, cook in syrup and tin into 24 cans with labels. David said straight away that he would pay for all the costs and made an immediate payment on account. By this offer, they established a partnership principle where each was more generous to the other than they were to themselves. In effect, they made sure that there was always more than 100 percent of goodwill to be shared.

David then wrote to Sir Warren Fisher, Permanent Secretary at HM Treasury, who he also knew from his time working there, saying that Keynes had suggested he write. He offered to supply the Indian army with prunes at a price which, when delivered, would be twenty percent less than they were currently paying.

Keynes had said nothing of the sort, but David knew that unless his letter came by way of an introduction it would go no further. He also wrote to the Earl of Birkenhead, the famous F.E Smith, who was Secretary of State for India, and to Sir Laming Worthington-Evans, Secretary for War, saying the same things. He reminded them of the million men of the Indian Army who served with the Allies in the Great War, and the health benefits of prunes. With each letter, David sent six tins of prunes for their examination and tasting.

When quizzed, Keynes couldn't remember a David Daunier but he didn't contradict, since he was well apprised of the problem and could remember speaking about it on more than one occasion.

Mysteriously all three letters, minus the tins of prunes, made their way to the same small room in the War Office; not an insignificant feat given the building had over 1,000 rooms on seven floors with over two and a half miles of corridor. Each letter had written on it the words 'please action' or something similar.

Letters flowed backwards and forwards as terms were negotiated and agreed. It was therefore a very satisfied David who, to Leon's great surprise, as he had almost forgotten about their agreement, arrived unannounced at his factory with a confirmed one-off contract for 25,000 tins of prunes: 12,500 tins for each of the Indian North and South Armies.

Leon protested that it was impossible to scale up and scale down his tinning factory for this one order. David argued that this provision was not in their agreement and pointed out that if each man in the Indian Army were to consume one tin of prunes every month then it meant the possibility of supplying over 200,000 tins a month. Provided Leon delivered a quality product, David was sure that there would be more and bigger contracts.

Leon ran through the figures with David, the profit was good, very good. What convinced Leon to honour his bargain was that the contract came with a British Government Bill of Exchange, endorsed by Standard Bank. It meant that, immediately the whole consignment passed over the side of the boat in Cape Town, and bills of lading were issued, they would get paid.

The Tinicheaski family's reputation for fair dealing was always more important to them than money, and Leon was of this mind too. Remembering how David had paid up front for the trial tins, and that there was no minimum or maximum order size in their agreement, they shook hands with each of them knowing that, of the two of them, Leon had the bigger task.

A loan from the richest member of Leon's synagogue, at an extremely high interest rate, enabled him to buy the extra equipment and hire the additional people he needed. With David's help, Leon then placed small orders for dried plums with all the major growers in both Capes, so everyone got a small share of their new customers' requirements.

Confident in future Indian army orders, David was the first person who refused to sell his plums to the UK buyer at the same price as he had been paid for the last five years. He demanded a twenty-five percent increase knowing this would not be accepted and he would settle for ten percent. If there was going to be a problem in their nascent tinning business, it would be in the supply of dried plums. Albeit David said nothing, the loose tongue of the British buyer meant that David's demand spread like wildfire amongst the fruit growers and, each buoyed with Leon as their new customer, the price was eventually set at twelve percent higher. Most importantly, they now all got paid immediately the plums left their farm gate. This meant a cash injection in each of their businesses, just at a time when, because of the worst recession in history, cash was getting very tight.

David's prediction was proven to be correct; the prune contract was extended time and time again until there was a regular order to supply 50,000 tins a month. He then won a contract to supply 5,000 tins of peaches. This time only charging fifteen percent less than the Indian Army was currently paying. Leon had mixed feelings, for although the tins were to be twice the size, the amount of work in preparing the fruit for canning was also twice as much. What offended Leon's sensibilities the most about this new contract was the specification for the label which read, 'Peaches, Officers for the use of.'

For most of the fruit farmers, the increase in the price of plums was not enough to offset the serious effects of the Great Recession. Fruit farms were regularly being put on the market and David, as a result of the profits he was making from his canning joint venture with Leon, was one of the few who had an ability to buy, and at the moment he was not spending his money.

The original vines from Château de Gressier took to the soil of South Africa as naturally as nature had intended. They had become well established and with careful cutting and grafting of the original vines, by September 1939, David had forty-five acres of land producing red and white grapes. There was only one snag. He could grow the grapes, but he had no idea how to make wine so, with a certain amount of dissatisfaction, he sold his crop to the local wine making cooperative. It was this frustration which regularly reminded him of his sister Juliette, her husband Étienne and the de Gressier winery. He would wonder wistfully how they were getting on.

Chapter 5

Bamberg September 1932 – January 1933

THE FIRST DAY of each academic year was one which would haunt Heinrik for the rest of his life. It was the day he discovered his father dead.

Dressed in his new uniform, provided by his mother as Otto neglected every item of his son's care, Heinrik went to say goodbye to his father before heading to school. The first sign something was wrong was the door to Otto's study was locked. It was never locked. The next clue was Otto's bed. It hadn't been slept in. Without alerting anyone else to his concerns, he went outside and finding the study window open just a fraction, Heinrik opened it fully and climbed through. His father was slumped in his chair. The accoutrements of his death, needle and two files of heroin, lay neatly on his desk. An empty brandy bottle was placed carefully on the floor next to where he sat.

Immediately, Heinrik phoned his mother using the phone on his father's desk. Through sobs of distress, he told her what he had found and what he thought had happened. "Father's dead! He's killed himself," he announced. For years afterwards Heinrik was cross with himself for crying. Like everyone else around Otto, Heinrik had no love for his father. The fact that he was his father, he decided, was not a good enough reason for tears.

There were constant knocks on the door and questions from the vets, nurses, and office staff as they turned up for work, but Heinrik had closed the window and drawn the curtains so they could not peer through. He refused to answer or let anyone in. It was only when his mother came that Heinrik unlocked the door. He let only her in before he rapidly locked it again. Lisa and Heinrik cuddled together as they gazed upon Otto's body. They shared a relief at his death.

Their nemesis was no more. A few minutes later the police and ambulance came, and they took control.

Before Otto's body was taken away, Heinrik gathered his possessions and moved out. He was going to live with his mother again in the small cottage where he was born. Heinrik had always felt strangely responsible for his father, but now, with him dead, a burden was lifted. He felt a huge sense of relief. He left his father's surgery confident that his life was about to start all over again, but this time with a positive, rather than a negative, spirit.

Otto's death was a shock, but not a surprise. For a long time Heinrik had known his father was drinking far too much and had secretly wondered if he was self-administering painkillers. Not for one moment did he think that his father would commit suicide. He was certain Otto was enjoying his power and his success far too much. But this was not to see the world through his father's eyes. While he appeared to have everything, he could not bear his self-loathing; just one extra file would put him out of his misery for a few moments longer, he had thought, as the needle punctured his skin. Like all the animals Otto had put to death, his heart simply stopped beating. His body overwhelmed by the drugs he had taken.

Lisa's biggest surprise came when Otto's Will was read, for he had not disinherited her as she had expected. A codicil made shortly after Heinrik was born left his son some money, but otherwise Otto's Will was unchanged from the day they were married. Lisa could not say the same thing.

Otto's inquest was quickly held. His death was recorded as misadventure which his insurance companies joined together to challenge. If the verdict had been suicide, as they would have liked, then they would not have had to pay out on the substantial life insurance policies which he had taken out as part of the banking arrangements to buy each of his vets' practices.

Otto's funeral was a strained affair. Over the years, he had lost all his friends, so they didn't come. Other than Lisa and Heinrik the only other attendees were his employees from all over Bavaria. They came out of duty and inquisitiveness. It was not to pay their respects to a man they had grown to dislike.

The fact was that the content of Otto's Will had become widely known, as was the requirement that a vets' practice could only be owned by a qualified vet. The senior vet in each of Otto's practices came to his funeral for one purpose; to register their interest in buying the practice in which they worked with the executor of Otto's estate. So started a whirlwind of disposals of Otto's vets' practices on the same terms as he had bought his first one.

Otto's bank, wanting to keep its lucrative business, lent to every one of the buyers. So keen was everyone to get the deals done, that the contract to sell the last vets' practice was signed on Monday 30 January 1933. It was the day that President Paul von Hindenburg named Adolf Hitler, führer of the National Socialist German Workers Party (Nazi Party), as Chancellor of Germany. It was three months ahead of Heinrik's twelfth birthday.

Lisa only kept two things of Otto's: his car because she needed one and the aeroplane because no one wanted to buy it. Heinrik kept his father's college dissecting kit. It was of the highest quality and an item to be treasured. He was sure he would need it one day. Otherwise, everything of Otto's was sold, even his cufflinks. Dr Lisa Friedman was now a very wealthy widow for, despite very many requests, Otto had denied her a divorce.

Chapter 6

Bamberg September 1935 to June 1939

USING THE PROCEEDS from the sale of Otto's vets' practices, Lisa bought the cottage which she had taken over renting. She also purchased an apartment in Bamberg close to the hospital where she worked. This enabled her and Heinrik's life to move into a simpler routine. They lived in the apartment during the week and at the weekends they went to the cottage.

Each day after school Heinrik would go to the hospital to get something to eat from the kitchen. There he would do his homework as his mother always worked until late. So familiar was Heinrik's routine that he became as much a feature of the hospital as anyone else who worked there. In the school holidays, and when he had nothing to do, he voluntarily attached himself to the portering staff, joining in, and then beating them at their practical jokes. It brought a sense of humour to a place where laughter was a rarity.

On the first Monday of the month following Heinrik's fourteenth birthday, Lisa watched proudly as her son, wearing his new summer uniform of black shorts and brown shirt, enrolled in the Hitlerjugend[8], as all his friends had done. Her faced beamed as Heinrik confidently swore his allegiance to Adolf Hitler.

Heinrik loved the activities of the Hitler Youth as it closely followed military training for its harshness and focus on physical fitness. Camping, hiking, and late-night marches were all part of his inculcation into the Nazi Party and the thesis that Germany was to live, even if individual Germans had to die. With his blonde

---

[8] Hitler Youth. From 1933 Hitlerjugend was made the sole youth movement for German boys. The Boy Scouts movement in Germany was later been banned in 1935.

hair and blue eyes, Heinrik was immediately identified as an Aryan German. So started his indoctrination. He was taught that amongst his Aryan race there was no class, for they were so much better than the rest. Above all, he learnt that the Jews were the enemy of the people.

It was in the second year in the Hitler Youth that Heinrik applied, and was accepted, to join the elite Flieger Hitlerjugend[9] for, with an aeroplane in his back garden, he thought it stupid not to take the opportunity to learn to fly. Heinrik joined a year-long glider training course where he learnt to build, and just about fly, a glider. For all his efforts, Heinrik never received the Aeronaut Certificate in Sailplane Flying that he coveted. Nevertheless, amongst his teachers, he found pilots who, just for the pleasure of getting into the air again, were ready to teach him to fly his father's Albatros aeroplane.

Although his age made it illegal for Heinrik to fly solo, after about ten hours flying and no more than 30 take-offs and landings, he took to the air on his own. He had never felt such freedom. At first, he did no more than circuits close to the landing strip at his home. Then he explored much further away, always following the roads, rivers, or train tracks to places like Nuremburg.

Once Heinrik had discovered the pleasures of solo flight, the Hitler Youth held no further interest for him. Instead his mind became focused on one thing: getting enough money to pay for fuel for his aeroplane which his mother point blank refused to fund. She thought his hobby dangerous, so she made it her task to do everything possible to discourage him.

It was the need for funds which made Heinrik approach the hospital administrator to get paid for the porter's job he had been doing voluntarily for more than two years. After a formal interview with the director of the hospital, Heinrik was given the job of Theatre Porter, working evenings, weekends and during every school holiday. It was an arrangement which suited Heinrik well for if he wasn't at school he was at the hospital, and if not at the hospital he was with Flieger Hitlerjugend and if he was doing none of these things, then he

---

[9] Flying Hitler Youth

was at the cottage flying his aeroplane; even in conditions when those older and wiser would have stayed on the ground.

"Better to be down here wishing you were up there rather than being up there and wishing you were down here," said an experienced pilot to him in the early days of his training. One day, after fog had rolled over the hills and hidden his landing strip from view until he was just feet above the ground, a terrified Heinrik took the expression to his heart. From then on, his personal safety moved high up Heinrik's agenda. It was something he became fastidious about, planning and preparing for every conceivable eventuality.

It was an easy move for Heinrik from theatre porter to scrubbing up and assisting as a theatre nurse on operations, particularly at times of emergencies, or when they were short of staff. It was on rare occasions that he helped his mother, who specialised mainly on organ and soft tissue operations. The other two surgeons who worked in the hospital and operated on everything, including orthopaedics, encouraged his involvement. When his mother was operating it became Heinrik's job to write down, in long hand, everything she said, for it was part of the quality control procedures of the hospital that the surgeons had to talk through their operations. A protocol too often ignored by her colleagues. Instead, they conscripted Heinrik to work at the sharp end passing sterilised tools, holding clamps and suction tubes, shining lights, and taking away limbs and other body parts as soon as they had been detached from the patient's body.

The mixture of working with his father's vets on animals at a very young age, writing up his mother's words and through observation of what happened in surgery whether it be something simple, such as the removal of inflamed tonsils, or the more complex, such as an above-the-knee amputation, gave Heinrik a practical medical education which surpassed the training received by many a qualified doctor.

For Heinrik, and all those who mentored him, it was obvious that, after school, he was going to follow in his mother's footsteps and become a surgeon; that was until one unfortunate moment changed Heinrik's destiny for ever.

Chapter 7

Bamberg June 1939

HEINRIK NEVER KNEW what it was that stopped him walking straight into the operating theatre. Perhaps it was the unusual rhythmical sound coming from inside. Perhaps it was just habit. Whatever it was, he stopped at the double swing doors, as he had done many times before, to check before entering.

As he looked through the gap, he could see his mother was bent over, laying across a hospital wooden trolley, her face looking straight towards him, as though on look-out, but she wasn't seeing. He could see her fingers were spread out wide, sometimes clawing at the wooden surface. Heinrik studied his mother's face and her mouth which at one moment was open and panting and the next grimacing. Her lips were pierced tightly together as her blonde shoulder length hair fell over her face which she kept sweeping away. He watched as she rested her chin, and then the side of her face, on the wooden trolley. But what he noticed above all was the bright yellow knitted jumper she was wearing. Then, seeing Herr Schmidt behind her, Heinrik realised that his mother was wearing nothing below her waist. Herr Schmidt, the surgeon whom he had so often assisted, was lying across his mother's back, sweating profusely, and performing just as he had seen many a snorting bull or boar at mating time. Heinrik's eyes were glued to the scene in front of him. He didn't want to watch, but all the same he had to see.

He took his eyes away to look up and down the corridor as though he were their lookout before moving back to look through the gap in the door. It was then that he saw his mother jerk involuntarily until she rested her head back down on the table. Heinrik watched as a wide smile developed across her face, which sang into his heart, for she rarely smiled. It looked as though she were genuinely happy. Heinrik turned away and tiptoed down the corridor somewhat confused for, at forty-four, wasn't his mother far too old to be having sex?

Heinrik said nothing to his mother or Herr Schmidt. The only tell-tale sign that he had seen anything, came from the disappearance of the yellow jumper. He couldn't bear the thought of seeing her in it again. He smuggled it out of their apartment and threw it away in the trash at school.

The constant embarrassment of seeing Herr Schmidt, and each time being reminded of that moment with his mother, was a sore which would not go away. It was the sole reason that Heinrik applied to join the Luftwaffe, rather than go to medical school as had always been planned.

When Heinrik told the Luftwaffe that he wanted to join them because he could already fly, his application was rejected. He was thought to be a fantasist as, although he'd been given the opportunity, he had failed to qualify as a glider pilot. It was only when he reapplied with letters from those that had taught him to fly that his word was accepted, and he was admitted to a Fliegerersatzabteilung[10].

---

[10] A recruit training depot

Chapter 8

Europe and South Africa September 1939

ONE THING UNITED the Dovingdon family on Sunday 3rd September 1939 for, although estranged, they were all sitting, ready to listen to the radio, and the British Prime Minister's broadcast to the nation and its empire. David was on his farm near Paarl. David's parents, Col. Sir Stoddart and Lady Primrose Dovingdon, were at home in Hertfordshire and his sister, Juliette Guégan who had reverted to using her first husband's name, was with her daughter Victoria at Château de Gressier in France.

"I am speaking to you from the Cabinet Room at 10 Downing Street," said Neville Chamberlain. On those words David stopped hearing. He remembered the room he once knew well. In fact, the day before World War 1 was declared, he had sat around the same cabinet table from which Chamberlain was now speaking.

"This morning the British Ambassador in Berlin handed the German Government a final note stating that, unless we heard from them by 11 o'clock that they were prepared, at once, to withdraw their troops from Poland, a state of war would exist between us," continued Chamberlain. David started listening again. *"I have to tell you now that no such undertaking has been received, and that consequently this country is at war with Germany."*

There was not a man or woman who fought or was involved in World War 1 whose blood did not freeze with those words: *"This country is at war with Germany."*

David's heart sank as he became overwhelmed with despair. For four long years he had seen the hell of war and now, twenty-one years after the last one had ended – the war to end all wars - his country was fighting Germany once more. It was unimaginable, inconceivable that they would have to repeat the agony of the past.

What about France? What about France? screamed Juliette inside her head, and then she heard Chamberlain say:

"We and France are today, in fulfilment of our obligations, going to the aid of Poland, who is so bravely resisting this wicked and unprovoked attack on her people. We have a clear conscience. We have done all that any country could do to establish peace."

On the realisation that France was at war too, fear and dread filled Juliette's body, for how do you tell people who were not there what war is really like?

"What does this mean? Do we have to leave? Should we go to England?" asked Victoria seriously as soon as Chamberlain had stopped speaking.

"What and leave everything here?" replied Juliette sternly. Then she paused. "I don't know ... leave Étienne and Victor here?" she asked ponderously

Victoria didn't answer for she found it an odd response. How could her father and twin brother be taken from their graves?

David paced around his large kitchen like a caged tiger. He didn't know what to do for the best. The Great War had weighed heavily on his mind throughout all the time he had been in South Africa. Now he wanted to go home to fight; to finish the job they didn't finish last time, but he knew, because of his military record, that was impossible. He would be arrested as soon as he appeared on England's shores. His conscience was only slightly assuaged by his age; now fifty, he convinced himself that he was too old.

Col. Dovingdon, Primrose, David, and Juliette each worried about the other for the rest of the day. Each of them was nervous, agitated, and restless. At night-time, unable to settle, David and Juliette deliberately went outside and looked skywards.

In the moonlight, David walked down to his vines now well established. He thought anxiously about his sister, perhaps she should come here, he wondered. From an announcement placed in The Times, he knew she had twin children, Victor and Victoria, but keeping to his vow, he had never been in touch. They should all come, he decided. It would be far safer for them all here in Paarl. As he thought more, he realised that Étienne' her husband, would never leave France, and he knew Juliette would not leave without him. David had no idea of Juliette's change in circumstances. That her son and two husbands were dead.

At the same time as David was thinking of Juliette, she was standing on the gravel drive of Château de Gressier all alone. She looked across the fields before she gazed skywards.

Albeit they were nearly eight thousand miles apart, David and Juliette stared at the moon as they recited a poem they had learnt in their childhood:

"When the moon is high
and its beam shines bright.
Then think of me, for
I will think of you."

Please David, please, please come home, prayed Juliette.

Unknown to David and Juliette, their father was doing the same thing in the garden of his home, Imptice House. He was truly a lonely and frightened man.

Chapter 9

Château de Gressier September 1939

THE NEWS OF war left Juliette feeling bereft and very lonely. She needed wise heads to discuss alternatives, and without her first husband Étienne, her brother David, or her Father for counsel, she didn't know to whom she should turn.

It was a strange lack of confidence for, released from the hypnotic influence of her second husband, Juliette, had very quickly rediscovered her true and original persona. She had recaptured the strength of character which she had used so effectively during her war time nursing career. It made her then, as it made her now, a highly capable and formidable woman. In fact, common with many people who find themselves free of a cult, she had the zeal of a convert. As a result, she engaged in the running of Château de Gressier, and in the activities of the neighbouring Latoire Village, with an energy and determination not seen since she first had her children.

The day after war was declared, Juliette drove into Bordeaux to see Dominique Hilaire. She had decided to ask her, and her husband Henri, what they thought this all meant.

Juliette was forty-five years old. Although she looked at least ten years younger, she didn't have the confidence in her looks which her appearance deserved. It was why she would always take an inordinate amount of care to choose what she would wear whenever she went to meet Dominique. The two women had the strangest of relationships. They both had good cause to loath the other, but they did not. They found a deep bond in their tangential history. Each time they met they were like friends who had never been apart. It was as if, had they chosen a sister, they would each have chosen the other.

Dominique lived close to the Jardin Public in Bordeaux. As a result of Henri's seniority in the Gendarmerie and the fact that he had led a modest and sober lifestyle before they were married, meant he had saved a considerable sum. This enabled them to afford a large house in one of the best areas of Bordeaux.

It was Dominique's skill which turned the house into the most elegant of homes. It made Juliette a little envious for everything in de Gressier was old and antique whereas Dominique's style was modest, understated but nevertheless very chic. None of their furniture matched, but each piece had been carefully chosen and then blended by colour across each of the rooms. Every item complimented the other as though it was meant to be.

It never occurred to Juliette that neither Dominique nor Henri would be available. In their absence, she went first to the offices of her accountant, Monsieur Delmas Junior. He had changed little since they first met nearly twenty years before. She then went to see Monsieur Liard, her lawyer. He was old when they first met and he had aged badly. His frailty was plain to see. He was well past the age when he should have retired. Juliette sought to discuss the implications of war, but neither man had the strategic vision she sought. She left these meetings unsatisfied.

In the hope she would now be at home, Juliette returned to Dominique's house at lunch time. Still she was not there. Instead she found her son, Stephen, by Dominique's first husband, Georges Bellanger. Stephen was tall and handsome with thick hair. He was twenty-three years old and at the start of manhood. He was at that stage in life where his body was beginning to fill out. There was something incredibly attractive about his demeanour, which came, not from a vanity, but from a confidence in his person and his purpose. Every time Juliette saw Stephen, she could not help but wonder if he wasn't Étienne's son for, they had too much in common.

"Mother's collecting Pierre," said Stephen immediately he saw her. "She will not be long. You must come in and wait for her."

"How old's your brother now?" asked Juliette, referring to Dominique's son by Henri.

"He's three; just started nursery school."

Juliette nodded. "I've come to ask your mother what she thinks will happen now we're at war." With those few words the conversation, which she had been looking for all morning, started.

"Germany lost the last war because she was starved to submission," said Stephen stridently. "It will try to do the same to Britain this time," he predicted. "France can feed itself, but neither Britain nor Germany can. This means it will be a war for the control of the seas," he said confidently. "To do that Germany will want to occupy of our ports along the Atlantic."

"Won't Poland's farmlands help feed Germany?" commented Juliette.

"Yes, they will," confirmed Stephen. "But they had possession of those last time, and they still ended up starving."

"Why?" asked Juliette out of genuine interest. "We only had rationing in England in 1918 and only then because people started hoarding food the year before. Until then we had a reasonable amount to eat, even on the Western Front. It wasn't particularly appetising, but we weren't hungry. If there were problems, it was in the logistics of getting food to the front."

"Last time, Germany thought solely about the war. They denuded their fields of men," replied Stephen. "We can't expect them to make the same mistake again."

"Will we get invaded?" Juliette asked anxiously.

"They might try, but we should be all right. We've built the Maginot line deliberately to defend ourselves against the German army. They will find it extremely hard to attack and cross that," said Stephen, confidently.

"Do you think we will be safer here than in England?" she asked.

"What, in Bordeaux? Of course. We'll be a long way from any fighting, and in any case, the war will be in the air and on the seas."

"Are you sure?" asked Juliette. "You just said Hitler would want to capture our port here."

"I think so, yes. But if we can get and keep control of the air, then our tanks will be able to stop any advance and then drive on to Berlin."

"Russia is not on our side this time," commented Juliette.

"It can hardly be said they were on our side last time, given the way they gave up," rebuked Stephen.

"We only won last time because the Americans came into the war, and that's not going to happen this time, is it?" she asked.

"We were winning before the Yanks came in," said Stephen, "but the fact that they did come made a huge difference. But I think that's right. Germany will try hard to avoid upsetting the Americans."

"What does this all mean for Château de Gressier?" asked Juliette.

"You sell to Great Britain, don't you?" said Stephen, more as a statement than a question.

Juliette nodded before mumbling, "Yes."

"Well, that market's gone. It's going to be almost impossible to transport luxury cargo like wine across La Manche."

"And the US?"

"My bet is that market will remain. As I said, Germany is going to take a lot of care not to bring the US into the war against them."

The two stopped talking for a little while as they contemplated their discussion.

"There's going to be a shortage of petrol," said Stephen confidently. He paused, "and the chemicals you need to keep your vines clear of disease."

"Why do you say that?" asked Juliette alarmed.

Stephen didn't answer. "You might think about producing industrial alcohol – ethanol, instead," he replied.

"Can we do that from wine?" asked Juliette.

"I think so, but I believe maize, wheat, potatoes, and things like that, are best."

"Are you saying we can make our cars run on alcohol?"

"With some modifications, I think so, yes," said Stephen.

"Do you know how to do that?"

"No, but I'm sure I can find out. You most probably have much of the equipment needed already in your winery."

Juliette was impressed for although Stephen's remarks were off-the-cuff, she thought they were well made. "What are you doing now?" she asked.

"I'm doing the same as my father before he was conscripted into the army. I'm an aeronautical engineer."

"That's lovely, well done," said Juliette, and she beamed an encouraging, but nevertheless embarrassed, smile.

"I completed my master's degree last year, but the company I work for hasn't won a government contract to put its latest plane into production. I've been told that my job finishes at the end of this month," he said in a depressed tone. "It's why I'm here. I'm going to Paris tomorrow for a job interview." Stephen paused as it seemed Juliette wanted to speak.

"I am sorry," she said empathetically.

"Getting work in aeronautics is extremely difficult," continued Stephen. "It's all dependent upon government spending, and this government hasn't been spending anything like enough," he added angrily. "They're about to spend now but it is far too late. They should have been doing it years ago."

"Do we have enough planes to defend ourselves?" asked Juliette quickly.

"On paper, yes. Britain and France together have about the same number of planes as Germany, but only the Dewoitine D520 has any chance against a Messerschmitt, and we have far too few of those."

"So we could lose the air war," said Juliette alarmed. "And, if this happens, from what you are saying, their tanks could come this way, rather than our tanks go theirs?"

"Perhaps it's a bigger risk than I previously thought," acknowledged Stephen pensively. "However, I am sure the country which controls the skies and the seas will be the country which eventually wins the land war," he added emphatically. "Its why losing my current job is so ... frustrating."

For the first time since Étienne had died, Juliette was having a strategy conversation with someone who analysed things in the same way as her brother and husband used to do.

"Would you like to come and work with me at de Gressier?" she asked wistfully.

"What would I do?"

"You would help us prepare for the war ahead," she answered. "You can work with us until you get a job working with aeroplanes again."

It was probably one of the best, and certainly one of the worst, questions she would ever ask in her life.

Chapter 10

South Africa September 1939

'IT IS A truth universally acknowledged, that a single man in possession of a good fortune must be in want of a wife,' wrote Jane Austen at the start of Pride and Prejudice. Certainly, it was a truth acknowledged by the mothers of the nubile women of Cape Town. Knowing David was unmarried, they saw him as potential husband material for their daughters. However, fearing his secret could be discovered at any moment, David had decided that marriage and a family was strictly off his agenda. The mothers and daughters came, presented themselves, and with so many women disappointed, rumours were started amongst the unkindest of them that his appetite lay elsewhere.

When making it clear to his last huntress that, for personal reasons, marriage was not possible, it dawned on him that he had missed out on a woman's touch for far too long. He had been managing his domestic affairs without finesse. He ate the simplest of food. It was a task he performed to provide his body with fuel rather than for pleasure.

It was a conversation with Leon which persuaded David it was time to take a housekeeper. "The last war was great for the tinning business," said Leon on the telephone the day after war was declared.

"I know," replied David. "My father always said war creates an opportunity to make a profit."

"How long will it go on for?" asked Leon.

"If France and England are not defeated in weeks then it will last years," David replied confidently. "It will all depend on when America enters the war. If the last war is anything to go by then, let us guess, five years?" he continued.

"Then we need to secure an extra supply of plums and peaches, but I think we should do apples and pears as well," said Leon.

The two men talked some more, and as they did so, David knew what his war effort would be. He was going to supply the Allied military forces with as much tinned fruit as he possibly could. To do that he was going to need some domestic help.

David considered the servants he had working in the house, on his farm and living in the local villages. He concluded that none had the sophistication or training he was looking for. In his mind's eye he knew exactly what he wanted; a mirror image of the housekeeper his father employed during all his growing-up years.

David decided he would recruit through an agency in Cape Town. With this mission in mind he parked up near the Castle of Good Hope and walked the length of Longmarket Street towards Shortmarket Street where, he had been told, he would find the best agency in South Africa for domestic servants.

It was past one o'clock when David arrived at the agency only to find it closed for lunch. He cursed and then wandered aimlessly back down Longmarket Street heading away from the heart of the city. The day was hot, and it was hard to be anything but lethargic. His strolling led him into a rough and rundown market established on some scrubland. David recognised it immediately as primarily a place where dayworkers were hired, and where they were returned at the end of the day. It therefore catered primarily for this customer base. Those lucky enough to be selected had gone to their labours. Those who were unlucky had drifted off, either for a day of petty crime or slow soul-destroying hibernation.

David had hired day workers from a similar market outside Paarl many times, so he was familiar with their set up. Without the fear which would have kept most Europeans away, he wandered around the stalls with his attention being drawn to the local craftwork, admiring the colourful shirts and the skills of the leather workers. His only precaution was to keep a firm grip on his few possessions, knowing that the local pickpockets would have stripped him clean of his money faster than a Piranha could strip the flesh off a bone.

At the back of the market there was a crowd of men gathered, mostly heavily set bearded Boer farmers. Interested by the hubbub, David moved forward to see what was happening. There was a makeshift platform of planks placed across up-ended empty oil barrels. On the platform was a young black girl dressed in a long white Victorian nightdress. There was a lot of jostling as some of the men fought to get to the front. The girl stared at the ground, cowed into submission as the shouting went on around her.

David watched, wondering what was happening, but it was when the man acting as the master of ceremonies shouted 'sold' that he knew exactly what had taken place; he had stumbled into an illegal slave auction. A shipment of boys and young men had already been sold and now it was the turn of the women, with the youngest last in the auction as they were expected to achieve the highest price. David watched as the young girl was led off the stage to the side of the highest bidder where money changed hands between him and the auctioneer. Every one of the men around him looked and smelled as though they had not bathed or washed for weeks.

Another girl appeared on the platform who looked like the girl just sold: young, petite, maybe a bit taller, wearing the same kind of white cotton Victorian nightie. As the auctioneer moved her around the stage, making her twizzle around, stretch her arms, upwards, outwards, sideways and forcing her to touch her toes, David could clearly see through the thin denier of the nightie.

"Christ, the poor girl's wearing nothing underneath," he said, aghast and out loud; a statement too obvious to all the other men who, if not bidding, had come in the hope of a peek at a naked woman.

On hearing David's comments, the girl looked directly into his eyes, holding her gaze. It was as though she was imploring him to bid for her. David looked away embarrassed for her and for him, but when he looked back, she was still looking at him; this time her head was cocked slightly sideways in a questioning pose. He thought he saw her start to mouth something, and then she stopped.

The bidding had already started when David's focus turned away from the girl to what was happening around him. In anger and disgust, he started bidding, and every time he was outbid, he raised his hand to bid whatever amount the auctioneer proposed. This was one auction he was not going to lose.

"Sold!" shouted the auctioneer, quickly dragging the girl to David's side, who was unaware of how much he had bid. The auctioneer clicked his fingers impatiently as David counted out the money from the wad of cash he had on him.

No sooner had David's money been taken than the auctioneer started again. Another girl came forward, looking almost identical in every way, but this time there was no imploring look. Instead, etched across her face was the look of sheer terror. David started bidding again. Once again, he had no idea how much he was bidding, but as the process went on, every instinct in his body told him he was in a rigged bidding ring, so he suddenly stopped. He watched as the girl was taken to the highest bidder's side, but the fact that no cash changed hands confirmed what was happening. Another girl came on stage, older, taller, sexier than the others, but dressed the same. She carried an air of disgust and defiance. This was the last and prized lot of the auction. David looked around the crowd. He was certain that there was no one around who was prepared to pay what he had paid for his first girl. David called the auctioneer forward.

"I will pay you one thousand rand for both this girl and the last," he said.

"Last girl sold," said the auctioneer.

"Yes, back to you. I repeat one thousand rand for both girls."

"Fifteen hundred," said the auctioneer.

"No, I paid five hundred rand for the first girl and I will pay the same price for these two."

"But they are good virgins, I guarantee it. Look at that girl," said the auctioneer, pointing to the eldest of the three, "what a great fuck she will be."

David shook his head. "Twelve hundred rand, but you and the girls will have to come to the bank so I can get the extra money, or it's one thousand rand because that's all the cash I have."

The auctioneer thought for a moment, spat on his hand, and then, taking David's hand, shook it vigorously confirming a deal done at one thousand rand for the last two girls.

As David drove back to his farm, he realised he had not achieved his objective of a housekeeper. Instead, he had created a problem for himself. What the hell was he going to do with three girls, any of whom might have come from his surrounding villages? What would everyone think when the news broke out?

The eldest girl, who was the last to be auctioned, called Destiny, sat in the front of the car with Satutu and Newday sitting in the back. Satutu was the one who had looked at him with pleading eyes and a questioning tilt of the head. None of them knew their ages and, apart from Satutu, their level of English and their accents made it hard for him to understand what was being said. Questions about school appeared to fall on deaf ears, suggesting to him that they had little or no education.

David could not help but be fascinated by Destiny for she had an allure and style of behaviour which he found disconcerting. As they travelled, she deliberately slid down into her seat so that her head rested against its back. As she did so, the darkness of her nipples showed through the V neck opening of her Victorian nightdress, and she deliberately lifted her buttocks and opened her legs so that the light cotton fell to accentuate the upthrust of her pubic bone. She was deliberately making it obvious that she wasn't wearing any underwear.

David kept looking down at Destiny's hips and legs as he wondered why she was deliberately posing like that. As time went on and she extenuated this provocative pose, it became obvious to him that this girl's experience was not as the auctioneer had described. Was she seeking attention or was she using her sexuality to get what she wanted? Whatever the reason, David's antennae shouted danger, and he started to worry. For a start, he was certain it would be a criminal offence to buy slaves, and with a girl like that by his side, he knew he was in deep trouble. He needed to find a way out and fast.

Immediately David arrived in Paarl he parked his car, and in a very embarrassed state, he took the three girls into the local dress shop where the European owners' immediate reaction was to protest that they didn't serve black women. David dismissed their complaint quickly arguing that they weren't serving them but him, as they were coming to work on his farm and in his house as servants. He demanded that they were to be equipped with school clothes, servants' clothes, and underwear to last a week. David then excused himself, leaving the girls behind in the shop, as he drove the few hundred yards to the local police station. There he reported what he had done; arguing that he had not bought slaves but instead had purchased their freedom. It was immediately obvious to David that a black slave market in Cape Town was of no interest to the two white policemen he spoke to. It was as a matter of courtesy to David that they both agreed to write what he had told them in their notebooks. Simply to shut him up, they agreed that the Station Sergeant would be out at his farm the next day to take his statement in full.

Back at the dress shop, the three girls were dressed either in light blue shift dresses, which were part of the school uniform for the local girls' school, or in black pleated skirts with white blouses and white aprons, as might be worn by a servant. There was a debate as the shopkeeper reluctantly agreed to accept David's promise that he would come back the next day and pay.

David had not done much to the house since he bought it, apart from normal maintenance and regular painting. It was a big family house, but he only occupied three rooms: his study, his bedroom, and the kitchen. In his study, at pride of place on his desk in a silver frame, was his treasured photograph of Drew Stubman. He never went into the sitting room, dining room, or playroom. Even after twenty years, they were still not furnished.

David loved his library for it was just as the previous owners had left it, with the fine carvings on the Victorian desks, tables and chairs matching those on the built-in cupboards and bookshelves, all exquisitely made in cherry wood and polished to a glossy hue. It reminded him of his father's library and that at the Reform Club. It was one of the few bits of England he had surrounding him. He had to pay extra, a lot extra, for this room to stay as it was. It was therefore strange that he rarely went in, other than to take, replace or read another of its books, but every time he sat in there, he knew it was worth every penny of what he had paid.

Two of the five spare bedrooms had always been made up since David bought the house, although no one had ever slept in them. He was certain that the sheets and blankets on the bed in one of the rooms had been untouched for over five years. The other he had recently washed and aired in the expectation of a housekeeper.

The servants' quarters were at the back of the house and upstairs in the roof space. The rooms were uncomfortably hot in summer and cold in winter, but mercifully they were completely empty for, just as the owners before him, David did not have live-in servants.

Immediately on the girls' arrival at his house, David showed them where they would be sleeping. He insisted that they bathed and changed whilst he cooked supper. Sitting formally at the kitchen table, David gave them all pen and paper and asked them to write their names and ages. It was obvious that Satutu was the only one who could read and write. She was also the only one who helped serve, clear away and wash up. Although Destiny had stopped her sexual teasing, her attitude was now one of slothfulness, shared also by Newday. David found it exceptionally irritating, not least because it was something which he knew would have to be dealt with. After supper he sent the girls to their bedrooms and went into his study to work. The next day there would be a serious discussion as to their duties.

When David came into the kitchen in the morning, he found only Satutu there. The kettle was on and she had laid the table for one, ready for breakfast.

"Good morning!" said David. "This is impressive, thank you."

Satutu nodded appreciatively.

"Where are Destiny and Newday?" he asked.

"They left in the night," she replied.

"Left to go where?"

"I don't know. I just heard them leave."

"Why didn't you stop them?"

"I was in a different room and I didn't...." She stopped, not knowing what else to say.

"What time did they leave?"

"I don't know. It was still very dark."

"Did they take anything?"

"I looked in their room and the clothes you bought for them yesterday, they're gone."

"I thought you were sharing the room with Newday?"

"I was, but last night Destiny told me to change with her. She said she and Newday were cousins."

"Where on earth are they going to go? Do they know where they are?" asked David.

Satutu shook her head.

"They don't have any money so they can't get far. We'll have to look for them."

"They have, mister," said Satutu, this time nodding her head.

"How?"

"Destiny stole it from the selling man."

"But she had nothing on her but a nightdress so she can't have done."

Satutu held her bottom indicating where Destiny had hidden the money, and David grimaced at the thought.

"How much?"

"I don't know, quite a lot, I think."

"Have they taken anything from here?" asked David.

"I don't know."

David quickly looked around the house. A couple of holdalls and some trinkets from the hall which were not worth much had gone, but thankfully his most treasured possession, the photograph of Drew, remained safe. The bigger worry was the two kitchen knives missing from the drawer. The girls now had weapons; but then, given what had happened, David could hardly blame them. No money had gone, for there was none in the house and David had none on him. His bidding for them yesterday had taken all the cash he had.

David returned to his chair at the kitchen table, and as Satutu poured him a cup of tea, he could not help but feel very foolish. He was cross with himself. He felt cheated, and yet at the same time, relieved, for the burden of looking after them was gone.

"Do you want to leave too?" David asked Satutu.

She shook her head.

"Are you sure?"

She nodded.

"Good," he said, and with that Satutu smiled and David smiled back.

Chapter 11

Château de Gressier September 1939

"RUSSIA'S JOINED THE war," said Juliette, as Stephen Bellanger sat down at her kitchen table in The Cellar. It was his first day of work at Château de Gressier.

"Really?" he questioned, his voice sounding surprised.

"Yes, the Red Army marched on Poland yesterday."

"On our side?" he asked.

"No, of course not, on its own side," said Juliette, her voice giving away her slight frustration at him not knowing that Russia would only do something if it was in its own best interests.

"So, we're now fighting to get both Germany and Russia out of Poland, are we?" asked Stephen, sounding both annoyed and perplexed at the same time.

"No, we've no treaty obligation to protect Poland from Russia. In any case, those two countries have been fighting over the position of their borders for years and years," said Juliette.

"Perhaps Stalin's being an opportunist. He'll know that Germany cannot win a war if it has to fight on two fronts," said Stephen. "Maybe he has decided to use the war with Britain and France to expand his empire. If you were Stalin, wouldn't you declare war on Germany, when it's militarily weakened, to win the whole of Poland? Of course you would!"

"It's going to be the Great War all over again," said Juliette, joining Stephen's look of depression. "This is about finishing off the job we failed to do last time, but I fear it's going to be more complex than that."

"There will be only one winner of this war," pronounced Stephen, after he had thought about the matter for some little while. "It will be Russia. Germany will be destroyed, and we will be bankrupted."

"My brother said roughly the same about the last war," said Juliette.

The two debaters sipped at their coffee saying nothing, as Victoria, Juliette's daughter scurried in and out of the kitchen. At fourteen years old, it was obvious to Stephen that Victoria was going to grow into an attractive woman. Just like her mother.

"I've been thinking about our last conversation," said Stephen changing the subject.

"Which part?"

"I don't think you should keep all your stock of wine here at the Château. It's far too risky. You sell into both the US and Britain, don't you? You should move some of your stocks there. Do you have bank accounts in those countries?"

"Yes, why?"

"So they'll have somewhere to pay you," said Stephen, not making it clear who 'they' were.

"I have a personal account in London and the Estate has bank accounts in London and New York. Étienne had to go there just before he died to open an Estate account because Joseph wouldn't pay us in France. He said it was too difficult for him to keep paying us here and insisted we had to be paid there."

"Joseph?" asked Stephen.

"Joseph Kennedy."

"He's a business partner of yours?" he asked, surprised.

"Yes."

"The guy who's the US Ambassador to Britain?" asked Stephen.

"Yes," said Juliette, getting frustrated at the aggressiveness of Stephen's questions.

"Yeh, well he's the guy who's determined to keep the US out of the war this time. He's definitely no ally of ours."

"I've known Monsieur Kennedy for a long time. Let me tell you, he is no one's ally, except his own!" said Juliette firmly, "but for all that I quite like him," she added softly.

It was following this conversation with Stephen that Juliette decided she was going to divide the wine stored at de Gressier into three parts; twenty-five percent would go to her agent in England via Spain, thirty-five percent to her agent in the United States, and the rest would stay behind. So started a frantic process of bottling and packaging the wine, which had, until then, been stored in huge barrels in the de Gressier cellars.

Juliette selected wines from the 1936 de Gressier harvest and earlier, along with wines from La Maison de Louis harvested a year later for bottling. In fact, as things worked out, although the proportions of the wine stock she sent abroad remained the same, it was the less familiar La Maison de Louis wine which comprised well over sixty percent of the wines which remained behind.

Almost at the same time, the grapes on the vines became fully ripe. There was a feverish effort to get them picked and sorted, removing any rotten or raisined grapes, leaves and petioles, before putting them into the winery for their primary ferment. The job was done slowly and carefully with not a grape wasted. It had been drilled into all those who worked on the Estate, by the long line of Guégans, that it took eighty grapes to make a glass of wine, and each drop of wine in that glass paid their wages.

Once the harvest was in, there came the moment of 'the great debate'. How much yeast should be added to the black grapes to start fermentation? There was already natural yeast on the black grapes, and in the air, but extra yeast had to be added to help convert most of the sugars in the resultant red grape juice to alcohol. For the Estate's white grapes there was no such debate as it was always the same amount each year.

Every worker in the vineyard and winery thought they were experts on the amount of yeast to be added to create its famous red wines. Each had an opinion and expressed it loudly. But the secret was held with the Guégan family, passed down from father to son, and now it rested with Juliette.

During the years when Hugo Coudace was the General Manager of the de Gressier vineyards and winery, Juliette did not interfere with the winemaking. Immediately after his departure she had taken control. Fortunately, she remembered everything Étienne had taught her about making de Gressier wines. Once again, the midnight trips to the winery, which Étienne used to make, were re-started, but this time it was Juliette who made sure that the pressed grapes in the fermentation tanks were doing everything they should, for one of the skills was to keep a constant temperature. The 1939 wines from de Gressier turned out to be prize-winning. The first time a prize had been won since Étienne's death. It was, in no small part, down to the skills of Juliette and the calm organisation of Stephen.

Chapter 12

Bordeaux May - June 1940

EACH DAY THERE was no actual fighting lulled Juliette, Victoria, and Stephen into a false sense of security. The British Expeditionary Force which landed in France had learnt very little in the twenty years since they had left at the end of the Great War, but their presence along the Belgian coast added to the feeling enjoyed by everyone at Château de Gressier and in Latoire Village that, perhaps this time too, the war would pass them by.

The last bottle of wine destined for the United States left on the day that the French Prime Minister Édouard Daladier told the French people in a radio broadcast: *"For us, there is more to do than merely win the war. We shall win it, but ... in this world of masters and slaves ... we must also save liberty and human dignity."* It was fighting talk, but enough to persuade everyone at Latoire Village and the Estate de Gressier to feel confident about why France had joined the war. Men started to receive their call-up papers leaving, in their ones and twos, with cheers and tears.

But fighting talk was not enough. What became known as the phoney war suddenly ended on 10th May 1940. It turned into a war of lead and steel when the Germans attacked; but not the Maginot Line as had been assumed. Instead they invaded through Holland and Belgium, with Germany's primary mechanised force attacking through the largely undefended Ardennes Forest. On that day, almost everything came to a stop on the de Gressier Estate as no man wanted to go into the fields. Instead, they wanted to listen to the radio and prepare themselves, both mentally and physically, to join the fight.

Every other day since he started work at Château de Gressier, Stephen Bellanger phoned the Armée de l'Air asking to be conscripted.

If he couldn't design and build aircraft, he could either fly or help maintain them, he thought, but he got more and more frustrated as no one ever came back to him. The fact was that all branches of the French military were underprepared for, and overwhelmed by, the task that faced them. It was the same for the British Army.

The confidence, at de Gressier and Latoire village, in a French victory started to collapse when the BBC reported that over half a million French and British soldiers were surrounded at Dunkirk. Juliette's standing in the village fell to rock bottom when the British Army was evacuated from the beaches. "Your countrymen are cowards," she was told disdainfully. "You've abandoned us to save yourselves," was the consensus. She agreed it was shameful, not knowing that one third of those evacuated were French who were very quickly repatriated to France.

Late afternoon on 12th June, Juliette called everyone who worked on the Estate together and formally announced that she and her daughter were women of France. They would not be running away. It was no co-incidence that it was the same day that the French government raised the white flag of surrender, and with it one and a half million French and two hundred thousand British soldiers were interned as prisoners of war.

On 14th June, the German army occupied Paris and Juliette turned off the lights of Château de Gressier. The beacon, which shouted, "all is well" and had shined across the valley all night and every night for the last five years was extinguished. "They'll stay off," said Juliette, "until the damn Germans have gone home."

On 28th June, the German army peacefully entered Bordeaux in accordance with the armistice agreement. Commissionnaire Henri Hilaire, along with all those who heard the crunch of the jackboots of the Wehrmacht for the first time, would long remember the dread and total despair they felt.

Hilaire's misery was made worse by the fact that, together with his Commandant Divisionnaire, he had been taken by armed guard first thing the next day to meet Feldkommandant Ernest Kuene-mann, the German officer in charge of running the Bordeaux Region. Also there were Kommandant Wagner, Kuene-mann's deputy, and General

Kleinst, whose army of occupation had just marched through the city's streets.

Attending the meeting on behalf of France was Bordeaux's Mayor, Adrien Marquet, a dentist known to be a good friend of the German Ambassador. He had, the previous day, publicly welcomed the arrival of the Wehrmacht. Also present was Pierre Alype, the Prefect of the Gironde, who was known to be a strong supporter of Pétain and his Vichy Government. Alype came with his deputy, Georges Reige, who was also pro-German.

Hilaire was surprised to find himself at this meeting. At all times, his demeanour was one of detached politeness and precision. His colleagues would describe him as distant, some would say aloof, which is why he was rarely the first choice to represent the Bordeaux police. It was probably his reputation for fearless determination which had secured his place around this table.

Hilaire was shocked to find that the only other Commissionnaire de Police there was Pierre-Napoléon Poinsot. He had been invited by Alype. For good reason, Poinsot was generally disliked by his work colleagues. Assigned to work from the police station at Gare Saint Jean, he oversaw a special unit tasked by Pétain's government with the hunt for communists; a role he undertook with unnatural zeal and vigour.

The meeting was unusually cordial with Kuene-mann apologising for the inconvenience caused by the occupation. He assured them that his soldiers would be going home as soon as hostilities with the British stopped. "It will be in your best interests to persuade them to seek peace," he said, and then added after a pause, "and sooner rather than later, for they are bound to lose."

The meeting then dealt with the formalities of the armistice agreement. The first item on Kuene-mann's agenda was the arrangements for payment of his occupying German soldiers, for it was a condition of the armistice that France would pay for the occupation. Ringing in his ears were the clear instructions of Hitler: "We will take everything that we can make use of."

The second item on the agenda was getting Kuene-mann's men into the French military Camp de Souge and into billets in the city as fast as possible. The third priority was for the Sûreté Nationale to identify all Jews.

The concern of Mayor Marquet, and the fact that thousands of civilian refugees had swarmed into the City, doubling its size from 300,000 to 600,000 people in just a few days, was of no interest to Kuene-mann.

While Hilaire was in his meeting with Kuene-mann, his wife, Dominique was experiencing a different side of the German army. Her car had been stopped at a brand-new checkpoint set up on the road less than one kilometre from the turning towards her fisherman's cottage, which was close to the edge of the Garonne River. She had bought it shortly after her first husband had been killed in the Great War. It had been her pride, her solace, and above all the home in which, during those long lonely days, she had raised Stephen from a mere babe in arms. She had dreaded the thought of Henri asking her to sell her cottage, when they got married, so they could afford their home close to Jardin Public, but thankfully he had fallen in love with it too, and so it stayed, a family treasure. Now she was aggressively being denied access to her home by German soldiers brandishing guns. It was, she was told, no longer in bounds. She would have to move elsewhere.

That night Henri and Dominique's conversation was very subdued as they talked quietly of their day, lest their housekeeper heard them. After dinner, rather than each go about their chores, Henri moved to the piano and started to play Chopin's Nocturne No.2 in E-Flat Major from memory, for it suited his mood. Dominique came and sat by his side and slowly joined in, for they found something incredibly special in their duets.

As Henri sorted through the sheet music for their next piece, Dominique suddenly bounced on the stool to sit facing him. "We have a problem," she said, softly. Her voice was earnest.

"Monsieur Lussier is a Jew."

"Who is Monsieur Lussier?" asked Henri, puzzled.

"My headmaster, Thomas Lussier, you know that!" said Dominique crossly.

"Don't be silly! Lussier is as French a name as there can be."

"His wife is Jewish."

"Really?"

"It means he and their children are Jewish," she informed him.

"How come?"

"Because the Jewish religion follows the female line."

"I don't see why this is our problem," added Henri, not realising that Dominique, with her liberal arts philosophy, was about to make it their problem.

"They can get a visa from the Portuguese Consulate-General to cross the Spanish border and leave."

"How do you know this?" Henri asked.

"Because Father Bruntein asked me for a donation to help another Jewish family, and he told me how they were getting out."

"And you paid."

"Of course, why not?"

"Because aiding and abetting is a crime," said Henri. It was his turn to be cross.

"Don't be silly. I haven't aided and abetted anything!"

"I am not being silly," snapped Henri. "There are thousands of edicts coming from the Germans and the Vichy government every day. It's chaos; believe me, in that lot, there will be something about helping Jews. You can be certain of it."

"Well it's done, and if I am asked, I will do it again," said Dominique defiantly.

"Then don't tell me, I don't want to know."

Dominique looked puzzled, for not once had Henri ever raised his voice or given her an instruction like that before. He never asked and never ordered her. He had only ever requested.

Dominique turned away from him and faced the piano where she stamped out the first few bars of Hava Nagila in protest. Henri very gently placed his hand over hers and the music started to fade.

"We are living in very dangerous times," he said, and with his arms around her shoulders he pulled her close into him.

"I cannot know these things," he said. "Remember my position. For the safety of all of us, not just you, Stephen, and Pierre, but everyone around us, I must not know these things. You understand, don't you?"

Dominique nodded lamely as she looked into his eyes and, with fear seizing her stomach, she sighed a heavy sigh of despair. She knew it was true. They were going to have to take very great care.

"We have a problem with orphan children," said Henri, returning to his earlier thoughts. "We have over two hundred, maybe five hundred, in the city who have become separated from their parents."

"What!" said Dominique, appalled. "How?"

"In the panic to leave Paris ahead of the German army."

"How did they end up here?"

"It's the end of the line. The church is taking care of them, but they need somewhere to live. Can you see if you can help? We have room here for three, maybe four?"

Dominique nodded. Henri didn't see her leave the room, so he was startled to see her back within half-a-minute with her coat and hat on. "Where are you going?" he asked.

"To give a home to some children."

"I didn't mean now. In the morning will do."

Not being one to procrastinate, Dominique was out of the door and set on her mission before she heard Henri shout, reminding her about the curfew.

Hilaire's first call the next day was to see Aristides de Sousa. He told the Portuguese Consulate-General that his authority to issue visas was revoked until his position had been re-accredited by the German authorities. In this one sentence, a lifeline, which had saved nearly 300,000 people, was closed and thousands more, who might have escaped, were sentenced to death. Then, with as much circumspection as he could muster, Hilaire mentioned that he thought that the person responsible for the illegal issue of visas was very unlikely to have their accreditation renewed and it might be best if they left Bordeaux.

His next call was to see Kuene-mann. He had expected to be kept waiting, but instead was shown in almost straightaway. Unlike the first time they met, when there were no greetings, the two men saluted each other.

"Illegal visas were being issued through the Portuguese Embassy," said Hilaire, immediately. A soldier standing by Kuene-mann's side translated into German, for although his French was good, he wanted to take extra care to make sure he was understood.

"They were being used to emigrate Jews out of France. I have told the Consular-General that he has no authority to issue visas until he is re-accredited by the German authorities, whether that is you or someone else, I don't know."

"So you've stopped the export of our little Jewish problem," said Kuene-mann. "I am not sure that's particularly helpful."

Hilaire was taken aback, for it showed how easily something could be misunderstood. "No, I said I had stopped the illegal issue of visas." It was a phrase he was to repeat to himself many times over the weeks ahead, but with little comfort.

Kuene-mann simply nodded.

"There is another point. My family can't get to our house near Bec d'Ambès. It's by the side of the River Garonne, upstream from where it merges with the Dordogne to make the Gironde estuary. There's a roadblock stopping us this side of Saint-Louis-de-Montferrand. Apparently, we need a permit, and I understand I get this from you."

"Yes, yes," acknowledged Kuene-mann impatiently. "Once the area is secure, you will be able to apply for a visa in the ordinary way."

"I am sorry, but it can't wait. My job depends on me having access to the Ambarès-et-Lagrave peninsula, so I need an authority letter signed by you. In any case, my family needs to get to our home."

Kuene-mann stared at the man in front of him as he weighed up how much he needed this French policeman. The information on the Consulate General was a good sign. It showed that this Commissionnaire was prepared to work with them. So it was that, one hour later, Henri had in his possession four letters on the Wehrmacht's headed paper signed by Kuene-mann giving Dominique, Stephen, Pierre and him the authority they needed to get in and out of the restricted zone.

Chapter 13

Château de Gressier June 1940

FROM THE MOMENT France surrendered, Juliette cursed her stupidity for not having sent Victoria to England for safety. She feared that, as English women, they would be interned as aliens. The immediate feeling of stupidity turned to cold-blooded fear when a German staff car, followed by an army lorry, headed up the drive to Château de Gressier. She was certain they had come to arrest her. She gave instructions for Victoria to hide, and with her stomach in her mouth, she went out to greet them.

The officer in the passenger seat got out of the open top car and saluted Juliette who was now standing in the driveway. The officer was very smartly dressed in the light blue-grey uniform of the Luftwaffe. As she looked into his face, memories of the young injured German soldiers she had nursed years before flooded into her mind.

"I need to billet twenty men," said the officer, in broken French.

"I nursed many German soldiers in the last war," said Juliette, for no other reason than the men before her looked as young as those she had nursed then.

"I need to billet twenty men," repeated the officer, taking no notice of what she had said. Instead, he spoke more slowly and carefully.

"Why here?" she asked. "There's no airport nearby."

"It's halfway between Ribérac and Merignac Airports," the officer explained.

Juliette frowned because she could not believe that was true. "Have you tried Saint-Émilion?" she asked. "They've far more spaces in their village than I've got."

"Yes, I have men billeted there too, but their mayor sent us to you!"

By this time Stephen had run to be by her side.

"We have La Maison de Louis available," said Juliette, knowing that there was no point in arguing. Her objective was to keep them out of her own home. Then, remembering how the Mayor of Montreuil charged for each British soldier who stayed within the town boundary during the last war, she asked, "How much rent are you paying?"

"We are not paying rent, madame," said the officer, confused because this had never been demanded before.

"The British paid us rent in the last war. Four and a half francs per soldier per night, and I expect no less from the German military," she continued confidently.

"I will see," said the officer.

"No," said Juliette. "We will agree on five francs per soldier per night."

"I have no authority to agree that," replied the officer.

"Then I have no authority to show you to your billets. If you get the authority, then I will be more than pleased to show you around."

Stephen was aghast. He could not believe that Juliette was choosing to argue with men with guns.

"Madame, please show me around and I will do my best to get the authority," said the officer almost pleadingly, at which point Stephen suggested to Juliette that this was a good compromise.

With the officer at the wheel, Juliette in the passenger seat and with his driver and sergeant sitting in the back of the staff car, she directed them out of Château de Gressier, past Latoire village, over the bridge, where she made a point of not looking into the river spot where, her son, Victor had drowned but up towards La Maison de Louis. Long before it had been purchased by Juliette it had been nicknamed 'La Bête Blanche' by Étienne, Juliette's deceased husband. The officer counted the rooms as she showed them around.

"This will take ten officers or twenty-six other ranks," he declared to his sergeant.

"Ten, twenty-six?" questioned Juliette.

The officer went through his calculations again, this time in appalling French. "It could be sixteen officers," he said, after doing his sums again, "but we will call it ten."

"And we will call the rent fifty francs per night for the whole house," said Juliette.

"If you insist madame," said the officer as he got back in the car, conceding the point as he had decided it was not his concern.

"There is also billet space here. Please show it to me," said the officer, immediately they had returned to the drive at Château de Gressier.

"You want to move into my house as well?" asked Juliette, her face yielding serious disapproval.

"I'm told Château de Gressier is two houses, madame," said the officer.

"You appear to be very well informed," said Juliette, cursing the mayor of Saint-Émilion under her breath.

Reluctantly, she showed the officer around the east wing of the château known as The Cottage. This time the tour was accompanied by Stephen who agreed to move out of his room and into a room next door in the west wing of the house known as The Cellar.

"Please show us your wine cellar, madame," instructed the officer, at the end of the tour. His voice carried an officiousness not previously displayed.

"Our wine?"

"Yes, the cellars now, please," and with that he shouted instructions to his sergeant who shouted further instructions. Soon there was a small army of soldiers traipsing between the cellars and the lorry loading case after case of seized wine. Juliette had the presence of mind not to protest. Instead she moved to the back of the lorry where she counted the number of cases which had been loaded.

"Where do I send my invoice for 47 cases of wine?" she demanded, after the tailgate of the lorry had been shut.

"Heil Hitler," saluted the officer.

"Is that at the Reichstag, Berlin?" she continued, and with those words Juliette added to her reputation as an eccentric. More importantly, in her defiance, she was accepted as being a true patriot of France.

"No madame. Send it to Marshal Pétain," shouted back the officer as he marched off.

That night Stephen went to sleep in Victor's bedroom. No one had slept in there since he had died nearly seven years before. For Juliette it made perfect sense, as Stephen was developing into her surrogate son. A substitute for the one she hadn't seen grow into manhood.

Chapter 14

Château de Gressier July 1940

THE SUMMER OF 1940 saw Château de Gressier fall into an 'occupation' routine. Juliette's efforts in getting rent paid for the airmen billeted at La Bête Blanche was unsuccessful. Instead, in the need to generate cash, she set up The Cottage[11] as a mini hotel where the accommodation was provided free, but she charged handsomely for meals, drinks, hot water and clean sheets, which she demanded be paid for by the pilots themselves, and up front. No credit, not even for one meal, was allowed.

Juliette's wine continued to be openly purloined, de-nuding de Gressier's cellar as their 'foreign guests' stole bottles and cases of wine, but they never touched the wine in the barrels. In defiance, Juliette had Virgil Beauvais, one of her most loyal vineyard workers, build a partition which sealed off one-quarter of the cellar space, allowing a secret store to be created. When the 1939 vintage came to be bottled it was here that Juliette hid half her stock of Château de Gressier wines. The rest was spread around the Latoire villagers.

Being in the countryside, and with her vineyard transformed, in part, as an approved and licensed livestock farm, Juliette offered a standard of cuisine not available in the German military airfields and rarely found in Bordeaux. In fact, Château de Gressier became the Luftwaffe's little secret, kept from the other forces of the Wehrmacht.

---

[11] Château de Gressier comprised two separate, but identical, houses which were joined by a Gallery suspended high above a separating drive way and all built under one long roof. The Cellars was in the west wing of Château de Gressier and The Cottage was in the east wing. The Cellars was built first. It was the wing which, together with the Gallery, was where the ruling family traditional lived with the Cottage as the home of the heir to the Estate

Pilots, flying missions from Bordeaux's Merignac Airfield, would try and take their off-duty days at Château de Gressier. Such was the demand that the 'visitor' accommodation was expanded into the bedrooms of The Cellar, but here there was a room charge. It meant that Stephen had to move yet again; this time from his bedroom in The Cellar to Maison Presson, the house he had purchased from Juliette five years before but had never moved into. Slowly as the billeted men moved out of The Cottage, for which Juliette was not being paid, she filled it with paying guests. No one from the Wehrmacht objected because no one noticed.

Nearly every time one of her 'guests', as she referred to them, left to return to their duties they would scavenge something and, if they were returning to Germany, then they always scavenged far more. They saw nothing wrong in denuding de Gressier of its silver or paintings and even its linen sheets and tablecloths. It was a common sight in Bordeaux to see an officer walking around with a suitcase full of purloined bounty.

Madam Guégan, as Juliette insisted on being called, was the grit which made de Gressier an oyster of an experience. It meant that she could let her rooms two or three times over. This made it best for her guests not to upset her for she had a reputation for being a tyrant with any miscreants. Firstly, she deprived all her guests of the same thing that had been stolen. She would write a note of apology in German saying that the missing item was entirely the fault of the airman, whom she would name, stating he clearly thought himself more important than anyone else. On one occasion she provided only forks to her pilot guests to drink their soup as a protest at one of their pilot colleagues who, on his departure, had stolen a set of silver spoons. When they remonstrated with her, she provided them with straws. Then she added ten francs to everyone's bill to compensate her for the loss. When they complained she told them to reclaim the money from their colleague who'd stolen her spoons. Everyone paid.

Eventually, after one Oberstleutnant was given only a spoon to eat chicken stew, in retribution for some carving knives which had been stolen the previous day, an instruction went up on the inside of the front door of The Cottage, on Wehrmacht headed paper, signed by the same Oberstleutnant, instructing that nothing was to be removed without the approval of an officer of his rank or above.

Should any offender be unwise enough to return, which they rarely did, then every night was deliberately made uncomfortable. One of the advantages of a girls' boarding school was how naughtiness was passed from one generation to the next. Once you had learnt how to make itching powder, from rose hips or the seeds of the maple tree, then these are skills never to be forgotten. Juliette would never admit what had caused their rashes, and if anyone said anything, she would simply say that it was God's way of punishing those that stole.

In this way Juliette established a code of conduct which not only saw excellent behaviour from her guests but created a partnership feel. Not least because every airman who worked in the vineyards of the estate was provided with half a carafe of wine with their evening meal as payment.

There were murmurs of disapproval in Latoire Village. Some thought the Englishwoman had become a *'collaborateur'*, but she was doing what every other French person was doing; trying to survive in incredibly difficult times.

Chapter 15

Ribérac Aerodrome August 1940

THIS WAS THE moment Leutnant[12] Heinrik Klugman enjoyed most about flying. He would describe it as floating. The high work rate required to set up the aeroplane for landing was done and, with the runway coming up beneath the belly of his plane, all he had to do was gently pull back on the joystick helping the plane to defy gravity, keeping it in the air, for as long as possible, until the tyres kissed the grass.

He always found this moment flying bliss except, on this occasion, Klugman was far from relaxed. He was landing for the first time at Ribérac Aerodrome. It had recently been established by the Luftwaffe as a training school for Fliegerfuhrer Atlantik[13] and he knew critical eyes would be upon him. He wanted to make a good impression with no bounce, just the perfect landing on this perfect day. It was his nineteenth birthday.

It was the end of a journey which had taken Heinrik from flying school as a trainee pilot to Ribérac Aerodrome as a pilot officer in the Luftwaffe.

Heinrik would later complain that his first six months in the Luftwaffe of square bashing, performing drill and the hours spent on physical training, suffering the same misery as every recruit who joined the armed forces, was the biggest waste of time in the whole war effort. The only elements in the first six months which were relevant to being a pilot were wireless training and map reading.

Suitably infused into the disciplines of military life, Heinrik

---

[12] Lowest rank of Pilot Officer.

[13] Aviation Command Atlantic.

then went to a Fluganwärtelkompanie[14] at Bromberg, just south of Stuttgart, where he studied general aeronautical subjects. After two months he moved to an A/B school where he flew Klemm 35's, Focke Wulf 44's and Buecker 131's. He got his A1 licence in record time proving what he had said in his joining interview: he could already fly an aeroplane. To say that Heinrik was frustrated with his speed of progress would have been an understatement. It had taken him six months in the Luftwaffe to get to a stage he had achieved as a sixteen year old school boy.

To get his A2 Licence was far more challenging academically as Heinrik had to study all the subjects he thought he should have studied during his first six months: aerodynamics, aeronautical engineering, elementary navigation, meteorology, and flying procedures. He also had to learn to fly heavier, higher performance twin engine aircraft which he absolutely loved.

In July 1940, eleven months after first appearing on the parade ground as a new recruit, Lisa Klugman watched proudly as her son passed out as Leutnant[15] Klugman with his Luftwaffenflugzeugfuehrerschein[16] and his Flugzeugfuehrerabzeichen[17] His log book showed just over 150 hours in the air and not one of those had been spent in combat training.

There were two things which differentiated Heinrik from his fellow students. He had been identified, by each instructor, as a natural pilot. What set him apart was a rare gift, enjoyed by only about one in ten thousand pilots or navigators. He instinctively knew where he was in the sky. Wherever he flew, and for however long, he could always find his way home. He had the same homing senses as a pigeon. He would, like all other pilots, study the maps and plan his routes carefully. When deep over the ocean, where the only sight was sea, he would record his course assiduously, but it was his instinct which, above all else, always brought him home safely.

---

[14] Flight School.

[15] Pilot Officer

[16] Pilot's Licence

[17] Pilots Wings

The second difference came from the lessons he'd had when he was a young boy when one of his instructors, on learning of the use by the Royal Air Force of safety check lists and mnemonics to remember them by, had created his own and then learned them by heart. He was constantly teased by his fellow trainees for their use, but he didn't care. He knew it made him a safer pilot and, as with everything involved with flying, he was sure that forethinking meant he was forearmed.

Like all German pilots, Heinrik had hoped that his Ergaenzungseinheiten[18] would be a Stuka School but it was his skill in navigation which ensured Heinrik's first active posting was to the Seeluftstreitkrafte[19], a newly formed branch of the Luftwaffe devoted to flying long-range maritime reconnaissance and anti-enemy shipping missions.

Heinrik was both scared and thrilled when he finally received his combat orders. He was to meet his crew and fly a brand-new Junker JU88A-4 dive bomber aeroplane which was renowned for its pinpoint bombing ability. He was to collect it from the factory and fly to Ribérac Aerodrome in France where he was to undergo a three-week training course. Afterwards, he was to join his operational unit, Fliegerfuhrer Atlantik[20] at Bordeaux's Merignac Aerodrome.

At the factory he learnt he was only getting two crew members: a co-pilot who would have to double up as the navigator and a bombardier who was magically expected to operate the radio, the ventricle gun and aim the bombs all at the same time. Very formally, the three men introduced themselves. Each of Heinrik's new crew doubted whether a pilot so young had the ability to take them hundreds of miles out to sea and bring them back again safely.

It was the lack of a Junker factory produced check list which first worried Heinrik. The handling matrices of the aircraft, such as the take-off speed, were simply handed over in a verbal briefing. However, what made Heinrik wonder about what he was climbing into was when he was told by the test pilot, that despite whatever

---

[18] Operational training unit

[19] Marine Air Combat Force

[20] Aviation Command Atlantic

anyone else might say, he shouldn't try and deliver his bombs with a dive angle of greater than 45°. "We don't normally tell pilots this," said the test pilot, "but the airframe really isn't strong enough to take a dive greater than that, particularly when fully loaded."

The apprehension felt by Heinrik as he took to the skies in his brand-new plane with his brand-new crew was matched only by the sickening feeling he felt on the first day he reported for training as a pilot.

After flying 1,700km over two days, and using dead reckoning navigation, Heinrik found Ribérac Aerodrome without making any final course alterations and then landed perfectly. It was with huge relief that he taxied his aeroplane along the grass runway. With judicial use of the twin propellers and the brakes, he squared up and parked neatly alongside the other planes. He switched off the engines, opened the hatch and breathed deeply as fresh air streamed through the window. Heinrik looked straight ahead over the planes' bulbous glass nose, over the grass runway, through the crop of maize, into the trees in the distance and the blue sky above. He was enjoying the silence after two days of engine noise. Slumped back in his seat, Heinrik closed his eyes and then said out loud to his two-man crew, "Welcome to the war." It was his way of acknowledging that they were now on combat duty.

There was only one question on the crew's lips as they reported to their new commanding officer. It was the same question asked by every German who was following the fortunes of the Luftwaffe as they fought over the skies above the English Channel in the Battle for Britain. How was the battle going? The news was good. The Luftwaffe were confident of a win. Although the fighting was tough, the overall view was that the Royal Air Force could not continue to suffer the loss of aeroplanes and crew at the same rate. It would only be another couple of weeks before the English were defeated in the skies and the invasion of Great Britain could take place; and with Britain defeated the war was surely won.

Chapter 16

Ribérac Aerodrome - August 1940

AT RIBÉRAC AERODROME, Heinrik was taught the basics of his job. He was to patrol the Bay of Biscay between Bayonne in the south and Brest in the North, and way out into the Atlantic. He was to sink any British ships or submarines found in the area and if he couldn't sink them then he was to identify the boat and plot its speed and direction. He was part of a command structure which was to keep the German shipping and submarines, stationed along the Atlantic sea wall, safe. Of importance were the submarine pens at Saint Nazaire and harboured deep inland, upstream on La Gironde River, in Bordeaux.

After one week of theoretical training, one week of shadowing an operational crew and a final week of having an experienced pilot as his co-pilot, Heinrik, his crew and plane were transferred to Bordeaux Mérignac Aerodrome and made operational. He had still not fired his guns or dropped a bomb in anger.

If you are going to war and love flying then, as Heinrik had concluded, he had been given a lucky number for his was not an arduous task. Not once, in the whole time Heinrik was stationed with Fliegerfuhrer Atlantik was he attacked by an enemy aircraft. The only times he was directly fired at was when attacking a British frigate or destroyer, usually en route between the Mediterranean and the English Channel. At these times, he concluded that the odds of not being hit were significantly in his favour just as his bombs missing an enemy boat below were in theirs. When one of his bombs landed on the deck of a boat, he considered his shot lucky, although his bombardier would claim otherwise. When his plane was hit and damaged, he would consider himself unlucky. His worst ever damage was from flak, which destroyed one engine. It was through skilful flying that he brought his plane and crew safely back to their base. Like his colleagues, he found attacking British submarines from the air an impossible task. Once it had spotted him, the submarine would turn rapidly and dive in defence, making his bombs ineffective.

Most of the time Heinrik and his crew were out deep over the Atlantic they saw little of the general shipping which kept well to the west and north of their patrol area. The most effective part of what Heinrik did was to provide shipping intelligence to German Naval High Command, not least the activities of the French fishing boats.

Heinrik's posting was made luckier by the delights of France, the Bordeaux region, and the Luftwaffe pilots' open secret of Château de Gressier. It provided a haven of tranquillity where the quality and quantity of food and wine belied the fact that there was a war going on.

Chapter 17

Château de Gressier August 1940

VICTORIA GUÉGAN FOLLOWED the men from a long way behind. She kept close to the hedge, as they walked, ran, pushed, jumped, and teased each other on their way to the river, which passed between the vineyards of Château de Gressier and those of La Maison de Louis on the other side. These young men, who at the call of an alarm would suddenly be in charge of the most modern of killing machines, were like lambs at play. Each was, at this moment, without a care in the world.

At the river's edge, the men stripped naked and dived in to cool themselves from the very hot afternoon sun. As their bodies hit the water, Victoria felt affronted for this was her spot, her mother's spot, above all else it belonged to her brother, Victor. In defiance of all her instincts, Victoria strode to one of the two benches placed underneath the plane trees planted along the riverbank. The bench she chose to defend by possession was engraved with Victor's name. She was determined it was not going to be used by any German pilot. They could use the other one with her name on it.

Not one of the men noticed her. Without a stitch on they climbed out and dived or bombed back in, splashing, and ducking each other. It was done with a joy which Victoria found quite infectious. With a lightened heart, her eyes focused on the men in front of her for there was an amazing sameness about them. They were all roughly the same height, had the same erect body, tight leg muscles, firm buttocks, and broad chests. She thought they looked beautiful. As she watched more closely, she noticed how each moved with an athletic grace, their bodies doing exactly as their brain commanded. Amongst this group there appeared no sign of the arrogance or officiousness which had been demonstrated on the day The Cottage was requisitioned as the billet for these young pilots.

Heinrik Klugman climbed out of the river using the concrete steps which had been cut and placed deep into the riverbank. They had been laid to make swimming in the river much safer after Victor, Victoria's twin brother, had drowned there.

Heinrik wiped the water from his face and turned to choose his next victim whom he would swamp with a dive bomb. As his eyes swung through the panorama, Heinrik spotted Victoria sitting demurely on one of the two bench seats. He was not the first of them to spot the girl, but he was the first to walk curiously towards her, his hands naturally moving from his side to his front in a gesture of modesty.

Victoria studied him carefully, her eyes moving rapidly between his face and his groin as he started his journey towards her. Then, just a couple of metres away, realising his nakedness, he turned and jogged back to gather his towel. How come men have such fantastically shaped bottoms, she thought as she studied his muscular buttocks move gracefully from side to side, almost in slow motion, driven by the power of equally muscular legs.

Heinrik wrapped a small towel around his waist. As he turned and walked towards her, Victoria visibly started to bristle. Her first motive of getting closer to the naked swimmers might have been prurient voyeurism, but the reason she was sitting there now was to defend her brother's bench from enemy occupation, and the enemy was now rapidly approaching that very bench.

Heinrik's run had drawn the attention of his colleagues to Victoria, but it was he who was the first to sit next to her. Both sat stiffly with their bodies facing straight ahead looking towards the river. From Victoria's periphery vision, she could see that his towel had fallen to reveal a muscular thigh beginning to turn red with sunburn.

Suddenly, in continued silence and unison, they both turned their heads, without moving their body one iota, to look in the other's face. The moment their eyes met they smiled. Immediately each suffered an inexplicable feeling of panic and anxiety which ran from their chests to the pit of their stomachs.

"Bonjour, mademoiselle," said Heinrik.

"Bonjour, monsieur," replied Victoria.

With one hand clutching his towel, Heinrik offered his other hand by way of introduction and greeting. Victoria took it tentatively in her grasp and, at that moment of touch, they both felt an intensity for which neither was prepared. They gazed deep into each other's eyes and they knew, not only a heart stopping, breath taking desire, but with certainty that their lives were destined to be intertwined.

"Romeo et Juliet," said Heinrik, for he could think of little else to say to break the palpable tension.

"Romeo et Victoria." she replied. As soon as she had spoken, Victoria cursed for the clumsiness of her response.

"Heinrik et Victoria," he said, taking her lead.

Victoria repeated his name and nodded her head approvingly.

Quel âge avez-vous? asked Heinrik, his French very Germanic in its pronunciation.

"Quinze, ... et vous?"

"Dix-neuf," and he held up his hands to count out his age on his fingers.

Victoria giggled and turned away to look straight ahead.

They sat still saying nothing. They did not know what else to say. Instead they held hands again, as though they were saying hello for the first time. They gazed into each other's eyes until the jocularity of Heinrik's colleagues caused them to break apart rapidly. Both were embarrassed for they knew they had held on to the other too long for the situation they were in. Two people on either side of a dreadful war.

Now swarmed by young naked athletic men speaking loudly in German, some taking less care of their modesty than others, Victoria suddenly felt intimidated. Instantly, Heinrik felt her fear. He shouted at his colleagues with ferocity. She did not know exactly what he had said but it was obvious from his words that he was claiming Victoria for himself.

Victoria rose from the bench. She stood still for some moments to claim the ground as hers. She wanted to make it clear she was leaving, not running away. As she stood there defiantly, all the men around studied and scored her figure and beauty. There was not a man there who was not envious of Heinrik having met her first.

As Victoria strode away Heinrik stood up and leapt to walk by her side. She noticed he was tall, but not too tall. He spoke in German. She ignored him. He spoke again. Still she ignored him. "Je m'appelle Heinrik," he said using his limited French.

"Oui," she said brusquely. "Je m'appelle Victoria." She paused. "Parlez-vous français?" she asked.

"Non, parlez-vous anglais?" he asked.

"Yes," said Victoria fluently

"I speak better English than French," said Heinrik confidently.

Victoria didn't reply. Instead the two walked side by side in silence, off the grass and onto the path leading up to the Château. At the path's edge Victoria stopped. This man had come quite far enough dressed in nothing but a towel. Any further and they would attract the attention of the men attending the vines.

Victoria twisted her index finger in a circle indicating he should turn around and return to his colleagues. Not a word was spoken. Now for the first time they looked deeply into each other's face. His eyes were blue. Her eyes were brown. His hair was blond. Her hair was brunette, lightened by the sunshine. His face was square with an angular jaw line. Her face was oval. What they had in common was their smile. Both rarely, if ever, smiled, but when they did their mouths beamed and their eyes shone with a warmth which would have enraptured the whole of humanity. It was with such a smile that Heinrik and Victoria parted, for each knew that they would have to see the other's smile again.

Chapter 18

Château de Gressier October 1940

HEINRIK HAD NEVER done an hour of manual work in his life, until now. His time on farms with his father was spent, not in the fields, but in the sheds, stables, and pens of the animals they were looking after. His time with his mother was spent either at home or in hospital. Both had expected him to exercise his brain muscle as they valued knowledge and thinking above almost everything else.

In his aeroplane Heinrik was beginning to resent the hours he spent over the sea in stupefying boredom as the view never changed. His only thoughts were on his designated course and its navigation so he could find his way home again. These hours of tedium were occasionally peppered with periods of intense activity as they attacked an enemy ship and were shot at in turn. These attacks gave his mission some purpose but, flight after flight, they saw nothing and did nothing. The monotony had the effect of draining Heinrik and his crew's soul for they were not fighting the war which they knew had to be won if they were to go home again soon. That war was being fought over the skies of England and the Channel.

Unquestionably it was Victoria who drew Heinrik to Château de Gressier, but it was the contrast to his former life and current job which attracted him to work in the vine fields every time he visited. With the help of Heinrik and the other pilots who worked in the fields of both La Maison de Louis and Château de Gressier, the 1940 harvest was collected from the fields and sorted in the fastest of times.

Usually the last day of harvest ended with a celebration but all the old hands knew that the 1940 crop of grapes was not as good as the previous year. It meant that year's harvest festival was a sombre affair. The estate workers and villagers were not in the mood to celebrate, particularly with so many Germans in occupation at Château de Gressier, La Bête Blanche and in Latoire Village. Their mood was made worse by the expectation that any wine they produced would, immediately it was bottled, be stolen, and shipped back to Germany.

On the day of the harvest festival Heinrik and his colleagues were equally muted, but for a different reason. A whisper had gone around the dining room at Château de Gressier that Operation Sea Lion was over. Hitler had ordered that the invasion of England be postponed. With winter approaching, the conditions in the Channel were now going to be less than ideal. They were going to have to wait until the spring or summer of next year to defeat Britain. The pilots in the dining room took the news badly. They knew it meant the Luftwaffe had failed to defeat the Royal Air Force in the skies. It was the first battle that the Luftwaffe had not won, and each man felt it personally.

"The war will go on another year," said Heinrik, speaking to Victoria much later, when they were alone in her mother's dining room. Ostensibly, she was teaching him French, but his learning rate was poor as they spoke to each other mainly in English.

"Why?" she asked perplexed. "We've already surrendered.

"It will get worse here not better," Heinrik predicted, not answering her question.

"Why?" she asked again but this time with greater stress in her voice.

"It will give those Frenchmen who don't like us hope," he said. "With England defeated they would have had no hope and given up ... well now they have a reason to intensify their struggle."

Victoria said nothing.

"The terrorism will get worse, and so will the response," continued Heinrik. "It makes it bad for us," he said.

"Us?" she asked in a questioning tone, having quickly noted his use of the word. "You mean you, don't you?"

"No, I mean you and me, we have to be careful."

"Careful," repeated Victoria.

"Yes, and it shouldn't be like this. We just want peace. We just want to be able to go home."

"Why are you here then?" she asked with angered annoyance sweeping into her voice. "We're not enemies, you and me?"

"I'm not sure I know anymore," said Heinrik. "I thought I did once but not now. I think we're fighting the last war all over again and that makes no sense to my generation. We got what we wanted, what we needed, an end to the unfairness of the Treaty of Versailles, but now it all seems a bit ...." He did not finish his sentence. He didn't know how to describe how unnecessary he felt it all was.

As Heinrik spoke, Victoria noticed how vulnerable he appeared. In his officer's uniform he seemed strong and assured but, as he expressed this uncertainty, he showed signs of vulnerability, even humility, and that made him more human. However, it didn't change the fact that he was the enemy, and that made everything between them complicated

Chapter 19

Château de Gressier Autumn 1940

JULIETTE, WITH STEPHEN close at hand, supervised the winemaking, for what became a distinctly average vintage. They had just finish storing their wine in barrels when Heinz Bömers, the Weinführer for the Bordeaux region, made an unannounced inspection.

Bömers was head of Germany's largest wine importing firm, Reidmeister & Ulrichs, and had been importing Bordeaux wines into Germany for many years. He had earned a reputation for fairness. It was he who had persuaded Herman Goering that the German plunder of France's vineyards would very quickly result in Germany having no fine French wines available for import, and a fair price had to be paid if the industry was to survive. It was his job to negotiate that price.

Château de Gressier had sold only small quantities of wine to Germany before the war, and never anything to Bömers. Juliette's negotiations with him over de Gressier's 1940 production were tough. She successfully argued that she should be allowed to supply her customers in the United States on the grounds that it was in Germany's best interests to keep America placated so that it didn't join the war. It was something Bömers accepted, meaning that de Gressier was only one of five or six vineyards authorised to export to the US. He also agreed that a certain amount of stock should remain for the billeted pilots and those flying from Bordeaux military airports. The rest, he insisted, had to go to Germany for which Juliette had no initial argument, as they made a good replacement for the English market she had lost. They agreed on what Juliette thought was a fair price in French francs, but when she was told she would be paid in deutsche marks, their negotiations broke down, for the official exchange rate for the deutsche mark had been set artificially high. Juliette quickly calculated that the price meant a rapid reduction in income for the Estate. It was not something she was prepared to accept.

It was when Juliette presented Bömers with the bill for the wine stolen in the previous year that their negotiations fell into serious difficulties. Juliette stubbornly insisted that she be paid for the wine which she had already supplied, albeit at gunpoint. There would be no shipping of her wine, she told him, until her outstanding invoices had been paid. "I would prefer to pour it into the ground rather than be cheated time and time again," she told him angrily. There was an impasse in their negotiations. Juliette knew she had a very weak hand and was being stupidly bloody-minded, but she could not help herself. She incorrectly thought that Bömers could seize her stock at any moment, but the truth was that, even if he did have that kind of power, he did not have the resources.

After much wrangling, Bömers, agreed that Juliette would be reimbursed with the cost of the corks, labels and bottles for the *requisitioned* wine, and this total cost would be spread across that year's production by way of an additional price paid per bottle of wine. While it only worked out at a few centimes per bottle, it nevertheless meant that Juliette got the highest price for a bottle of claret anywhere in the whole of the Bordeaux region that year; including those which were from world famous vineyards.

Not only did she get that price for the Château de Gressier wines, but also for the wines of La Maison de Louis, which normally sold at a much lower price. Not known then, but equally importantly for later, the price for the 1940 de Gressier and La Maison de Louis wines set the price level for every other year's negotiation with Herr Bömers. When she and Stephen finally did their sums, they calculated that they might be able to break even without laying off any staff, provided the Germans stopped their stealing.

Juliette's fight with Herr Bömers went into the folklore of Latoire Village and added to her reputation for eccentricity. With it, came the affectionate nickname of 'Le Singe Fou de Latoire' – The Crazy Monkey of Latoire, but the nomenclature was given with a large measure of respect.

Chapter 20

Château de Gressier January 1941

THE WINTER OF 1940/41 was one of the coldest on record. For sixty-six days in a row the temperature was below freezing and for some days it consistently fell below -10°. There was no coal to be bought. It was with timber scavenged from the local woods that Château de Gressier was kept warm and became a haven for those who came to stay. The same could not be said for the airmen billeted at La Bête Blanche, where only one fire was allowed, and that was simply to stop the place from freezing over.

It was in these inordinately harsh conditions that, late one January afternoon, Juliette was summoned to the front door of The Cellar.

"Madame, I believe you have a problem with your water," said Eric Dubois, nervously.

"I don't think so," said Juliette, standing in the doorway. "Who told you this?" she asked puzzled.

"You've had a phone call from Monsieur Philidor?"

"No," said Juliette dubiously. "Why?"

"Because he was to introduce me."

"Well, I'm sorry but he has not," she replied sharply. "In any case, who's Monsieur Philidor?"

"He says he knows you," replied Dubois. "Are you not English, madame?"

"Can you tell?"

"No, madame I cannot."

"I'm a French woman," said Juliette, firmly. "I'm a citizen of France. My husband was French. My son was French. They are buried in French soil. My daughter is French. My husband fought against the Germans in the last war. I think that is enough to prove I am French."

"Yes, and you nursed the English soldiers who were injured, did you not?" added Dubois. "So you are a patron of England too."

"I am a patron of France, monsieur. I say nothing more, but why do you ask? Who is Monsieur Philidor? I know no such name."

"He says he knows you and that you would be able to help," Dubois replied, quickly.

"And how do I know that you are a patron of France too?" asked Juliette cautiously. She then added, "Sadly, much is not what it seems these days."

"That's true," said Dubois, "but there comes a time when you have to trust, for there is nothing else left to do, and that's the position I'm in now."

"It seems to me we're living in times when you survive longer and do better if you trust no one," said Juliette, still not sure who or what she was dealing with.

"I can prove to you that I am a patron of France, madame," said Dubois.

"How?"

"It's in my van."

"You know there are Germans billeted here?" she asked.

"No!" said Dubois, the alarm palpable from the change of tone in his voice. "Can I show you somewhere else?"

"No," said Juliette emphatically.

"Then please come with me," said Dubois, as he moved his shoulders in response to the excruciating pain in his neck, made worse by the intense strain he was under.

It was with a degree of trepidation that Juliette walked cautiously behind Dubois towards the small plumber's van which he had parked curiously with its back close to the wine barn. Juliette stood back as Dubois opened just one side of his van's back door to reveal two uncomfortable English pilots, still in their uniforms, squatting on the van floor, both shivering from the immense cold. It took just milliseconds for Juliette to assess the situation. Without anyone saying anything, Dubois shut the van door.

"Are you mad?" retorted Juliette very quietly, as she started back to the warmth of The Cellar.

"We knew the Germans had taken over La Maison de Louis, but not here," whispered Dubois apologetically.

"They've been here for over six months." Her tone indicating not only the exasperation she felt, but the fact that she was acutely aware that, what a few moments ago had been Dubois's problem, had now become hers.

"It's just our plans suddenly changed," said Dubois, "and we thought you might be able to help."

"How long for?" asked Juliette instantly, correctly assuming he wanted her to hide the two pilots.

"One night, maybe two."

"Come with me," she said, without hesitation. Juliette returned to the van and climbed into the passenger seat. There she gave instructions to Dubois to drive to Maison Presson. She knew Stephen was with his mother in Bordeaux, his house would be empty, and she guessed, in hope, that it would be unlocked. Not a thought of Maison Presson's notorious past entered her head as, for the first time in her life, she walked in. She was too busy concentrating on the present.

Even though Stephen Bellanger now lived at Maison Presson, he had made no effort to make it into a home. It was in virtually the same condition as it was when Juliette cleared it out and had it repainted from top to bottom before selling it to him five years ago.

"They will be safe in here for a day, maximum two," said Juliette as she found the stairs to the basement and bundled the three men down into the dark. I expect it will be taken over as a German billet any day soon.

"Can you feed them?" asked Eric.

"Oui," she replied resisting the temptation to speak English as she knew this would give her away if the airmen were ever captured and forced to talk.

Back at The Cellar, Juliette bundled up some pillows, blankets, candles, bread, cheese, and wine. In the darkness, she forced Dubois to take them back to Maison Presson by himself. She did not want to see those English pilots ever again.

Chapter 21

Château de Gressier January 1941

JULIETTE DIDN'T SLEEP a wink. She was petrified at the risks that had been brought on Victoria, Stephen, and herself. As she got out of bed, she was determined that the two pilots would have to leave that very day.

Early in the morning, Juliette got the phone call from Monsieur Philidor which she had been told she was going to get the previous day. After the briefest of pleasantries, Monsieur Philidor suddenly asked, "How are my two parcels, did you receive them?"

"Monsieur Philidor," said Juliette formally. "I don't know how we know of each other or what you are talking about." The hairs on the back of her neck were standing on end with fright.

"I was at school with your husband," he replied.

"Which school was that?" she asked.

"St. Joseph's."

"And where did we meet?"

"At your husband's funeral; the service was in your village church. It started at 11.30am. Dominique Bellanger, now Madame Hilaire, sat by your side" he added, to prove he was there.

"How can I help you?" asked Juliette, now more confident in the man she was talking to.

"We're having difficulty in moving your packages. They need to be in Agen tomorrow night. I was wondering if you might be able to help move them with one of your vans."

"Are you crazy? No," responded Juliette, crossly. "It's over ninety kilometres away." She then lowered her voice and whispered, "It means going through La Ligne and that's impossible. I have no reason to go."

"But you have a lorry," replied Philidor, not to be defeated.

"Which needs petrol," she protested.

"I must go," said Philidor suddenly. "Please think about it," and then he hung up.

For everyone living in Latoire, La Ligne, as the demarcation line was known, was a constant reminder that France had lost the war, for it divided their country in two. The Demarcation Line ran east west from near Geneva to Tours and then south to the border with Spain. Fifty-three of France's departments covering the northern half of France and down along the Atlantic coastline were designated as being in the 'Occupied Zone' of which forty-one were occupied in their entirety. The land to the south and east of La Ligne was treated as being in the ostensibly 'Free Zone'. Bordeaux, the Dordogne Department, and the village of Latoire were firmly in the Occupied Zone.

In practice, the demarcation line was not as neat as it sounded, for when the Germans planted their 1.5 metre poles painted in red, white and black, the colours of the German flag, and laid stretches of barbed wire and even mines, they took into their possession anything which looked agreeable. La Ligne was constantly patrolled on the occupied side by German soldiers and military police in groups of four, either on horses or motorbikes, and very often accompanied by an Alsatian dog.

On the Free French side, the Vichy Government had tried to make the demarcation a buffer zone. It was in an ill-conceived attempt to protect its sovereignty, but in the process, had made matters much worse for its citizens living along La Ligne. Immediately after the armistice, when the two zones were announced, all communication, including telephone, post, trains, and cars, was stopped. People could not get to their doctor and children couldn't get to school. Eventually, for the *frontaliers*, those living within five kilometres of La Ligne, it was possible to get a daily pass, but for those living in Latoire it meant either going to Paris or Angoulême to get a pass which was only issued if they had convincing business.

It was in total panic that Juliette replaced the receiver. She felt completely trapped. She wanted to phone Philidor back straight away, but she had no number for him, nor did she have the telephone number for the mysterious plumber who foisted the 'packets' on her in the first place. Juliette had already concluded the name he had given her was probably false. It was then that she remembered the words of her father, repeated by Étienne when his mother died. "In a crisis make a cup of tea and write a list." Shortly afterwards she recalled another of her Father's other sayings: "It was a lack of thinking which got you into this mess and its only thinking which is going to get you out of it!"

On the way to the kitchen, Juliette called one of her maids to fetch Virgil Beauvais. Étienne had a method of judging people. He would ask, if stuck adrift on the seas, would he want that person with him in his lifeboat? Juliette had already decided that, if that moment ever came, Stephen and Virgil were the two people living closest to her who would fit that bill. So it was that Virgil was given the job of looking for Stephen and then, in the silence of her kitchen, and with pen and paper in hand, she started to work out a plan.

"Stephen," said Juliette, immediately he was presented to her by Virgil, "we need to go for a walk. Virgil, please stay here and make a cup of tea," she instructed. "We need to talk later."

Setting out along the same route as she and Étienne would take on their evening walks, Juliette stopped about 200 metres from the house so that Stephen could catch up.

"Why weren't you called up as a soldier at the start of the war?" she asked.

"Because I am an aeronautical engineer," Stephen replied in a semi aggressive tone, as he was affronted by the way she had asked her question. "It's a reserve occupation. I was turned down from joining the Armée de l'Air for this reason."

"Do you by any chance have a copy of the Défense de la France?" she asked.

"The underground newspaper, no," said Stephen, quite shocked.

"Have you ever read it?"

Stephen paused, for they both knew it was a dangerous question. "I have read it many times, but I make sure I never have a copy," he said, lowering his voice. "The damage to Mother, Henri or Pierre if such a thing were to be found would be too horrendous to contemplate."

Juliette nodded sympathetically.

The sky was clear and the temperature well below freezing, but deep in worry, Juliette hadn't felt the cold. Nevertheless, for the first time she shivered as she knew she was about to ask Stephen to do something which would risk his whole family. Was this something she should do? She walked on in silence. At the river's edge she stopped. It was completely frozen with the marks of skaters gouged into the ice.

"Do you know any *passers*," she asked. "I need to get something into the free zone."

"What, people who will take you across La Ligne?" asked Stephen, seeking clarification, because it was another very leading question.

Juliette nodded.

"No, we live too far away. Why do you ask?"

Juliette made a point of ignoring Stephen's question. Instead, she asked: "What do you think of Marshal Pétain?"

"That man...." He swore under his breath. "None of his generation represents me," he replied angrily. "Do you know that in 1916 the Germans attacked Verdun for ten months without capturing it at a cost of 162,000 Frenchmen's lives; this time it was taken in little more than a day with a loss of 200 men. They have all let France down."

"What's your feeling towards the British?" she asked.

"Do you really want me to answer that one? You might not like what I say." The sarcasm in his voice gave away his opinion.

Juliette nodded.

"I think they've been contemptuous," he continued. "They evacuated 240,000 of their soldiers at Dunkirk leaving us behind to face the slaughter alone, and then they had the nerve to sink three of our battleships at Mers el Kebir. What do you think I would think?"

Juliette walked on in silence not knowing what to make of Stephen's remarks.

"Do you know that in May 1918 the English had eighty-five divisions in France? In May 1940, nine months after the war started, they had just 10!" he continued.

"Are you being fair?" she asked. "One set of your figures is at the end of one war and the other at the beginning of the next. Does it not take time to mobilise?"

"Britain will get invaded, just like us. What did General Weygand say to Pétain?" He paused to summon up the exact expression. 'Britain will have its neck wrung like a chicken in three weeks'. You wait; in the summer, when the German army can cross La Manche, it will be defeated just like us. I don't know why they don't seek surrender terms now. If they did, the Germans would leave France and we could all go back to how we were."

Juliette took a few paces along the riverbank leaving Stephen where he was. She was not sure that his answers really told her what she wanted to know.

"Stephen," she said, when she was back by his side and leading them both back up the hill, "tell me, what do you think of me?" Juliette was now resolved. It was the answer to this question which would decide what she did next.

He stopped them both from walking and looked straight at her, for he knew she was seeking reassurance that with him she would be safe.

"You are our 'Singe Fou de Latoire'," he said. "Everyone here loves you and admires you."

"Is that my nickname?" she asked, "To be called a mad monkey is hardly a compliment."

"But you are from England, and everyone from England is mad and the monkey is a spirited animal we all want to keep as a pet," he explained. "It's a lovely nickname – it's always said with affection."

Juliette accepted the explanation for what it was, although she wasn't sure why. "What do you think about me?" she asked abruptly, this time stressing the word 'you'. "Am I your Singe Fou too?"

"You are my family," said Stephen. It was said with such heart, calmness, and clarity of purpose that the message was clear. "My Mother, Pierre, Henri, you and Victoria, you are my family. Étienne made it so when he sort of ... adopted me."

"And the meaning of family?" she asked.

"Right now?"

"Yes, right now."

"Love, trust, loyalty, friendship, support; all those kinds of things. I am sure it has the same meaning for the English as it does for the French," he replied.

"Unconditionally?" she asked.

"Yes, unconditionally!"

"I am always, always there for you too," said Juliette earnestly. The dampness of her eyes gave away the relief she now felt at having someone else with whom she could share the burden of the two English pilots.

Something unusual then happened. For the first time in their lives, Stephen hugged her and rubbed her back to reassure her that everything would be all right. It was the sign that this man, of the younger generation, was at one with this woman, of the older generation, whatever might come.

On the walk back up the hill toward Château de Gressier, Juliette told Stephen of the packages hidden in the basement of his house and 'their' problem. Stephen was immediately excited at the thought of being able to contribute, to what he wasn't exactly sure, and then he fell silent. He had started to concentrate on solving what he now saw as 'his' problem.

Chapter 22

Château de Gressier January 1941

"I HAVE A problem," said Juliette to Virgil, and then she paused, "and I, we, need your help. Only the three of us here will know anything about it."

Virgil said nothing.

"And it will stay that way," she emphasised.

Still Virgil said nothing.

"Hiding in Maison Presson are two British pilots. We don't know how they got there," she lied. "They were probably dropped off because of my English background."

"Where, at Stephen's place?" asked Virgil, making sure he understood what he was being told.

"Juliette nodded. "We have to get them into the free zone."

Virgil yielded not a sign of emotion on the news. It made Juliette wonder whether he understood not just the risks but all that was involved. Instead, he simply nodded in return.

There was a scraping of the chairs against the tiles on the floor as the three conspirators sat closer around the end of the kitchen table.

"I have had more time to think about this and I have some thoughts which might work," said Juliette. Stephen and Virgil started to focus intently on what she was saying for they had both, on hearing their challenge, thought it to be an insurmountable task.

"I'm told there is a *passer* in Agen who will take them to the Spanish border. We just have to get them there."

"That's over ninety kilometres away," said Stephen, making the same protests as Juliette had made to Monsieur Philidor when on the phone.

Juliette nodded frantically in agreement, frustrated that her thought processes had been interrupted. "But our coopers[21] are there," said Juliette. "It means we have a reason to go."

"Mise en Rose," said Stephen to Virgil, interpreting coopers for both.

"I thought we might take them over La Ligne de Marcation on the flatbed lorry, hidden inside wine barrels."

"They won't fit in there," exclaimed Stephen, "and certainly not for that long."

"Did you know that the first person to go over Niagara Falls in a barrel and survive was a woman," added Virgil, very quietly. "She did it by increasing the air pressure inside the barrel with a bicycle pump." It was a strange contribution, and the authority with which this abstract and disjointed knowledge was presented, surprised both Juliette and Stephen into a moment's silence. "Except it wasn't an ordinary sized barrel," he added.

"La pipe sized barrels will probably work," said Stephen. "La tonne barrels are far too big, except they're the ones which we really need mended."

"No," said Virgil, vehemently. "Move la tonne barrels and they'll be finished. You'll need new ones and they're very expensive. There's a few more years in 'em yet," he continued. "We've some old pipe barrels which we could use."

"Won't they suffocate?" puzzled Stephen.

"We'll put air holes in the barrels," said Juliette.

The look on both their faces suddenly made her feel as though she had said something stupid.

"Obviously the holes will have to go where they can't be seen," she said, as her voice expressed its annoyance at their inability to take on board the obvious. "We're going to need about a hundred litres of petrol," she continued, immediately re-imposing her authority on the meeting.

"How the hell are we going to get that?" asked Stephen, shocked by the size of the problem.

"Ribérac and Merignac Aerodrome," said Juliette. "They both

---

[21] Barrel makers

have huge supplies. We just have to arrange a barter system, petrol for wine."

"Gaspar Mesny is best at doing that," said Virgil. "He's a natural blagger."

Juliette nodded in agreement and both she and Virgil smiled as they remembered the never-ending line of mischief he had caused their German guests.

"It needs to be made part of his job," said Stephen, "the Estate's Chief Scavenger. There are so many other things we need. We will have to supply him with things to trade, like butter and bacon."

"If and when the Wehrmacht cars come here, we'll get them to park differently so we will be able to syphon a few litres out of each of them without them knowing," added Virgil, suggesting that he too could be a skilful scavenger.

"What about an Ausweis?" asked Stephen.

"Laissez-Passer," corrected Vigil, upset that German had been brought into their discussion.

"We get that from Angoulême," answered Juliette.

"That's an impossible journey with all the checkpoints that are now about," commented Stephen.

Juliette nodded.

"You'll need to get Heinz Blömer to write a letter of support. I'm sure he'll do it as he quite fancies you," said Stephen.

Juliette raised her eyebrows; half flattered by the fact that a man could still fancy her and half by the fact that Stephen had noticed that she could be attractive to another man.

"Virgil, your job is to convert the barrels and make them comfortable and safe for our guests."

"That's going to take days," said Virgil, "and I can't use the barn, everyone will wonder what I'm doing."

"You'll have to do it at Maison Presson," responded Juliette.

"And if the Germans turn up? They could requisition it at any moment," said Virgil, making a point which they all feared.

The meeting fell silent as the consequences of what they were doing sank in.

"We don't have many days; we have two, three at the very most," added Stephen.

No one said anything else. It was on Stephen's observation that the meeting ended with Juliette shooing the two men out of her kitchen and to their tasks.

In a short telephone call, which was clearly being listened to by the operator, Juliette sweet-talked Blömer into providing her with the letter she needed. Then, with a small suitcase she cycled to catch the last bus into Bordeaux. She stayed that night with Dominique and Henri who were the most perfect and loving hosts, before setting off the next day to meet with Blömer. It was true, she thought, he does fancy me, as Blömer extolled both charm and grace in a meeting which took far longer than the task warranted. It meant that Juliette was late for the train to Angoulême, but luckily it was later than her.

Juliette stood in a long queue in the Ausweis office in Angoulême which was manned by French nationals protected by two very bored German soldiers. Out of devilment, she applied for a multiple visa for one year which she got very easily, but a pass for Stephen was refused. Every applicant had to appear in person, she was told. Very quietly, and without getting cross, Juliette pleaded for a Laissez-Passer for Stephen and whilst the words of the counter clerk were quite intransigent, his eyes told her something else. She left the counter, waited discretely before re-joining his queue some ten minutes later. This time, when she re-presented the application form for Stephen, she slipped a twenty franc note, enough to buy one hundred baguettes, and two of her food ration sheets between all the supporting papers and 'voilà', out came a year-long visa for Stephen too. In all her life, Juliette had never paid a bribe, and as she walked out of the building, she did not know whether she was pleased or disgusted with herself. She soon realised it is what everyone does when needs must!

Juliette had a tedious journey home by bus. It was much cheaper than train, but it was pure myth that it was easier than going via Bordeaux. She spent a very cold and uncomfortable night in the bus station in Chevanceaux where, because it was after the curfew, she had her papers inspected time and time again, albeit that everybody was locked in.

As the hours dragged by, Juliette wondered why she had insisted on such a long period for their Ausweis, as she had no intention of making another journey across La Ligne. She found no answer but if she had asked anyone who knew her, they would have explained. Deep down, she was still the same person who, all those years ago, had read maths at Cambridge and, just as then, she needed to prove to herself that she could play the system and win.

By the time Juliette returned to Château de Gressier, Virgil had done an excellent job of converting one of their old barrels. Building a barrel is a complex and difficult job as each stave is carefully crafted to be free standing, held in place, next to its neighbouring stave, by the pressure of five outer steel rings. The steel rings force each stave, not only into each other, but also into the top and bottom lids, so as to create the perfect seal. In normal circumstances, it would take some two to three hours to build a wine barrel around a man, even if all the staves had been pre-shaped and were ready to go. This made Juliette's idea totally impracticable.

Virgil found a way of short cutting the process by gluing the staves together in one quarter sections, and then fixing two of these one quarter sections to two of the iron circumference rings so that they stayed in place, whilst allowing some flexibility of movement during reassembly. With the man to be hidden, first standing, and then squatting on the bottom lid of the barrel, the remaining two quarters of the staves were then hammered into place around the man, who held the top lid in the right position. Once everything was in place, the remaining three outer rings were then banged down around the barrel which forced everything together. The barrel was complete again.

Initially the smell of alcohol, which had penetrated deep into the oak, would have knocked someone unconscious within minutes, but with the lid off, the staves apart, and after very many washes, the aroma had started to evaporate. With holes drilled into the bottom of the barrel, and with the bung left out, there was just enough air for the pilots to breathe. Whether, at the end of their journey, they left the barrel intoxicated, was something they would have to find out.

Virgil had even installed a small seat which both Stephen and he tried. Very quickly they realised that, even with a torch, it would be humanly impossible to stay inside the barrel for a two-hour journey.

Their plan had to change. The pilots would have to ride in the cab with them to somewhere, just before they crossed through the checkpoint. There they would stop, and the men would be hidden in the barrels. It meant that they had to find a way of taking apart a barrel and rebuilding it, with a man in it, in just a few minutes.

At the outset, it seemed an impossible task, but patiently, Virgil went back to work. His solution was to fix three of the one quarter sections together and to two of the outer rings, leaving one quarter of the barrel free for entry. Then he reduced the diameter of the top lid so that, once the barrel had been reassembled, it was the final thing to be put in place. The reduced lid was rested on new wooden blocks, screwed into the inside of the barrel staves. The lid was then clamped down from the inside so it could not be pulled open from the outside. The barrel didn't have to be watertight. It just had to look like it was, and with a bit of dirt and oil mixed together and forced into the gaps, it did just that.

All three conspirators were concerned that, stopping to transfer the pilots into the barrels, would significantly increase their chances of discovery. With two escapers without identification papers, they knew it would only be seconds before they were arrested and then....? They needed to get each of the pilots a set of papers, but how? They had no idea.

In all their planning, the person whom they thought had been given the hardest job, found it easy. Gaspar set a barter exchange rate of two litres of Château de Gressier wine for five litres of petrol; three litres of wine if they provided the can. Very quickly he had a surfeit of cans and a surplus of petrol.

Every evening, just before eight o'clock, the mysterious Monsieur Philidor would phone Juliette. When would she be sending him the cases of wine he had ordered, he would ask. On each previous occasion she had been deliberately non-committal, but tonight the answer was different. It would be with him tomorrow, and they would be travelling without the pilots having their much-needed false identification papers.

Chapter 23

Château de Gressier January 1941

IT WAS AT 6am on the sixth day after Juliette had shared her problem with Stephen and Virgil that they gathered around her at Maison Presson. It remained bitterly cold. Stephen had spent the night there. With clothes provided from Étienne, Stephen, and Virgil's wardrobe, the two pilots blended into their surroundings.

The two airmen wanted to keep their wings from their uniforms, so they had carefully unpicked them and hidden them in their new French outfits. Stephen was furious when he found out. He angrily threatened to leave the whole mission if they didn't give them up. It may have seemed a silly argument, perhaps reflecting the tremendous anxiety each had for the journey they were about to undertake, but Stephen's concerns were real. Caught as Englishmen in civilian clothes the pilots would be shot as spies. This would not happen to them if they could prove they were pilots, which the badges would help them do. However, for Juliette and Stephen, as collaborators with the English enemy, there would be no mercy. Stephen was adamant that their risk profiles had to be the same. Juliette very tactfully explained the issue. Gracefully the two men gave up their badges and immediately offered their hand in apology. No one saw Juliette secretly slip the badges deep into the palms of her gloves. She knew she couldn't let the two men be shot if she had a mechanism to save them.

The bench seat of the Citroën lorry was designed to take three people and now it had to take four. When Juliette took her place at the steering wheel, it was Virgil's turn to protest. He'd always assumed, guided by old fashioned chivalry, that it was Stephen and he who would be making the journey. It was only when Juliette showed him that the Laissez-Passers were in Stephen and her names, did he relent.

It was still dark when Juliette and Stephen left Maison Presson with the two pilots between them. Neither of them knew their names. They had never asked.

The four companions travelled in complete silence. About five kilometres from Blasimon, where they were going to cross La Ligne, Juliette and Stephen spoke for the first time, as they sought to find a small side road where they would be unobserved.

Finding a small gap, closer to the village than they would have liked, they stopped, and the pilots were helped into the barrels. It was not an easy task, because the modified barrels in which the pilots would be travelling were surrounded by other barrels. It meant that each of these had to be moved to get access to those prepared for their human cargo.

They arrived at the crossing point, which was at a small crossroads about one kilometre outside Blasimon, just before 8.00am when the guards would start allowing people to cross. They had deliberately chosen to be there at this time as they had expected a crowd to have built up. Their hope was that the crowd would put the guards under pressure and give them less time to search the lorry. The trouble was that their crossing point was not a popular one. It meant that no one else was around waiting, just the guards. Neither of them could remember ever having been so scared; their hearts pumping uncontrollably fast as the adrenaline poured through their bodies.

At the barrier, Juliette, hunched up against the cold, handed over their papers through the window.

"Raus, hier raus," shouted the soldier ordering them out of the cab, clearly angry that he was being forced away from the fire roaring away in a nearby old oil drum.

Stephen and Juliette moved and stood close together in front of the engine, their hands placed over the bonnet to keep them warm in the biting chill. They said nothing. They didn't dare. As one soldier carefully examined their papers, the other searched under the bench seat looking for stowaways. Instead, he found two bottles of de Gressier wine which had been deliberately brought along as a distraction, expecting it to be found. Pleased with his find, the wine was quickly confiscated by the soldier and their papers returned. Not a single question had been asked. Not a barrel inspected. The barrier was opened, and they were on their way. It had taken all of one minute and yet it had seemed like a lifetime. As they drove away, Juliette and Stephen had never felt so alive.

"*Vache de choix,*"[22] said Stephen, under his breath, and they both burst into a nervous fit of giggles.

Leaving Blasimon, Juliette and Stephen carefully checked to make sure they took the south-easterly road towards Cleyrac, otherwise, having successfully crossed out of the occupied zone into the free zone, they would have returned to the occupied zone again at Sauveterre-de-Guyenne.

The plan had been to stop a few kilometres from the checkpoint to release the pilots from the hell of their coffins and take them back into the warmth of the cab. However, overwhelmed by the 'fight or flight' instinct which took control of their minds, they simply needed to get away from the checkpoint as far and as fast as possible.

The agreed drop-off point was a well-chosen spot halfway between Sauveterre-de-Guyenne and Agen. It was at a Y-shaped junction where there was a coppice of trees in the bottom of the V of the Y. It would make an excellent hiding place for the pilots until they were collected. Either side of the road, on the tail of the Y, were bus shelters with bicycles left all around. Stephen and Juliette first drove past the drop off point but quickly realised their mistake.

In another sheltered spot, the two pilots were released from their black holes but there was little joy in their faces. They were both blue and shaking involuntarily from the cold. It was obvious that the two men were suffering from hypothermia. They needed to be warmed up before they could be abandoned to whatever fate was next in store.

With the two pilots back in the front seat, Juliette drove in circle after circle so they could be warmed up by the heat of the engine, some vegetable soup, which Virgil's wife had considerately packed in a vacuum flask, and their shared body warmth.

It was nearing midday when normal colour was back in the two

---

[22] Prize winning cow - the French nickname for the German soldiers and military police after the medallions which they wore around their necks.

airmen's faces and they agreed that they were warm enough to be dropped off.

Parked at the edge of the copse ready to say goodbye, Stephen suddenly asked, "Do you have any money?"

"Why?" asked Juliette, surprised.

"They'll need money for the next part of the journey."

"But surely the next person...." but she stopped mid-sentence, for there was no point in arguing.

"Do you have any money?" Juliette asked the pilots. They both shook their heads, so she dug into her purse and handed out two 10 franc notes to one and a 20 franc note to the other. The whole expedition was costing her a fortune. Then, she translated Stephen's instructions for the two pilots to hide deep in the woods until they were called for, adding that it should be today or tonight that they get collected, but she could not say when. There were then warm handshakes, plenty of smiles and words of well wishes, as the two men scampered into the woods and were gone.

Juliette and Stephen both thought it wise to continue with their plan, so with Stephen driving, as Juliette's arms were physically aching from the weight of the steering wheel, they made their way to the coopers' yard at Agen where they unloaded seven aged wine barrels for alleged repair. They brought back Virgil's two modified barrels, with the excuse that they were beyond repair.

It was late-afternoon when they got back to the checkpoint at Sauveterre-de-Guyenne, choosing the shorter route for their return journey.

There was no search of their lorry, for on the back were just a bundle of staves and four-barrel lids for anyone to see. There was a cursory examination of their papers, and they were back in the Occupied Zone.

At Sauveterre-de-Guyenne, Stephen stopped the lorry in the Place de la République just outside the Hôtel de France. "I think we should celebrate," he said. "I certainly need something to eat."

Juliette smiled in agreement. Inside the lounge they sat either side of the fire and there, whilst taking a simple plate of bread and cheese with several glasses of wine, the kinship of successful warriors grew between them.

"We happy few, we band of brothers," said Juliette very quietly in English, raising her glass in a toast to Stephen. He didn't respond. He had no knowledge of the saying. Then she added, again in English, "He today that sheds his blood with me shall be my brother."

Stephen listened to her French translation and raised his glass in response. As they tapped their wine glasses together there was, for the first time, an explosion of sexual chemistry between the two of them which tingled and excited. And so they stayed many an hour in front of the fire, eating, getting intoxicated and flirting as would normally be the preserve of teenagers or illicit lovers.

Chapter 24

Château de Gressier Spring 1941

IT WAS SOME six weeks after the mysterious Monsieur Philidor had phoned Juliette to thank her for the safe delivery of two cases of wine that he telephoned again. "I have another order for two more cases of wine for you to deliver," he said.

"No," said Juliette firmly, and paying little attention to the fact that the local telephone operator was almost certainly listening in, she exploded. "I have an invoice for four hundred francs to repair some barrels that didn't need repairing. This whole exercise has cost us well over six hundred francs, probably more. Some might assume we are rich, but we are not. Since the Germans have stolen most of our wine we are now very hard up. We only have the income from the German airmen who stay here, and that is not very much."

"We will help," said Philidor, but his commitment was not heard.

"Do you know how hard it is to get petrol nowadays?" she asked.

"We will help," repeated Philidor.

"Like you did last time?" Juliette added sarcastically.

"The packaging will be with you tomorrow."

"Then make sure it comes with the right paperwork. Last time there was nothing and it makes the task far, far too risky."

"We'll do our best," said Philidor, and with that the phone went dead.

Three more times Stephen, Virgil and Juliette worked together to get English pilots across La Ligne and into free France. Not once were the airmen provided with the identification papers Philidor had said he would try and get. They did exactly as they had done on their first trip, but there was one small, but significant, difference.

On the third and fourth trips when they stopped at the Hôtel de France, just as they had done on their previous journeys, things changed. In the excitement of what they had achieved, the lack of inhibition created by alcohol and the frisson that Juliette and Stephen had for the other, they stayed the night. In the silence of their bedroom, Juliette felt nothing of the anxiety she felt when she undressed in front of Étienne or Hugo, and they had seen her naked for the first time. She was later to think it strange given their age difference. Instead, her focus was only on one thing: she wanted Stephen to take her, to satisfy her. In response, her young novice proved to be the most energetic and generous of studs.

After they had stayed the night, Juliette and Stephen would drive back to Château de Gressier without speaking. Theirs was never an embarrassed or shameful silence. It was merely that each was contemplating the other. They knew that these moments could only ever be fleeting, and certainly not something which could continue at de Gressier. Theirs was a different love. It was an enduring love which comes from a shared danger for they each knew, without a word having passed between them, that the other would die to save them. Had Étienne felt about the same way about her, she wondered.

"Pas un groupe de Frères,"[23] said Stephen as they drove back through the gates of Château de Gressier after they had stayed away for the very first time. "Peut-être un groupe d'amoureux,"[24] he added, as he very quickly squeezed her hand and looked at her with a beaming smile. "I looked up your saying," he added.

---

[23] Not a band of brothers

[24] Perhaps a band of lovers

Chapter 25

Bordeaux June 1941

IT WAS WITH a mixture of fear and flattery that Juliette arrived at the Grand Théâtre de l' Opéra National de Bordeaux to hear a performance of Felix Mendelssohn's Midsummer Night's Dream. She had been invited as the guest of Herr Bömers and had wondered long and hard whether she should go. Fearful that he might take her refusal as an insult, she had reluctantly accepted. Deep down she was scared that, at any moment, she would be discovered as English and immediately interned. It was therefore with some relief that amongst the crowd of Nazi black uniforms, there were some of the other major wine growers of Bordeaux in the audience.

On their greeting, Bömers took Juliette by the hand and, as though she were the guest of honour, accompanied her around the auditorium introducing her to everyone as he went. She mentally kicked herself after she had curtsied to General Morizt von Fabier, now the senior officer in Bordeaux, known for his special interest in wine.

There was only one subject for discussion: the German assault on the Soviet Union army in Eastern Poland the week before. The talk constantly returned, with pride, to the size of the invading army: two million men, 3,200 planes and 10,000 tanks all attacking at once along a front of 300 kilometres. All the early reports were that the battle was going far better than could possibly have been expected. The early successes of the Wehrmacht gave the whole evening a buzz about it. At the start of the concert, to Juliette's great surprise and embarrassment, Bömers accompanied her to the very best of seats where he placed her on his right hand in the front row which had been reserved for the German High Command of Bordeaux.

Shortly after they were settled, a young German woman, oozing with confidence whilst carrying the bounce of youth and wearing the most gorgeous of emerald ball gowns, came and sat on his left. Bömers stood up to make the introductions. Juliette did not catch her name for her attention was being caught by the dazzling matching emerald and diamond jewellery which the young woman was wearing with obvious pride around her neck, wrist, and in her ears.

'Grande horizontale', thought Juliette, summing up the young woman's relationship with Bömers perfectly. It was also some relief for whatever Bömers intentions were for Juliette, it seemed they were not as inappropriate as she had immediately feared.

The young woman had no appreciation, nor would she have cared, that her jewellery had been confiscated from its former owner, a Jewess now surrounded by barbed wire, locked up in the Great Synagogue of Bordeaux, waiting with her family and friends to be sent on a cattle train to one of the extermination camps in Poland.

The concert started and finished early to allow the guests to get home before the curfew started. With the memory of music still dominating her thoughts, Juliette walked lazily back to Dominique and Henri's house where she had changed earlier and was now going to spend the night.

As she walked, she reflected on how many things had changed since she had first visited. Gone was the simple, neat, and organised household which had been the hallmark of Dominique's domestic life. Now it was a chaotic dormitory for distant relatives, lost children, and a bed for the night for those who, like Juliette, needed somewhere to sleep when passing through. There was only one room unchanged. It was Henri's study where, in his refuge and behind a locked door, his pencils and papers remained as neat and orderly as ever. Meanwhile Dominique looked quite radiant. She buzzed with organisational efficiency and, whilst she looked much slimmer and more highly toned, she worked with joy and enthusiasm in her new found purpose. Once again, Juliette wondered whether she was slightly jealous of her, but then concluded that, perhaps whatever her feelings, they were more akin to one of overwhelming admiration.

It was late in the evening, and all the children were in bed but not necessarily asleep, when Henri, Dominique, Stephen, and Juliette met on the terrace and savoured the peace. Their simple but beautiful garden was, in common with most other houses in Bordeaux, gone. It had been replaced with a carefully tended vegetable patch.

It was exactly one week to the day after the longest day and the sun had just fallen behind the roofs of the houses which backed on to their garden. The earlier warmth of the day was turning into a chill. On the table were gathered the remains of the chicken, eggs, cheese, and wine which Juliette had brought, making her a highly honoured guest, for this quantity of fresh food was a rare treat for a ration-card bound city.

Juliette and Stephen sat next to each other, but not once did they share those furtive looks only known by lovers, for this was neither their time nor their place. After a long pause in the conversation Juliette asked Henri, "What do you think will happen now Germany has attacked the Soviet Army in Poland?"

"We got that one wrong, didn't we?" said Stephen, interjecting himself into the conversation.

Henri and Dominique looked confused, unaware of Juliette and Stephen's conversation the day after Germany had invaded France.

"Only because we weren't aware of the deal between Stalin and Hitler to divide up Poland," replied Juliette defensively.

"Now we have one psychopathic crook stealing from another, all hell will be let loose," said Stephen confidently.

"Stephen," exclaimed Henri, "please. Walls have ears and comments like that put us all at risk." Stephen took his rebuke well, for he knew he had spoken foolishly.

"This is plainly crazy," added Dominique, her voice much lower following Henri's chastisement. "Germany invaded Poland so that made Germany our enemy, but when Russia invades Poland, for some strange reason, it is not our enemy when, if the same principles were to apply, it should have been. Now Germany has invaded the bit of Poland which Russia had illegally occupied; well, the whole of Russia has suddenly become our ally. Am I the only one who has lost the plot?" she asked.

"My enemy's enemy is now my friend," said Stephen. "Throughout history it has ever been thus."

"What will happen, what will be the outcome?" asked Juliette.

"Exactly the same as I predicted last year," said Stephen confidently.

Juliette reached across and touched him gently on the thigh and, by way of a very patient look, she indicated it was not a question she wanted Stephen to answer, but Henri.

"It depends," Henri answered cautiously. "I can tell you the unofficial view of the High Command in Bordeaux. If they stop, after having taken Poland and all the land as far down to include Romania, and then seek a peace treaty with Stalin, then they think they will be able to keep control of everything they will have got. Importantly, they will have won the prize of the oil fields in Romania. If they cross the border into Russia and move on Moscow, then they think Germany might eventually lose the war. They think the same thing if Germany invades Ukraine, because the Russian orthodox church originates from there. It means they are passionate about those lands too. Although, they're feeling confident now, those who think seriously about these things know it is too far to the North Pacific Sea. Germany cannot control such a large land mass. It means they will always have a Russian enemy to fight somewhere. They think the omens are not particularly good."

"But that fails to understand Stalin," interjected Juliette. "His political survival is now dependent upon beating Germany."

"I agree," said Henri. "But the German High Command thinks Stalin will not survive politically. They will keep attacking until he is gone. Their hope is that there will be a new leader suing for peace. Just like last time."

"They also don't understand Hitler," responded Juliette. "Men like that never settle for half-a-cake. He'll keep on going until he's won everything."

"I have a hypothesis," said Henri. "Russia, after retreating and applying a scorched earth policy to its own land as it did in 1812, will eventually defeat Germany going all the way to Berlin and on to its border with France. Why there you might ask?" He paused before answering his own question: "Because Russia will not allow itself to be invaded for a third time."

"A third time?" asked Stephen.

"Yes," said Henri. "Napoleon invaded Russia in 1812, nearly getting to Moscow, where his army saw the Russian's setting parts of their city on fire so there would be nothing for them to occupy. They were invaded a second time by Germany in the last war, and now."

"Do you think if Russia defeats Germany, they'll stop there?" asked Dominique. "What's to stop them from invading us, going all the way through to the Atlantic, travelling in exactly the opposite direction to Napoleon? After all, now we have no army or air force, there's nothing to stop them, and Britain is not going to take on the might of Russia alone, is it!"

"Will Russia do that?" asked Stephen. "Will Russia invade us once they get control of Germany?"

"It's possible. I am not sure Stalin will be able to resist the prize of controlling the largest land mass in the world; from the Pacific to the Atlantic," replied Henri.

"Russia will do whatever is best for Russia. It's her only consistency," commented Juliette, repeating the long-standing view of her brother and father. "It has always been imperialistic in its attitude; look at what a vast country it is; the biggest in the world. If they can take Germany and France into their dominion, with little cost, then they will try to do so," she added, pessimistically.

"Whether they cross the border into France or not, France will always be France and the French will always be French," said Dominique stridently. "Whoever occupies us, whoever tries to run us, they can never take away from the people their love of this country."

"Vive la France," said Henri, standing up and raising his glass in a toast. The others stood and together they toasted the country they loved.

"The Americans might join the war," said Stephen, "but it doesn't look likely."

"I agree" said Juliette, remembering the attitude of her friend, Joseph Kennedy. "Britain might now have the support of the US through the Lend-Lease Act, but I think they're a very long way from joining the fighting."

"That's another conversation," said Henri abruptly, "right now it's time for bed."

Later that night when everyone was asleep, the two lovers were having contrary thoughts. Juliette waited patiently, almost expectantly, for Stephen to join her, having made sure that everything she wore would make her easily available to him. Stephen's thoughts were as distant from hers as they could possibly be. He was in deep contemplation about their earlier conversation. It was now clear to him that the winners in this war were going to be the communists. It was they who were going to defeat the Nazis and it was only they who would be able to provide the new leadership which he thought France so desperately required. He didn't care that the Communists were an illegal organisation. To him it was a political injustice which had to be righted. It was where the true fight for France was going to be carried on. If the red flag of Russia, with its gold hammer crossed with a gold sickle, was going to replace the swastika of Germany over the buildings of Bordeaux, then he was going to be part of that corps of influencers. It was, he decided, time to join the Communist Party.

Chapter 26

Château de Gressier August 1941

"DO YOU KNOW we met exactly a year ago today," said Heinrik to Victoria as she served him a cold beer in the dusk of the evening. He was in an area where her mother had, before the war, tried to establish an English styled walled garden with little success. It was a sanctuary of peace but, in the heat, showed little beauty.

"Did we?" she said. "It doesn't seem that long ago."

"It is, I remember the day."

"I remember the day," said Victoria. "I just don't remember the date." She smiled at the thought of that moment.

"It seems to have been a very long year," said Heinrik, as he sipped at his beer. He appeared to be quite melancholic

"What do you think about the invasion of Russia?" asked Victoria. "I thought you were hoping the war would have ended by now, but this will make it go on even longer."

"Please don't tell anyone but ..." He paused. "I really don't understand it," said Heinrik leaning towards her and speaking quietly.

"Why?" asked Victoria sitting down next to him.

"I thought we would invade Britain this summer. She would have been easily defeated and then this war in France would have ended. The resistance is getting worse everywhere, just as I predicted. Only when we had truly won in the West should we have attacked Russia."

"I heard it said that Germany had no alternative but to attack. I am told it was a pre-emptive strike because Stalin was preparing to invade Germany through Poland at any moment. Apparently, Hitler offered half of Poland to Stalin, who now thinks Hitler didn't honoured their deal."

"What makes you say that?" asked Heinrik somewhat shocked.

"I heard it from your guys in our dining room," Victoria replied.

"Apparently German High Command's analysis of where Stalin had placed his troops was interpreted as a battle plan for an imminent attack.

"No, really?" said Heinrik surprised.

"Yes, really," replied Victoria assertively. "It's why Hitler felt he had to attack first

Heinrik pulled a face as he thought about what he had just been told. If it was true, then the change in strategy made sense.

"I don't think it matters. We are winning the war against Russia. Look how far we've got so far. In less than two months we've already got as far as Kiev and we control the skies over every battlegroup. Leningrad will be taken in days, said Heinrik. His melancholy was lifted with the thought of Germany's success.

"Have you made it back to Germany, made it back home since the war started?" asked Victoria seeking to change the subject.

"No. I've had leave but it's such a long way to go. I've preferred to come here instead."

"Do you not have a family? No brothers or sisters to go and see?" she asked.

Heinrik looked straight into her eyes, puzzled by the question. "No, there's just my mother and me," he replied quite sternly. Then he added more softly: "I think I should've liked a brother." He paused. "Or a sister, but it was not to be."

"Oh," said Victoria noncommittally, noticing the wistful nature of his reply.

"My parents lived apart for a very long time," offered Heinrik. "My father was a difficult man. I didn't like him very much."

"I didn't know my father," said Victoria. "He was murdered when I was young."

Heinrik didn't show any sign of outward emotion as he absorbed her news. "My father committed suicide," he added almost as a throw away remark.

"Oh, ... I am sorry," said Victoria. "That must be so much worse."

"Why?"

"The sense of responsibility that everyone around will have. That feeling of letting him down, of failing him," explained Victoria.

"They said he was depressed because of his job; putting down so many animals. I think it was because my mother was having an affair with a surgeon in the hospital where she worked. I don't think my father could bear the shame."

"My father was having an affair when he was killed," said Victoria very quietly. "But that wasn't why he was killed. He was killed out of jealousy by a man who wanted to marry my mother and take control of this estate. It was horrible and he was quite ghastly. We've never been allowed to speak about it since."

"Would you have liked to have a brother or sister?" asked Heinrik, seeking to change the subject.

"I had one once," she replied. Victoria stopped looking at Heinrik. Instead she stared down at the table. "I had a twin brother. He drowned in the river when we were ten. He duck-dived into some weeds, and never came up again." She sighed heavily.

"I am so sorry," said Heinrik with real feeling.

"I miss him dreadfully. There's not a day goes by when I don't think of him." Victoria took her hands off the table and, in a sign of distress, she started to rub her arms to give herself comfort through her own embrace. "I live every day as though half of me is missing. I can't explain it. I think only another twin would understand."

"What was he like? asked Heinrik.

"I don't know," replied Victoria and then she added, "I do know but then again I don't. After he died my mother removed every photograph of him from around the house. She made it as though he didn't exist."

"So you have no photograph of him?"

"No, I have a memory of what he looked like, but now....I'm not sure."

"What was he like ... as a person?" asked Heinrik sensing a sudden tension in Victoria's demeanour.

"Do you know, I've never spoken to anyone about him? Not from the day he died."

"Why not?"

"It seemed to upset everyone, so it was best not talked about."

"What was he like?" Heinrik asked again. His instinct told him that she needed to say. There was warmth and sympathy in his voice.

"He was strong, so strong not just physically but mentally. He was so determined. Nothing would make him give up. My God could we argue. He would tease me. I would retaliate but then this was our fight, no one else could join in. If they did, we'd unite and turn on them.

Victoria looked at Heinrik carefully to see if he understood what she was saying.

"He was my very best friend," she continued. "There was nothing he wouldn't do for me."

Victoria stopped speaking and swallowed hard. "He made me feel so very safe. He would have slain every Dragon in the land to protect me," she said, and then smiled as she enjoyed her allegory.

Heinrik reached across and took hold of Victoria's hand. "Will you let me slay those dragons for you now? he asked.

Victoria said nothing, she simply smiled.

"We're quite similar you 'n me," he said.

Victoria nodded very gently to agree.

"Both only children, brought up by a single mother following the death of our fathers. Both feeling that something is missing from our lives. The thing is" ..., Heinrik paused. "The thing is, I think I've found what I've been missing."

Victoria looked puzzled.

"I think the missing thing. No, I'm sure the thing missing from my life is you," said Heinrik as earnestly as he possibly could.

How could he say such a thing she wondered? They hardly knew each other.

"I don't come just for the wine, the food, and the open spaces," said Heinrik. "I promise, I come here to see you,"

Chapter 27

Latoire Village September 1941

ONE OF THE constant pressures on Juliette was the need to find flour and sugar to make the bread, cakes, and biscuits for those staying at Château de Gressier. Bread was a staple diet of everyone, but the home-made cakes and biscuits were a delicacy reserved only for those guests who were paying: the pilots of the German Luftwaffe.

Bakers in all the five villages surrounding de Gressier were conscripted into providing Juliette with one kilogram of black-market flour and half a kilogram of sugar each week. These were in addition to the amounts permitted under the ration cards which she collected from her guests. These black-market purchases were deliberately small amounts which would not be missed from each baker's supply, but together it mounted up. With de Gressier wine as the trade, it was an arrangement easily established by Gaspar Mesny. As the war went on, food became very scarce, and despite having the food ration stamps of the Luftwaffe to use, even one kilogram of the very basic ingredients became too much for even Gaspar to blag. There were shortages everywhere so making do was the necessity of every day.

It was one of Victoria's jobs to cycle each day to the designated village to collect the few contraband goods still available and bring them back in her basket, along with the other things that de Gressier needed. Long gone were the days when grocers made house calls.

As Victoria cycled into the village of Latoire, she saw a black sedan car of the Wehrmacht parked in the square. It was an unusual and therefore worrying sight. She slowed down, as the wheels of her bicycle bounced across the cobbles, to take stock of what was happening. As Victoria passed Monsieur Dufour's tabac, she was surprised to see that some of the tables and chairs, usually two deep outside his café window, were no longer in their usual place. Some had been moved across the road and placed on the grass in the shade of the trees, which were just beginning to turn to an autumn brown.

For many months, Monsieur Dufour had worried about having German customers fearing that they would immediately drive away his existing clientele. So, on that day, he put into action for the first time the plan he had prepared. As soon as the three Luftwaffe pilots appeared at his café, he took a table and moved it, and them, across the street and onto the grass opposite, telling them that this is where his tables should be. His family was still serving drinks from that same grassy spot 65 years later.

Victoria noticed that there was no one sitting at the tables under the trees. Instead, it was used as a dumping ground for coffee cups, caps, and jackets. Three men, in German uniforms, were standing around an area of hardened gravel playing pétanque. Seeing this, Victoria relaxed a little, for they were clearly not in the village on official business.

Victoria went into the baker's shop and collected and paid for her regular quantity of flour and sugar, which she placed into the wicker basket on her handlebars. She remounted her bike and set off across the street and then onto the gravel path which traversed the brown lawn in the middle of the square. She was heading towards the post office to collect whatever post might have arrived for the de Gressier Estate.

As she pedalled, Victoria looked carefully at the three airmen and, as one of them turned, it was obvious to Victoria that he was the ever so handsome Heinrik Klugman. She waved. He didn't notice her. As she got closer to the pétanque play area, Victoria waved again. In her excitement, she didn't see the pothole which she had missed hundreds of times before. This time her front wheel dug deep into the hole and her bike came to an immediate stop, throwing its passenger straight over the top of the handlebars. Victoria's hands, knees and face were torn on the gravel, with stones digging into her skin and cutting the skirt of her dress into shreds as she slid along the ground. Overcome with shock, Victoria rapidly stood up and jumped around on one leg and then the other. She shook her arms and hands in agony. She leaned forward for the pain in her knees was suddenly making her feel nauseous. Within seconds, Heinrik was at her side. Ignoring her suffering, Victoria was overcome with embarrassment, not just because Heinrik had seen what had happened but because she had made such a spectacle of herself in front of the whole village.

Heinrik and one of his colleagues held Victoria by the arm as they assisted her to limp back to where they had been seated. The third carried Victoria's bike with its buckled front wheel. Heinrik gave an order for one of his colleagues to get water and cloths from the café and the other to get bandages and plasters from the chemist. It was only when Victoria was sitting that, in shock, she started to cry.

Pouring water from the jug, Heinrik very gently washed the gravel out of Victoria's wounds. Thankfully, there were no deep cuts but nevertheless the bleeding was quite profuse for large areas of her skin had been torn away. Taking a bottle of cognac, which Monsieur Dufour had brought out, Heinrik poured some brandy gently over Victoria's grazes, arguing that the alcohol would be a good disinfectant. She screamed violently as the stinging aggravated the pain she was already suffering. Rather than making her feel better, it made her feel much worse.

The villagers from the shops gathered around Victoria wanting to protect one of their own from the Germans, but when they saw the care and attention Heinrik was giving her they moved away.

Taking one of the glasses of water which had been served with their coffee, Heinrik filled it one third full with cognac and instructed Victoria to drink it. She did as she was told but, instead of sipping gently, she took a mouthful as though she were drinking wine, causing another burning sensation, but this time on her lips and in her gullet. Heinrik, seeing her mistake, reached for the glass to slow her down. "Woah, Woah, petite, petite," he said.

Victoria looked into Heinrik's eyes. She saw the biggest, kindest smile. Once again, she noticed his blond hair and his blue eyes which were nothing like Victor's but the shape of his face, the shape of his nose, his ears and chin were incredibly similar to those of her brother. But it was the way Heinrik smiled which captivated her. It was a loving, supportive, cheeky smile just as her brother would share, and seeing it, Victoria felt a calm which she hadn't felt for a very long time.

With the glass of brandy emptied, Victoria felt decidedly lightheaded as she climbed into the back seat of the Luftwaffe's sedan car, for the journey back to de Gressier. Heinrik sat next to her in the back seat. His two companions sat in the front, with the front passenger nursing Victoria's flour and sugar, which luckily had not been damaged in her accident. Her bike, with its crunched front wheel, was placed in the dickie seat which folded out from the boot.

Feeling bruised and a little intoxicated, Victoria slumped in her seat and closed her eyes as she travelled. She did not notice that, with her skirt badly torn, she was revealing the whites of her inner thighs. Heinrik had seen similar sights when he had worked with his mother in her hospital, but nothing was as appealing or mesmerising as this. His first intention was to cover Victoria and protect her modesty, but instead very gingerly he placed his warm hands on her legs just above the bandage on her knee. Then, very slowly he started to rub her leg and then very tentatively the inside of her thigh. Such was the excitement created by Heinrik's touch that Victoria no longer felt the stings of her wounds. When the car came to stop in de Gressier's drive, Victoria wished it not so, for she didn't want the sensation, which was streaming throughout her whole body, to end.

Their patient was placed into the safe arms of Juliette who, rapidly deciding that Victoria had been well looked after, forsook her daughter's needs. Instead, she went through the formalities of signing in the three airmen. They were staying for three nights, a few days of rest away from their air war.

It was late afternoon when a very dirty and sweaty Leutnant Klugman knocked at the side door of The Cellar and asked for Victoria. She left the kitchen table and hobbled through the hall to the door. They smiled the instant they saw each other. Victoria once again thanked him for rescuing her and, out of habit Heinrik saluted and clicked his heels in response. He had, in his hands, Victoria's bicycle with the front wheel repaired.

It is impossible to make a bicycle wheel completely straight again when it has been buckled, because once the metal has been stretched, it cannot be shrunk. However, with spokes salvaged from another wheel and others straightened in a vice, and by patiently standing on the wheel frame to force everything back into shape, it was possible, using the limited tools in the de Gressier garage, to get something which ran reasonably close to true. The wheel was never going to be as good as new but Heinrik's repair enabled the bike to be used in reasonable safety once again. Strangely, the toughest job was mending the inner tube because the rubber had been badly cut. It took the patience of Job for Heinrik to make the vulcanised repair. Many times he wanted to give up but he kept going, for as history has shown, the beauty of a woman has driven lesser men to greater things.

In the delight of having her bike back again, it didn't take much encouragement from Heinrik for Victoria to try it out. Feeling the stiffness of her bruises and her wounds being stretched open, she started to cycle tentatively at first and then feeling the freedom which she always felt when riding her bike, she chose to pedal down the hill towards the river. Heinrik ran by her side, watching the front wheel run through the front forks. It was running about 2mm either side of true which meant that at one time the wheel touched the right brake pad and then the left. Nevertheless, both Victoria and Heinrik were pleased with his work.

Victoria cycled away towards the river's edge where she stopped, turned around to make sure Heinrik was following, and then dismounted. She walked, pushing the bike, to her bench; the bench with her name engraved on it. There she lowered the bicycle to the ground before she sat down.

De Gressier's need for that scarce resource, food, meant that every scrap of land had to be cultivated. The lawn, where Heinrik and his colleagues had run around before swimming naked the summer before, had been dug up. Now there were just two strips of narrow lawn in front of each bench running straight down to the river's edge. Growing around each seat was a crop of maize which was now very tall, creating for each bench its own private den overlooking the river, with the fields beyond and towards the sky.

By early evening, the grey rain clouds, which had given rise to an autumnal feeling in the morning, had blown away. There were now white puffball clouds floating high in the blue sky, racing inland from the sea. The maize creaked as it moved gently in the breeze.

Heinrik threw himself on the ground and whilst he was sitting at Victoria's feet, he spoke to her in German. Although she had been trying to take German lessons, Victoria didn't understand. She replied in French. In turn, he spoke some stultified French which she helped correct. There was an intensity as he studied Victoria's face, willing her to understand him. In return. she spoke to him in the language they shared, English. At this point his face beamed and she saw it again, her brother's smile. Victoria blinked several times, to check what she was seeing; it was still there, her brother's smile. Confused, she smiled coyly in return.

"Mademoiselle," said Heinrich, formally. There was stiffness in his approach. "May I say I think you are beautiful," he said in English.

"May I say I think you are beautiful," repeated Victoria, very softly. She said the words as though each syllable was bouncing in delight around her taste buds. She smiled back.

Heinrik sat at her feet as they talked of her wounds. They laughed at her embarrassment at her crash, and they admired his engineering ability to put her bike back together again. Most of all, they reminded themselves that they had met for the first time at this very spot just over a year ago, when Heinrik had no clothes on.

Once again, Heinrik very gently touched Victoria's legs and immediately she warmed with the sensation. He then moved to kneel in front of her where he kissed the bandages on her knee, and then very gently, very slowly he started to kiss either side of her inner thighs. Unconsciously, Victoria slowly moved her legs apart to allow him to continue whilst, at the same time, she forced her dress down between her legs. She watched his oily, dirty hands stroking the outside of her thighs, but she didn't care. There was something both wondrously right, and at the same time frightening, about what he was doing. She took hold of his head and with his hair held tightly in her hands, she ruled this far and no further.

The excitement was too much for Heinrik. He knew he had to stop or he would embarrass himself, so he moved to sit beside her and holding hands, they kissed. There was no need for words. The kisses were short touches at first but quickly they turned into full embraces. Heinrik's dirty hands undid two of the buttons at the top of Victoria's dress, and as they continued to kiss, he slipped his hand under her bra and on to her breasts. Upon this touch, and as his fingers gently circled her nipples, she forced her mouth more firmly onto his. The look in her eyes told him that he should not stop.

It was then that they both heard the shouts across the fields. "Victoria, where are you? Victoria are you all right?"

The newly found lovers quickly adjusted their dress and were sitting formally next to each other when the search party came into view.

"Do you know Leutnant Klugman speaks English?" blurted Victoria, revealing a fact which was already widely known.

Chapter 28

Château de Gressier September 1941

"MAY I BUY the motorbike in the barn?" asked Leutnant Klugman, in stilted but much improved schoolboy French. He had presented himself smartly at Juliette's front door in his uniform.

"What motorbike?" replied Juliette, not realising what Heinrik was talking about.

"The big motorbike in the barn," repeated Heinrik. "There's only one. It's the black one with the dented and rusty petrol tank and the torn seat. It's dirty, filthy dirty." As he spoke, so he became more confident in his French and his speech started to become reasonably fluent, aided by the fact that he had discussed the pile of metal with Stephen Bellanger earlier.

The instant Heinrik mentioned the words 'torn seat' Juliette knew he was talking about Étienne's motorbike. It had been left lying there idle since it had been returned by the police after his accident some ten years before.

"Does it work?" asked Juliette.

"I don't know," said Heinrik. "I haven't tried to start it yet."

"Don't you think that you should find out, before you try to buy it?" she asked.

"Then, if it does, you'll want more money for it."

"True, but who says I want money?"

"You want something else?" asked Heinrik, realising the negotiations had already started.

"Yes, I want my tractor back. The one you stole!"

"I've stolen nothing, madame," protested Heinrik, before he realised Juliette was referring to the confiscation by the German army of motor machinery wherever it could be found, taken in raid after raid, throughout France in the previous fifteen months. Juliette's car and the two estate vans had already been taken. Her flatbed lorry only escaped the same fate because not only did Virgil remove the rotor arm and cap but, he took off the starter motor making sure it could not be taken anywhere, otherwise than when they needed it for their *passer* work.

"It's impossible! I can't get a tractor Madame," said Heinrik.

"Then it's impossible for me to sell my motorbike," announced Juliette triumphantly.

"May I try and start it?" asked Heinrik.

Juliette signified her agreement and walked away without comment. It was just something else which the Germans would steal, and to be fair she would be happy if it were gone. It was something which always caused her distress whenever she saw it, but then again, she could never bring herself to let it go.

Back at the barn, Heinrik tried to move Étienne's motorbike. It was incredibly heavy with many of the parts rusted together, such that the back wheel had to be dragged because it would not move freely.

Heinrik's first task, once he had the bike out in the sunshine, was to wash it. A sheet had protected it from ten years of bird droppings, but nevertheless, the general filth accumulated over that time made everything dull and nasty to touch. He spent the first day cleaning, scrubbing off rust with wire wool, and then coating everything he'd cleaned with a very fine layer of household oil. By the end of the day, he had freed the wheels, loosened the forks so the handlebars moved freely and had the brakes working properly.

The next day, Heinrik tackled the engine. The piston had not seized but the inside of the cylinder had, in the absence of oil, become pitted with rust, which needed to be rubbed free. Very patiently he took everything apart and put it back together again. Then, with petrol and oil purloined from the estate's lorry, Heinrik tried to kick start it. He tried several times, but nothing came to life. Sitting on the bike and moving it with his legs swinging from side to side, he started rolling it down the hill towards the river. As the bike gathered speed, so he released the clutch in an attempt to bounce start it. All that happened was that it came to an almost abrupt stop. Depressing the clutch, Heinrik tried again going a little faster this time before he engaged the gears and got the piston moving. The bike coughed once, coughed twice, and then roared into life before it died again. One more attempt, and with much better choke control, Heinrik had Étienne's bike working. His mission was achieved, for with this as his means of transport, he would be able to leave Bordeaux whenever he had a day off to come and see Victoria at Château de Gressier.

It was an oily and very dirty Heinrik, who presented himself to Juliette to conclude his purchase of the bike. He had been able to locate a 1930's Eicher tractor in Bamberg. He knew it had worked two years before but now he wasn't certain. He presented the terms of his proposed deal to Juliette. He would organise for the tractor to be sent to Château de Gressier, and once there, he would swap the bike for the tractor. In the meantime, he would leave a cash deposit with Juliette in case the tractor didn't arrive. Given that Heinrik could requisition the bike without payment, it was a bargain Juliette had no difficulty in accepting.

Chapter 29

Château de Gressier September 1941

THE BROKEN BAFFLE in the exhaust pipe meant that Victoria heard the roar of a motorbike long before it came into view. Although she had another five kilometres to pedal before she reached the neighbouring village of Génissac, she stopped at the side of the road. She watched as the motorbike went past, swung around, and came back towards her. The sound of the engine seemed to cause everything to vibrate.

"I thought it was you," shouted Heinrik, as he stopped the engine.

"I knew it was you," she replied.

They smiled sweetly and chatted for five long minutes, sharing admiring words as young men and women do.

"Would you like a lift?" asked Heinrik.

"No thank you," said Victoria.

"Come on, leave your bike here. We'll go into the village. You can do whatever you have to do, then I'll bring you back here. It will be fun."

Victoria looked up and down the road before answering. She wasn't sure. She wanted to say yes but didn't want to be seen.

"Just to the edge of the village?" she instructed. "Where you'll wait for me?"

"If that's what you want," said Heinrik, moving forward to make room on the back and pointing to the footrests.

Victoria climbed up, swung her leg over the back seat and sat down. Heinrik stood up, kick-started the engine, and as he sat down, he slid his buttocks back pressing them between Victoria's thighs. Taking one of her hands at a time, he wrapped her arms around his waist and yelled for her to hold on. He roared the engine, slipped the clutch, and sped off. Quickly, he changed gear once, then twice more as he accelerated the bike as fast as possible. Victoria hung on tight, feeling the air being forced into her mouth and making her eyes water as her hair streamed behind and about her face. She found it both exhilarating and frightening at the same time.

Heinrik leaned the bike into the first corner, accelerating as he went. She squeezed her legs around his buttocks and tightened her grip around his stomach. At the next corner and going still faster, he leaned the bike in the opposite direction. She squeezed him still tighter. The vibration of the bike underneath her set every one of her sensations alive.

In less than 5 minutes, they were on the outskirts of Génissac, but Heinrik kept going until they were just a little way from the centre, when he stopped. Victoria dismounted with everyone looking at her. Although Heinrik was not in uniform, there were disapproving looks from the villagers as they all assumed the driver was a German soldier. No Frenchman had a motorbike anymore and if they did, they had no petrol to start it.

Victoria ran to the baker's shop taking with her the bag which Heinrik had carried on his petrol tank. She bounced from one foot to another as she waited impatiently to be served. It seemed to take an age, but it was only seconds before Victoria had her supply of flour and sugar and was out of the door and running back to where Heinrik had parked.

Heinrik took Victoria's bag, and balanced it back on the top of the petrol tank, as she remounted the motorbike. With her grip tight, they shot off, heading back to where Victoria's bike had been left, but they didn't stop there; instead, the happy young couple raced around the lanes of the Gironde, both thrilled by the speed, the sound and holding each other tight.

It was about an hour later when Heinrik returned Victoria to her bike. Both were laughing from the effects of the adrenalin in their bodies. Neither could remember when they had had so much fun.

Immediately Victoria had dismounted, Heinrik grabbed her with one hand around her waist and pulled her into him. It was a masterful touch which was followed quickly by a passionate kiss on the lips, all of which surprised and delighted Victoria, who quickly broke away in the fear that she might be seen.

Taking her shopping, Victoria retrieved her bike and started to pedal back towards home. Frantically, she shooed Heinrik away. "I'll see you back at de Gressier," she instructed. "Now go!"

Heinrik roared into the distance and was quickly gone from sight. There was now peace in the air; just the sound of Victoria's slightly wobbly bike moving along the road. But there was no calm for she was pedalling just as fast as she could to get back to de Gressier. Not only was she late, and her mother would be worried, but she had to get back so Heinrik could kiss her like that once more.

Chapter 30

Bordeaux October 1941

HEINRIK HAD BEEN away from Château de Gressier for only a few days. He had left just before the end of the harvest but, now he was back. Victoria was certain he was different. She could not say what it was. He was now in the uniform of a Hauptman,[25] but it was more than that. As he stood in the hall of The Cottage, there was no man more confident for, along with his promotion, Heinrik was being transferred to the most prestigious flight in the Wehrmacht. There is one thing about confidence; it's an aphrodisiac, and one to which Victoria was not immune.

Once again, the Cottage had mistakenly been overbooked with German aircrew. Very much to Juliette's chagrin, it meant she was forced to use the spare bedrooms of The Cellar. However, there was one room which was inviolate to the enemy. It was Victor's former bedroom, next to Victoria's. Tonight, it was going to have its first 'foreign guest' sleeping there since Stephen had moved out; and that honoured guest was to be Heinrik.

Victoria and Heinrik left the Cottage where Heinrik had registered, walked under the Gallery to the side door of the Cellar where they climbed the stairs. In Victor's bedroom, logs were burning gently in the grate. It made the room feel warm and inviting. In the privacy of the bedroom, Victoria gracefully swayed a welcoming dance around the pilot, who was resplendent in his new uniform. Heinrik placed his small case on the bed and hung up his coat and hat.

Although it was not cold, Heinrik moved to warm himself in front of the fire. As he did so, he offered Victoria his hand and as she took it, he tugged and then, with the other hand taking her around the waist,

---

[25] Captain

he pulled her into him. She yielded to his kiss. It was tender, gentle, and passionate. Neither wanted the moment to end. For the first time, Victoria was feeling the masculinity of the male; the hardness of his muscles and the strength of his frame. Heinrik was feeling the softness of her breasts and the gentle curve over her hips. Each was captivated by the smell of the other. Embarrassed, they broke away, only to resume kissing just a few moments later.

But something was wrong, Victoria could sense it. Heinrik was nervous - apprehensive - which made her feel worried, very worried. Her mind went back to her bicycle accident and their first kiss by the river. She remembered their exhilarating ride on her father's old motor bike after which he pulled her tightly into his body, but it was when he took her into his arms and they kissed, just before he had last departed, that she knew there was something very special between them. Now his touch was like none of those moments. Had he not said that she was 'the thing missing from his life.' Had he not said that 'he only felt truly complete when he was with her.' Had he changed his mind, she wondered But then his kiss just now; how could he possibly be lying to her when he kissed like that?

You need to come to the kitchen," said Victoria breaking from his touch. "We've saved you some soup and bread. I think there may be some cheese and pâté as well," she added.

Moments later, with her hips swaying from the mere pleasure of having him around, Victoria led Heinrik into the informality of the family kitchen. There he was prompted to sit at the head of the table. Juliette was already there and she instantly noticed the difference. "You've had a promotion Leutnant Klugman," she said sharply. "What's your rank now?"

"Hauptman," he replied, thrusting his chest out in pride.

"Congratulations!" said Juliette as she wondered why, of all their German 'guests', it was only this young man who was consistently invited into their kitchen.

"I am to be posted to the Führer's flight," he said proudly. "This is my last time here. I've come to say goodbye or perhaps I should say au revoir." His accent remained stilted but otherwise his French had improved significantly.

"Congratulations," repeated Juliette, as she heard Victoria make a short-muffled gasp.

"Why you?" asked Victoria breathlessly, her voice rising in pitch from emotional stress.

I'm a good navigator pilot; one of the best," he boasted, "and the Führer wants only the very best."

"I'm sure it's a great honour," said Juliette, as she looked towards Victoria who was stunned into silence. She hadn't heard his reply. Her brain was screaming inside her head: 'You're my friend, you're my best friend. You can't go. You can't go!'

"Where will you be going?" asked Juliette.

"I am not allowed to say," said Heinrik and then, after a pause, he added, "Berlin" for the answer was obvious. He looked towards Victoria whose face was ridged, so determined was she not to show her emotions.

When will you be going?" asked Juliette, thinking about her bookings more than anything else.

"I meet him the day after tomorrow," said Heinrik proudly as he ignored the question.

"Who?" said Juliette, instinctively knowing exactly who he was talking about, but not wanting to give Heinrik the satisfaction of presuming she knew.

"Herr Hitler, the Führer. He's stopping off in Bordeaux on 23rd October. I've been ordered to meet him on the Fuehrerzug[26]. It's his special train. It's called 'Erika'. You mustn't tell anyone. No one is to know."

"Of course not," said Juliette lying. She would tell Monsieur Philidor as soon as she could.

"His train is stopping just to meet you?" asked Victoria, both impressed and incredulous at the same time.

"No, not just me, but with the local High Command too," said Heinrik. "I feel very honoured."

"I am sure you do," said Juliette, the obvious sarcasm being missed by Heinrik through his limited French but instantly noticed by Victoria.

---

[26] Leader's Train

"I am here tonight and tomorrow night and then, after I've seen the Führer, I catch the next available train from Bordeaux to Paris."

Victoria said nothing. She had sunk deep into the kitchen chair as her brain screamed even louder. "You can't go. You mustn't go." Instead she smiled sweetly. She didn't know what else she could do.

Chapter 31

Château de Gressier October 1941

AS EVERY PARTNER of every soldier, sailor or airman will tell you, there is a mass of emotion pressing down on your body when you know that your loved one is about to be posted away. It is so powerful it squeezes every element to your core and yet, under this enormous pressure, you want to make those last few moments together very special. You don't want to be apart for a second until that moment comes when he or she must leave.

That night, long after Château de Gressier had fallen fast asleep, there were two people wide awake. Heinrik and Victoria were each busy thinking of the other and the kisses they had enjoyed earlier. Victoria found the situation was emotionally overwhelming. With her mind spinning she became convinced that the reticence she'd felt from Heinrik's kisses earlier had been caused by the news he didn't want to share - that he was leaving. Nothing had changed. She was still, as he had once said, 'the person he'd been looking for'. She was sure of it.

For Victoria, the thought of being away from Heinrik was proving too much. He was leaving in two days and she needed to spend as much time with him as she could before he went. She just needed to. He had to know that she wanted him to come back to her. It was with these feelings that Victoria, dressed only in her nightie, very quietly tiptoed down the corridor, into Heinrik's bedroom and into his bed. Heinrik welcomed her under the sheets. Not a word was spoken as she slowly rested her head on his chest, swung her leg across his and moved herself to lay in the sanctuary of his arms.

Night after night, when he was alive, Victoria would snuggle up to her brother in his bed, so cuddling up to Heinrik was the most natural thing in the world for her to do. Except this time was different. Heinrik was strong like her brother, but the movement of Heinrik's hand excited her whereas Victor's had been soothing. Lying with Victor seemed permissible, for they had been side-by-side before they were even born but now, with Heinrik by her side, it seemed risky and dangerous as though she were eating forbidden fruit.

They stayed motionless for a long time until they moved in unison to lie on their side so that their bodies naturally fitted into one another. As they cuddled, Heinrik snuggled up into Victoria's back with his arm wrapped protectively around her shoulders. The nervous excitement Victoria felt was made more electric by the way Heinrik twisted and played very gently with her hair, curling it around his fingers until there was no more hair to curl when it would fall away. He would do the same thing, time and time again just as her brother would do. Was this a sign she wondered? Was Victor telling her that he approved of Heinrik as her future husband?

Victoria's thoughts of Victor did not linger long as her mind was distracted by the sensuousness of Heinrik's warm hands as they moved up inside her nightie and, ever so gently, explored every part of her naked body. She was tingling to his touch. Moving very slowly, and only a millimetre each time, she gently pulled and pushed her bottom backwards and forwards into his groin as Heinrik, overcome with embarrassment as to what was happening with his body, kept his hips motionless. Neither spoke, nor did they sleep. In the magic of the moment it was all they could do to breathe.

Chapter 32

Château de Gressier October 1941

VICTORIA WAS BACK in her own bed when those in the Cellar started to wake. When she came downstairs at her normal time, Heinrik was not in the kitchen or in either of the dining rooms. He had taken himself for a swim in the river which, when she heard, Victoria thought quite mad as it would be freezing cold.

Throughout the day they drifted in and out of each other's company. Usually Heinrik would seek work in the vineyards but with the harvest collected the only thing for him to do was to relax. He lolled about in the library of the Cottage, shared some faint banter with his colleagues until they walked into Latoire Village for lunch and then back again.

Victoria completed her household chores and from mid-morning until late afternoon she attended to her studies. Although the war had stopped formal schooling for her age group, Juliette remained determined that Victoria was going to university, just as she had done, war or no war. It meant a tutoring program which was as extensive as Juliette could devise.

Heinrik had dinner that night with his military colleagues in the dining room of The Cottage where, as she always did, Victoria acted as waitress. They shared furtive, secret glances as lovers do on such occasions. It was the little twinkle in each other's eyes as their gaze touched which they found exciting.

Once again, long after Château de Gressier had fallen fast asleep, Victoria tiptoed down the corridor to Heinrik's bedroom. This time, standing on the edge of his bed, she undid the buttons to her nightie and allowed it to fall to the ground. Naked, she climbed in beside him where she found him naked too. His pyjamas of the night before lay abandoned in the expectation of this very moment. With his confidence boosted by the wine he'd drunk over dinner, Heinrik nervously, tentatively, but with tremendous care and consideration, became the most ardent and persistent of lovers. It was a union so perfect, so right that, in their breathlessness and afterglow of love making, Victoria found she loved him even more.

In the morning, just as the house started to stir, Victoria tiptoed out of his room but this time, rather than going back to her bedroom, she retrieved the key to the Gallery and unlocked and unbolted its door. It was the very first time since the Germans had arrived that the door had been opened. She went to her father's desk, which had remained virtually unchanged from the day he died. There, in the bottom right hand drawer, she found the two gold pocket watches given to Victor and her by their grandfather when they were born.

Taking the two watch cases, Victoria returned to Heinrik's room to find the fire ablaze. Heinrik was partially dressed and sitting on the floor tying up his boots. "I want you to have this," she said handing him her brother's pocket watch in its velvet green case covered in a cardboard protective sleeve.

Heinrik accepted the box but he didn't immediately open it. His attention was taken by Victoria's long legs silhouetted by the light from the fire which shone through her white cotton nightie. It would be a sight he would remember forever.

"It was Victor's," she explained before pausing, "it's one of a pair alongside mine."

Heinrik nodded, for they had already talked in depth about Victor's death. It had made them the same, only children brought up by a single mother. It was therefore with some solemnity and great care that Heinrik pulled the green velvet jewellers' box from out of its cardboard outer sleeve. He flipped the lid open and, like everyone else who had seen the golden pocket watch before him, he had to take it out of its box and touch its majesty. The cleanness of its lines, the simplicity of its pattern, the brilliance of the diamonds at each hour point and, above all, the magnificence of its gold, made it unquestionably an object of desire.

"See, they're the same," said Victoria, taking her watch out of its case and showing it to him. "The only difference is the engraving; mine says Victoria and Victor's says, well, Victor obviously." She giggled nervously.

"I can't possibly take this," said Heinrik, shaking his head and putting the watch back to nestle where it had always lain in its cream silk bedding.

"Please," said Victoria, her eyes now moist with emotion. "If you have it, I know you will come back to me."

"Honestly, Victoria, I can't take it."

"I'm lending it to you," she replied, an urgency developing in her voice. "It will bring you luck." The fact that it had failed to bring Victor luck was, at that moment, not obvious to either of them.

Heinrik closed the lid, placed the velvet box back into its outer cardboard box and handed it back to Victoria who was now squatting beside him. He rubbed the back of her calves, the curve of her bottom and the small of her back in a token effort to bring some comfort after his refusal.

Victoria stood up and stepped back. Taking one of his shirts, she wrapped it around the package and then placed it deep inside his leather bag.

"You must bring it back," she said, with a questioning look on her face. "When this war ends, as it will, then you must bring it back to me."

Heinrik nodded.

"Promise?" she said.

"I promise," said Heinrik.

"I will be waiting for you," she said. "I will wait forever."

Heinrik stood up and, standing very proudly before her, took hold of Victoria's hands and looked deeply into her eyes.

"I will treasure it, keep it safe and bring it back to you," he said, "I don't know when, but it's a promise, I swear."

They kissed slowly and gently and then, hearing voices and people moving, he urgently shooed her out, as he didn't want her to be compromised by being seen coming out of his room. But it didn't matter to Victoria for now, in her womanhood, she walked with a newfound confidence. It was as though all the secrets of the universe had been revealed. But most of all she knew, beyond doubt, that Heinrik would come back to her. They loved each other too much for it not to be so.

Leaving his motorbike behind, Heinrik left de Gressier without seeing Victoria again.

Chapter 33

Erika – Bordeaux 23rd October 1941

YEARS LATER, WHEN Heinrik would try and offer an explanation as to how Hitler became so powerful, he would say it was his eyes: "They were like meteors. Lost in space, frozen and disconnected from any human emotion. They stared at you with an intensity which, when coupled with the energy that radiated around him, made him frighteningly intimidating."

"I'm told you're joining the F.d.F."[27] said Hitler to Heinrik, after the two men had first saluted and then shaken hands.

"Do you know SS – StandarttenFührer Hans Baur?" asked Hitler, referring to his personal pilot.

"No Führer. I've heard of him, of course, but we have never met," said Heinrik.

"I don't like flying. I only fly with Hans Baur. He's been my pilot for over eight years but apparently there is now so much work he needs more pilots in his squadron."

Heinrik said nothing as he watched Hitler study him carefully.

"Ever crashed?" Hitler asked.

"No Führer."

"Ever shot down an enemy plane?"

"No Führer. We don't get many enemy planes in this area of the Atlantic"

"Then what have you done? Why have they suggested you join my flight?" There was genuine puzzlement, perhaps even a little sarcasm, in Hitler's voice.

"I've bombed two British frigates in the Atlantic, Führer," said Heinrik with a certain amount of pride.

---

[27] Fliegerstaffel de Führer – Aviation Squadron of the Leader

"Did they sink?" Hitler asked.

"No, but they were badly damaged; enough to put them out of the war for a long time," said Heinrik assertively in his defence.

Hitler looked at the briefing papers in front of him.

"You've been in Bordeaux a long time."

"Yes Führer, fourteen months."

"What do you think about the French resistance in Bordeaux?" asked Hitler. "I've just ordered an increase in the number of hostages we shoot for each man of ours the French Resistance kills down here. Fifty appears to have little or no effect so I've increased the number to one hundred. That will stop them. You've lived here a long time. Was that the right thing to do?" he asked.

Was his question rhetorical, Heinrik wondered. He wasn't sure, for Hitler had stopped looking at him.

"I'd let the French police do their work," he said. "I think most of them are with us. Get them to find the murderers and bring them to trial." Heinrik wanted to go on. He wanted to say that reprisals would only make the French hate them more, but he could see that Hitler wasn't listening. Their meeting was mentally over, even if it still had a few minutes to physically run.

It was with the Wehrmacht slogan, *Jeder einmal in Paris*[28] in his mind that Hauptmann Heinrik Klugman boarded his first-class carriage at Bordeaux Railway Station for a few days in, what he had correctly heard, was one of the most amazing cities in the world. His final destination remained Berlin and Tempelhof Airport.

Immediately after he had settled into his seat, Heinrik looked at the gold pocket watch Victoria had given him. He stroked its smooth glass and shiny outer casing. I am going to come back here, marry Victoria and make wine, thought Heinrik. He was certain he was going to settle down somewhere close to Latoire village. He knew it was where his heart would always want to be.

---

[28] Everyone should see Paris once.

Chapter 34

Bordeaux, Nantes and Château de Gressier October 1941

VICTORIA GLANCED AT her watch all day on 23rd October. She kept wondering whether it was 'right now' that Heinrik was meeting with Hitler. She felt a strange sense of pride for knowing a man who would be working so closely with him; albeit she knew of her mother's disapproval of 'the Corporal', as she would secretly call him. If Victoria had known that Hitler had asked Heinrik about his decision to order an increase in the number of French hostages shot in reprisal for the shooting of Dr Hans Reimer[29] she would have been appalled.

The very next day, just after midday, three lorries left Bordeaux and headed west for the Camp de Souge in Martignas-sur-Jalle.[30] The convoy was preceded by a sedan car in which two German officers were seated in the rear. In the first two lorries were fifty French communists all handcuffed together singing La Marseillaise. In the last truck were armed German soldiers. At Camp de Souge, the

---

[29] On 20th October 1941, Leutnant Colonel Karl Hotz, Feldkommandant of Nantes, was killed by a commando unit of the French Resistance made up of Gilbert Brustlein, Marcel Bourdarias and Spartaco Guisco. On 22nd October 1941, 27 hostages were shot at the Camp de Choisel in Châteaubriant and 21 hostages were shot in Nantes in retaliation for the killing of Hotz. The youngest person executed was Guy Môquet; he was just seventeen years old. On 21st October 1941, Dr Hans Reimer, a military lawyer, was strolling gently through the streets of Bordeaux, going about his work as a customs border officer, when he was shot twice in the back by Pierre Rebière, a communist militant, and died.

[30] Souge had been a French military camp since 1915 and had been taken over by the Germans serving from July 1940 to the spring of 1941 as the headquarters of Erwin Rommel's 7th Panzer Division.

hostages were lined up, three at a time, and with every man refusing a blindfold, they were executed. They were singing patriotic songs as they died.

At the same time as the three lorries drove into Camp de Souge, there was a loud and consistent scraping of heavy tyres and screeching of brakes on the driveway of Château de Gressier. The sound announced that there was something wrong, very wrong and everyone on the Estate froze in a deeply chilling, sweaty, and sickening fear.

The first vehicle through the gate was a motorcycle with sidecar and mounted machine gun. Next came a black Mercedes Sedan of the Gestapo. It was followed by an armoured car, and finally at the rear was a lorry loaded with German soldiers.

At that moment, Juliette and Eric Dubois were walking towards his plumber's van. Another two packages in the rear were being delivered to be taken across La Ligne. Juliette's first instinct was to run, but where to? Instead she walked purposefully towards the black Sedan as though she was greeting any guest. Then, very serenely, revealing her English upper-class upbringing, she offered her hand to the plain-clothed officer. The smile which she fixed onto her face was immediately enchanting. "Pardonnez-moi," she said, "I had no idea one of our guests was so important that they got their own escort."

"What?" said the Gestapo officer puzzled, as the soldiers rapidly alighted from the back of the lorry and spread themselves around the Château.

"Are you not a guest, monsieur?"

"No," he answered, for a moment confused by the question. "I have come for Stephen Bellanger."

"Why?" she asked, using a very gentle tone which was designed to disarm. If she had felt fear before, Juliette was now in complete terror. Her head began to spin, and she started to feel faint. She looked towards Dubois for comfort, but he stood stock-still by the side of his van. There was no expression on his face.

"For questioning, madame. Where is he, please?"

"Search the house," ordered the leutnant to his soldiers, as he left the security of his armoured car.

"He's not in the house. He will be in the office in the barn, or in the fields," said Juliette, confidently. "Let me walk with you."

No sooner were those words out of her lips when she saw Stephen walking purposefully towards her. There was a briskness in his step and a scowl upon his face. The soldiers, who were ordered to the barn, ran past him, not appreciating that this was their quarry.

Stephen said nothing as he came by her side.

"They have come for you, Stephen," she said with an unfortunate emphasis on the word you.

At this news, his face gave her the biggest smile and his eyes sparkled in the relief that it was him they wanted and not her.

"Stephen Bellanger?" asked the Gestapo officer. "You are wanted for questioning, come with me."

"Of course," said Stephen, "always happy to oblige." There was jollity in his voice and the smile remained on his face disguising whatever his true feelings were.

Stephen was ordered into the back of the Sedan where he sat by himself looking out towards Juliette. He nodded and looked straight into her eyes. With his face framed through the window, he smiled his most handsome and cheeky smile. One which only a man possessed with supreme confidence could muster.

Immediately she saw his smile, Juliette recognised it. It was the same assured smile, yielded at moments of adversity, as Étienne's. Could he be Étienne's son she wondered for the thousandth time?

As quickly as the soldiers had dispersed in their search, they were ordered back in the trucks, and with the convoy sweeping around the drive, they left with the same speed as they had arrived.

Juliette walked slowly towards Dubois gathering her composure. "The answer is no, emphatically no!" she cried angrily.

"Can you hide them?" he asked.

"No," she almost shouted. "Stephen's house will now get searched and there is nowhere here. The Germans are everywhere. You have to go, it's the end," and with that she walked away. There would be no change of mind, at least not until Stephen was free.

Looking out at the whole scene from a top window of The Cellar was Victoria. She was in deep shock. Her Stephen, the Stephen that everyone, including her, expected to marry; the Stephen who was her nearest and dearest friend, had just been taken prisoner by 'the enemy'. It then dawned on her. She was in love with one of the enemy. "How could this be?" she wondered out loud.

Chapter 35

Bordeaux October 1941

THE TWO WOMEN arrived outside the café a few moments apart. It was the same café where Étienne and Dominique had started their affair, but the irony was lost on Juliette as she did not know of the connection. It was two days after Stephen had been arrested. Their greeting was one prolonged embrace as, in silence, they each sought to comfort the other. They now sat opposite and held hands across the café table. Still neither had spoken. Both women looked dreadful, both overwhelmed with fear, exhausted and yet unable to sleep.

It was Juliette who started the conversation. "Do you know where Stephen is?" she asked Dominique.

"Yes, Dhose and Poinsot have got him in one of their cells in La Bouscat."

"Oh God," said Juliette, her voice breaking with emotion for Friedrich Dhose was head of the Gestapo and Pierre Poinsot was the zealous Bordeaux commissioner well known in police circles for his Machiavellian behaviour. What scared the two women most was Poinsot's infamy throughout Bordeaux for the use of torture in his interrogations. Everyone pedalled like a madman when they cycled past the Gestapo buildings in La Bouscat for they feared hearing the howls of the men inside as they were beaten with blackjacks, hung by their thumbs, immersed in bathtubs, had cigarettes burned in to their bodies or had their heads squeezed until they fainted from the pain.

Juliette shook her head in despair and started to feel physically sick. "Do you know why he was arrested?" she asked.

Dominique didn't move or say anything.

"I think I do," said Juliette, feeling the need to fill the gap made by the lack of response.

Dominique looked quizzically at her as the remark registered.

"Stephen was part of a line which helped British pilots escape," whispered Juliette.

"How do you know that?" asked Dominique, disbelieving what she was being told.

"He told me," she said, knowing her explanation was a lie, but seeing Dominique's distress she couldn't bear telling her the complete story.

"That's not why he was arrested," said Dominique confidently, indicating, for the first time, she knew the answer. "He was on some bloody list as a communist."

"Stephen was never a communist," retorted Juliette.

"Henri's made extensive enquiries. Apparently, Poinsot found Stephen's name on an application form after a raid on one of the offices of a communist cell."

"That can't be. How do you know that?"

"Because he took great delight in telling Henri of Stephen's arrest, and the reason why. He even told Henri the date he joined the communist party. It was Monday 30th June!" There was irony in her voice.

Juliette tilted her head questioningly.

"It was the Monday after we'd had the conversation about the winners of the war being the Russians; the bloody communists."

"What after the concert .... late in the evening?"

"Yes," said Dominique, her voice giving way to her frustration at how slow Juliette was at grasping what she saw as the obvious. "On the Sunday, he was calling the Vichy regime odious; complaining that their policies weren't imposed by the Nazis but came from their own right wing. He was arguing against everyone and everything: the Catholics, the freemasons, the nationalists, the capitalists, everyone. The only people he had a good word for were the Unions." Dominique leaned closer. "He was equally as passionate in his loathing of Hitler and Pétain."

"So you don't think it had anything to do with the escapes Stephen worked on?" asked Juliette.

"I'm sure if he'd been involved in the resistance, he would have told me." Dominique paused. "Even if he's not a communist, and he's not," she said strongly, "they still have him as a hostage. Do you know ..." Dominique paused to get control of her emotions. "Henri says that Hitler has now ordered one hundred Frenchmen shot in retaliation for each German murdered?"

Juliette said nothing as her hand involuntarily grasped her mouth in horror. It was the first time the two women had broken hands since they sat down. They stopped talking and each stared into their untouched cups of coffee made from roasted chicory and grain.

"Dominique," said Juliette in a conspiratorial whisper, "I promise you Stephen was a *Passer* and a very, very brave one."

"How do you know?"

"Victoria worked with Stephen on the escape line," she lied again. "They worked from de Gressier."

Dominique stared into Juliette's eyes seeking confirmation that it was true.

"I'm so sorry. I am so very fond of him," said Juliette, deliberately. "He is exactly the way I wish Victor would have grown up. So clever, and he really cares." With those last few words Juliette's voice choked and her eyes welled up for everything reminded her of the pain of losing her son. She recognised the paralysing fear that was now dominating Dominique's senses, as she too was feeling it all over again.

"Stephen told me that you can get a visa to leave France through the Portuguese Embassy. Do you know anything about this?" asked Juliette, wiping her eyes dry and finding her composure.

"They were shut down over a year ago," replied Dominique. "Why? Have you got to get someone out?"

"We think our lines been compromised. As soon as Stephen is free, we need to get him and Victoria safely to England. They can stay with her grandfather."

"Really, did Stephen do as you say?" asked Dominique, seeking reassurance once again.

"Yes, and not once but many times; please I can't say more."

"And Victoria's life is now at risk?"

"Yes," said Juliette, for she was sure that even if Stephen was arrested for being a communist, he would soon, under torture, give up his *Passer* secrets, after which, she and Victoria could be certain of their arrest.

Dominique reached across the small table and once again the two women held hands and leant in close. "I can get them out," she said.

"How?"

"On a fishing boat from the harbour. It then rendezvous with a British ship or submarine out at sea."

"But they search the fishing boats before they leave, don't they?" asked Juliette, already knowing the answer.

"Yes, but they are canoed out by a fisherman and then get picked up by the fishing boats after they've left the harbour. It's all after the searches."

"The riverbank's a restricted area, it's almost impossible to get in or out," protested Juliette. "I've been turned back more than once."

"Yes, but I have an Ausweis because of where my cottage is. More importantly, I have a letter signed by Feldkommandant Kuene-mann. Because of this I never get searched."

"Does Henri know?"

"About the Ausweis, yes, he got it for me, as to the rest … Good God, no! He's really struggling. Ever since the *chasse aux Juifs*[31] started. He thinks the French police are acting as though they are part of the German occupation force, doing far too much of their bidding. This conflict is making him sick with worry."

"I'm so sorry," said Juliette. "I'd heard the Bordeaux Gendarmerie had become unsafe because no one knows who to trust. It must be awfully hard for him."

"We have to take great care," continued Dominique. "It's really frightening. A few days ago I got a phone call from a stranger asking if I was a patron of France."

"I had one of those," interjected Juliette.

"I hope you didn't say anything?"

"No."

"Because it's a trap. I was pestered several times. We think they were testing Henri and me."

---

[31] Hunt for the Jews

"What did you do?"

"It happened just after Stephen was arrested. Henri now thinks it was Poinsot seeing whether he or I were involved with Stephen's communist group."

"Mon Dieu!" said Juliette. "This means that Henri can't even trust his colleagues not to try and trap him, never mind you."

Dominique nodded, "It's very sad," she said, "and er, ... so very distressing."

"I think I need a cognac," admitted Juliette. "Would you like one?"

"If you are having one so will I," said Dominique, "although I can't remember the last time I drank spirits."

"I do. The morning Hugo was executed," Juliette admitted. "I thought it would calm my nerves."

"On the morning before I married Henri," confessed Dominique, "although I don't know why. I was sure I was doing the right thing."

"How is Pierre?" asked Juliette, after the brandy had been served.

Dominique sighed and slowly shook her head. "He's stopped being happy and has become very withdrawn. He needs me all the time which is a change because he was such a father's boy. They were so very close. Henri now frightens him, not in an aggressive way, but he senses something is wrong and doesn't know what it is. He's confused, very confused."

Juliette nodded sympathetically and squeezed Dominique's hands in an effort to provide some comfort.

"How's Victoria?"

"Very upset and very scared."

"I sometimes wonder if they might marry one day, Stephen and her," said Dominique.

"So do I," said Juliette enthusiastically, before adding "but of course, she's still very young, but they're very natural together. It's nice to see them. Unfortunately, she got quite attached to a German pilot but, thank God, he's been transferred back to Berlin to work directly for Hitler."

"Do you want me to see if I can get her and Stephen out of France?" asked Dominique.

"To England?" asked Juliette, as she nodded in the affirmative.

"Where else?" replied Dominique, with a frown of confusion set on her brow. "What happened to the line Stephen was working on?" she questioned. "Couldn't they get out through that?"

"Maybe but after Stephen was arrested it was shut down. He only told me of one man. He never met anyone else. I suspect, after his arrest, that the people immediately before and after him on the line will have gone into hiding."

"Were you involved?"

"Yes, but I had a very small role," she lied.

"And you were doing all this under the noses of the Germans billeted at Château de Gressier?"

"The packages, they were always referred to like that, were kept in Stephen's cellar at Maison Presson."

"What!" exclaimed Dominique. "If he was doing that then he was bound to get caught one day, wasn't he?"

"Is it safe?" asked Juliette, ignoring Dominique's point, instead referring to her escape route. "The seas can be very rough at this time of year."

"No, but it's worked every time so far."

"How many times?"

Dominique very gently shook her head indicating it was not a question she was prepared to answer. "Do you want me to try?" she asked, pressing Juliette on the point.

"How far do they canoe out?"

"The fishing boats always pick up between Ile de Cozeaux, Ile Patiras and Ile Margaux, so the time in the estuary is quite short; and because they are so low in the water, unless you know where and what to look for, the canoes are very hard to see. The biggest risk is a full moon as that makes them too easy to spot. There's the risk of another search as the estuary narrows at Royan but these are thankfully rare." As she spoke, Dominique realised how proud she was to be involved.

"Can I think about it, please?" begged Juliette.

"She and Stephen will get only twelve, maybe twenty-four, hours warning, that's all."

Juliette nodded.

"And she can't bring or take anything with her; just her identity papers and a bag no bigger than this." Dominique waved her hands in the air indicating the very smallest of cases.

"And what about Stephen?" asked Juliette, "What do we do?"

"Mon Dieu, I see. You're scared that Stephen will, under err ..., say something about Victoria being a *Passer*."

"No, no," protested Juliette too easily, for although the scenario was correct, her fear was not that Stephen would say something about Victoria, but about her. In the confusion of her thoughts and emotions, Juliette started to cry. "I want him out," she said with fire in her voice. "How do we get him out? We need to get him out!"

Chapter 36

Bordeaux October 1941

LATER THAT SAME day, Stephen Bellanger was hauled from the floor of his 1.2metre by 2.5metre bare concrete cell, handcuffed and thrown into a German military lorry. He had endured the most appalling torture but had told them nothing. How could he? He knew nothing about the communist party he had joined, except who its Bordeaux leaders were, and the Gestapo already knew that.

Not once was his work as a *Passer* mentioned in interrogation. In his cell, late at night, lonely, cold, and scared, he often wondered if he did say anything whether it might stop the hell he was suffering. Logic told him it would just cause more suffering. When in the agony of drowning, being burned by cigarettes or crushed under blow after blow of the baton, he had no ability to think of anything for every thought was destroyed in the dark red and white mist of trauma.

Stephen recognised none of the men in his lorry. Each had been savagely beaten. There was no joy in this group of heroes, for each knew they had been physically defeated. Their minds remained strong and resolute, but there would be no singing of patriotic songs, for none could bear the thought of the rifle butt bringing more pain on themselves, or on those around them.

Twenty minutes from La Bouscat, Stephen's lorry, with its escort of motorcycle, sidecar and machine gun in front, and an armoured vehicle at the rear, started to drive through the woods of tall, burnt looking pine trees, with their pathetic, unattractive canopy of branches and pines. Using a cut in the canvas canopy of the lorry, Stephen could see where trees had been felled and the land lay barren. As the lorry crossed a stream, which started to run alongside the road, he could see the white and silvery coloured water, flowing through brown peaty loam. Finally, the lorry turned into Avenue 57 ri, and the formal entrance to Camp de Souge.

Stephen's lorry stopped at the spot where the firing squad had already been prepared. Like tens of thousands before, and after him, Stephen was shot dead by German soldiers carrying out their orders. We do not know Stephen's last words. All we know is that he was not amongst friends; just with those who loved France. The history books have never revealed for which event his life was taken in reprisal.

Chapter 37

The Wolf's Lair November 1941

ANY ROMANTIC THOUGHTS that Heinrik might have had of working from Templehof Airport in Berlin were quickly disabused when he reported there for duty. Immediately, he was sworn in to Leinstandart SS Adolf Hitler, the Führer's personal bodyguard.

After three short flights with Hans Baur to test his competence, Heinrik was ordered to fly a newly delivered Junker Ju 52/3 to Rastenburg. This was the airfield closest to Hitler's new field headquarters known as Wolfsschanze, or the Wolf's Lair, where he was to be based.

The Wolf's Lair was the first of Adolf Hitler's Eastern Front military headquarters. He had it specially built in the dense Goerlitz forest so he could command the invasion of Russia. It was made up of three Security Zones. The highest security one, and in the middle, contained the Führer's Bunker, with its conference rooms, and ten other bunkers each built, partially above ground using two-metre thick steel reinforced concrete. Each bunker was connected by underground passages. Hitler's accommodation was on the northern side of the top security zone to avoid direct sunlight, which he disliked. The Wolf's Lair was noted for its constant hum from the air pumps which provided ventilation into the bunkers. It was a noise which grated on every one's nerves.

Heinrik was stationed in the Security Zone 2 which housed the quarters of several Reich Ministries and the military barracks of the Reichssicherheitsdienst, the SS security force of Nazi Germany. His accommodation was in a wooden hut which was too hot in summer, when it was plagued with insects, and cold and damp in winter. What made everything worse was the food; nothing but regular military rations.

Life at the Wolf's Lair was anything but pleasant. It was isolated with no entertainment. The forest was dark and oppressive. Its ambience was both dismal and gloomy. It was in sharp contrast to Bordeaux's Merignac Airport and Château de Gressier. Heinrik knew that, if he hadn't the freedom of the skies, he would have gone mad there from claustrophobia.

Like every pilot in the F.d.F. Heinrik never had a day off. Supplies had to be flown in every day and Hitler's constant demand to see senior officers in his military meant that Hans Baur was running a 24/7 air taxi service, and Heinrik was one of his taxi drivers.

It was after a few days of flying for F.d.F. that Heinrik realised there were some fundamental differences to his previous job with Aviation Command Atlantic. Firstly, he was working much harder, constantly flying which brought with it a feeling of permanent exhaustion. Secondly, with landmarks, navigation was much easier and therefore the level of concentration was less. But it was the realisation that, if he crashed on land, he had a much better chance of surviving than if he crashed into the sea. It was as he contemplated this likely change in outcomes that he remembered the motto "failing to prepare was preparing to fail." It had been drilled into him by his first flying instructor.

It was with this thought that Heinrik took inordinate care to prepare a small escape bag which he started to take with him religiously on every flight. He packed it with a small medical kit, a small wash kit, a compass, a bottle of water, chocolate and biscuits, a tiny camping stove full of paraffin together with a spare flask of fuel, a small tin containing matches, pins, needles, fishing hooks, string and yarn and a rubber backed canvas ground sheet. He included a small leather tool bag, with a knife and its attachments of hammer, screwdriver, file, and saw, which a grandfather had given him as a young boy.

Heinrik added two things of sentimental value to his escape bag. Somehow, he couldn't imagine being without them. One of these was his father's college dissecting kit. It was a roll of the finest quality leather with slots for a cutthroat razor, scalpels, scissors of various sizes, serrated and non- serrated forceps with needles and probes all different shapes and sizes. He also packed Victor's gold watch still in its cardboard outer case. As he put the watch in his bag, Heinrik thought of Victoria and wondered how she was. He had been so busy he'd hardly had any time to think about her at all. Most times it would be as he was climbing into bed but normally these thoughts didn't last long. He was so tired that, as soon as he put his head on the pillow, all thoughts he had of her evaporated with his unconsciousness.

Chapter 38

Bordeaux and Château de Gressier November 1941

JULIETTE WAS PETRIFIED. She expected that, at any moment, the Gestapo would bang on her door and arrest her for being a *Passer*. She had correctly guessed the terrible torture Stephen had endured and was sure that he would give her name away to stop, even for a little while, his living hell.

She wouldn't, she couldn't blame him, as she knew she would be no different; except, other than Stephen's name what else did she have to say? Nothing, and so she knew her pain would go on and on relentlessly. Scared rigid about what she might say under torture, Juliette decided that, if they came for her, she wouldn't be taken alive. To this end, she had retrieved her brother, Penrose's[32] pistol from his caravan which she had rescued from the Western Front at the end of the last war. She loaded it with old bullets and put it in her bedside table. Juliette had no idea whether the gun or bullets would work, as she had not been able to test them. In anticipation of failure, she had placed a long-sharpened kitchen knife in her bedside table as well.

Juliette had not slept properly since Stephen was arrested. A nervous, sick feeling was constantly with her. She moved from room to room, starting and stopping jobs but settling at nothing. To make matters worse, Juliette was also mithering about Château de Gressier and La Maison de Louis' wine business because their fortunes were not good. Six weeks of very cold summer weather, coupled with prolonged rain and a complete lack of copper sulphate to treat odium and mildew fungus meant that the wine harvest for 1941 was half the quantity of the previous year, possibly the worst in Bordeaux's

---

[32] Now known as David Daunier.

recorded history. The only saving grace was that Juliette's vintage was as weak and pathetic as her competitors.

However, she had a problem which her competitors did not. Louis Eschenauer was Bordeaux's most prominent négociant. He bought wine in bulk, bottled it, and then sold it to his customers throughout the world. With the Third Reich as one of his biggest customers, he had managed to secure a monopoly on the manufacture of all new bottles, other than those needed by the Grand Cru houses, where Blömer's influence had come to their aid. However hard she tried, Juliette could not get the quantity of bottles she needed. She was certain that Eschenauer, in an effort to force her to sell her bulk wine to him, had used his purchasing power to stop bottle manufacturers selling to her. With no bottles she had no ability to turn her wine into much needed cash.

If there was one thing that she and Étienne had learnt in the funding crisis, which hit them just after they had taken over Château de Gressier, it was how to do cash flow projections. With the 1941 harvest in its barrels, Juliette knew that, with the price Blömer was prepared to pay, she would run out of money before the next harvest. She had to implement a drastic redundancy programme and urgently if she were to stave off bankruptcy. The thought of doing this filled her with dread. These weren't just people she would be putting out of work. They were true and loyal friends and colleagues.

It was only the 'hotel' business run out of The Cottage, with its high-spending Luftwaffe officers, which was just about keeping her solvent; but for how long? They came because she was always able to offer a table of food not available at their airbase. However, as food shortages took hold, and the controls and demands increased, the Estate had less of its own produced food to feed her guests. This was despite the low-lying fields on both sides of the river being denuded of their vines and turned over to growing maize and corn. Even millet was now being grown between the vines.

In normal times, Juliette might have sold a lorry, van, or car to help her through. But over time, piece by piece, most of these, together with her stable of horses, had been requisitioned into the German army. She sobbed as her horses were led away, leaving behind just one old nag, long into retirement, which was now back pulling a plough and trailer.

Juliette desperately wanted to escape, just run away. She thought long and hard about leaving and how she would do this. As soon as Victoria was in the fishing boat and on her way to England, she would cross La Ligne using her Laissez-Passer, head to Spain and get to England that way, where she and Victoria would be reunited. It was a simple plan but with so many people dependent on Château de Gressier she felt trapped. Measuring the idea of escape against her responsibilities for Château de Gressier, and those in Latoire Village, was an impossible equation to compute. Above all else, she would forever judge herself as a deserter and she wasn't going to be that.

It was early evening when the phone rang. She had not received a call for days, so the sound of the clattering bell shocked Juliette, who instantly froze with surprise. Her hand was physically shaking as she picked up the receiver.

"Hello," she said.

"Juliette? It's Henri, Henri Hilaire." Immediately Juliette knew that something had gone dramatically wrong.

"Henri," she repeated.

"I'm sorry to say....," Henri stopped speaking. Juliette could hear that he was fighting his emotions, struggling to talk.

"Henri?" she said, checking if he was still there. His silence made her more scared.

"Stephen's dead," he blurted out suddenly.

"No!" shrieked Juliette. "No, no, no!" she yelled, and then, with desperation in her voice, she asked, "How? ... When? ... Where?"

There was another long pause.

"We think five days ago, we're not sure. He was executed by the Gestapo."

"Why?" Juliette asked, for whilst she was petrified of the answer, she needed to know.

"For being a communist," he replied, with anger biting out of every syllable.

"No," she exclaimed again, "that can't be."

There was silence as Henri held the phone away from him, not wanting his grief to be heard. "They say he was executed in a reprisal, but we don't know for what."

There was a long silence as both were in shock and neither knew what else to say.

"How's Dominique?" asked Juliette gently after a long while.

"She doesn't know yet."

"Why?"

"I haven't been able to get hold of her. I'm going home now."

There was another long pause.

"Juliette?" Henri asked. "Could you come and be with her tonight, possibly tomorrow. It's just you've lost...." He didn't say a son, but in the silence, it was obvious what he was thinking. "I am sure you will be the best person. You will understand how she's ..." Again, he didn't finish his sentence.

"Where are you?" asked Juliette.

"At work."

"How did you find out?"

"I was told about five minutes ago. We haven't had anything formal. I pulled rank and made enquiries this afternoon as I couldn't bear the silence, the not knowing, any longer. I am told Dominique will be getting formal notification tomorrow."

"Of course, I will. I'll be with you tomorrow morning, first thing."

"Thank you," he whispered, becoming overwhelmed once more.

"Take care, Henri," she said. "Please give Dominique my love," but he didn't hear her as he had already hung up.

The overwhelming relief that Juliette immediately felt on hearing of Stephen's death gave her cause to feel guilty for the rest of her life. It was a secret she only ever shared with her diary and only many years later. Stephen's death meant that the chances of him giving her away under torture had gone. If he had said anything before he was killed then she was sure she would have been arrested in the last five days.

Juliette's relief was followed by a grief so painful that she screamed for Victoria as she ran up the stairs to look for her. Immediately, Victoria saw her mother, she knew.

"Stephen's dead, isn't he?" said Victoria, emotionlessly.

Juliette nodded, tears falling down her face, unable to talk.

"Oh God, oh no," said Victoria, and then her persona changed as she welled up with tears too. "He was so very special."

Victoria followed her mother into her bedroom. For the next two hours they lay on the bed and for the first time since Victor died, they spoke as mother and daughter should.

"Can I share a secret with you?" asked Juliette, at one stage in their conversation.

Victoria nodded.

"I always thought, perhaps wished, that you and Stephen would get married one day."

There was a long pause. "I did too," said Victoria. There was wistfulness in her voice. "He was very good-looking, and so wise, but somehow I think he thought me too young. I always hoped that one day I might grow up just that little bit more so he would like me."

"He liked you, darling," said Juliette. "He liked you a lot. Of that I'm certain."

"He liked you too, Mummy," said Victoria. He liked you a lot too, didn't he? I always thought there was something very special between the two of you. There was, wasn't there?"

Juliette nodded and swallowed hard. The way Victoria spoke made her think about her times with Stephen in the bedroom at Hôtel de France. Did Victoria know, she wondered anxiously.

"He was a lot like your father, very bright and practical," said Juliette wondering as the words left her lips. "It meant we could share a lot together."

"I know. It made me think, well you know what happened between Dominique and ...... well. I couldn't help wondering if he was Papa's son too. Was he – what do you think?

"I asked myself the same question too – many, many times, to the point I couldn't think about it anymore."

"It's just you never encouraged us, did you?" said Victoria. "I thought it may be because you knew we shared the same father."

"No darling, that was never it. It was just the wrong time for you and him. The right time might have come, but now ...." Juliette's voice faded away as she thought of the things which might have been.

Three lovers and all now dead, thought Juliette. How can that possibly be? And with that, she held her daughter's hand extra tight, not wanting to let her go.

Chapter 39

Bordeaux November 1941

HENRI AND DOMINIQUE'S house was in chaos when Juliette arrived. None of the children had gone to school but, recognising something was wrong, had a sullen calm about their behaviour. Milling around were a collection of adults, none of whom seemed to belong but who, for that moment, had to be there. Henri was doing his best to cater for everyone's needs but there was a pressure cooker atmosphere which Juliette sensed immediately. Recoiling from her memories of Victor's death she recognised Dominique was under the same impossible strain: trying to be a hostess whilst suffering the physical pain of grief.

Leaving the parcel of food she had brought with her on the kitchen table, Juliette took Dominique's hand and led her out through the front door into some peace and quiet and, more importantly, some fresh air. The two women didn't talk. They just walked. A little way around the corner from Dominique's home was a café which, despite it being close, she had never been in before. Taking a table at the side of the front door, the two women sat down as the autumn sun, in a cloudless blue sky, streamed through the window.

"What happened?" asked Juliette, after they had ordered. She looked directly into Dominique's eyes which were bloodshot and puffy from crying. She could see Dominique was in complete shock for there was a disconnection between her brain and the external stimuli around her; something very normal when the brain is overtaken by emotion.

"All we know is that he was shot at Camp de Souge last week. Apparently, the fucking Germans in their fucking ruthless efficiency will be writing to me," she replied angrily.

"Where is his body?" asked Juliette, shocked to hear Dominique swear so profoundly.

"I don't know. The coffins of all those shot are delivered in batches of two or three to churches all around Bordeaux for burial."

"Why?" asked Juliette, puzzled.

"They don't want where they're buried to become a shrine to martyrs."

"So you don't know where he is buried?"

"No, but Henri is going to travel to all the churches and make a list of the most recent graves and see if we can work out something from there."

"That's just dreadful, unforgivable," sympathised Juliette.

"He's like his father, lying somewhere in an unmarked grave to be forgotten." The despair in Dominique's voice wanted to make Juliette weep too.

"He won't be forgotten," said Juliette, defiantly. "He will be remembered. You and I will make sure he is."

The two women sat silently each in their own thoughts.

"Henri is in a terrible state about it," Dominique added. "He said that when Poinsot told him...."

"Pierre Poinsot, the Préfet de Police?" interrupted Juliette.

"Yes. It was him who told Henri that Stephen had been executed. Do you know, when telling him, he smiled? Can you imagine that? He bloody smiled."

"Why?"

"Henri always thought Poinsot was dangerous. He has no emotion. He's been given immense power by the Germans. With Inspectors Laffargue and Langlade and his two brothers all working together, he has a *brigade des tueurs*[33]."

"Why would Poinsot be involved?" asked Juliette, getting confused, for she was convinced that Stephen's arrest had been by the Gestapo.

"It's Poinsot who makes the list of those who are to be executed by the Germans in reprisals. The Gestapo and Poinsot are virtually one and the same. Poinsot is probably worse."

---

[33] Brigade of killers

"Are you saying that Poinsot deliberately chose Stephen to be executed because he was Henri's stepson?"

"Yes."

"Why? It makes no sense," said Juliette, now feeling quite nauseous.

"It does in Poinsot's world. It proves that he is more senior to Henri."

"But he's not, is he?" said Juliette. Her despair at the illogicality had now crept into her tone.

"Yes, he is. Poinsot's now a Préfet de Police while Henri is a Commissionnaire. Also, he has far more influence with the Germans than Henri."

"That makes Henri's job almost impossible, doesn't it?"

"Yes, he can't bear the thought of arresting someone for a crime, very often for a crime which he doesn't think is a crime at all, like being a member of the Communist Party and then, the next minute, they're on some ridiculous list to be shot in some damn German reprisal." Dominique paused and then said reflectively. "It's getting him very, very depressed."

The two women drank more coffee, a glass or two of wine and talked for nearly three hours swapping their stories; it was a given between the two of them that Henri should never know. Juliette told Dominique the truth about Stephen and her *Passer* activities. Before she had said it was just Stephen who'd acted, but now she explained exactly what Stephen and she had done together in helping British pilots to escape. She told it as an adventure story from beginning to end, always just stopping before she and Stephen would climb the stairs to bed.

Juliette described, in the minutest of detail, the heroic smile which Stephen gave her as he sat in the back of the black sedan car waiting to be driven away; for it was a picture engraved in her mind which she would never forget. It was news that Dominique needed to know for it gave her a new found pride in her son.

As Dominique told Juliette of her stories of working with the fishermen of Bordeaux to get resistance leaders out of France and back to England, she wished that she had shared these adventures with her son too.

Dominique was visibly much calmer when they returned to her home. She had relived in conversation with Juliette every part of Stephen's life. It was something she needed to do, to tell someone who would listen and would understand.

It was on the last bus back to Latoire Village that Juliette decided there would be a grave reserved for Stephen in the village churchyard. As an Estate worker he deserved to be buried there. If he was Étienne's son he was entitled to be there. His spot would be right next to Victor's. It would be his place irrespective of whether his body was there or not.

Chapter 40

Château de Gressier Christmas 1941 and January 1942

FOR THE SECOND year in a row the winter was incredibly cold. This meant that the fighting came to a virtual standstill. Planes were unable to take to the sky and vehicles were unable to move as engines were frozen solid. With the forecast showing little change in the weather those lucky Luftwaffe pilots, who knew the secret of Château de Gressier, decided it was the place to go for Christmas and the few days afterwards. It was so busy that, once again, the guests overflowed from The Cottage into the bedrooms of The Cellar.

If there was one thing which united the French in a common cause it was the search for food. With the need to feed paying guests, particularly at Christmas time, Gaspar Mesny's role as Estate scavenger took on almost biblical proportions. Every time the Germans requisitioned something from the Estate, he took pride in stealing it back, or at least something of equivalent use or value. Added to this, there was not a Latoire villager who didn't have a sideline as a baker, fromager, butcher, cook, kindler or even poacher. It was in this way that the cottage food processing industries enabled both villagers and de Gressier to become almost self-sufficient. They were their own micro-economy.

Stephen's death undoubtedly brought Juliette and Victoria closer together. For the first time since Juliette had announced her fated engagement to Hugo Coudace, mother and daughter enjoyed being with each other as they prepared for the Christmas festivities.

On Christmas Day, they each laid their handmade wreaths on the graves of Étienne, Victor and on the place now reserved for Stephen. His future grave was marked with a wooden plaque secured against the outer wall of the churchyard with Stephen's full name and his dates of birth and death. Underneath, inscribed in large letters, were the words "A Hero of France." Everyone who saw those words knew exactly what they meant.

Any blame and resentment that Juliette and Victoria might have felt towards their paying guests for Stephen's death was deliberately absent. They had placed the blame equally between the Gestapo and the collaborators within the Bordeaux police, and there it lay. So resolved, they kept de Gressier warm, served the limited amount of food they had and allowed their poor-quality wine to flow freely. It meant de Gressier had an atmosphere of joy, although neither woman was truly happy. Victoria pined for Heinrik, disappointed that there was no letter from him wishing her well. Juliette yearned for the return of the days when Étienne was alive.

It was on New Year's Day that, for the first time, Victoria came downstairs late, looking white and pasty. She was feeling nauseous and unable to serve breakfast. She had been sick. Over the next few days mother and daughter worried about what bug Victoria might have caught, whether she was infectious, and questioned whether she should be serving at table at all. It was while standing at the kitchen sink, with her housekeeper, tackling the never-ending washing up that it suddenly dawned on Juliette; Victoria was pregnant. Her heart sank, then she felt an enormous surge of anger as she immediately guessed the father - the ever-visiting Hauptman Klugman.

Immediately, one of the sights of the Great War which Juliette had found most frightening came into her mind. It was as clear in her memory as if it had happened yesterday. A crowd of angry French women, probably thirty or forty in number, were attacking five women in the square of a small town near Lille, as a crowd of men, a little smaller in number, looked on and did nothing. The five women had been bound and stripped to the waist, their skirts and dresses torn to shreds. Their hair had been viciously cut short and, using tar from a boiling vat, their hair, breasts, backs and sometimes their buttocks had been smothered in the hot black glue, badly burning their skin, which was then covered in old chicken feathers.

It was just as the women were being tied to two posts in the middle of the town square, that Juliette's ambulance arrived. The women's crimes? They had slept with German soldiers. Juliette watched completely shocked from the front seat of the empty ambulance, as her sergeant drove through the crowd to where the five women were bound. Their arrival on the scene didn't stop, but only abated the appalling attacks which the five women were suffering.

Juliette's sergeant, determined to take control, fired three shots into the air with his rifle, at which point the crowd fell silent and moved back. Each of the women was shaking with fear, their bodies in shock from their burns. Juliette remembered being terrified as she got out to go to the women's aid, for she and her sergeant were hugely outnumbered. As she did so, the women's mothers, fathers or brothers forced their way through the booing, jostling, and dangerously angry crowd to rescue them. Covered as best they could by their rescuers, the tarred women were led away back to their homes.

A virtually naked girl was left behind whom no-one claimed. The sergeant untied her and led her to the back of the ambulance where Juliette wrapped her in a sheet and tried to clean her and attend to her wounds as best she could. It would take surgical spirit at the hospital to get her clean again, and more cutting of her hair to get the tar out. The girl was Victoria's age. What Juliette remembered most was the fear in the girl's eyes, and the way she continued to shake violently for a long time after her rescue. She saw the girl a few days later, clean and in a hospital bed. She was a woman with nothing and no one - no family, no friends, no home, no job and with no reason to hope.

Seeing the young girl's face in her memory, Juliette stopped what she was doing. She dried her hands and sat down in despair. She wondered how much more she had to bear. Did Victoria not know the consequences of being a *collaborator horizontale* and giving birth to a child with a German father. It would be bad enough during the occupation, but should Germany lose the war the consequences would be unimaginable. Did Victoria not hear the talk, already in Bordeaux, of creating the crime of *indignité nationale* punishable by *dégradation nationale*? [34] she wondered. How could her daughter have been so

---

[34] Dégradation nationale meant the loss of all political, civil, and professional rights, including the right to a pension.

stupid as to give herself to a German pilot? Juliette questioned herself angrily.

It was whilst Juliette was sitting quietly working through the consequences of Victoria's actions that her daughter arrived in the kitchen looking quite shaky.

"You stupid, stupid girl!" scathed Juliette, her eyes narrowing as she looked at her daughter from the chair she was sitting on. "You're pregnant, I think you're pregnant," said Juliette, continuing her stage whisper in English so that no one else could hear.

Victoria froze and said nothing. The thought had not even occurred to her.

"You're going to have a bastard child. Heinrik Klugman's bastard child!" continued Juliette, wanting to make it obvious that she knew who the father was. "Do you know what this means? Have you any idea?"

"It's not possible," said Victoria urgently, but as these words left her lips, she knew her mother was right. In a flood of tears, she ran from the kitchen to her bedroom, where she locked the door and collapsed sobbing on the bed.

There was no rapprochement between mother and daughter all day, each feeling as angry and as cross with the other. In addition, Victoria was totally bewildered at the thought of being pregnant. Motherhood had taken little or none of her thoughts to date, for next week would be her seventeenth birthday!

Late in the evening of the following day, Juliette sat at her desk writing her diary. She was recording with honesty the events of the previous day, and how she felt and why. Victoria sat in one of the armchairs near the log fire, and neither had said anything.

Juliette turned from her writing and said, "You know you can't stay here, don't you?"

"What! Are you throwing me out? Why?" asked Victoria, completely shocked. The thought of being made homeless frightened her rigid.

"Do you not understand the shame you've brought on us? Getting pregnant when you're not married is one thing. It's a double shame when everyone discovers the father is German. The damage it'll do to the name of Château de Gressier will be untold. How could you hurt your father's legacy like that?" asked Juliette weakly.

There was silence between the two women.

"You and your baby are going to be outcasts, do you understand that?" continued Juliette.

"Only if you make us," said Victoria defensively.

"No, at the end of the last war 'giving comfort to the enemy' was made a crime. If we win this war, it will be the same again. You'll go to jail. You'll lose the right to vote. You'll not be allowed to go to any public functions. You'll be excluded from any kind of senior job. You couldn't even become a director here, and you can forget the idea of going to university. It's not going to happen!" There was resignation in Juliette's voice as she catalogued events which she thought showed a life being thrown away.

"Papa wouldn't send me away," Victoria added defiantly.

"Be glad your father doesn't know!" spat back Juliette.

"We could say the baby's Stephen's?" suggested Victoria quietly, and after a long pause.

"No, don't be ridiculous," said Juliette emphatically. "How could you lie to Dominique like that? Imagine what traitors we would be if she were to find out."

"How would she find out? Stephen's dead. He was alive when ... you know ...".

Juliette looked at her daughter with such an expression of disapproval that even the strongest man would have wilted.

Victoria's silence signified her acceptance that it was not an idea her mother was prepared to approve.

"I think we have to get you to England to stay with your grandfather."

"You've not spoken to him in years, certainly all my life," said Victoria completely shocked by the suggestion. "He might even be dead for all you know."

Juliette had wondered the same thing.

"If he's gone, then Jack Morris will help you get established. He's been here many times and has always been a good friend to me and your grandfather. There's also Judith Perfett. I am sure she will help too if I write to her. We have money there," she added, by way of encouragement to the plan she was mentally developing. "Certainly enough for you to have a home and live on without going out to work."

Victoria gave no reaction. She just sat with a sulk on her face.

"Hells bells girl!" said Juliette angrily. "Most families would throw you out to fend for yourself. At least I'm making sure you're looked after."

Still there was no reaction from Victoria.

"There, you can be Mrs Stephen Bellanger and the child can be his if you want," added Juliette. "It's a story you can create there, but not here."

"How do I get there?" asked Victoria, her voice revealing that she was beginning to resign herself to the inevitable. "Walk and then swim?" she added sarcastically.

"No, there's another way to get you out, but it will take time to organise."

"Well, I'm not going out in a wine barrel."

"You know?" said Juliette, in surprise.

"Of course I know. Stephen told me what you and he were doing. He had to."

"Why?" There was both alarm and puzzlement in Juliette's voice.

"Because I was suspicious as to why you two were spending nights away. And, I still am. I'm not sure he told me the whole truth," she added accusingly, whilst looking straight into her mother's eyes.

Juliette baulked at the thought her daughter might know of her relationship with Stephen. Did she really know, or had she guessed, she wondered frantically?

"There was something very odd about his and your behaviour on the day he was arrested," continued Victoria. "It was as though he was rushing to save you, and once he'd done that, he was happy."

Suddenly, someone had said what Juliette intuitively knew, but had never consciously recognised. It was an observation which cut her to the quick.

"I'm not throwing you out," said Juliette defensively, deliberately changing the subject. "I'm trying to protect you. In the last war I rescued a woman who had been tarred and feathered for sleeping with a German soldier. It was dreadful, my most frightening experience of the whole war. I've never forgotten it. I must protect you ..." Juliette paused as she remembered the scene. "I have to protect you from that. I just have to!"

Victoria sensed the desperation in her mother's voice, and with that she reluctantly acquiesced to Juliette's plan.

"There's one thing you have to do before you leave," said Juliette. You have to know exactly how Stephen and I got the airmen across La Ligne, and you'll have to be an expert on the German defences in Bordeaux; what happens at the aerodromes at Merignac, Bergerac and Ribérac and, of course, the submarine pens on the river. In fact, everything and anything we can find out."

"Why?" asked Victoria, genuinely surprised.

"Because it will immediately make you useful when you get home. There will be people who will want to know these things."

"Home?" questioned Victoria, "as a spy?"

"Home, of course, home. It was my home country. It will be yours from now on." The strength with which Juliette spoke the last sentence told Victoria what she needed to know. Her future had been decided. She was about to become an Englishwoman.

Chapter 41

Château de Gressier January 1942

VICTORIA LAY ON her bed, pen in hand staring at the writing paper under her wrists. She knew what she had to write but she didn't know how to write it. Eventually she started and suddenly her words fell easily on to the paper:

> *Château de Gressier*
> *Latoire Village*
> *Dordogne*
> *France*
>
> *7th January 1942*
>
> *Dear Heinrik*
> *I pray you are well. I have some news to share. I am going to have a baby. You are going to be a father. I am sure this news will come as a surprise. I hope it is a nice one.*
>
> *At first, I was shocked, even frightened. War time is not a good time, but having thought about it I now know that there is nothing more I want than to have this baby, your baby.*
>
> *The news was not well received by my mother who now tries to make plans for my future away from here, but I am not sure these are for the best.*
>
> *We now must think and prepare for two of us; me and our baby. I need to know what you think. Do you want to marry me? Do you want me to come to you? Will you look after us? Where will we live?*
>
> *I can only say that I am sure we will be very happy. Do you remember, on the night we made our baby, we both thought it*

impossible to contemplate us not spending the rest of our lives together. I am as certain of this now as I was then.

I have a love for you, my darling, which I know will never die. It will last longer than a lifetime; until we are reunited once again whether it is in this life or the next. My hope is that you decide that we should be together very soon.

Please take care and keep safe for you are more precious to me now than my life itself.

I can't wait for your reply

All my love.

Victoria

As Victoria signed her name and blew on the ink to make sure it was dry, she felt nauseous with anxiety. She truly feared for her future. What would he say, she wondered? Would he write telling her to come to him? She prayed he would. She felt certain that he would want her to be with him just as much as she wanted him with her. But then, so much had gone wrong before and she was scared that it might go wrong once again.

Chapter 42

Templehof Airport January 1942

VICTORIA POSTED HER letter to Heinrik from Bordeaux's main post office. She feared that there might be local gossip if she posted it in Latoire Village. The efficiency of the German military meant that Heinrik received her letter in the officers' mess at Templehof Airport only five days after it had been posted.

It was the French stamp on the envelope which first drew Heinrik's attention but then, recognising Victoria's handwriting, he knew the letter was from her. Heinrik chose to sit away from his colleagues to read her letter. He wanted the moment to be a private one.

He opened the envelope and started to read. His heart sank on the news that he was going to be a father. He couldn't be, not now he was working so close to Hitler!

Heinrik's mind raced. What did it mean for his job? He didn't know. Would it matter that he had a son and was not married? Could he get married, he wondered? Would Victoria, being French, risk his bodyguard status? Would he still be trusted? To each of these questions he had no answer.

It couldn't be. He just wouldn't allow it. Only when the war was over, when it was won. That was the time to be a father, he said to himself. Not now!

Heinrik sat completely still for five minutes, thinking only about the news and what it meant. Suddenly, and with a heavy heart, Heinrik tore the letter into small pieces and then, striding across the room, he threw it into the mess room fire.

He gathered all his things and walked outside, back to his aeroplane where he settled himself in the cockpit. Despite the bitter cold, he found it was a place where he was at peace, where he could think.

He had nowhere to fly and, even if he did, his aeroplane was not yet ready. He was angry with himself. He was angry with Victoria. Angry that his aeroplane was not being made ready to fly. Most importantly, he was damned angry with the war.

Chapter 43

Bordeaux and Château de Gressier January to March 1942

VERY QUICKLY A new routine was established for Victoria. Over breakfast and dinner she would listen intensely to the German pilots' discussions, often breaking into their conversations by admitting that she had been near one of their aerodromes and innocently asking about what she saw; the speed, height, navigation equipment and armaments on their planes. Each fact, she recorded to memory, only to write it down later. She was surprised at how, over the last two years, she had become reasonably fluent in German.

After breakfast, Victoria would catch the bus to Bordeaux taking her bicycle, and there she would cycle incessantly, pretending to be a wine delivery girl. She noted anything which might be relevant; the names and identities of the military units in the city, where they were barracked, the defences and gun casements. She carefully remembered each fact and then, making sure she was unobserved, she wrote everything down on a piece of paper which she concealed in the handlebars of her bicycle. Even though it was very cold, and sometimes drenching wet, she found the freedom of cycling, and what she was doing, very exhilarating.

Impatiently, she waited for a letter from Heinrik. When it didn't come, she wrote again. She repeated the news that he was going to be a father, said she couldn't wait to see him again and even suggested that she should come to Berlin to get married. She thought carefully about mentioning in the letter that she was being sent away to England, but dismissed it, knowing it would cause untold problems for her mother. Victoria was certain that as soon as Heinrik knew about the baby he would come and collect her. Years later Victoria would describe these cycling days, when she lived in the naïve expectation that Heinrik would return to her, as some of the happiest in her life.

Each evening, Juliette and Victoria would secretly listen to the BBC as, other than with her mother, Victoria rarely spoke English. After the German invasion they had stopped speaking English to each other, but now, using the copious notes which Victoria had made, her mother would test her in English on what she had seen and discovered. It was treated as a memory game, as though she were learning the complete works of Shakespeare to perform on stage.

It was a strange and often strained time between mother and daughter, for while the rapprochement which had been made after Stephen's death continued, each knew that there would soon be a parting. For this reason, and at every opportunity, Juliette took great pains to share with her daughter her life's learnings as a mother and housekeeper.

Sometimes Victoria blamed herself for what was about to happen, sometimes she blamed her mother. What she did know was that she wanted Heinrik's baby more than anything else in the world.

Chapter 44

Bordeaux and the Atlantic March 1942

THE CALL FROM Dominique was a long time coming. The tides, the moon and weather all had to be just right, and a naval frigate had to be available to be tasked to rendezvous with the fishing boats of Bordeaux.

It was late March when Juliette and Victoria said their goodbyes at Dominique's house in the centre of Bordeaux. It was as painful a parting as any mother and daughter had ever known. Both hearts were breaking, each torn apart in their torment. As a result, each froze their outward emotions making their parting clinical, formal and one they would both regret forever. *Why didn't I take her in my arms and cuddle her one more time,* Juliette would ask herself time and time again.

Dominique drove them to her fisherman's cottage in Henri's car. Victoria had no idea what was about to happen. Dominique's familiarity with the guards meant that they went through the German checkpoint giving access to the Ambarès-et-Lagrave peninsula without any papers being shown.

It was early in the evening when Victoria sat in the same chair that her father would have sat in when he visited. Like Étienne before her, she was enjoying the views over the river as the sun went down. It gave Dominique an opportunity to study Victoria. Sometimes she looked like her mother, at other times like her father, but it was her mannerisms which showed Victoria to be a daddy's girl. It then dawned on Dominique why she was doing this; she owed it to Étienne to make sure that his daughter got to safety.

Slowly, over the course of the evening, men would arrive very discreetly in ones and twos until there were six of them in total plus

Dominique; three fishermen, skilled in canoeing and who, from the banter they shared, were very good friends. There were two other Frenchmen, who appeared to know each other but hardly spoke. They were obviously under huge strain. To make matters worse, the two Frenchmen were highly suspicious of Victoria. It was only when she was vouched for by Dominique, explaining that her mother was English, her father French and that she had been working as a *passer*, did they accept the uninvited guest into their midst.

"Do we have authority to take her with us to London?" asked one of the two Frenchmen.

"Yes," lied Dominique, making it clear that she was not going to debate the subject.

It was just past 11 o'clock at night when the gang of six, plus Dominique, stepped out of the fisherman's cottage to the water's edge, taking with them three flimsy wooden and canvas two-man canoes. These were normally stored in flat pack state in Dominique's garage, but earlier in the evening, they had been built up, with their staves keeping the body rigid.

The night was incredibly still, with little cloud. It meant it was very cold and allowed any sound to travel. The moonlight was almost too bright for safety.

At the water's edge, Victoria and the two men were bundled into sou'westers, bulky life jackets and given seal-covered gloves. The canoes were lowered, one at a time, into the water, which was at high tide. They were then pulled parallel, hard against the riverbank. Each passenger was put in the front seat first, followed by their small bag of possessions which was placed between their knees.

In Victoria's small bag was Victor's pillowcase. She wanted to take his whole pillow with her as she couldn't imagine ever being able to go to sleep without it, but it was too bulky. Taking just his pillowcase was the minimum bearable compromise.

Laying on her tummy, Dominique held each canoe close to the edge of the riverbank, as each fisherman canoeist climbed in. Once he was settled, she handed the canoeist his paddle. Immediately that was in his hand, Dominique used it to gently push the canoe out towards the middle of the stream. Victoria's canoeist expertly, and very rapidly, powered their little craft away from the shore and into the middle of the river.

"Keep low," Victoria's canoeist whispered to her. She slid down further inside, causing the spray, made by the canoe's bow bashing against the waves, to sting her in the face. The ease with which each canoeist saw the other in the middle of the estuary made each of the venturers frightened that they would be seen. Any man looking out over the water could not have failed to spot them.

The speed and skill with which the three canoes were taken across the river was incredible. With the lack of wind, it meant that they got to their waiting point downstream between two of the islands in far less time than they had allowed. It was out of the current of the river, and with the high tide just about to ebb, it was as safe and quiet a resting up spot as might be found.

Victoria and her canoeist heard the fishing boats long before they saw them. There was some distance between them, for each fishing boat had a line of rope laid out behind on either side, kept afloat by an attachment of corks placed about a metre and a half apart.

"You have to catch one of the lines," explained Victoria's canoeist. "There will be six boats in all so don't worry if you miss one, we have a lot of others to go for. If, at any time, you think we are going to tip over then for God's sake let go! If we end up in the sea, we're dead!"

Victoria nodded frantically.

"Do you understand, we're dead! If you think we are going over, let go," he repeated urgently.

The first fishing boat quickly spotted the fleet of canoes which had now moved into the middle of the river waiting for them. It slowed down and navigated directly between them, dividing two canoes on one side and one on the other. Victoria's canoeist took them carefully alongside the rope which she picked up, but she was not ready for the abrupt jerk as the canoe came under the strain of the rope, so she immediately let go of it. The canoe on the other side successfully latched on, and she watched, disappointed, as it sailed into the distance.

The next fishing boat divided the two remaining canoes in half. Once again, the two canoes worked themselves to be alongside the floating lines. Both passengers grabbed their rope, and Victoria was just picking up the strain when what was happening with the rope on the other side caused her to let go. The passenger in the other canoe had held on too tightly. With the canoeist unable to steer them back on course, their canoe was suddenly dragged sidewards. The passenger was pulled horizontally into the sea and, with his arm tangled around the rope, the passenger could not let go. He was pulled, like a popping cork, out of the canoe and was now being dragged through the fishing boat's wake. His canoeist was tipped into the water where he was left floundering next to his upturned craft.

"Merde," exclaimed Victoria's canoeist. He paddled rapidly to try and help his friend, but the current was sweeping him away, and the next fishing boat was almost upon them. There were more boats behind, if he could signal to them, then it would be far better if they went to his friend's aid rather than him. He knew his priority. It was to get his passenger onto the fishing boat.

Once again, Victoria's canoeist skilfully lined up their canoe, this time alongside one of the ropes from the third fishing boat. Victoria picked it up and allowed some of it to pass through her gloves, each time holding it a bit tighter. Suddenly she felt the canoe tip. Rather than let go she allowed some of the rope to slide through her hands until the canoeist had the little boat lined up again, then she held on for dear life as her canoeist kept the little craft pointing straight ahead. Once latched on, the captain of the fishing boat hauled them alongside his craft. A rope net had already been laid down its side and was being manned by an eager crew. Almost in unison, Victoria's case was taken, and she and her canoeist were lifted out. No sooner were they on the deck than the canoe was with them. It was a smooth, well-practised and perfect operation which thrilled all those involved, until they heard Victoria's canoeist shout out in a panic: "André or Vincent have capsized! They're in the water."

Immediately there were shouts of man overboard, and within an instant the boat's captain followed the agreed drill and sounded five short and two long blasts on his horn, warning the three boats behind that one of the canoes was upturned with two men in the water who needed rescuing. No sooner had the last blast on the horn faded away than Victoria heard the engine noise rise as the revs were increased. She felt the boat physically speed up through the water. Like the canoeist, the captains of the fishing boats, with resistance agents on board, knew their priority. They had to rendezvous with the frigate.

The following day was spent fishing in the coastal waters of the Atlantic, where Victoria began to feel quite seasick. The smell of the fish, the diesel, and the rolling of the boat in the swell of the sea made her quite nauseous; that was until she was in the wheelhouse, watching the captain and his crew go about their work. With her eyes able to see the horizon, her seasickness abated.

That night, all three fishing boats made their rendezvous with a British frigate. Victoria found the transfer from the small fishing boat to the much larger frigate petrifying. She was certain that, when told to jump, she was going to fall between the two boats and into the sea, where she would be crushed to death. Four times she failed to make the jump when told. On the fifth attempt, she had no alternative but to go as, propelled by the forceful shove of a couple of fishermen, she flew into the arms of sailors sent down the rope netting to capture her.

On board the frigate Victoria was delighted to be reunited with her other two escapees, as she was certain that one of them had not made it. The man who had capsized his canoe was in a lot of pain as, with his sou'wester and lifejacket acting as an enormous brake, he was pulled through the water by the rope wrapped around his arm. The strain had dislocated his arm at both his elbow and shoulder and torn his tendons. He didn't know what had happened to his canoeist, but the consensus on board was that, unless he had been rescued within twenty to thirty minutes, he would have fallen unconscious from hypothermia and drowned.

This news, and the sight of the injured man, shocked Victoria. She had no idea of the risks they were taking. Until that moment, she had thought it all as a huge game of German hide and seek. Only now did she realise the risks these very brave men had taken for her freedom. It left her feeling very humble and rather ashamed. She knew that when she got to England, she would have to do her bit; whatever that bit was. Her only caution came from a feeling of responsibility to Heinrik and his child, but then, he had abandoned them, had he not? It was on this last thought that Victoria knew where her duty would lie. It would be with England because then, it could be with France too.

Chapter 45

Plymouth and London March 1942

VICTORIA AND HER two travelling companions arrived in Plymouth three days after they had boarded the frigate. To avoid German submarines, they were unable to take the most direct route. Victoria had spent her time sleeping and writing out everything that she had memorised from her notes. As she wrote, so she remembered things that she had seen but not previously recorded. At the quayside, after the frigate had docked, there was some consternation as the greeting party were expecting just two agents and not her.

Why, they asked the captain, had he brought three people when his instructions had said two.

"I was given three and I wasn't going to leave one behind in the bloody Atlantic," was his gruff and dismissive answer, as tiredness overwhelmed his body. For the last three weeks he had not slept for more than two hours at a time. For his own health, and that of his crew, he needed to be back in port for a rest.

The escapee with the damaged arm was taken straight to Plymouth hospital while Victoria and the other fellow escapee travelled into London by train. She never learnt his name, but he made a most engaging travelling companion. Away from the Germans, the resistance, and the collaborators, the agent gradually 'decompressed', and in so doing he found fun in the smallest of things, which Victoria found quite infectious.

"She's not a plant," said Vera Atkins confidently to Col. Maurice Buckmaster, Head of the French Section of the Special Operations

Executive[35], when he came to review how this mysterious French woman had managed to infiltrate their highly secret network.

Victoria had been taken from Plymouth straight to SOE's Baker Street offices where, over two full days, she was interviewed. At the outset, her questioning was calm and gentle, but deliberately it became aggressive and intimidating as they tested what she had told them.

"I've interviewed her and most of her story stacks up," continued Atkins. "She speaks fluent French and English and has reasonable German."

"Is she on some German wanted list?" asked Buckmaster.

"No, not as far as we know."

"Then why is she here?"

"She says she worked with her mother and husband as a *Passer* getting pilots through the demarcation line. Her mother thought she was in danger and wanted her out."

"Do we know her? Can we prove her mother worked on the Comet Line?" asked Buckmaster.

"From the debrief of half a dozen pilots who've got back, we can prove her mother was a *passer* but not this girl. She's far too young to meet the description. And it wasn't the Comet Line her mother worked on. It's one we haven't been able to fully identify."

"So why didn't she come across the Pyrenees to San Sebastián like everyone else?"

"She said, after her husband was shot, their line stopped working."

"Why was he shot? Do we have a record of this?" asked Buckmaster.

"She's not sure. It might be because he was a *Passer*, but she thinks it's probably because he was arrested as a communist and was simply unlucky to be chosen for one of their reprisal shootings. She was very honest on all of this. I am in no doubt this man was executed as she says."

---

[35] Special Operations Executive ('SOE') was set up by Prime Minister Winston Churchill to conduct reconnaissance, sabotage, and espionage through occupied Europe. Vera Atkins was Col. Maurice Buckmaster's assistant. She was a brilliant intelligence officer. She has specific responsibility for its forty-seven women agents. These included Noor Inyat Khan, Violette Szabo, and Odette Sansom (also known as Churchill) whose names and exploits were to become famous after the war. Very many were not to survive.

"So the wife of a dead communist just happens to thumb a ride on one of our frigates," commented Buckmaster sarcastically.

"Her mother's friend owns the fisherman's cottage which is used regularly when we need to get people out of Bordeaux using their fishing fleet."

Col. Buckmaster looked down at his desk as he contemplated what he was being told. "What about the information she's brought us? Anything in there that is new, or are we being sold re-cycled stuff to get one of their agents into our midst?"

"Some of it's very useful; it means we will be able to identify far more from aerial photographs. I have arranged for her to spend some time examining those we have for Bordeaux to mark them up. They have a big air base and submarine pen there which we're very interested in."

"How did she get it?" asked Buckmaster.

"Her mother ran a guest house for German pilots on leave. Also, once she knew she was coming here, her mother made her cycle through Bordeaux looking for information which she thought we might need. It was all good and thorough, whilst being too haphazard to have been put together to trick us."

"Do we know her mother?"

"No, except I've been able to verify that she's English, went to Girton and served as a nurse in France during the last war."

Buckmaster grunted. "Can we train her and send her back as a radio operator?" he asked.

"No, she's pregnant. In any case, she's only seventeen. She brought her birth certificate with her to prove her identity, so we know her age. It's the one thing in her story which doesn't stack up. She says she was married, but I'm not sure that's true. It might be his child, but I don't think they were married."

"Why not?" asked Buckmaster.

"She didn't bring her marriage certificate with her. It's not the kind of thing a married woman would leave behind, particularly when pregnant; and her identity papers were still in her maiden name. As a married woman, it would be one of the first things you would want to get changed. Also, her wedding ring was quite old. She said it belonged to her grandmother, which doesn't surprise me. It was the way she was fiddling with it. I would say it had only been on her finger a few days rather than a few months."

"Why the hell have we got her? Why didn't Special Branch take her?"

"Because she came in with our people," replied Atkins.

"So what the hell are we going to do with her?"

"Her plan, or I should say her mother's plan, was for her to go and stay with her grandfather." Atkins looked down at her notes. "He's a Colonel Dovingdon. He lives in one of the villages, somewhere in North Hertfordshire."

Buckmaster sat back in his chair and started to light his pipe. "You say she speaks German. What's it like?" he asked.

"Reasonable, good enough for basic conversation. Sir, there is one thing you should know about Dovingdon," added Atkins.

Buckmaster's attempt to light his pipe had not gone well so he stopped as he listened to what Atkins was about to say.

"Dovingdon's son was sentenced to be shot for murder, desertion, and a whole host of other things in the last war. His son was injured and escaped before the sentence could be carried out. It was a very controversial decision; many thought his son should have received a medal instead."

"Indeed," said Buckmaster dismissively, not understanding the point Atkins was making.

"It's just that the Colonel supported the army in its Court Martial decision against his own son. The old man's unimpeachable."

"Good," said Buckmaster firmly, "then get her to him and tell him that she's there, and not interned, on his surety. Tell him we can't have her running around, and he needs to look after her."

Vera nodded.

"He can't be far from Station X, can he?" asked Buckmaster, referring to Bletchley Park and its highly secret code-breaking activities.

"I would say it's a decent journey, well over an hour by car," answered Atkins. "In any case she can't work there, it's too risky."

"I thought with her German she might ... no, you're right," said

Buckmaster. "But there's a listening post out at Chicksands, which must be close by," he added, regrouping fast. Let's get her posted to work there; her language skills will be useful."

"After the baby's born?" asked Atkins.

"Before, after, I don't care. I'll leave that to you." It was Buckmaster's last word on the subject of Mrs Victoria Bellanger.

Chapter 46

Hertfordshire March 1942

COL. SIR STODDART Dovingdon didn't consider himself an old man, but now aged eighty-two everyone else did. His wife, Lady Primrose, had died a few years before, and with her death he had become lonely and self-centred. He had very few friends, and apart from a fussy housekeeper, he still lived in Imptice House, but alone. The chauffeur and groundsmen had, once again, all gone to war.

Dovingdon tried hard not to think of Penrose and the shame he had brought on the family, but of course a father's love for his son can never be overridden by willpower. The pain of his lost relationship still hurt him, even after twenty-four years. The fact that Juliette had not returned home once in that time, not only upset him but made him terribly angry every time he thought about it. He felt she had no right to castigate him so. He still could not understand it, for they were a father and daughter team who were, at one time, so close, and yet they were now so very far apart. It was the root of their problem; they were so alike.

The telephone conversation between Vera Atkins and Col. Dovingdon, telling him that his granddaughter was coming to live with him, had not gone well. It was clear that the Colonel had an imperiousness which suggested he was not to be trifled with. It made Atkins nervous as to the prospects of their meeting. However, the reception she and Victoria got could hardly have been more different.

Dovingdon was choked with joy at seeing his granddaughter for the very first time. He could not miss the obvious; what an extremely attractive young woman she was, and to Victoria's total amazement, her grandfather sobbed as he took her in his arms for their first introductory embrace. What Victoria could not see, but her grandfather immediately recognised, was how much she looked like her mother. It was as though Juliette were coming home.

"Mrs Bellanger is to stay with you on your surety," said Atkins, rather loudly, incorrectly believing the Colonel was getting deaf. "We think you would prefer this rather than her being interned in some camp somewhere," and then added, "particularly as she's pregnant." Atkins was repeating everything she had told him over the telephone. Dovingdon, being an old stalwart, took on board Victoria's married name and the news she was going to have a baby, without a murmur.

"Mrs Bellanger arrived with eight hundred French francs," continued Atkins. "We need the currency, but we'll credit her bank account with the equivalent in sterling as soon as she has one open. I have organised identity papers, coupons etc. plus some extra ones for clothes. We didn't have time in London to buy much. She'll need to register with the doctor immediately to arrange her confinement."

The no-nonsense efficiency with which Atkins delivered her messages appeared to completely disarm the Colonel, but that would be the wrong interpretation. He was simply thrilled that Victoria was coming to live with him, and he didn't care what conditions were attached.

"Oh," said Atkins, addressing Dovingdon as she was about to get in her car. "I've organised a job for Victoria to have after her baby's born. She'll need to learn morse code. I'll try and get her on a training course before her confinement date. We'll be in touch about that." With those few words, Atkins returned to her car and was gone.

"We've got your mother's old room made up for you," said Dovingdon excitedly, as he carried Victoria's few possessions into the house. There was not a happier man in the whole of England.

Chapter 47

Bordeaux and de Gressier March 1942

JULIETTE DIDN'T HEAR the phone ring. It was only when she was called to the telephone did she wonder who wanted her.

"I thought you'd like to know that it's arrived," said the voice abruptly, without any introduction.

"Arrived, who's this?" asked Juliette, not sure who she was talking to.

"It's Dominique. I wanted you to know that your parcel arrived safely, that's all."

"Oh, thank you, thank you," said Juliette, now understanding the message. She was being told Victoria had made it safely to England.

Juliette closed her eyes and bowed forward as she offered a mental prayer of thanks.

"Have you read in the paper ... about the drowned fisherman?" asked Dominique.

"No ... why?" asked Juliette.

"He was a friend of mine and Victoria's."

"Oh, I'm sorry ...," said Juliette, again not really catching what she was being told. "Should I tell her?" she asked, bewildered.

"No, no, she already knows," said Dominique quickly.

"She's safe?" asked Juliette seeking reassurance.

"Yes," said Dominique. "She's safe. The thing is ... the fisherman's funeral service is the day after tomorrow. I think it would be good if you were there."

"I didn't know him," said Juliette, with a mixture of puzzlement and alarm in her voice.

"But Victoria did," said Dominique, making it clear that she wasn't making a request but giving a command.

"I'll be there," said Juliette, eventually putting two plus two together and getting four.

"I'll see you there. I'll be able to explain," said Dominique, putting down the phone without saying goodbye.

Immediately the telephone went down, Juliette sat on the stairs. She felt herself physically weakened, as wave after wave of relief flowed throughout her body. She wanted to shout; to shout out loud her news, but she had no one to tell. It made her feel the loneliest person in the world. There was no one left in her family. No one. They had all gone! After a little while, Juliette rose and climbed the stairs. For the first time since Victoria left, she was going to her daughter's bedroom. She needed to see, to touch, to smell something of hers. She didn't know how she was going to carry on.

Hope, she decided, after she had sat on her daughter's bed for a long time, holding Victor's pillow, without its case, close to her breast. It was hope which was going to get her through this; hope and defeating the Germans. Now Victoria was safe, Juliette knew she should do more, she could do more. Tomorrow, she would find Monsieur Philidor and this time volunteer to help the Resistance. It was the least she could do.

Chapter 48

Bordeaux July 1942

"THEY WOULD DISAPPEAR under cover of Nacht und Nebel,"[36] said General Keitel, in response to Hitler's decrees of 7th and 12th December 1941. It required all political activists and resistance helpers to be imprisoned or killed. A few weeks later, in January 1942 at the Wannsee Conference, the Third Reich would approve 'die Endlösung' – the Final Solution - to exterminate the Jews throughout the whole of Europe.[37] There was no secrecy to this policy which required an industrial effort to put it into effect.

"What's the screaming?" asked Henri Hilaire anxiously as he sat outside the Kommandant's Office at the German army camp near Merignac airport. He was waiting with Pierre Poinsot, the Préfet de Police, to join a meeting. He hated being there. Just to be close to that man made him angry.

---

[36] Night and fog

[37] Very soon after the Vichy government had been established in July 1940, it set up a Commissariat General aux Questions Juives, and by October 1940 the Statut de Juifs came into law. It was the first in a long line of legislation which excluded Jews from public service and the professions, forced them to wear a yellow patch on their clothes, and banned them from all public places including cafes, restaurants, theatres, parks and gardens; even their phones were disconnected. Throughout France there was little concern amongst the ordinary French men or women as to the extra difficulties faced by the Jewish population from an ever-growing list of restrictive regulations. The hardships of daily living in a war-torn France were taking all their focus. It was only in the French police that the Jewish problem was at the forefront of their minds. In July 1942, René Bousquet, General Secretary to the Vichy Government, under a policy labelled as 'Chasse aux Juifs', urged his préfets to "liberate your region of Jews" in a program he euphemistically called "migration, evacuation and settlement".

"They're separating the children from their parents before they're deported," came an anonymous and unemotional reply.

Henri got up and looked out of the window. Below was a scene he would never forget. Children were screaming, yelling, crying as they were forcibly snatched and then dragged from their desperate parents, who were frantically labelling their children in an attempt to ensure they would get reunited.

"Why are they being separated? Where are they going?" asked Henri, getting distressed at the sight below him.

"The adults are going to Gare Saint Jean and then, I think, to Poland. The children are going to Velodrome Hiver," he was told matter-of-factly.

"What, with no parents, why? What's at Velodrome Hiver?" asked Henri.

"It's a sports stadium on the outskirts of Paris."

"Why are they taking their name tags off?" protested Henri, as he watched the guards snatching them off the children's clothes. "Their parents have only just put them on!"

"Oh, they won't need them anymore," he was told, in as dismissive a way as it was possible to make.

With those words, Henri instinctively knew what he was being told, and the children's fate. With every child he saw loaded on to the truck, he ached in despair and raged in anger, as he identified each and every one of them with his very precious son, Pierre.

The reports Henri heard later from the Bordeaux policemen who accompanied the children to the sports stadium were worse than could be imagined. Babies and young children were being kept without food, water, or sanitation for days. So distressed were the returning policemen with what they saw that they petitioned Pierre Laval, the Prime Minister in the Vichy government, to stop it. "They must all go," he replied, completely unmoved. The only concession Laval would make, so as to stop the policemen from being upset, was to add children to the trains taking the men and women straight to Auschwitz. This way the police would no longer have to endure the desperately upsetting scenes where women and their children, and babies, some just days old, were separated.

It was immediately after Henri had seen children being ripped from their mothers' arms at Merignac army camp that Dominique started to see a physical and mental change in him. He no longer ate, and his hands physically shook. He started to get home promptly and then just before 6 o'clock, without saying a word, he would climb the stairs to his study, close and lock the door. Very carefully he would unwind an extended aerial which he would connect to his radio. In great secrecy, he would tune into BBC Radio London and listen intensely. Henri had no interest in the progress of the war. He was only after hearing one thing; what was happening to the children who had disappeared. He heard nothing, but every day the rumour mill grew. The train drivers returning from delivering their human cargo to Auschwitz didn't keep secret what they had seen. Stories of an enormous labour camp and the execution of those too ill or too young to work now circulated freely amongst the Bordeaux police, as did the reports of the constant acrid smell from its chimneys.

"What's the matter?" asked Dominique as she stood by Henri while he watered their vegetable patch with his hands shaking. The evening had just started to cool.

Henri shook his head. He couldn't speak. He had been to Merignac Camp that morning. It was one month to the day since his last visit and still they were separating Jewish children from their parents before they were deported and sent to the gas chamber.

"What have you seen?" she asked. All the time he had been in the police force he'd never got used to seeing a dead body. It always distressed him for days afterwards, and so Dominique would patiently nurse him through these few days until he got better, but this time his depression had gone on much, much longer and was far deeper than anything before.

Henri shook his head signifying he didn't want to talk, but then his knees involuntarily collapsed, and he fell sobbing to the ground, the watering can he had been holding bounced on the ground, soaking him all over as the water was flung out.

Henri rolled into a little ball and physically shook, for whatever he did he could not get the pictures of the children's faces out of his mind. Not one or two but twenty or thirty babies and small children, each picture different, except for two things: the fright in their eyes and the terror in their mouths, which were screaming for all their worth, but in his head there was no sound. One by one, the pictures went through his mind like cards being flicked through a Rolodex.

Dominique's first reaction, because he was shaking so badly, was that Henri was having an epileptic fit. It was his gentle rocking backwards and forwards which told her that her immediate diagnosis was wrong. Very slowly, and with a huge amount of sympathy, Dominique coaxed Henri onto a dining room chair which she had brought outside. There she insisted he took a sip of brandy. He'd always hated the stuff as he found it burned his gullet and stomach, but with the first sip the slideshow of pictures in his mind slowed down, and after a few more sips it stopped altogether.

"What's the matter?" asked Dominique again.

"We're killing children; we're murdering children," he said desperately, shaking his head from side to side.

"How do you know?" Dominique asked very gently.

"I can see them. I can describe every child I saw being separated from their parents and taken away, every one!" There was desperation in his voice.

"Every time I see Pierre, I see them, every time I see these children in my head, I fear for him."

Very slowly and painstakingly, just as though he was giving evidence in court, Henri shared with Dominique what he had seen and what he knew was happening.

"It's happening in my France," he shouted in despair. "In my France, the France of the good. The France of liberté, égalité, fraternité. It cannot be. It cannot be," he said, as he started to repeat himself.

Henri rubbed his eyes hard and then stroked his forehead.

"I'm a policeman. I'm supposed to catch murderers, but I can't! This is state organised, and I can't stop it!" Henri was now almost yelling, so strongly was he feeling about what he was saying.

Dominique was seriously worried about what Henri had told her, but her immediate concern was her distressed husband and the fact that the neighbours might have heard his yelling. There was no doubt about it. Henri was a broken man, unable to function.

"When did you last eat?" she asked, as softly and as gently as she could.

"I can't eat," he mumbled, shaking his head.

"Come you must eat something," she said, as she led him to the kitchen table; shooing everyone out before her. There she broke some crusty bread into small portions. Making an exception, she spread on both butter and jam before handing them to him one at a time. She made some tea and using the very last of their rations she made it very sweet. Henri took the mug from her in both hands, as he was shaking too violently to hold it in one. He took one sip and then another.

"There will be no work for you tomorrow. I'll take in a message saying that you have the flu," she said.

Henri was too exhausted to argue.

The little nourishment Henri had taken was enough to see an improvement in his disposition. "I'm going to see Father Luke," he announced, after he had changed out of his uniform and put on his best suit. It was, noted Dominique, very strange for Henri to put on his best suit to go to church but then she dismissed it from her mind as she was seriously worried about what Henri had just told her.

Whatever happened at church, Henri was much calmer on his return. He greeted Dominique as he usually did, when he came in from work, with a kiss.

"I feel much better now, thank you," he said. "I need to do some work." It was on those words, and with a bottle of wine and some bread and cheese, that he headed to his study. Very carefully, Henri unpacked the three mixed packets of pills he had purchased earlier that day. He set fire to the packaging in the grate, making sure that there was nothing left other than fine ash. Then, picking up his pen, he started to write in the neatest hand on white bonded paper. He wrote fluently, without mistakes, for he knew exactly what he wanted to say. He didn't sign his name. Instead, he took out his police medals from the bottom drawer and rested them on the top of his desk.

It was nearly 10pm when Henri shouted to Dominique that he was going to check his motorcycle as he needed to use it the next morning. In their small garden shed, with the door shut, Henri started the engine. Sitting on paper laid out on the floor and with his face nearest the exhaust, he breathed heavily. He coughed and choked a couple of times but kept breathing deeply as fast as he could; in and out. Sometime after he had begun to feel the effects of carbon monoxide, depriving his blood cells of the oxygen his brain and muscles needed, he cut the engine and made his way back to his study. With his head feeling thick and heavy, he locked the door. He combed his hair, tightened and straightened his tie and sat down at his desk. He counted out half of the pills and swallowed them down with red wine. The other half he wrapped in camembert cheese before swallowing them too. He neatened his jacket, signed the letter with his full name, and slowly sipped more wine. Henri very deliberately allowed himself to fall into a deep sleep and then a coma from which he never awoke.

As one person was leaving this life another was entering. Victoria was giving birth to her son; Henry Victor Guégan Bellanger. While the new-born baby was being nursed, Col. Dovingdon opened a bottle of champagne to celebrate the birth of 'his' son, albeit a great grandson, who had come into his life.

Chapter 49

Bordeaux July 1942

"I WILL LEAD the funeral service," said Father Luke, after he'd spent a few minutes in Dominique's sitting room offering his condolences, "but Commissionnaire Hilaire cannot be buried in the church cemetery," he added. "You will understand why."

"I don't, why?" asked Dominique, completely shocked.

"As Henri is Catholic, it is only right I conduct his funeral service," said Father Luke, pompously. "Also, I've been asked by the Préfet de Police to do it because they think that there will be a lot of people who will want to pay their respects. Henri was widely liked and highly respected."

"Why can't he be buried in the cemetery?" asked Dominique, returning to the key point which was worrying her about what he had just said.

"He committed suicide," said the priest defiantly, presuming Dominique knew and was trying to cover things up.

"No, he didn't, don't be ridiculous. You don't know that," said Dominique, trying to hide the fact that the priest had just articulated her own fears about Henri's death.

"You don't know what I know," said the Priest. "I took Henri's confession the night he died."

"What are you saying? Henri told you in confession that he was going to commit suicide? I thought you were supposed to keep everything you were told in confession absolutely secret until you died!"

"Dominique," said the Priest quite firmly, "you know I can't talk about what is said in confession."

"Henri's death certificate says he died from a heart attack," she retorted.

"That might be what the police want us to think."

"It's not the police, but the doctor who signed his death certificate."

"The police doctor," replied Father Luke, stressing the word 'police' as he spoke.

"You have to accept what's on the death certificate. It's the law," Dominique argued.

"Man's law maybe, but it's not God's law. Under God's law I cannot bury a man in consecrated ground who has committed suicide. Do you not see, if I did so I would be defying God on this earth?"

"God's law doesn't permit babies and little kiddies to be torn from their mothers either, but you do nothing about stopping that, why?" she snapped. Dominique was just about to lay into him about his hypocrisy, and that of the Catholic Church, when she decided to hold her tongue. She needed a funeral service for Henri, and she was not going to have him buried in some municipal grave. It was a fight for later.

"Henri left this letter for you, Father," said Dominique. "I don't know what it says but I suspect it is something he would like you to read out in church. He always talked about such a thing."

"He did, he did," acknowledged the Priest, as he took the envelope into his hands. At that moment there was little more to be said between them.

As soon as Juliette heard of Henri's death she rushed to be by Dominique's side.

They had not seen each other since the fisherman's funeral. This time the two women went into Henri's study to talk. It was as organised and immaculate as he had left it. Still on the desk were his medals. The only change was the letter which had been handed to Father Luke. Dominique offered Juliette one of the two reading chairs which were circled around the unlit fireplace. As they sat down, both leaned forward to talk in the quiet conspiratorial way they now seemed to conduct all their conversations.

Juliette immediately noticed that Dominique's grief was different. It was not the physical, broken grief which followed the death of her son, but something far more circumspect. It was deeper and more thoughtful.

"Father Luke says Henri killed himself," said Dominique, as her opening sentence once they had sat down. She had not said anything like this to anyone else. She had closer friends, but she felt unable to share with them the things she shared with Juliette. Perhaps it was because she lived far away, and wasn't there to gossip about her, that she knew their conversations would be kept secret. Perhaps it was because, through Étienne, they knew each other better than anyone else, although he had been dead for twelve years. Why was it only in times of strife or tragedy that they seemed to meet up, each asked themselves privately?

"I heard he'd had a heart attack," said Juliette.

"That's what the medical certificate says." Dominique paused. "Henri had a sort of nervous breakdown earlier in the evening before he died."

It was at that moment Juliette recognised the grief Dominique was suffering. It was predominantly one of guilt, for failing to save him. It was a common reaction of families of suicide victims.

"Very strangely, Henri went to confession just before he died," said Dominique casually.

"I didn't think Henri was the type of person who would do that," said Juliette surprised.

"Once a Catholic, always a Catholic. What do the Jesuits say, 'give me a child until seven and I will give you the man'. It's the biggest indoctrination force in the world," commented Dominique, angrily.

Juliette frowned slightly and reached across to hold Dominique's hand in sympathy because she could feel how angry she was getting. "What makes Father Luke say what he says?" she asked. "Did he leave a suicide note or anything like that?"

"He left a letter to his precious priest, that's all," said Dominique sarcastically. Do you know that wretched man won't bury him in the church cemetery?"

"Why not?"

"Because he says Henri killed himself." Dominique's voice yielded a sign of frustration at Juliette's lack of speed in joining the dots. "I hate that wretched place. That man has the hypocrisy to insist he conducts a catholic service because Henri's a catholic and then wants him buried in the municipal cemetery."

Juliette got off her chair and kneeled at Dominique's feet so she could hold both her hands.

"Henri and I have supported that damn man and his damn church way, way beyond … and this is what he does to us."

"Would you like Henri to be buried in Latoire Village church?" asked Juliette.

"Can he be?"

"In the Guégan family row, I can't see why not."

"But it's a Protestant church."

"It seems to me that his church has deserted him in his hour of need, so why not?"

"I'm Protestant," said Dominique, not that it would have made any difference to where Henri could be buried.

"So am I," said Juliette.

"In fact, I'm nothing," said Dominique.

"So am I," repeated Juliette, enjoying the commonality of thought.

"Can I be buried there with him?" asked Dominique. As soon as it was said, both women knew it was a loaded question, but not deliberately so, for laying just a few yards away would be Étienne. Juliette thought rapidly. She did not want Dominique consorting with Étienne again, even in his death. What if Dominique died before her, then they would be together first. She knew she wouldn't like that.

"Would you want your own plot or to be buried with Henri?" asked Juliette.

"Oh, with Henri," she answered, instinctively.

It was the correct reply, for Juliette smiled her agreement and Dominique smiled back. Both women knew exactly what the other had been thinking.

Chapter 50

Bordeaux July 1942

THE CHURCH WAS packed for Henri's funeral mass. Dominique's friends and family, including those from her first husband, George Bellanger's, family attended. Henri's police colleagues turned out in force. Juliette and Dominique came in together and sat side by side. Dominique had already decided that Pierre was too young to attend.

Father Luke had already read Henri's letter carefully two or three times. His initial reaction was to ignore it. Instead, he worked carefully crafting his eulogy. It was only at the last minute, as the church was filling up with so many policemen with their medals, and politicians with their sashes and chains of office, that he had a change of mind. He could not explain what caused it. Perhaps it was, he wondered afterwards, the smugness of the congregation which had prompted him.

"My brothers and sisters," said Father Luke, after the procession had placed Henri's coffin before the altar. "Before we begin this funeral mass in celebration of the life of Henri Valoire Hilaire and we commend his spirit to the safe keeping of God the Father, I have a letter from Henri which he wrote before he died. He asked that I read it to you."

Father Luke slowly took out his glasses as he moved from the centre of the aisle to his right, in front of the pews where the dignitaries of Bordeaux were sitting. Gathered immediately behind them were members of the Bordeaux police force. Henri admired some, and would have wished that those whom he thought evil and loathed had not come, but none of them were his friends. His only true friend in the congregation was his wife Dominique. She was sitting on the other side of the aisle bolt upright, determined not to yield to any emotion, for only metres away were the men she was blaming for Henri's death and killing her son.

Father Luke deliberately made a show of unfolding Henri's letter. He started to read:

"*Dear Father Luke,*
I have not said goodbye to those that I love. Perhaps you would be so kind as to read these few words at my funeral service so I may do so. This is my dying wish.

To those who are gathered here today I would like to say thank you. I do not know what I have done that has persuaded you to give up your free time to be with me this one last time, and in doing so, support my family, but you are being most kind.

I would also like to say sorry to all those I have caused pain and anguish. To those who have suffered from my anger, intemperance, injustice, rudeness, and many other unforgivable actions, I truly apologise. I am in no doubt that the fault was entirely mine. I do not make these apologies in the hope that God will judge me less harshly. I do it because it is the right thing to do. My God will not forgive an insincere apology".

Father Luke paused, half turned and looked towards where Dominique was sitting.

"*To my family, I wish to say thank you, for you have been the inspiration for my ambition, joy and happiness. From my earliest days with my parents, with my brothers and sister and then with my wife Dominique, our son Pierre and her son Stephen, the love and affection I have enjoyed has known no bounds. It went far beyond anything I ever deserved.*

I would like to publicly acknowledge Dominique's indomitable spirit. She kept me going long after I had wanted to give up. She is wise and clever, brave, and resourceful. Her beauty, care, compassion and kindness means she is genuinely loved by everyone, and I have been a far better man for having her by my side.

To Pierre, my precious son, I would like to say how proud I am of you. Even at your tender age I can see that you will be a good person. I ask, do not seek wealth because it will not bring you happiness. Be a joy seeker and bringer as, in this happiness, the world will be your oyster, even in the most terrible of times.

I love you both with all my heart and I will always do my best, wherever I am, to look after you. If God is gracious enough to put me in heaven then I will seek out Stephen and tell him that he is our hero, never to be forgotten."

Father Luke paused again, smiled graciously at Dominique, and then turned directly towards the great and the good of Bordeaux. He continued:

"When I was in school, Victor Hugo's 'Les Misérables' was one of the books on the curriculum. Like all in my class, I was enthralled by the story; the generosity of the church which allowed Jean Valjean to renew himself to lead a life of good and godliness. The love shared between comrades-in-arms, the fractious love of the Thénardiers, the unrequited love of Eponine, and the unrelenting belief of Javert in the righteousness of the law, all come together to make a great story; but in its greatness, the biggest lesson is often forgotten. Its moral is that the law without compassion, the law without morality, the law for the sake of the law, is nothing. It is like a man without a conscience, a man without a heart, a man without a soul.

It was the moral of Les Misérables which encouraged me to become a policeman, for I promised myself that I would not just uphold the law, but I would do so with morality and compassion in my heart.

Today, far beyond anything in our history, there is now a lack of morality and compassion in our policing which I could no longer bear. It is causing deep upset, and a fission in our society. It is like a canker spreading and rotting the whole body which will be very hard, if not impossible, to heal if it is not cut out.

It starts so very easily and is so understandable. The police know who the criminals are. They know those who make their living from crime. What does it matter if they plant evidence on a criminal to see him convicted of a crime he hasn't committed. If he wasn't guilty of one, he was surely guilty of another. Haven't the police served society by keeping a habitual criminal off the streets and in prison? What has been done may be corrupt but wasn't it done in a good cause? Does this not make it justifiable? Does it not make it right?

Our ethical system is grounded in the belief that how and why you do something is far more important than the results of your behaviour. This means that if your actions are inherently bad it doesn't matter whether the outcome of your behaviour is good, those actions will always be bad.

When a policeman uses unethical and sometimes illegal means to obtain a result, in the belief that it benefits the greater good, then they are doing nothing of the sort; for their actions will always be unethical and illegal.

Those who practise good cause corruption, for it is now widespread in Bordeaux, argue that theirs is the greater morality; that the ends justify the means. However, when good people do bad things because they believe the outcome will be good, then they cross the line from being a good person to being a bad one.

Today, too many of my colleagues seem unable to recognise that they are doing things which they would deplore in others. They have lost sight of the 'Golden Rule' found in every religion throughout the world. It teaches us that we should treat each other as we would like that person to treat us.

It requires you to wish and bring upon others only that which you would wish brought upon yourself, and no one, not even the police themselves, would want the actions of today's Bordeaux police brought upon them."

Father Luke looked up and stared directly at Pierre Poinsot and then along the row at his colleagues. There was an icy chill in the atmosphere. He started to read again:

"The most frightening thing about good cause corruption is the belief that its practitioners have in the righteousness of their actions. Their belief that killing someone, or deliberately injuring them, is justified because their actions will result in a better outcome for society is truly frightening. Science has, for a long time, taught us the fallibility of our beliefs.

At one time, people believed the earth was flat. Another time they believed our world was the centre of the universe and the sun went around it. They did not know then that these beliefs were false. Recognising the fallibility of mankind, I question how anyone can have a belief which is so strong that they can put aside the moral judgement of all humanity.

How can you believe, with such conviction, that your God and your disciple is better than their God and their disciple? How can you believe, with such certainty, that your political system is better than theirs? How can you be sure that your judgement is better than their judgement?

The answer to these three questions is that you cannot. There is no certainty in any belief, and categorically not to any extent which makes it lawful to do the unlawful, or moral to do the immoral.

Any person possessed of the commitment to make the world a safer place who, for whatever reason, becomes convinced of their righteousness, such that they will go to any lengths to advance their belief, is unquestionably dangerous. Such a person strikes at the heart of a good society. They do not belong in the Bordeaux police force. Consequently, it befalls on each and every one of us to stop such a person, or group of persons, for the harm they do will be immeasurable.

I have often wondered why there are Ten Commandments when only one is needed. It is the sixth commandment - do not steal. All the others are simply different versions of this. Do not steal God's authority. Do not steal another's possession. Do not steal someone's life. Do not steal another man's wife. Do not steal their reputation. Do not allow jealousy to steal your soul, and do not steal another's grace and dignity by doing them harm.

Someone entrusted to uphold the law, and who breaks the law in the commission of their duty, is committing the biggest crime of all. They are stealing justice not just from one person or group of people. They are stealing from the whole of mankind and a theft of that magnitude can never, ever be forgiven.

A small, but highly influential, element of the Bordeaux police is now, each day, breaking the law for the benefit of their beliefs or because, cowardly, they break the law on the instructions and beliefs of others. These are the very laws which, on becoming a policeman, they swore to uphold.

These policemen do not serve the people when they break the law, for however justified they feel, the harm that their actions are doing to the reputation of policing, not just in Bordeaux but throughout France, is a price which is far too high. A civilised society needs an honest, and uncorrupted and incorruptible police force."

Father Luke paused to take breath and as he did so he wondered whether he had been wise to read the letter. Should he stop now, he pondered. It was when he looked at the face of the mayor, who was paying particular attention to every word, he knew he had to continue. He started reading again:

"Throughout time, all societies have created bad laws. A law which requires an innocent baby to be torn from its innocent mother's arms, is not just bad, it is immoral and plainly wrong. It is not the duty of the policeman to carry out immoral acts in the name of the law. It is their God-given duty, as it is of all of us, to use their discretion in the way that they exercise their powers. There is no obligation placed on a policeman to do an immoral act. On the contrary, his duty, as a human being, requires him to ignore any immoral law and permits him not to enforce it. In this way, the police never need be an instrument of the state, but an instrument of morality, as judged by the Golden Rule.

When I look at myself, when I look into my conscience, I see a man who has failed to tackle the biggest crime of all. It is the crime of corruption and statism in our police force.

Unquestionably, I have failed in the promise I made to myself to learn the lessons of Javert, and thus police with compassion and morality. For that I am deeply sorry.

When I look at my inactions, I am ashamed at what I see. Too often, I have cowardly concluded that the risks to me, the risks to my family, the risks to my friends and colleagues in speaking out, in doing the things I should have done to stop these atrocities, was too high; and for this, other people have needlessly suffered and died.

Unlike me, others have time to repent, to change their ways, to end the corruption they practise every day, and thus seek their saviour in this life before they go to the next. It requires no bravery on their part. It just means stopping their evil behaviour. Is that too much for a dying man to ask?"

Father Luke stopped. He didn't read out Henri's last three words: *Vive la France.* Somehow, they didn't seem appropriate. Instead, he stood there, for some time. He allowed Henri's message to linger in silence amongst his shocked and offended audience before he folded the letter shut.

Dominique and Juliette had stopped breathing. They were in awe at the magnificence of Henri's message. They now understood his motive. Like Henri, they knew one man making a protest would be a voice in the wilderness. But to commit a form of self-immolation, and explain why, would create a political storm which would be carried far and wide. Sadly, with no free press, the impact of Henri's letter, which had created a tidal wave inside the church, was to dissipate into a ripple outside, and then into still waters beyond.

"Let us pray," said Father Luke after some while.

Immediately after the service, Dominique and Juliette didn't stay to talk. Another time they might have done, but both knew they could not cope with the reaction from Henri's letter. Instead, together with the vicar from Latoire Church, they accompanied Henri's coffin to the Guégan row in the churchyard. It was just the three of them who saw him buried in the spot next to that reserved for Stephen. Dominique wept when she saw the plaque in her son's memory, for she had not seen it before. She had known of Juliette's promise but now it was tangible.

"You've created a family of heroes," said Juliette. "Georges, Stephen, and now Henri. It's quite remarkable."

"Remarkably painful, you mean," replied Dominique.

"Pierre can be very proud of his Dad. We'll get a copy of his letter to make sure he is," said Juliette, before pointing to Étienne's grave and adding: "It's where I'll be."

Dominique looked and nodded. "Then we won't be far apart," she whispered mournfully.

The two women linked arms and walked away in a friendship which they knew should not be, and yet they also knew it would be as strong in death as it was in life.

Chapter 51

Pitomnik Airfield, Stalingrad January 1943

"YOU'RE FLYING TO Pitomnik Airfield," instructed Baur to a group of F.d.F. pilots gathered in the crew briefing room in the Wolf's Lair. "You leave first thing in the morning, have a brief stopover at Morozovskaya to refuel before going on to Pitomnik. You'll then return via Königsberg[38] to drop off the wounded." he continued.

Heinrik had forgotten how many times he had flown into Pitomnik and on to Königsberg in the last month. It had become his default job if Baur didn't assign him something more important. The fact was that the German 6th Army and 4th Panzer Army at Stalingrad was surrounded by the Soviet army. Pitomnik's narrow, hard rolled snow runway was their only lifeline. F.d.F. was now part of an air bridge which was working to keep Hitler's army in Stalingrad supplied.

"What's the mission?" asked one of his pilot colleagues.

Heinrik thought it a damn silly question, for the mention of Königsberg meant it would be the same as the previous trips they had made into Pitomnik.

"Everyone's taking in supplies and bringing out the injured," said Baur. "The Führer has ordered that every spare aeroplane be committed to the relief of Stalingrad," he added sharply.

"Are we getting fighter cover?" asked another one of the assembled crew.

Another stupid question thought Heinrik, for they had never been provided with fighter cover before.

Baur ignored the question. "Make sure you get the liaison officer's briefing before you leave. The situation on the ground is fluid and constantly changes."

---

[38] Now known as Kaliningrad.

Baur looked around the room and the solemn faces in front of him. He could detect that each of them thought they were being sent on a suicide mission. It was exactly how Heinrik felt each time he had been ordered into Pitomnik, for it was one hell of a flying challenge.

"I'm not asking you to do anything which I haven't done myself," said Baur responding to their mood. "I've flown in and out several times, so I know how tough it is, but then, as we all know, we have to think of our colleagues fighting there. They need us, no question, so let's get ready and go." Baur left the room. He had nothing else to say. In any case, he was dining with Hitler, as he did on many of the evenings they were together at the Wolf's Lair, and he could not be late.

Heinrik's plane was maintained and loaded with supplies overnight so that, at first light, he and his crew were ready to take off in the falling snow. Sandwiches and warm ersatz coffee from a thermos kept them sustained on their journey. Heinrik found Morozovskaya airfield without difficulty and, despite the poor quality of air traffic control, he landed easily. There he found a crowded airfield in organised chaos as aircraft were loaded from the stacks of supplies and ammunition accumulated to be airlifted on.

At Morozovskaya, while his plane was refuelled, Heinrik and his crew were able to get a refill of coffee and sandwiches from the very limited facilities. Heinrik rechecked his sums. Just as Baur had suggested, the lighter load of only wounded soldiers picked up at Pitomnik meant that they would not need to return here to refuel. Instead, they would fly directly to Königsberg where they would drop off the wounded, and then refuel before returning to their base.

The snow had stopped falling and the airfield was blanketed with fog when Heinrik took off. As soon as they were in the air, his only gunner fired a short burst from their central gun to make sure that it would work in the freezing cold. They flew above and through low cloud cover to avoid enemy fighters and flak. They tuned into the radio beacon which was broadcast by Pitomnik airfield to navigate there. As they flew, Heinrik and his co-pilot took great care not to be tricked by Russian radio operators broadcasting similar sounding beacons. That would have caused them to head towards a Russian airfield with the guarantee of attack from both the ground and the air.

The flight time from Morozovskaya to Pitomnik Airfield was just fifty minutes. Heinrik found the primitive landing field on the snow bound Russian steppes without difficulty. It was earmarked by a few parked Ju 52 aircraft and several wrecked fuselages which had crashed landed. The problem was that the landing field was cratered with shells and the Junkers undercarriage was notably very weak. Heinrik quickly identified the red landing cross and finally, as he circled the field, he saw the green light giving him permission to land.

Heinrik landed on the narrow-compacted snow runway where, at the end, he was waved off and instructed to stop. He left his engine running as men swarmed to unload the supplies he had brought. No sooner was his plane emptied than it was hurriedly loaded with scared wounded soldiers; unlike before no medic was coming with them as none could be spared. Heinrik wanted to take off quickly before the weather cleared. He was certain that, as soon as that happened, Soviet fighter planes would come into the air increasing the risk of an attack. However, as soon as he was ready to leave, Heinrik was denied permission. Germans 6th Army Group had given an instruction that no one was to take off until it had given its specific authority, so concerned were they to control the exodus of its surrounded army.

"Can you not see who we are? Our orders come directly from the Führer not General Paulus," shouted Heinrik angrily before pushing the throttle and heading for the runway. One more shell, one more crater and it would be impossible to take off.[39]

Heinrik flew directly west using the same defensive strategy of low cloud cover as he had used on his inbound journey. He knew

---

[39] Hauptman Heinrik Klugman's aeroplane was one of the very last to leave Pitomnik Airfield which was captured the very next day on 24th January 1943. General Paulus, who headed the 6th Army Group, was promoted to Field Marshal on the 30th January 1943 and surrendered his headquarters a day later. By 2nd February 1943, the rest of the German Army at the Battle of Stalingrad had also surrendered. The Battle had been won by the Russians. It is estimated that, from both sides, over 2 million men and women were either killed, injured, missing, or captured during the battle.

he could not relax until he was well inside the German controlled area and outside the reach of Soviet fighter planes. This meant that Heinrik was ready when, a few minutes after take-off, just as there was a break in the cloud, his plane came under heavy attack from anti-aircraft guns on the ground. To avoid the flak, Heinrik swung his plane violently in the air from left to right. Those injured in the back of the plane screamed from the added pain his defensive manoeuvres were causing them. In a few minutes they were through the worst and the plane settled down to straight and level flight. Heinrik set a north-westerly course for Königsberg and started to relax. From now on everything should be routine, he thought confidently. His co-pilot could take command for the next couple of hours while he took a bit of a rest.

Chapter 52

The Wolf's Lair - Hitler's Field Headquarters February 1943

"COME WITH ME," said Hans Baur, to Heinrik. It was said with unusual familiarity. He had just returned after a two-day round trip and looked as he felt, scruffy and exhausted. Now was not the time for one of Baur's debriefing meetings which he insisted on holding after every three or four missions.

"Now," said Baur firmly.

Heinrik obediently followed Bauer as he took him from their quarters into Sector 1 and into a room which had a huge map of the Eastern front laid out on a table. Hitler was by himself pacing around the map when Baur and Heinrik entered. Until that moment Heinrik had no idea who he was going to meet.

"Heil Hitler," said both men instantly standing to attention with a click of their heels and a smart salute. Hitler lifted his hand in half-hearted acknowledgement.

"Führer, I would like to introduce you to Hauptman Heinrik," said Baur. "He's the pilot I mentioned to you. He flew one of the last planes in and out of Pitomnik Airfield. He has asked me to apologise for his attire, but he and his crew have just returned from a mission to Bratislava. They landed only a few moments ago."

Hitler looked at Heinrik with great intensity. "We've met before," he said after a long pause.

"Yes Führer, we met on your train when it was in Bordeaux, just before I joined F.d.F."

"Tell me about Pitomnik Airfield. What was the situation there? What was it really like? Why did he have to give it up? Why did he have to surrender?"

Hitler never mentioned any name but Heinrik instinctively knew he was referring to Paulus. Heinrik could sense an agitation in Hitler's demeanour. He was like a lit fuse waiting to explode in anger at any moment.

Heinrik decided to speak very softly as he told of the situation as he saw it. He started to tell of the chaos on the airfield and the bravery of the men on the ground. Hitler invited Heinrik to sit down. Baur remained standing as he looked on pleased as the two men continued the conversation. If there was one thing Hitler like to hear about it was the bravery of his soldiers. Their conversation was stopped after about ten minutes by Col. General Wilhelm Keitel[40] entering the room carrying a small presentation box which he handed to Hitler. Heinrik sensed Hitler would have liked the conversation to have gone on. Nevertheless, he stood up and so Heinrik followed.

"Hauptman Klugman, it gives me great pleasure to award you the Order of The Iron Cross 1st Class, congratulations," said Hitler. For the first time in their meeting he smiled. In normal circumstances Hitler would have placed the ribbon, with the medal attached, over Heinrik's head so it rested on his neckline. Instead, almost absent mindedly, he handed Heinrik the presentation box he was holding.

"Thank you," stammered Heinrik completely surprised. He paused as he looked inside the box at his award. "It will make my mother very proud." It was all he could think to say.

Just as Heinrik was being dismissed, Hitler turned to him and asked: "Have you just come from the field?"

"Yes," said Heinrik. "I'm just back from Bratislava."

"Ah, it explains his dress," said Hitler to Baur and they looked at each other as though they were conspirators in a shared secret. It was clear they knew the name of his passenger. Heinrik did not. At the signal for dinner Hitler and Baur left the room. Heinrik was not dismissed. He was simply treated as though he were no longer there.

As he walked back to his quarters on his own, Heinrik felt confused. Baur had told Hitler where he had been. Had he not heard, he wondered. But it was his medal which made him feel uncomfortable. It was nice to be recognised, but was he brave? Not really, he was just

---

[40] Chief of Staff Oberkommando de Wehrmacht

doing a job which, had he refused, would have been treason. There were far braver men than he at Stalingrad and it made him feel quite humble.

It was only much later when Heinrik got his citation that he understood a little bit more for it said that, of all the F.d.F. pilots, he had flown more missions into Pitomnik Airfield than anyone else. But even then, it made no sense. There were transport pilots who had flown far more missions than him. There was another reason which Baur was later to admit to Heinrik. Hitler needed to meet a hero from Stalingrad. Baur could have chosen any one from his flight and found a reason for them to be honoured, but he felt no one had the same emotional intelligence as Heinrik. What he thought Hitler needed, at that moment, was a combatant from the field. Not a colonel or general, but an ordinary officer who might be able to empathise with Hitler's plight of losing an army.

Chapter 53

Kropyvnytskyi, Ukraine January 1944

THE GLOOM WHICH hung over the Wolf's Lair was not relieved in any part by the fact that it was a New Year which normally brings with it renewed hope and optimism. Since the surrender at Stalingrad, eleven months before, every discussion of counter-attack was bogged down in the practicalities of getting enough supplies to the German forces now defending 2,000 kilometres of the Eastern Front; a situation made more difficult by the ever strengthening partisans who attacked the railway lines at almost every strategic point.

The F.d.F. and Heinrik were kept busy as, more frequently, Hitler demanded that his Generals be brought from the battlefield to report to him directly. He no longer fully trusted the written reports he was getting from his High Command. Sometimes Heinrik knew who he was flying, but most times secrecy dictated that he did not. He would fly to an airfield where his passenger would be waiting. No one dared to be late for the Führer or his aeroplane.

Such was the reason for Heinrik's second flight to Kropyvnytskyi[41] Airfield. He'd been instructed to return the very depressed Generaloberst [42] Karl-Adolf Hollidt who had been given command of the reconstituted 6th Army after its surrender at Stalingrad. He had been brought out three days before to see Hitler who had ordered him back to his troops without any promise of reinforcements or the extra supplies he had asked for. Hollidt knew this meant he was going back

---

[41] Until 2016 Kropyvnytskyi was spelt as Kirovohrad in Ukrainian and Kirovograd in Russia. Kropyrnytskyi was occupied by the Germans on 5th August 1941 and recaptured on 8th January 1944.

[42] Colonel- General

to be captured or die, but it was not his fate that worried him.[43] As a professional soldier he had long ago accepted the risks which came with his occupation. What made the Generaloberst's mood far worse was the fact that Hitler had denied his request for a few days leave to see his family, possibly for the last time. The Generaloberst knew that, now the Russians had breached the natural defensive barrier of the Dnieper River, nothing was going to stop them until they reached Berlin where his wife and daughters lived.

As often on these trips, Heinrik's instructions included the repatriation of injured soldiers. This time, for reasons which he could only imagine came from a warped sense of humour in the planning department, he was instructed to take the injured men to Nuremberg where they were to be admitted to 385 Station Hospital. Kropyvnytskyi to Nuremberg was over 1,900 kilometres which, even with the extra fuel tanks fitted to his plane meant refuelling at Budapest as well as Kropyvnytskyi.

Heinrik had seen Nuremberg airport from the air many times, but he had never landed there. For the first time since the war had started he was given permission to take two days leave to see his mother living 60 kilometres away from the airport in Bamberg.

The pre-flight briefing from the intelligence officer suggested that nothing had changed. The Ukrainian army attacks had been successfully repelled time after time and was still on the outskirts of the city. However, unluckily for Heinrik and his passengers, the Kropyvnytskyi airfield was on the eastern side of the Inhul River so, once again, his landing and take-off would be directly over attacking enemy soldiers.

What made matters worse for Heinrik's second trip into Kropyvnytskyi airfield was that, after a long flight and with his fuel tanks almost empty, he could not find the airport. With low cloud and thick snow, which gave repeated white-outs, he found it impossible to

---

[43] In 1944 Hollidt was dismissed from his command. In 1945, he was taken prisoner by US forces. Hollidt was convicted at Nuremberg of the unlawful use of prisoners of war and of the deportation and enslavement of civilians. He was sentenced to five years of imprisonment. He died in 1985, the last surviving Generaloberst of the Wehrmacht.

identify where he was supposed to be landing, and his search for the airfield's navigational beam had proven to be equally unavailing.

Heinrik eventually retraced his route until he found the river. At a height of just a few hundred feet, he followed the silvery water until he came to the railway bridge. From there he knew that the runway was directly east. It was with huge relief that Heinrik eventually landed. Not only had it taken all his flying skills but, he had to admit, an incredible amount of luck

As soon as the plane landed Heinrik decided he should keep his three engines running. He feared that if, in the cold, they stopped it would be impossible to get them restarted

"Sir, will you please order the plane to be refuelled immediately," shouted Heinrik to the Generaloberst as soon as the plane stopped. "It's best we are not on the ground for too long."

"You can stay here and get fucked with the rest of us," replied Hollidt, with anger and sarcasm biting in his voice.

"Yeah, well Sir, I nearly got fucked the first time I came in to get you out and I'm probably gonna get fucked leaving here," replied Heinrik. "So we're all getting our fair share of ...." He didn't finish his sentence.

Hollidt looked at Heinrik in amazement. No junior officer had dared speak to him like that before, except there was one thing which Heinrik had quickly learnt about the F.d.F. It was the immense power which came just by being involved with it. Once again, Heinrik was exercising that power.

"Are you going to deny some of your injured men the chance to get to hospital?" asked Heinrik deciding not to throw his weight around but use reason instead.

"OK," said Hollidt, who had remembered it was not a good idea to pick a fight with an F.d.F. pilot. With this agreement, Heinrik nodded to his co-pilot to open the door and allow the Generaloberst out.

The plane was quickly filled with 10 severely injured soldiers each on a stretcher, and two walking wounded who were to look after them. Their place on the plane had been chosen by ballot. It was the refuelling which took the time. To hand pump gallons of fuel was a hard and laborious task, particularly in the freezing cold. Eventually, with the sun beginning to fall in the sky and with the wind coming from the south, Heinrik lined up his aeroplane on the north-westerly end of the runway ready for take-off. He stopped, looked at his co-pilot and visibly crossed his fingers. The co-pilot smiled back. Heinrik had never done that before.

Immediately Heinrik was in the air and over the perimeter fence of the airfield he knew he was in trouble. Partisans had fired shots into his aeroplane hitting the fuselage and wings, instantly killing two of the injured men. The rest of the damage had yet to unfold.

Chapter 54

Above the Suhokleya River, Ukraine January 1944

"WE'RE LOSING FUEL," said Heinrik's co-pilot calmly as the plane flew on its westerly course, headed for the Hungarian capital. "Look at the main fuel gauge. It's way below where it should be. Look at the gauge for the auxiliary tank. That's okay," he continued. They were only a few minutes into their flight and had just picked up the frozen Suhokleya River below. They were using it as their navigational aid.

Heinrik did as he was told. His co-pilot was right. They were losing fuel. "The fuel tank's probably been hit by the gun fire we went through?" he said without any alarm in his voice.

The two men looked at each other but said nothing. It seemed the logical explanation.

"We're not going to make Budapest. We'll need to stop somewhere," said the co-pilot.

"Where?" asked Heinrik.

"Vinnytsia?" suggested the co-pilot.

They both knew Vinnytsia in Ukraine well. They had flown into and out of it many times. It was the airfield which supplied Hitler's latest headquarters known as Werwolf [44]. It had been built in the summer of 1942 and occupied by Hitler from July of that year because he thought that the Wolf's Lair, being about one thousand kilometres behind the front, was too far away for effective command.

"It's about 300 km away," said Heinrik. "Do you think we'll make it?"

"Don't know, I don't think so, but I don't know anywhere else where we could make a repair and refuel," replied the co-pilot

---

[44] Werewolf

"What about Odessa? We must have an airfield there. It's about the same distance but its more direct to where we've got to get to."

Soon the starboard and centre engines started to splutter from the lack of fuel, so Heinrik turned on the fuel cock from the auxiliary tank to keep his engines fed with fuel and their propellers turning.

"What's happening?" asked the gunner on the intercom with alarm. He had left his station and until then had been attending to the wounded men as best he could.

"We're losing fuel. We're changing direction. We're going to land at Odessa," said Heinrik. He then added, "I have control."

His co-pilot replied. "You have control."

On those few words Heinrik turned the plane to port and on to a direction bearing of 205 degrees. It was a decision he would never be able to explain to himself.

Chapter 55

Ukraine January 1944

"WHERE ARE WE? I'm sure we are off course," said Heinrik to his co-pilot after a little while and in a conversational style. "I'm sure we've gone too far north," he continued, as he took the plane below cloud level to check where they were.

Both Heinrik and his co-pilot looked out of the window at the topography below to see if they could identify their position. In the white landscape, with the lakes frozen and the roads covered with snow there was little which they could use to identify their location. Of one thing they were sure; they were not where they were supposed to be.

"Makes sense," said the co-pilot after a little while, almost nonchalantly. "The starboard engine's not pulling as hard as the port one, so we're bound to have gone a bit off course. Yeh, more to the north, most likely."

Heinrik cursed himself for not appreciating the obvious but then why hadn't his co-pilot said something before now. After all, wasn't navigation his main job?

Just as they were both staring, eyes peeled and into the distance, the port engine stuttered.

"What have you done? asked Heinrik sharply. "Are the carb heaters on?" he yelled as he leaned forward to make sure the carb heat levers on all three engines were fully extended and thus working. At that height, in that cold, the injectors in carburettors quickly freeze unless heated. Failing to keep them warm was a common cause of engine failure. You didn't leave flight school without that issue having been drilled into your head.

Both men watched in horror as the port engine shuddered to a stop. Suddenly Heinrik was working frantically. He pushed hard on the right rudder peddle to keep the plane flying straight and feathered the propellers on the stationary engine to reduce its drag through the air.

"We're not going to make Odessa," said the co-pilot in a statement of the obvious.

"Then where?" asked Heinrik as he focused on flying the plane.

The co-pilot didn't answer.

"Then where?" Heinrik asked again, his voice giving a command rather than opening a discussion which the two men normally adopted in the air. "We control everywhere down there. There must be a bloody landing field somewhere," he added.

The co-pilot studied his map, but not knowing where they were made it an impossible task. "We're over the Ukraine," he said. "I don't think we control all the airfields down there anymore. The partisans are getting more and more effective. It'll be bloody dangerous to choose any airfield at random."

Heinrik puffed in response and the two men fell silent as each contemplated their options.

"Did I tell you the Führer asked me if I had ever crashed," said Heinrik. "I said no. It appears there's a first time for everything." He was now sure of one thing which was going to happen on this journey. "Let's keep on the same heading and go as far West as we can," he said philosophically. He pulled back on the control stick to get the plane to climb higher in the sky.

The journey continued, minute after long droning minute, until first the centre engine and then the starboard engine started to fail. Their fuel tanks were completely empty. His engines were running on nothing more than fumes.

"What's happening, what's happening?" yelled the gunner becoming aware that the crisis he'd known about had now become serious.

"Prepare to crash," shouted Heinrik.

"What?"

"Prepare to crash," repeated Heinrik sharply.

Just then the clouds, which they had been flying through, broke. It was just minutes before the last segment of the sun finally set. Dark orange rays streamed in beams along the snow. All was quiet, just the sound of wind rushing by. Heinrik scoured the view ahead, seeking somewhere to land. There were no options. Forest pine trees laden with a carpet of thick snow would be their landing field.

For the first time in months Heinrik thought of Victoria and his son. He was certain he had a son but didn't know why. He had received a second letter from Victoria, and it hurt him more to read it than her first. There was a hint of pleading in her stoical words for it seemed as though her mother was sending her away. Like Victoria's first letter, he tore it into small pieces but this time he burned it over an ashtray, mixing the ash into dust with his finger. It was something he would always regret.

How old would his son be now he wondered; eighteen months? What was he called? For the first time in his life Heinrik thought about dying. Until that very moment he had always assumed he was invincible, but now he was going to die without ever having held his son. He felt no fear, just regret for the things he was never going to do.

As the plane descended rapidly, Heinrik lifted its nose to try and make the fuselage the first point of contact with the trees, but the dead weight of the front engine made gliding virtually impossible. They were coming down at a very sharp angle and too fast. At the last minute, Heinrik used the air speed to lift the nose which allowed the plane to fly straight and level for a few hundred metres before the fixed undercarriage caught on the branches of the trees, as did the propellers and engine. Heinrik heard the screaming of metal as the wings and fuselage were torn from the cockpit. He continued hurtling forward, viciously buffeted and thrown about. Just as quickly as the noise had started so it ended. Heinrik found himself almost stationery, strapped into his seat, swinging gently in the branches and unhurt. Not even a bruise. Apart from a broken window the cockpit around him appeared to be intact.

Heinrik looked towards his co-pilot to seek comfort from their shared ordeal. He was obviously dead. With no sign of what had killed him, Heinrik checked by shaking his body. The co-pilot's head fell forward. Heinrik reached to feel for his pulse, on his wrist first and then in his neck. There was no question; his co-pilot's life was gone.

Heinrik looked behind him. There was nothing but open air. The rest of his plane, his gunner and the injured soldiers were not there; just open space with green branches caked in frozen snow. He looked two or three times because he could not believe what he was not seeing.

Heinrik started to plan his exit. His parachute would help lower him to the ground he thought. At that moment, the word parachute screamed into his brain. Why hadn't he instructed his co-pilot and gunner to parachute to safety as soon as it was obvious they would crash? He cursed his incompetence not appreciating that every part of his brain had been overloaded with the thought of keeping his plane in the air. The only comfort that Heinrik could take was that, deep down, he knew they would never have gone and left him on his own, just as he would never have left them.

Heinrik pushed at his co-pilots body and, with the use of the knife he kept in his escape bag, he cut free the webbed harness of the dead man's parachute. Unfolding it from its case, Heinrik sliced the silk of the canopy in to long white strips, each about four metres long. Carefully, he platted and tied them together until he had a rope which reached the ground. He tied the top end around the metal stave of a broken window frame but deciding this might not be strong enough tied it to his seat frame too.

Using the co-pilot's parachute cord, he lowered his escape bag and that of his co-pilot to the ground. "You're to have your own," he had insisted to his co-pilot and each crew member the moment they started flying together." I'm not sharing mine just because you couldn't be bothered to prepare one," he had told them. Now he had two.

Very cautiously Heinrik climbed out of his broken cockpit and, using his home-made rope, he lowered himself to the ground. There were many moments when, as a pilot, he had been pleased to have his feet on the ground again, but no moment felt like this one. It was then that he cursed out loud for he had left his map behind. In his mental preparations, it was the one thing he had sworn to himself that he would remember to bring.

Heinrik picked up the two emergency bags and, with his folded parachute still attached to his back, he made his way through the wood in the direction the plane had come. He found the body of his gunner on the ground long before he found the rest of the plane's debris. The wings and fuselage, both torn apart, were high in the trees. He called out in a loud whisper but there was no answer. He called again. Still there was no sound.

He couldn't stay here he told himself. At any moment the locals would come looking for the crashed plane and its occupants. If there were any man alive then they would save him. It was the rationale he used to leave them.

Heinrik dived into his bag to retrieve his compass. He would just head west until he reached Romania, or perhaps found the German army. Looking at his compass he started off into the undergrowth, a bag in each hand. He had to get away as fast as possible, and certainly before the sun rose in the morning.

Chapter 56

Ukraine January – February 1944

HEINRIK FOUGHT HIS way through the forest. He was growing anxious. He'd been travelling for about thirty minutes and, because the undergrowth was so thick, he felt he was making little progress. When he came to a small clearing he decided to head north as the pathway looked clearer. Alternating between a jog and a quick walk he started to cover more ground. It was so cold his lungs burned with each breath, his frozen vapour stung as it touched his face and his arms were aching from the two emergency bags he was carrying, but he knew he had to keep moving if he was not to be captured.

He came out of the forest into the cutting of an unmade road. The blackness which had surrounded him lifted. Now, with the benefit of the half-moonlight, he could see much further. He checked left and right then slowly eased his way forward. He was less than two metres away from the road when he fell, face first, deep into a ditch full of snow. It took him some while to stand upright and clamber out onto the road. Heinrik brushed himself down as best he could. He was unable to stop small icicles penetrating his clothing and biting at his skin. He was out of breath and every part of his body seemed to hurt.

Heinrik found his compass again and looked at it for far longer than he needed to make a decision. Straight ahead of him was another wooded area, the thought of which was deeply unappealing. It was with some relief he saw that, if he turned left onto the road, he would be heading west and in the general direction of the German army. How many hundreds of kilometres away, he did not know.

Heinrik headed off down the rutted track. His heart was thumping with fear as he expected, at any moment, a bullet to hit him. It was a fear which was as strong as it should have been irrational. It was a fear which made him stop every 100 metres, crouch down, listen hard and study the pathway ahead of him carefully. Only when he had gathered his breath and was certain that there was nothing ahead did he move off again.

At daybreak Heinrik realised he had to find somewhere to rest up. He was now in wide-open fields and an obvious target. It was time to head into some woods, make camp and get himself organised. Of one thing he was certain, unless he found some warmth soon, he would die from hypothermia.

The sun had risen when Heinrik got to the edge of the next set of woods which he headed into. There he moved away from the pathway and deep into the undergrowth. He laid down his two bags, took off his parachute and squatted down. He took the rubber groundsheet out of his emergency bag and spread it around. For the first time since his plane had crashed, he sat down and thought of nothing.

After a little while Heinrik opened his co-pilot's rescue bag, as he knew what was in his. Unsurprisingly, there were many things the same, another groundsheet, a luger pistol with spare bullets, a standard issue primus stove full of gasoline, a torch, candles, and other essential items. There were also things which Heinrik hadn't thought of. A thick woollen hat which he put on over his leather flying helmet, pulling it down hard to cover the top of his painfully cold ears. There was a scarf which he wrapped around his head and two pairs of extra thick woollen socks. At the bottom of the co-pilot's bag he found two things which surprised him; a Bible and an English German dictionary. The only think Heinrik discarded was the co-pilot's mess kit. He didn't need two cooking pots or two forks or spoons.

Heinrik opened his bag expecting it to be just as he had packed it. Yet, he found, at the top, sandwiches and the coffee flask which he had collected on their stop over at Lvov on the flight down. He was genuinely surprised because he couldn't remember rescuing them from the plane. The sandwiches were frozen like a board. He broke off small pieces which he tried to dissolve in his mouth, but it was only with a sip of luke-warm, but very sweet coffee that it softened so it could be swallowed. For the first time Heinrik realised it probably wasn't the partisans who were going to kill him. It was going to be the environment. The weather was so cold it would very quickly extinguish any form of human life. He had to find shelter and quickly.

Heinrik's life-line came in the form of his parachute. He spread out the second groundsheet and tied it to the sticks and saplings around him to make a roof which would keep him dry. He unfolded his parachute, wrapped it around himself many times quite loosely, making him look something like a puff ball before falling, head first, between the two ground sheets. He lay completely still, away from any breeze, as his body warmed up the air trapped in the layers of the parachute silk. Just as he began to feel that his situation was not hopeless, Heinrik started to curse. He had collapsed to the ground with his flying boots on. It was only on reflection that he decided that they had to stay like that. He would only be able to make a quick getaway if he slept with his boots on. It was a wise decision for another reason. With bare feet in that cold he would have had frost bite in minutes.

In the peace of the forest, Heinrik rested his head on his bag. He closed his eyes and, as he felt his eyelids freeze together, he made his plans. He would sleep in the day and travel by night. Nothing would be rushed. Everything would be taken very slowly and carefully. It didn't matter how long it took him to get back to Germany. The important thing was that he got there.

Then he heard, not too far away, a wolf howl and a shiver of fright went down his already frozen spine.

Chapter 57

Ukraine Steppes February 1944

HEINRIK LOST COUNT of the days since his plane had crashed. Further, he had no idea how far he walked on any night. The first few days of his trek he was sustained by the rations in his two emergency bags, but after that he became preoccupied with finding food as well as finding and keeping sticks dry.

Every morning, before he settled down to rest, he got a campfire going using his camping stove to get it started, as he had to save what little fuel he had. Even if he had nothing to eat, he could melt the snow and have something warm to drink. His main problem was getting the fire hot enough to counteract the bitter cold so the water could boil and, if he had found food, cook what he had to eat.

Slowly but surely Heinrik became better organised. He removed the suspension lines from his parachute which gave him rope to make the protective roof of his nightly bivouac. With the suspension lines gone he cut along one side of the parachute to make it easier to wrap around him and to fold it up afterwards. He used the pilot chute, which dragged out the main canopy, to wrap around his head to help keep that warm. The khaki of his groundsheet and the white of his parachute provided a natural camouflage in his domain of brown trees and white snow.

He used his parachute harness to make a back carrier for his two bags thereby freeing his hands. Every other day he would heat extra water to wash his frozen feet, tend his blisters and put on the socks that he had dried the day before by wearing them close to his body. Every three or four days he would heat extra water to wash. He would not shave as his beard provided some protection from the elements for his face. Another part of the parachute was used as a towel to dry himself quickly, in front of the dying embers, before the water cooled and froze to his skin. These small things not only helped to alleviate the boredom of sitting out the daylight hours but had the effect of making him feel better. Those few moments when ice crystals weren't hanging from his beard, or his eyelashes cracking when he blinked or his lips splitting with every movement, took him just that bit closer to feeling almost human again.

As Heinrik travelled west so the forests and woods in which he could hide away became fewer. There was just mile after mile of white barren land. From the safety of his last camp, Heinrik took out his yellowy-green marine binoculars, a memento from his Atlantic days. He thought they might be useful in navigation, and so they had become a late addition to his escape bag because he could find nowhere else on the plane to keep them. Staring through the lenses, he looked out for hour after hour wondering what to do. As his body froze, he studied others walking. He was surprised by the loneliness of it all. Rarely did anyone walk together and when people, coming from the opposite direction, crossed they did not stop and talk. They just kept on walking, wrapped in their blankets in a desperate attempt to keep out the freezing cold, made far worse by the wind, which sometimes whipped the icy particles into a blinding whirlwind, making all sense of direction suddenly impossible.

It was this observation of solitude, but most of all hunger, which drove Heinrik to be bolder and start walking the main roads of the great steppes of Ukraine. Still wearing his pilot's uniform, but wrapped in the white silk of his parachute, he joined the lonely road. His heart was pounding, with his finger twitching on the trigger of his luger, when he passed the first person who had been coming towards him. True to Heinrik's studies, the other person was just as scared of him as he was of them, so both looked at the ground and went, as quickly as they could, on their way. Time and time again he walked past others who ignored him and he them.

Although now bolder Heinrik remained extremely cautious. Sometimes he would sit for hours studying a cottage or an outhouse to make sure it was safe before making his approach. Usually he was able to steal a few potatoes, the odd turnip, beet or apple and if he was lucky some ground maize.

Now walking in the day, and setting camp in the early evening, Heinrik would heat some water and then cook just as much food as he needed to make a thick mulchy soup. He would pour half of what he had cooked into his thermos flask so that he would have something warm to drink the next day and then, very slowly, he would savour each mouthful, leaving nothing on the side of his mess tin.

As the days passed so the freezing cold started to abate. Instead, there came a drenching rain which turned the hard-frozen ground into a thick, sticky, oozing mud which clung to Heinrik's boots making it hard, if not impossible, to walk by the edges of the fields. Whenever it rained, he took shelter, sometimes for hour after hour, as he saw little point in getting drenched with no facility to get dry again.

It was when comfortably settled into this routine that Heinrik faced his biggest, obvious, and yet most unexpected barrier to getting home.

Chapter 58

River Bug Ukraine March 1944

HEINRIK STOOD ON the edge of the River Bug[45] on the outskirts of the village of Troits'ke. He didn't know it was called that, nor did he know that, in his navigation, he had unconsciously travelled much further south than he had intended. It was simply whenever he had an alternative, rather than turn right and north, as he knew he should have done, he found the easier solution always seemed to be to turn left and go south just that little bit further. What he now knew was that, if he wanted to get home, he had to cross the river in front of him. If he had been there two or three weeks earlier, he would have been able to walk across the solid ice, but now it would have to be swum.

It wasn't the swimming of the River which worried Heinrik. His concern was about keeping his clothes and kitbag dry during the river crossing as these were his lifeline for survival. Get his clothes wet, he kept telling himself, and he would soon die.

Heinrik walked up and down the riverbank for about two kilometres in each direction trying to find a place to cross, or to at least find something which might help him. There was nothing obvious. He did find an ideal spot to get in and out of the water except on the other side, just a few hundred metres downstream and about the same distance from the water's edge, was a cottage whose occupants might see him and raise an alarm

With the problem assessed and analysed Heinrik headed back into a small wood where he committed himself to the task of building a raft to take his things across. He had heard how the Russians had used

---

[45] Now known as Pivdennyi Buh River

makeshift rafts to cross the Dnieper River[46] as part of their attack, and now it seemed the obvious solution to his problem

Heinrik's first attempt at a raft was a lamentable failure. As he stood in the river bank naked from the waist down, packing his clothes into his rescue bags which he had tied onto his flimsy raft, he realised it was neither big enough or strong enough to take the weight of everything which needed to go onto it. Prudence, the lesson he had learnt over his many days of walking, made him abandon the attempt and head back into the woods tugging his failed raft behind him. He would try again tomorrow.

With the patient use of the saw attachment to his penknife, and with the cords from his parachute, Heinrik built something far more substantial. In fact, it was so heavy that, when nightfall came, his problem was getting it to the river edge. There it worked perfectly, riding high in the water with his two bags, parachute harness, boots and clothes strapped on.

Heinrik had no time to notice the brilliance of the moonlight in the clear sky, or the stillness of the air, as he entered the water completely naked. His body was truly hurting from the stinging cold as the water got deeper and deeper. He was taking short rapid breaths as he pushed the raft in front of him until he kicked off from the bottom. His shoulders went under as he started to swim. He had just taken two or three swimming strokes when he was caught by the most agonising cramps in his calf muscles, so painful that he had no option but to scream out as he thrashed about in the water. In the still of the night he would have been heard for miles.

It is in this moment that most people in Heinrik's situation

---

[46] The Battle of Dnieper was one of the largest operations in World War II. It involved almost 4 million troops and stretched for 1,400km. It started on 26th August 1943 and ran until to 23 December 1943. During its four-month duration, the eastern bank of the Dnieper River was recovered from German forces by five separate fronts of the Red Army. The first river crossing assault and bridgehead on Dnieper's western shore was established on 22nd September 1943. By the end of the month 23 separate bridgeheads had been established. The crossing of the Dnieper was extremely difficult with the Red Army soldiers using every available floating device to cross the river. They did so under very heavy German fire and took serious losses.

drown. The cold and the pain causes them to take a sharp intake of breath, involuntarily carrying water deep into the lungs from which unconsciousness and death quickly follows. In desperation, Heinrik clung onto his raft which just about kept his mouth above the water line. In a panic, caused by the pain, he kicked out for the shore. From his position in the water, the other side of the bank seemed a frighteningly long way away. What made matters worse was that the river current, swollen from the rain and the thaw, was taking him rapidly downstream.

Kick after rapid kick eventually got Heinrik to the river's edge on the other side. He manhandled his little craft up the riverbank where he collapsed in the mud, shivering uncontrollably. With superhuman effort he fought the wet bindings to untie his two bags and his harness from the raft. Still naked, he grabbed them and his boots and clothes before heading straight towards the cottage. Halfway there Heinrik stopped. He put on his leather pilots' jacket and reached inside his bag. He pulled out his Luger which he stuffed into his jacket pocket. He picked up his possessions again and ran to the cottage door. Without fear or favour, and naked from the waist down, he kicked it hard, first with the ball of his feet and then with his knee. It just flew open. Heinrik was hit with a heat which made him think he had just opened an oven door.

Chapter 59

River Bug Ukraine March 1944

THE INSIDE OF the cottage was lit by a stove which, in the dark, was glowing red with heat. Just as Heinrik's eyes were adjusting to the light a shadow appeared out of the gloom bringing a heavy stave down towards his head. His first reaction should have been to shoot his attacker. Instead, he parried hard, driving the stick easily away from its intended target as it was being wielded by an elderly and frail woman. With the loss of her weapon she let out an almighty scream. Heinrik responded by shoving his fist deep into her mouth which she bit hard. In agony, Heinrik threw her tiny body against the wall so hard that she was winded and fell to the floor.

Heinrik stood over her, but with only his jacket on, and no trousers, he felt completely vulnerable. The two combatants stared at each other, neither moving, until Heinrik, with his luger pointing towards her, eventually offered his hand to the woman to help her up. Once standing, he led her to one of the two chairs placed around a small rustic table. She sat down knowing she was defeated.

On the table was a lamp which Heinrik pushed gently towards her. She took a spill out of a jar and silently handed it to him at the same time as pointing to the fire. With the lamp lit, Heinrik looked around the cottage. It was just one room with thick walls and a heavily thatched roof made to be warm in winter, as it was now, and cool in the summer.

Taking a bowl, warm water from the kettle and one of the woman's cloths, Heinrik sat down to wash. He washed his hands first, wiped his bearded face and then the mud from his body, legs, and feet. The woman watched carefully as he dressed. She frowned as he wrestled to put on his boots, as in their freedom, his feet had swollen.

With his boots on but with their laces not tied up, and with his gun firmly thrust into the waist band of his trousers, he looked out of the window and then the door. The woman's screams had not been heard, or if they had they had been ignored.

Heinrik moved to the stove where he refilled the kettle from the nearby jug, then taking a pan he filled it with water too and put that on the stove. The woman watched him carefully as, taking his final items of food from his bag; potatoes, beats and turnips, he cut each of them into fine pieces and placed them in the pan. He pointed to the woman and, gesticulating with his fingers near his mouth in universal sign language, he asked whether she wanted to eat too. She said and did nothing. Instead she simply scowled her disapproval.

Heinrik searched through her cupboards for anything else that might be added to his broth. There, laid out on a shelf, were six fish caught in the river, gutted, boned and ready to be cooked. It was the way the woman earned her living. Heinrik took four of the fish and placed them in the same pot to cook. Not a word of protest was made. Again, using sign language, he asked if she wanted to share the food he was cooking. Without any change in her disposition, she nodded her acceptance.

Once the broth was thick and bubbling Heinrik filled his flask. He then shared the rest equally between them, adding to the table, half each, a pickled egg and some sauerkraut Heinrik had found. As he sat down to eat the woman pointed to the cupboard nearest the stove from which he retrieved what she obviously wanted, an old bottle of Moldovan wine. They ate and drank in silence and, as they touched glasses and smiled at each other in the shared pleasure of food and drink, the animosity that they had felt, one towards the other, slowly evaporated.

Suddenly, Heinrik needed to sleep. The heat, the wine, and the food made him feel very soporific. He knew he couldn't risk his prisoner being free while he slept. Using more parachute cord, he bound her wrists together. With the end of the rope tied to him, Heinrik led her to her bed. He insisted she go in first and nearest the wall, so she could not escape without him knowing. Heinrik kicked off his boots again and lay down to sleep. He could not remember the last time he had slept so soundly. Perhaps it was at Château de Gressier over two and a half years ago.

The woman was sitting at a table when Heinrik woke up. During the night she had freed herself, climbed across him without him knowing and was now unpicking his German insignia and ranking from his leather jacket. As he put on his boots, he watched what she was doing and wondered why he hadn't done it before. On the table the woman had laid out three slices of maize bread with a jar of plum jam ready for his breakfast. As he settled down to eat, she served him a weak milky tea.

It was mid-morning by the time Heinrik had sorted himself out. He folded his parachute and went through each bag carefully wiping things clean and arranging everything neatly. He left behind one of his camping stoves as it no longer had any fuel and one of the torches because its batteries were flat. Perhaps she would be able to make use of them.

At her front door, the two shook hands and smiled. It had been a very strange ten hours for both of them. Perhaps not so strange for the woman. Somewhere in Ukraine her grandson was serving in the Ukrainian army. He was a little bit younger than Heinrik. Her kindness was in the simple hope that somewhere someone was being equally kind to her grandson. The fact that Heinrik was the enemy didn't matter. It was the kindness of one to the other which was at the forefront of her mind, and after all, hadn't he started it by offering to share his food first.

Chapter 60

Château de Gressier June 1944

"IT'S HAPPENING," SAID a voice at the other end of the telephone.

"What's happening?" asked Juliette confused, for it was very late.

"ITS happening!" said the voice excitedly on the other end of the line.

"We've had our message ... from ..." Deliberately the voice didn't say. "We have to get ready. We need everything you've got, tonight, now!"

"I can't get out until the morning, the curfew," she pleaded.

"We know, but we're coming, first thing. We must," said the leader of one of Bordeaux's resistance cells to whom Juliette had provided support over the last two years, to the point where she was now hiding guns and ammunition in wine barrels at Château de Gressier, right under the Germans' noses.

It was 10.15pm on 5th June 1944. The next day would be D-Day. Juliette immediately phoned Dominique.

"Yes, we've had our message too," said Dominique, immediately after Juliette said her name. "But we mustn't ... Are you OK?"

"Yes!" replied Juliette with tears gathering in her eyes. "I don't think I've ever been better."

"Bonne Chance!" said Dominique, as she quickly put down the telephone. Nothing else was said.

Juliette was overcome with a sense of anticipation and excitement. Her heart beat faster and she was alive with adrenaline-driven energy. She found it hard to contain herself as she served breakfast to her German 'guests'.

By mid-morning the gossip throughout Latoire had brought the village to a virtual standstill. The eight o'clock news from the BBC had given warnings to anyone living 25 miles from the coast to leave their homes and towns and disperse into open countryside. It reported heavy bombing at Le Havre, Calais, and Dunkirk. Everyone took this to mean that the invasion was coming, but only a tiny few knew it as a fact.

Unable to bear not knowing exactly what was happening, Juliette used Étienne's old radio hidden in the Gallery to tune in to the BBC for the 12-noon news bulletin. It was the first time she had been in the room since Victoria had left. With her ears straining, as she had the volume as low as possible, she heard:

Tuesday, 6th June 1944.

Here is a special midday bulletin read by John Snagg.

'D' Day has come. Earlier this morning, the Allies began the assault on the north-western face of Hitler's European fortress. The first official news came just after half-past-nine when Supreme Headquarters of the Allied Expeditionary Force – usually called SHAEF from its intials -- issued communiqué No.One. This said:

"Under the command of General Eisenhower Allied Naval Forces supported by strong Air Forces began landing Allied Armies this morning on the Northern coast of France."

It was announced a little later that General Montgomery is in Command of the Army Group carrying out the assault. This Army Group includes British, Canadian and United States Forces.

The Allied Commander-in-Chief General Eisenhower, has issued an order of the day addressed to each individual of the Allied Expeditionary Force. In it he said:

"Your task will not be an easy one. Your enemy is well-trained, well-equipped and battle-hardened. He will fight savagely. But this is the year 1944. The tide has turned. The free men of the world are marching together to victory.

I have full confidence in your courage, devotion to duty and skill in battle. We will accept nothing less than full victory. Good luck, and let us beseech the Blessing of Almighty God upon this great and noble undertaking."

"Marching together to Victory," repeated Juliette, out loud. God pray it's true she thought.

Like the whole of the United Kingdom, the United States, and almost all of France, Juliette held her breath as, at first, the beaches were taken, then bridgeheads were established and finally the breakout to attack and liberate Caen. The Allies were beginning to win the war, but now at a horrible cost to the French, who were going to lose thousands of citizens from Allied bombings; more than Germany killed in its blitz attacks on London and Great Britain's other main cities.

In the moonlight of the early morning of 6th June, the different resistance cells around Bordeaux had set to their individual tasks. These mainly involved ensuring that the German forces in the region stayed where they were. The job of the resistance was to stop their mobilisation, and then hamper any attempt, should they try to move north, to counterattack the Allied Armies from the south.

Within days of 'D' Day, Juliette no longer had German guests staying at Château de Gressier. Only the airmen billeted at La Bête Blanche remained, and they appeared to have been confined to barracks awaiting orders.

The co-ordination between each resistance group and London was excellent. However, distrust over the events of the very recent past, coupled with fears of the motives and ambitions of the other cells, meant that the relationship between many local cells left much to be desired. This rivalry gave a confusing picture, certainly to Juliette, whose kitchen in The Cellar and in the absence of Germans, had become a feeding and planning station for numerous resistance groups. Juliette refused to take sides. Instead, she worked with all those who wanted to work with her. In a detached matriarchal form, she sat above them all. Listening carefully, she brokered many an informal deal between the leaders of the rival fractions. It was assumed that, because she was English, she was speaking with the authority of London. She was doing nothing of the sort

The jobs in the vineyard and on the farmland failed to get done. The execution of the war took top priority.

Chapter 61

The Community Hall near Parata, Moldova June 1944.

HEINRIK STARED AT the wooden hut for a long time, sometimes with his binoculars but mostly without. It was long, with windows facing out either side of its length which remained shuttered up after the winter. It had stone steps leading up to light blue painted double doors, with cracked, but still waterproof roof tiles.

The Community Hall[47] at Parata had changed little since Count Sacha Donici-Solokov had arranged for the two sides of his family to meet there in a unity lunch over 40 years before. Sitting around the table was Leon Tinnerman, then aged 13, with his father the Count, his mother Aliza and his two brothers and two sisters. Also there was the Count's lawful wife Karina, and her five children by him.

There was one thing which surprised Heinrik about the hut. It was the Christian crosses at either side of the building and above the door. Had he come so far west that he was now out of communist Russia he wondered hopefully? He knew that, just over 25 years ago, when the Bolsheviks came to power, they had banned all forms of religious ceremony for nothing was going to be allowed which

---

[47] The Community Hall near Parata was built as a traveller's resting place when the Roman Catholic Church, under Pope John XV, was trying to persuade Vladimir the Great to adopt their form of Christianity as the religion for Ukraine. Once the home of a catholic priest and about ten or twelve nuns, it served travellers on their journey. The hall was later abandoned under the instructions of Pope Stephen IX following the Great Schism in 1054. It had fallen into disrepair and refurbished many times over the next 850 years, with the last refurbishment being undertaken by Leon Tinnerman's grandfather and Brigita Solokov's great grandfather as temporary housing for the workers who came in from the city to work on the land at harvest time.

might challenge the authority of the state, not fully realising that the churches had been an instrument of the Russian state for nearly one thousand years.

Heinrik watched the two chimneys which stuck out of the roof carefully until he was certain there was no smoke coming out. This gave him the encouragement to walk a semi-circle slowly and very carefully around the hut, always keeping to the woods or covered ground. He was looking for any signs of movement. There were none. His real problem was that any approach he made to the building would be instantly seen by anyone around.

Heinrik decided he should sit it out. It had taken him five months to travel 650 km and he wasn't going to be caught now. It would be dusk in about two hours' time. He knew he had no alternative but try and enter then. He had to risk going in. He hadn't eaten for the last forty-eight hours and was now down to his last potato. It was imperative that he found food soon.

Heinrik moved back into the woods where he laid out one of his groundsheets and wrapped the other around the area to give him a degree of camouflage and cover. He was now so used to being outside that, with the improved weather, he was not finding it as much of a hardship as when he had first crashed. With his camping stove out of fuel Heinrik had been forced to improvise. He now used two tins, which he had found, to make a small stove. He had removed the tops and bottoms of the cans, then using his penknife he had punctured holes around the bottom circumference to let the air through. To get the fire going, he first lit the remnants of his last candle as he was now down to his last three matches. Next, using the candle, he lit the paper torn out of his co-pilot's bible which in turn set the drying kindling wood on fire. Once this was alight, he blew out the candle so it was there for another day. Slowly, surely, and most tenderly he fed his campfire with one precious stick at a time until he had a compact but very effective blaze. He then filled his mess tin with water from his water bottle and placed it on the cans around which his fire was built. He took his last potato, wiped off the dry soil and, with his knife, he cut it into about 6 pieces. He put the potato pieces into the water, which was beginning to get warm, and watched as the water simmered and it started to cook. Heinrik didn't know then but it was to be the last campfire meal he was going to cook for well over 15 years.

Re-energised by food, Heinrik packed up his camp, reloaded his bags which, once again using his old parachute harness, he secured to his back. He kicked out the fire and went to the edge of the woods. There he looked over the grass field which surrounded the hut. With his luger in his jacket pocket he stood, watched, and waited.

There is never a right moment to go. It can always be too late or too soon. Suddenly Heinrik could bear the tension no longer. Impulsively, he started to move. It was just before 11pm and it had, at last, become dark. He walked deliberately towards the front door of the hut as though he was meant to be there. He climbed the stone steps and tried the blue double doors. They were locked. He tried again this time giving them a shake, but nothing happened. He tried a third time with such ferocity that, on this occasion, the doors rattled so loudly on their hinges he worried about being heard.

Heinrik attacked the shutters at the first set of windows he came to but its wood had swollen in the damp making them fixed solid. The next set of shutters were quickly prised open to reveal a closed window behind. Heinrik examined the frame trying to find a way through without breaking the glass. Finding the fastening point, he thumped it hard with his fist such that the window flew back on its hinges. In theory, he should have been able to have climbed straight in but it was too high. Heinrik needed a step which he found in the form of an old abandoned wooden box. This made his climb through the window easy, if not ungainly, as he landed on a bed placed directly underneath it.

Once inside, Heinrik found it very dark. He climbed back on the bed, pulled the shutters tight and closed the windows. He fumbled in his bags looking for his candle and matches. Eventually creating a flame Heinrik was able to look around the room. It was the regimentation of it all which struck him first. It was in the style of a dormitory or hospital ward. Each bed was neatly made with each bedstead positioned under a window with a wardrobe equidistant between each bed.

Heinrik made his way down the centre of the room sweeping the flame from the candle from side to side. At the end of the dormitory, in the middle of a wall, there was a corridor this time with rooms on either side which led to an exit. It was something he had not seen from the outside. Near the start of the corridor was a wood burning stove with a cast iron chimney running up to the roof. He ran his hand over it and found it cold to touch.

As he moved down the corridor Heinrik stopped and leaned against the wall. The only sound he could hear was his heavy breathing. He was inside for the first time since he had left the old woman at Pivdennyi Buh River, and it made him feel strangely claustrophobic.

He checked the two rooms on the right. The first could easily be identified as a kitchen. The second as the bathroom with lavatories and wash basins. He then checked the room on the left. It was the same size as the kitchen and bathroom put together (explained by the fact that, in times gone by, it was where the priests slept). The room was sparsely furnished, a bed in one corner placed against the wall with its bedstead under the window, a table and chair and a wardrobe placed against the opposite wall. There was still the mark on the wall to show where the sign of the Cross had been before it was removed at the start of the communist era.

Heinrik scanned the room until his eyes fell on two candles each stuck to small upturned plates on the table. He moved across the room to examine them. Lying by their side was a box of matches. Heinrik lit both candles, blew out the stub of his own and pocketed it along with the box of matches. He stood back as the light gave an immediate warmth to the room which, even though it was June, had a damp chill about it. He put his hands out to feel their warmth and gazed at the flames for some time, mesmerised by the beauty of their dance. His mind was taken back to the flickering candles around the crib of baby Jesus in his church at Christmas time. It was then that, only for the second time since he had crashed landed, he noticed that his hands and feet were feeling warm.

With his bags still on his back, Heinrik lay on the bed. His eyes faced up looking into the pitch black of the ceiling. He listened intensely, straining hard to hear any outside sound which might give him a warning. There was none. He sighed deeply, breathed out heavily and tried to relax.

As he had done all the way through his escape, Heinrik started to prepare for a rapid exit. His Mother's mantra of 'failing to prepare is preparing to fail' ran through his brain. He checked the windows. They would open. He checked the shutters. They would not. He thumped them hard. Still there was no movement. It was only when standing on the chair, and after a swift kick, that he could prize them fully open, only for him to close them again; but this time keeping them slightly ajar.

Heinrik took off his backpack and lay down again on the bed. Cautiously, he kept one foot on the floor ready for a rapid exit. The chill which had seized his back for days had gone. Was he in Romania he wondered? If so, they were Germany's allies and he would now be safe.

Chapter 62

The Community Hall near Parata, Moldova June 1944

HEINRIK WOKE STARTLED by the noise of an invasion. Once, where there had been complete silence, there was now the sound of shouts and screams with bodies being dragged and pushed. First it came with a crash against the huts double doors which instantly flew open. Now it was in the dormitory. Heinrik had no idea what was going on, but there was no question; it was the undisciplined sound of a rugby scrum of men against a team of women and girls.

Heinrik's thoughts were only on escape. He knew from the noise outside that leaving by the window which he had carefully prepared beforehand, was no longer an option. He must hide. Under the bed or in the cupboard were quickly discarded from his mind as, although they were the most obvious, they left him vulnerable, with no line of attack or defence.

He looked up and there across one side of the priests' room was an old, black, and wide wooden beam which ran into a void in the roof space above the corridor, kitchen and bathroom. Kicking his bags under the bed he rapidly climbed, using the chair and the table, until he was perched high on the beam. He cursed as he looked down. He had left both his guns in his jacket and bags below. He cursed again as he moved further back into the roof void. As he went backwards, he bumped into a set of rusty agricultural tools and implements long forgotten about. He cursed again. Below him, one of the candles, although much lower, was still flickering and lighting the room. It was immediate evidence that someone had been there.

As Heinrik put his hand behind his back to remove a spike sticking into his leg, he came across a sharp blade. It cut into him as he grasped it. Changing his grip, he pulled the implement towards him. In his hand he found a shorthanded scythe. At last, a weapon to protect himself. With still about one third of his body resting on the beam he pushed back as far as he could go into the void. He could go no further. He was unable to breathe because of the tension, made much worse by the fighting, screaming, and sobbing which came from the next room. As Henry waited, he heard heavy summer rain hit the roof tiles close above his head.

The peace of the priests' room was disturbed by the door being thrown open violently. A Russian soldier[48], in a waterproof cape, backed through the door. In his arms, held in a tight bear hug, was a girl. Her legs were lifted off the floor and were kicking out wildly as she wriggled her body fiercely in a fight to break free. Turning round, the soldier spied the bed and, rotating his body, he threw the girl across the room and onto it with a thud. He kicked the door shut.

Russian soldiers, Russian soldiers, screamed Heinrik's brain. How were they here? He'd left them weeks ago fighting in Kropyvnytskyi. How had they got here? Where the hell was he, he wondered?

The girl on the bed was frozen with fear as the soldier moved to sit astride her. He pinned her arms by her side and under his legs. He then lent forward, pushed his left hand in to her throat and squeezed tightly. He was letting her know who was in charge. Without warning, the soldier released his grip on the girl's throat, pulled her head up by

---

[48] The soldiers were not only Russian. They were from the 4th Ukrainian Front under the control of Fyodor Tolbukin. After winning the Battle of Dnieper in December 1943 and taking control of the Dnieper the Russian army headed west reaching the Bug River in March 1944 just a few days after Heinrik had swum across. They had now reached close to the Dniester River where they had stopped to prepare for the invasion of the Balkans, including Romania and Moldova. The women attacked by the soldiers were returning from the leather factory where they worked 14 and 15-hour days as slave labourers making thick felt lined leather boots for the German army. They were heading back to the Community Hall, where they were billeted, when they were spotted by a troop sent out to scout the land ahead. The Russian soldiers assumed the women were Romanian and therefore trophies of war. Romania was, at that stage in the war, an ally of Germany but was very shortly to change sides. The women in the boot factory had, until the moment of their attack, considered themselves fortunate. Many women of their age had been forced to work in the brothels in Kishinev set up by the German army for the entertainment of their men.

the neck of her cardigan and then, in one movement, as he let her go, he slapped both sides of her face very hard as her head fell back. The girl screamed from the shock of the attack and then instantly fell silent. She instinctively knew that if she screamed once more, he would hit her again.

The soldier wiggled out of his cape and jacket which he threw on the ground. She stared as he undid his belt and buttons on the flies of his trousers which he pulled down to free himself. The girl looked at his shaft which he was pumping to stand direct and proud. She had never seen what made a man a man before but now there was no surprise. Her mind slowed down to register what she had just seen. She instinctively knew what was about to take place. The soldier leaned forward again and, this time, without lifting her head, he hit her hard in the face once, twice on each side but this time with a clenched fist. The power of his punch completely dazed the girl. This time there was no scream, more of a muffled yelp.

Heinrik slowly and deliberately slithered along the beam like a snake expanding and contracting its muscles. In his right hand he held the scythe, keeping it tight and ready to strike.

Moving backward, further down the girl's legs, the soldier pulled at her skirt to get it from under him. In doing so her arms came free and so, with his hands tugging at her pants, her hands came forward to fight him away. Without any form of warning the soldier hit her with an upper cut punch straight under her jaw, crashing her teeth together and shaking her brain so badly that she saw stars. In that moment, any fight which the girl might have had was gone.

Slithering slowly, the scythe held high, Heinrik prepared himself. Two more feet and he would be able to attack.

The soldier now grabbed frantically at all the girl's clothing; ripping buttons and tearing material as he fought to find bare flesh. He squeezed her now exposed breasts so tightly that she winced again in pain. With her dress bunched up high, and her body now naked from the waist down, she froze in fear unable to move. Her brain went into slow motion as everything was amplified.

Lying still on the bed the girl slowly but methodically studied her attacker. The shape of his face, his nose, mouth, and the colour of his hair. He was not that old, perhaps in his early twenties. He had rugged good looks and was, unusually, clean-shaven. She found there was no viciousness in his eyes. She watched as the soldier sucked on his fingers making them wet with saliva and then he smiled. Suddenly, his fingers dug deeply into her and from the pain of being physically torn open, she screamed loudly. It gave Heinrik the opportunity he needed to move.

The soldier leaned back and upright, now concentrating on aligning himself for her defloration. It was at this moment the soldier's head was directly below Heinrik's. For the first time the girl spotted him. Her eyes started to dart incessantly between Heinrik lying on the beam, the scythe held high in the air and her attacker.

Just as the soldier sensed that someone was above him Heinrik struck. He brought the scythe down so hard that the point sliced deep into the soldier's neck just below his Adam's apple. He yanked it up high and then, catching the man's jawbone, he jerked the soldier's body up-and-down determined to do as much damage as possible

In desperation, the soldier grabbed at the blade, cutting deep into his hands as he tried to lift himself off. The girl stared at the soldier's face; his eyes wide open in fear, as his blood pulsated into his hands which were now around his throat. Heinrik was determined not to release the soldier so he held him as high as he could, treating him as though he were a carcass on a meat hook. Slowly the soldier started to drown in his own blood before falling into unconsciousness.

Immediately Heinrik felt the soldier's dead weight on his arm, he took this as the signal for one final lift of the soldier's body so it partially came off the girl and the bed. With a sideward's swing, Heinrik made the man's body fall onto the floor, taking the scythe with it.

The girl squealed in a loud screech and immediately sat up right. She moved backwards in fright forcing her body into the corner and against the iron headboard. She had assumed that one attacker was going to be replaced by another. The girl pulled her knees up to her body and yanked her skirt down around her ankles. Tears started to fall from her eyes and her chest heaved in silent sobs.

Chapter 63

The Community Hall near Parata, Moldova June 1944

IT WAS THE noise next door which took Heinrik's attention. Whatever was happening in the other room, he felt certain it was a major threat to his safety and had to be tackled. He recovered his jacket and two bags from under the bed and very quickly found his two pistols. He checked to make sure they were fully loaded with eight bullets in each gun. He released the safety catches and, although the Luger were notorious for their accidental discharges, stuck one into the waist band of his trousers.

Heinrik made his way to the door. He rested his left hand on the door handle. He stopped still, to take just a few seconds to control his breathing and to put into his mind's eye the shape and layout of the room next door. He was physically trembling at what he had to do. He could have stayed there a lifetime, but it was a particularly loud scream which prompted his action. He pulled open the door and charged. The dormitory was in chaos. There were people everywhere. It was obvious that soldiers outnumbered the girls and women, but he could not tell by how many. In some cases, two soldiers were holding down one victim, taking it in turns to molest her.

Someone had lit a couple of oil lamps, so it was not as dark in the hall as Heinrik had expected. Slowly and deliberately he moved into the dormitory. Every time he came across a soldier, he shot him once, sometimes twice, at point blank range into their chest, back or head. Every bullet he fired hit its target. When his gun clicked on a misfire, he deliberately allowed it to fall so he could take his second gun out of his waist band. He rapidly shot two more men as he moved down between the beds.

One soldier, furthest away from him, grabbed what clothes he could and dived out through the window. Another, naked from the waist down, grabbed his rifle, cocked it, and fired a shot at Heinrik without aiming it properly. It went wide of him. Instead the bullet hit a colleague in the thigh who collapsed screaming with agony. Heinrik looked straight into the pleading eyes of the man who had tried to kill him. As the soldiers' arms went into the air in surrender, Heinrik shot him once, directly in the chest. Next to him was another man with his arms up. He shot him in the chest too, just for good measure.

There was no remorse or hesitation in Heinrik's action. More arms went up in the air in surrender. Heinrik could no longer keep shooting in cold blood. Years later when he reflected on his behaviour, he realised he had fired only one shot for his own protection. He didn't fire to stop what was going on. He didn't even fire out of uncontrolled red rage. As far as Heinrik was concerned, his killings were punishment executions for the attacks he had witnessed. There was only one thing he regretted. It was shooting the second unarmed man with his hands up. It was mean and merciless, but over the years Heinrik absolved his guilt by convincing himself it had been necessary.

Heinrik now had prisoners to deal with. With their arms held high, he looked at the scene of the semi-naked and frightened men before him. He knew he had to act. Gritting his teeth, so as not to speak and give his nationality away, he pointed at the girls and held his wrists together beckoning them to tie the men up.

The girl from the priests' room, who had seen Heinrik cut the throat of her attacker, understood immediately what he wanted. She took the lead and shouted at the girls to tie up each man, but many were in neither a mental nor physical state to do as she instructed. Each of the women were in disparate stages of undress and reacting quite differently. Some rushed to take their friends in their arms, to give and receive comfort. Others stood silently staring at the scene of dead and dying soldiers, others sobbed, while some purposely set about getting dressed and sorting out their affairs. There was no common reaction to the trauma they had each been through.

Jumping from foot to foot, ready to shoot any soldier who made the slightest move, Heinrik bounded around the room. He picked up his dropped Luger and collected the soldiers' rifles. He took out the firing bolts, to stop their guns from working, and threw them to the far end of the room. He tossed the disabled rifles onto the bed nearest the double doors. There he emptied their cartridges of bullets which he stuffed into his pockets. Deliberately he set aside two working rifles to take with him.

He knew he had to get out of this place and fast. The escaped soldier would soon sound the alarm and, even if he didn't, the sound of gunshots was bound to attract attention. The trouble was that it was taking too long to deal with tying up those men whom he had not shot, if it was happening at all.

Heinrik picked up one of the captured rifles. He checked to make sure it was full of bullets and switched off the safety catch. He then walked down the corridor firing straight into one foot of each soldier who was alive. The last man, number five or six, had worked out what was going to happen and so he slid his feet from side to side. Without hesitation Heinrik pointed the gun straight at the man's naked crotch and pulled the trigger, tearing through his artery at the same time as blasting his pubic bone into a thousand pieces. The man would be dead in minutes.

With each soldier now incapable of making chase, Heinrik started to make ready his escape. He gathered his bags from the priests' room, reloaded his two lugers and put on the safety catch. He took the loose rifle bullets out of his pocket and, together with the candles, threw them into his bag.

The girl from the priests' room, seeing that Heinrik was preparing to leave, decided they must all leave too. She was obviously not the oldest but nevertheless she barked out instructions ordering the others to sort out their clothing, coats, and boots. "We must leave. We must leave," she yelled out in Moldovan. "Hurry, we must get out." In their trauma the women found it easier to do as they were told. "We have to go to Kishinev," the girl instructed firmly.

Heinrik chose the back exit to leave, worried that the man who had escaped earlier might have been able to assemble a party to ambush him, but the girl from the priests' room held him back. Instead she ushered all the girls through the blue double doors outside into the darkness of the night. When the last girl was outside, she went herself.

Heinrik looked back on the scene of bloodied men and devastation before he finally left. His bags were on his back, and a captured and fully loaded rifle was in each hand. He didn't notice it had stopped raining.

Just as Heinrik was leaving, they heard a huge explosion. Unknown to them, the Germans had just blown up the bridge which crossed the Dniester River to stop the Russian army capturing it. It was the bridge which had been built, and rebuilt, by the Donici-Solokov family. They were former relatives of both the girl from the priests' room and Leon Tinnerman. For over 100 years, ending at the time of the Bolshevik revolution, the bridge had been the primary source of their family's wealth. Years of history now lay in rubble on the river bottom. The Bridge would never be rebuilt.

Chapter 64

Transnistra June 1944

ONCE OUTSIDE THE Community Hall the girls started to run, and run fast, towards the road. Heinrik followed on behind. They were all of one mind, to get away from there as fast as possible before another party of soldiers arrived. If the Russians had got as far as the Community Hall then they could be anywhere. At the end of the drive the girls stopped for a moment before turning left, westwards, towards the now destroyed bridge and, beyond that, Kishinev.

About a mile away from the bridge the girl from the priests' room waited for Heinrik to catch her up. She stopped him and grabbed at the sleeve of his jacket. She was leaving the group and, speaking Moldovan, she suggested with a tug that he should follow her. He didn't understand so she tried again. This time she spoke in Russian and signalled to indicate what she wanted. Heinrik nodded and the two of them left the road and headed north down a small side road which the girl knew well. They were heading towards the foundations of Valikey House. Now destroyed, it was where her mother, Brigita Solokov had once lived as a child, and where the girl regularly came to lay flowers at the graves of her grandfather, grandmother, uncle and aunt who had all died there during the Russian revolution.

Unknown to Heinrik, he was deliberately being led into a trap. If he had stayed with the other girls and kept to the road, for just over one kilometre, he would have come to the destroyed bridge and seen, on the other side of the river, his German colleagues making ready to defend Kishinev from a Russian attack. But, as the girl from the priests' room knew, her mother was deeply involved with the Moldovan partisans. So strong was her mother's hatred of their occupiers that she would prefer to throttle any German with her bare hands than give him even the time of day. She would know what to do for the best, thought the girl.

They jogged the length of the road making a dreadful noise as they went. As they passed through Valikey House cemetery the girl from the priests' room, acknowledging the family graves, made the sign of the cross upon her chest without stopping. Field after field, the girl kept running. Heinrik was struggling to keep up as his bags bounced up and down on his back and his arms ached from the weight of the two rifles. They came to a wood, into which the girl dived. About fifty metres inside she stopped for the first time since leaving the road to allow Heinrik to catch up.

The light from the midnight sky was lost in the canopy of the trees but the girl knew the path so well that, still walking rapidly, she sensed her way forward. After a long walk Heinrik stopped the girl and beckoned her to crouch down. Covering them with his groundsheet so as not to be seen, he lit a match above his compass. They were heading north. Heinrik gesticulated that they should head west but the girl shook her head furiously. Once he was packed up again and his breath recovered the girl tugged at his sleeve indicating he should follow her. Not since Heinrik had run away from his crashed aeroplane had he covered so much ground so quickly. His reward was an aching stitch in his side.

First light comes early in the morning in June and so it was, with some relief after more fields and woods, that they came to the eastern bank of the Dniester River. Heinrik's heart sank as he could not bear the thought of another swim like his last, except he told himself now it was summer the water would at least be warmer.

They walked along the riverbank almost at a dawdle. It was as though the urgency in the girl's run had gone. They came to a series of broken down and abandoned pig sties. The animals long gone from drowning in a flood many years before. In one of the sties the girl pulled out a coracle made from wicker with a patchwork covering of sown canvas, leather, and tar. She hoisted it on her back, and with paddle in hand, she walked slowly to the river's edge. It was something she had done many times until the Germans invaded and she was conscripted to work in the boot factory. The coracle would normally just take one person but today it would take two, plus Heinrik's load.

The gunwales of the coracle were just 2 cm above the waterline when they set off, but with Heinrik staying very still, and with the girl's expert use of the paddle, they were soon on the other side of the river.

As Heinrik placed his feet on the west bank of the Dniester River he felt an overwhelming sense of relief. There was now a natural barrier between him and the Russian army once again. Where his German colleagues were, he had no idea. However, he rightly, feared that he was still in partisan country and, as he had just seen first-hand and was to find out again, there was little as dangerous as a Russian hell bent on revenge.

Chapter 65

Moldova 1918 - 1944

IF, ON 17 July 1941, which was the date the Axis Powers [49] captured Kishinev, you had been asked to identify one person in the whole of Moldova who would be dead-set on revenge then Brigita Solokov would have been a top contender. On that day she was thirty-two years old and already a committed member of the Moldovan Partisans. Her daughter, Mayanna Solokov, the girl from the priests' room, was then just fourteen.

It would be hard to specify the day when Brigita first became a rebel. Some would say she started to be uncontrollable on 20 March 1918 when, hiding in the bushes, she witnessed Vilikey House, her parent's family home, burned to the ground by revolutionary Bolsheviks. Her mother, brother and sister were still inside. Only a few hours later her father was killed at work by the same people.

Except Brigita was not a rebel when she lived with her paternal grandfather, Count Sacha Donici-Solokov, at Pechea House. Sacha was one of the last of Moldova's Grand Boyars. Although grandfather and granddaughter lived together, for only a few months for he was to die shortly after she came to stay with him, there was undoubtedly a special bond between them. Perhaps, it was because it was her grandfather who, after she had seen her family home razed to the ground, had lifted Brigita from hiding in the bushes nearby into the safety of his arms.

However, it was probably on 20th April 1920, at the age of eleven, that Brigita's life was to change permanently. At the instructions of

---

[49] The Axis Powers was formed as a result of a tripartite pact signed by Germany, Italy and Japan on 27 September 1940 in Berlin. The pact was subsequently joined by Hungary (20 November 1940), Romania (23 November 1940), Slovakia (24 November 1940), and Bulgaria (1 March 1941).

Karina Donici-Solokov, her paternal grandmother, she was hiding in a specially created secret compartment in Pechea House with her Aunt Larissa and her four cousins. Through a spy hole, Brigita watched as Leon Trotsky's soldiers confiscated everything they had to eat, even the seeds, before mindlessly ransacking their home. Then, just before they left, they smashed the family's cooking range into tiny pieces. Finally, they took with them Brigita's Aunt Olga to be a 'soldier's wife'. At first, Brigita thought it terribly romantic but then, a few months later, when she discovered what it really meant, her character changed as she deliberately brought her bloody mindedness to the fore. She was determined that no such thing was ever going to happen to her.

The soldiers raid on Pechea House meant it was no longer safe to stay there. So, with her Grandmother Karina, Aunt Larissa and her four cousins, Brigita moved from living in luxury and grandeur in the large home of a former Grand Boyar to living in a Woodman's Hut. It was a place the family had used as a venue for summer holidays and getaways for over a hundred years. With Sacha Donici-Solokov's foresight it had, at the start of World War 1, been turned into a primitive survivalist hide away. He did it in the expectation that the German / Austrian army would invade Moldova and Kishinev. They never did. It was the Russian revolution, and Trotsky's soldiers, that first caused the Woodman's Hut to be used as a place for escape and safety.

The move into the Woodman's Hut meant Brigita had to stop the mixture of home and local schooling as it would take her an hour to walk each way. Her grandmother's solution was to send Brigita to live with a librarian and his wife in Kishinev so she could go to school there. Brigita would recall these as the three happiest years of her life.

As Brigita developed, she enjoyed the benefit of a good shaped teenage figure but, with her downturned mouth, it could not be said that she was pretty. In fact, the opposite would have been true. However, when she smiled her face was transformed for, with her mouth widened, her eyes would open, brighten, and sparkle. There was never any halfway. Smiling and Brigita became quite alluring and could captivate any man's heart. With her default expression of a saddened face, she would frighten them away.

When the librarian fell ill, Brigita had to leave. She went to live with her grandmother's doctor who, with his wife, also ran the local pharmacy. Whereas the librarian's wife would do everything for Brigita, the doctor's wife took the view that she should do her fair share of household chores. Brigita vehemently disagreed. Her grandmother was paying for her to be their lodger and not to do these jobs. She would argue strongly that they were not hers to do.

Given Brigita's personality, it was unsurprising that animosity grew between her and her hostess and, as the hapless doctor was to discover, any man who gets caught between warring women is bound to come out worse.

It is difficult to say who seduced whom; but there could be no doubting that Brigita's Lolita act, to get the doctor on her side, was a significant contribution to their sexual liaisons. As far as Brigita was concerned, this was not love. It was not even romance. It was a matter of power over a man, getting her own way, and her self-gratification.

In a scene worthy of the Tempest, after the doctor and Brigita were caught in 'flagrante delicto', the doctor's wife threw Brigita's things into bags and dropped them at the front door. She called for a horse and carriage and sent Brigita home to her grandmother.

Within hours, the reason for Brigita's expulsion was the talk of Kishinev's high society. Karina Donici-Solokov, Brigita's grandmother, didn't know what upset her more; the damaged reputation of her 'impossible' grand-daughter or the fact that she had to find a new doctor!

A year after she had been expelled from the doctors, and during the course of a few days at the village wine festival, with her head swimming in the joy of alcohol (but far from drunk) and with her face beaming, Brigita shared her favours with several of the boys and men of the village. She had them. She rejected them. She turned them on. She turned them off. It was as whimsical as it was sinister. It meant one thing, Brigita didn't know who Mayanna's real father was, nor did she care.

Finding she had become pregnant was neither a shock nor surprise to Brigita. Nor did it worry her that she had no husband to provide for her and her child. Using her dourest expression, she told every man who could possibly have been the father they would have to pay to support her. Many, knowing of Brigita's capricious behaviour that weekend, refused at first but, being no match to the strength of her character, eventually gave in. Thus, Brigita benefited from a series of secretly negotiated dowries which were, in the main, to last until the war started.

Karina's effort to discover the father of Brigita's child, and therefore force a wedding, proved less than satisfactory. She knew that, in the absence of a husband, polite society expected Karina to throw Brigita out of the house, but it was not something she could do. There was something indomitable about Brigita's spirit, which gave her such support that she could not bear to see her go. In any case, she argued, hadn't the Donici-Solokov family always been unconventional.

Brigita registered her daughter's birth under the name of Mayanna Solokov. Her first name, for Christian names were not allowed, was created through the combination of Maya, a young girl who she never knew but whose death she heard her grandfather talk passionately about, and Anna, after her mother, who had been killed by the Bolsheviks when Brigita was eight years old. However, the distinction didn't last long as the name Mayanna was quickly abandoned and she became known as Anna to one and all.

Through incredibly hard work, with everybody in the family being expected to work on the land surrounding the Woodman's Hut when they weren't at school, Brigita's grandmother slowly and very carefully carved out one hundred and forty hectares of scrub land from their communist seized farmlands and turned them into fertile fields. However, to be such a big independent farmer once again made the Donici-Solokov family Kulaks[50] and thus an enemy of Stalin.

It was Stalin's Holodomor[51] in 1932/33 when, once again, the Red

---

[50] Rich land owning peasants.

[51] Means to kill by starvation – an artificial hunger, organised on a vast scale, against a country's population. The Terror Famine in Ukraine and Moldova in 1932/3 led to 3.9 million deaths and 6.1 million deformed births. So bad was the situation the people, who no longer had the energy to move, would lay down in the streets and die; their dying bodies to be seen by anyone passing but who, being so weak themselves, had no ability to help. A woman doctor wrote to a friend in June 1933 saying she had not yet become a cannibal, but she was: "not sure that I shall not be one by the time my letter reaches you. The good people died first. Those who refused to steal or to prostitute themselves died. Those who gave food to others died. Those who refused to eat corpses died. Those who refused to kill their fellow man died. Parents who resisted cannibalism died before their children did."

Army marched into Ukraine and Moldova to seize food from the peasants to feed those who were working in the towns and cities, that Brigita's loathing of Russia and Russians became engrained in her very being.

So ruthlessly did the Red Army seize food to feed Stalin's mass industrialisation policy that nothing was left for any peasant or farmer to eat. Starvation was so intensive and extensive that, however much money you had, you could not buy food as there was none to be had. Mikhail Gorbachev, who would later become President of the USSR, would recall walking in the streets past dead bodies of those who had died from starvation. So desperate was the situation that the rivers were rapidly overfished so they yielded nothing, and the forests so widely hunted that there were no animals left to catch. These methods, which Karina had used to feed her family during the 1920 starvation, were not available to her this time for everything had been taken.

The only people with food were the soldiers who were taking it from everyone else. It was with this group that Brigita used her body to get the little food she could. She secretly fed Anna and herself. There was no question in Brigita's mind; the deaths of Grandmother Karina, Aunt Larissa and her four cousins in 1933 from starvation lay directly at Stalin's feet. She knew he hated the Kulaks as a class, and simply didn't care if they were wiped out.

Brigita knew that, with just Anna and her, she would not be able to survive at the Woodman's Hut for there would not be enough people to grow the food that was needed. The Donici-Solokov fields were once again left to fall fallow.

Brigita and Anna first went to Cebotari House, which had been the Donici-Solokov family home in Kishinev's city centre, only to find that it had long been taken over by squatters. In desperation she went in search of her Uncle Dmitry who worked as a doctor at the city's main hospital. He was not there but, by asking around, she found where he lived. It was a small, two roomed, apartment in the best part of the city but their reunion was not a happy one. Dmitry had typhoid. He had taken to his bed and was dying. Dmitry was to die from typhoid related pneumonia three days after Brigita had arrived.

Every one of Brigita's known relatives were now dead. She and

Anna were the only survivors and their survival depended on Brigita finding work in the city and fast. It was not an easy task for the reputation of the girl, now with an illegitimate daughter, who had seduced her family doctor, had not been forgotten.

Brigita and Anna had been living quietly, modestly, and very happily in Dmitry's apartment for seven years when in June 1941 the Germans attacked Kishinev with bombs dropped in air raids. Shortly afterwards Brigita and Anna were ordered to leave. "Join the refugee trail and go east like everyone else," they were told. Stalin had ordered the same be done to Hitler's army as the Russian compatriots did voluntarily to Napoleon's army in September 1812 when it occupied Moscow. After the Russian army had left the city, the Muscovites set two thirds of it on fire to deny Napoleon its use. Stalin's orders were clear. Nothing was to be left behind which the German's could use.

The day after Brigita and Anna left, their apartment was blown up by the Destruction Battalion[52] from the defending, but also retreating, Russian army[53]. By July 1941, without regard for any property, Kishinev city centre was completely destroyed.

Brigita and Anna did the only thing they thought sensible. They fled to the Woodman's Hut. They had been going there consistently between April and October since they left it eight years before. They would stay at weekends and on the few days off they got each year.

---

[52] Destruction Battalions were paramilitary units under the control of the NKVD which stands for Naródnyy Komissariát Vnútrennikh Del and means the People's Commissariat for Internal Affairs. First established in 1917, the NKVD was disbanded in 1930 only to be re-established in 1934 when it was given monopoly control of all USSR law enforcement including regular policing, the secret police, the courts, the prisons and the gulags (the forced labour camps). It was, in effect, the law enforcement agency of the Soviet Union Communist Party. The NKVD was the instrument of Stalin's Great Purge (1936-1938) which saw large scale ethnic cleansing and political repression involving long terms of imprisonment and mass extrajudicial executions. Its operatives were universally feared throughout the USSR. The NKVD were responsible for implementing Stalin's scorched earth policy making sure that, as the Russian army retreated, nothing usable was left behind which the German army might be able to use. The NKVD later became known as the KGB.

[53] Romania had ceded Moldova back to the Russians only the year before in June 1940

It was their hideaway from the noise of the city and so, equipped for living, it was ready for their use.

Maybe it was these life experiences which became the grit which created Brigita's character. Perhaps it was the genes of her grandfather who was famed for his arrogance, narcissism, stubbornness and intransigence. Whatever it was, Brigita had grown into a fearlessly impossible woman, fighting every injustice however slight.

With the German invasion, the partisans discovered one of their most ardent, but impossibly independent fighters, for while Brigita hated the Russians, she now hated the Germans even more, as they had destroyed everything she had worked for.

Chapter 66

The Woodman's Hut June 1944

ANNA SOLOKOV, THE girl from the priests' room, quickly hid the coracle in its usual place. Heinrik followed her further north along the riverbank until they came to a field which led up to a large wooden hut with a forest behind. Anna stopped and pointed to the hut indicating it was their destination.

As they climbed the slope of the field a rifle shot rang out, but it was too late for Heinrik to do anything about it. By the time he heard the bang a bullet had gone through his sleeve, grazing his arm. He hit the ground hard and started to take aim with his captured rifle when the girl, still standing, started shouting out loudly towards the hut where the shot had come from. After an exchange of words, Anna once again, tugged at Heinrik's sleeve. "Come on," she said in Moldovan. Heinrik had no idea what she had said but, like everyone else, he did as the girl beckoned.

Their arrival at the Woodman's Hut was not an amicable one. Anna was furious that her mother had shot at them. Brigita was equally furious. Not only had she missed her target, but the fact that her daughter had even thought about bringing an obvious German into their midst was beyond her comprehension.

"The only good German is a dead German had long been Britiga's motto. "Look at him, he's even carrying a gun" she said in support of her decision to try and kill him

Heinrik had no idea what was being said as the two women raged in an ill-temper. However, their behaviour was not what was worrying him. Spread around the hut there were some badly wounded men. From the sweet putrid smell, which made him feel as though he needed to vomit, it was clear that at least one, if not more, had gangrene.

Ignoring the row between the two women, Heinrik reached into his bag and pulled out his father's dissecting kit. Then he searched for the English word 'Doctor' in his co-pilot's dictionary. Interrupting the girl and her mother, he showed them his set of instruments and pointed to the word doctor. The girl and the mother understood immediately. Instantly, the girl tugged Heinrik towards one of the injured men but this time he did not move.

"Heinrik," he said, speaking for the first time as he pointed to himself. "Heinrik," he said for a second time and then he added the word "Rik," in the hope that this would be easier for them to remember.

"Mayanna," said the girl pointing to herself and then added "Anna ... Anna."

Heinrik repeated her shortened name.

The girl pointed to her mother. "Brigita," she said.

For the first time Anna's mother spoke to Heinrik. "Brigita Solokov," she said, with a scowl across her face.

Anna offered Heinrik her hand in welcome which he took. It was small and slender. It immediately reminded him of Victoria, except there was one difference. Anna's was covered in callouses developed from working in the leather factory. As they held hands the two of them looked into each other's eyes and for the first time they smiled; each liked what they were seeing.

Heinrik offered his hand to Brigita but she didn't take it. Instead, she deliberately ignored him with a look of disdain.

Introductions out of the way, Heinrik turned to the seven severely injured men lying around the room. They were not Germans and it didn't seem as though they were Russians. It was clear from their injuries that they had been fighting so Heinrik assumed that they were from a band of partisans, but from where he had no idea. He was sure it was the very people he had spent the last six months trying to keep well clear of.

Heinrik unwrapped the bandage around the leg of the first man revealing wet brown pus and a smell so foul that several times he retched but his stomach was empty. Heinrik had never seen gangrene before but he was certain that this was it. Using sign language, Heinrik made it very clear that unless the leg was amputated the man would die.

Brigita and Anna nodded their agreement furiously.

Anna picked up the dissecting kit, took out a scalpel and handed it to him. "Doctor," she said.

Heinrik shook his head and shrugged his shoulders to signal that he was no surgeon, but Anna was her mother's daughter through and through. Under no circumstances was she going to take no as his answer. She went to his bags, got out both his pistols and pointed them at him and then at the injured man, switching between one and the other many times indicating that, if he did not operate, she would shoot them both.

Heinrik could easily have disarmed Anna for she had not switched off the safety catch, but it was the scowl of Brigita, and knowing that if nothing happened very soon, the man's death was inevitable, which persuaded him to have a go. He nodded his agreement, at which point Anna moved into a fury of activity.

She boiled water, scrubbed the table, found sheets which she tore into bandages and administered large quantities of Moldovan brandy to their semi-conscious patient in the expectation that it would act as an anaesthetic.

Heinrik washed every implement in his father's dissecting kit and his toolkit and popped them into the water that Anna had boiling. In his kit bag, he found the set of sewing needles he had packed but they needed to be curved if he was to sew the man's leg back up again after the amputation. In sign language Heinrik explained the problem to Anna who gave it to her mother to solve. Brigita, not appreciating that the needle needed to be red hot if it was to be bent, snapped the first one in two. Her solution was to find a small fishing hook which she handed to Heinrik as a replacement. He responded by handing her a file with unspoken instructions to remove the barbs.

Anna rushed around finding other things that they might need; a tourniquet and several different forms of saws, all of which she scrubbed and boiled.

Heinrik sat down to think through the operation he was about to perform. From the age of seven or eight he had seen his father amputate the legs of domestic cats and dogs. From the age of eleven he had been in the operating theatre as his mother, or her lover, operated. Sometimes he took verbatim notes, other times he just observed or held something but always, it appeared to him, that he had to dispose of the discarded limb. He was sure he knew what to do but suddenly, as he was trying to calm himself down, his body started to shake uncontrollably. He held out his hand and watched it tremble. He could not operate like that. He knew his body was telling him it needed rest, but the chance of sleep was just not possible as, every time he closed his eyes, he could see the look on the face of the last man who he'd shot the night before when his hands were raised.

Anna started to bully him to get ready, but the look of true anger he shot back was all she needed to understand that he had to be left alone. Instead of being repulsed, as she should have been by his look, Anna poured him a small amount of brandy. As he took sip after sip Heinrik began to stop shaking and he drifted into a short sleep; just long enough to recover.

When Heinrik woke, a minute or two later, he signalled for pen and paper. He had to write everything down which had to be done to make sure he was prepared. As he was doing this, Heinrik realised he had nothing fine enough for the internal suturing work. He plucked three strands of Anna's hair over which he poured boiling water. One hair would not be strong enough but three plaited together might just work and so again with sign language Brigita was set to work. Her first attempts failed. Anna's hair was too fine but Brigita's was that bit thicker and seemed to work perfectly.

With his patient unconscious and on the kitchen table, Heinrik carefully chose the spot where he was going to amputate, well above the knee. With a wet crayon, he drew where he was going to cut so he would have the right amount of skin to make a flap to re-cover the patients flesh and severed bone.

With scalpel in hand and ready to start, Heinrik looked up into Anna's eyes. She nodded her approval. He looked at Brigita. She nodded too. Anna tightened the tourniquet and with his hands trembling, Heinrik tried to make his first incision. Nothing happened, he wasn't pressing hard enough. He put down the scalpel and picked up his cutthroat razor, pressed harder and cut through the skin which started to bleed. In response, Anna tightened the tourniquet. Working quickly, but very carefully, Heinrik identified blood vessels, nerve endings and tendons. Just as he had seen happen years before, Heinrik tied off blood vessels with his thread of human hair, cauterised the smaller ones with a red hot steel. The burning flesh disguised the smell of gangrene. He packed the nerve endings deep inside his patient's flesh to alleviate any post-operative pain. Cutting through muscles, tendons and flesh he eventually came to the femur bone.

Pushing a bandage under the bone so it would stop any chippings being left behind, Heinrik started to saw. He felt the blade slide along the bone, only scratching it, until he had the blade under control. He had heard the grinding of a saw on bone in amputations before but, when the grinding is matched by the vibration in one's hand, he found it one of the most appalling sounds in the world.

Once he had cut through the bone, Heinrik finished off the rest of the amputation quickly. He pushed back the flesh, cut the bone a bit shorter, and then, with the file attached to his knife's handle, he started to smooth off the end of the bone so it didn't cut or dig into his patient's flesh.

Just as Heinrik was sewing up the skin flap, which he had carefully prepared at the outset to cover the stump, the patient became semi-conscious and started to move. For the first time since the operation began, Anna ordered Brigita to help hold the man down. She did as she was told using a vice like grip and the weight of her whole body.

With the last stitch in the man's skin, and with the surface of the stump washed in brandy, Heinrik stood back to study his handiwork. He had finished. Brigita and Anna gently clapped their hands together in approval. Heinrik had no idea how long the operation had taken him. It seemed like a lifetime. It was just over 50 minutes from first cut to final suture; 20 minutes longer than his mother's lover would have taken.

Throughout Anna had been the most supportive of nurses, producing instruments and swabbing away blood as Heinrik's sign language had indicated. There was telepathy between them. With Heinrik at the sink, washing the blood off his hands, it was left to Anna to bandage up the man's leg. Would the man live? None of them knew. What they did know was they had given him the best chance possible.

When Brigita heard how Heinrik had saved Anna and the other factory girls from the attacking Russian soldiers, the immediate death sentence she had passed on him was suspended. Following his operation on her injured partisan colleague, Brigita had commuted it; to what she was not yet prepared to say.

That evening Heinrik cut off his beard and using, for the first time, the shaving soap he had carried all the way from where he had crashed landed, he had a close wet shave. When he looked in the mirror, he didn't recognise himself. He had lost a third of his body weight. Nevertheless, for the first time in six months he felt clean, and for the first time in four months his tummy was full. These gave him good reasons to be optimistic as to his future

Chapter 67

The Woodman's Hut June 1944

HEINRIK'S FIRST LEG amputation was followed early the next morning by an upper arm amputation for the same reason, gangrene. Heinrik set a badly broken leg using the metal strings from a Romanian cimbalom to hold the bones in place. In those early days, his most difficult operation was on a stomach wound where a bullet had ripped apart a man's guts. The man was in intense agony. He was the only one of Heinrik's batch of original patients who was to die. All the others were to suffer frighteningly high fevers but, through Brigita and Anna's nursing, and the patient's own determination, they were able to pull through.

The Woodman's Hut quickly became known by the partisans as their local field hospital with the result that a trickle of other patients started to arrive. They came mainly with bullet and grenade blast injuries gained from close quarter fighting. Soon the partisans started to provide anaesthetics, morphine and bandages stolen from the Germans.

The more patients Heinrik had and the more digging around he did, the more he learnt about the human body. It meant he became better at putting people back together. He knew he was hopelessly out of his depth and he hated himself for it. He had no idea how well he was doing. Some lived but too often, it seemed to Heinrik, many died. This was because he would remember his failures and not his successes. All he knew was that the patients kept coming and those that brought them had confidence that he would do the right thing.

The first time that Heinrik truly baulked was when he had to deal with an eye injury. The eye had been sliced right through and the socket smashed to pieces. Heinrik had no idea where to start but start he had to, for the man could not stay in agony like that. And so Heinrik's cutting, digging, and sewing continued with little sophistication but more care than a local butcher.

Long before his patients were well, but only after Brigita was certain that they would live, she would enforce their discharge from her field hospital. They got in the way of the other things she knew she had to do. She knew the Russians were coming back. She was determined to grow and hide food to see them through the winter. Under no circumstances was she going to allow herself and Anna to suffer from another Holodomor, which she was sure Stalin's defeat of the Germans would bring. It was why, when they were not attending to patients, Heinrik, Anna and any of their walking wounded were forced to labour in the maize and wheat fields.

It was Anna who decided that Heinrik should learn Russian; interestingly not Moldovan because, like Brigita, she knew the Russian occupation was on its way. They started with the names of medical instruments and then everyday objects. It was all done, as they ate, with pointing and mime in the late evening, after they had swum in the river to cool off after the terrible heat of the day.

It was a strange time for Heinrik. He knew he should leave to find his German colleagues and get back to fighting the war yet, every time he thought he would go tomorrow, another patient would arrive needing his attention. It gave him the excuse to stay. The fact was that the war was raging all around them, but not at the Woodman's Hut field hospital.

Chapter 68

The Woodman's Hut July 1944

HEINRIK NEVER REALLY knew whether it was the scrapped objects he found accumulated in an old shed next to the Woodman's Hut or the need for a source of permanent hot water which gave him the idea of creating an immersion heater. With an old stove, some copper tubing, a hose pipe and an old wine barrel and the principles of convection he managed to heat up a barrel of cold water inside their hut. For the first time an endless stream of hot water was available. It stopped the constant need to boil a kettle and thus reduced the damp which hung in the air from the steam. For Heinrik, even though it was summer, its first use had to be as a bath.

Being a gentleman Heinrik offered the warm water to Anna first. With curtains set up around an old wine barrel brought inside for the purpose, she stripped off, stepped on a box and plunged deep into the barrel squatting down, deep enough to cover her shoulders. Water poured over the barrel's edge falling through the cracks in the wooden floorboards to the soil below. Anna ducked her head under the water allowing the warmth to penetrate the pores of her face and scalp. Everything was perfect bar one thing. There was no soap. Nevertheless, for the very first time in a long time Anna felt truly clean.

When it came to getting out of the barrel Anna found she had a problem. She could raise herself by her arms but never high enough to get her legs over the edge. Try as hard as she might she could not get out without risking tipping the whole barrel over. Anna called for help. Heinrik looked cautiously behind the curtain as Anna beckoned him in.

"I can't get out," she whispered lowering her shoulders under the water to stop him seeing her breasts.

"Do you want me to lift you out? signalled Heinrik, with his hands going up and down and his head nodding.

"Yes please, no. Get me something to stand on," Anna instructed, pointing to the box which she had first stood on.

"It won't fit with you already in there," said Heinrik in workable Russian as he signalled the problem. He looked around the room. "I can't find anything. I will have to lift you. It's the only way."

Anna thrust her head under the water. As she stood up, it gushed down her sides as she wiped her hair into a ponytail behind her back. Subconsciously she let her hands fall to her side before taking hold of the edge of the barrel.

Heinrik deliberately avoided looking at Anna's breasts by staring straight into her eyes. He immediately recognised her expression. He had seen it before. It was the same look of vulnerability he had seen as she had lain beneath the Russian soldier on the bed in the Community Hall.

Heinrik took hold of Anna either side of her chest and, squeezing her tightly, he lifted her high into the air. He looked where he was going to place her but found nowhere comfortable. Without saying anything he settled her back down in the water as she looked at him quizzically. Taking a towel, he folded it many times and placed it on the sharp edge of the barrel to make a cushion. He then lifted her high into the air again and placed her to sit on the towel. Heinrik looked to support her as she swung her legs over the edge and then helped her down. She was standing completely naked in front of him. He was overwhelmed by her physical beauty. Almost in shock, he stepped back, picked up the towel which had fallen on the floor, shook it out and, without any form of embarrassment, he studied her figure before wrapping the towel around her. At that moment Heinrik found something quite magical about being so close to Anna. Why had he not noticed it before, he wondered?

Anna was bewildered. Yes, she was embarrassed, but something else had happened too, but she did not know what.

Brigita, back from the fields, was the next into the water. After hearing of Anna's problem, she took a milking stool in with her, so she climbed out without any difficulty. Heinrik was the last person in. Although the water was dirty, he too felt completely renewed.

Chapter 69

The Woodman's Hut July 1944

IT WASN'T JUST the night summer sky, and the fact that it was warm and muggy, which was keeping Anna and Heinrik awake. As they each lay in their own beds, each under a single sheet, they thought of the other and the moment when she came from the bath and stood naked before him.

Anna's mind was in total confusion. He had saved her from, she did not know what, but he sought no credit. He had worked opposite her during surgery and had shown no interest in her, except as a colleague. She remembered how, at the start of each operation, he would look into her eyes for encouragement and how, at the end, he would look again to see if he had her approval. She thought of the language lessons and how they would laugh together. It was only these which had ever created a little frisson between them, and now there was earlier today. It had changed everything. It was a sensation which came from his strength yet softness of touch that no words would ever be able to describe.

Anna got up, wrapped herself in her sheet, tiptoed around the few patients that were lying on the floor and stepped out onto the veranda. Hearing her move, Heinrik rose from his mattress, also placed on the floor, wrapped himself in his sheet too and joined her. They stood side-by-side looking down over the field, across the river and towards the east where the sun would start to rise in a couple of hours' time.

Heinrik reached out and gently took Anna's hand. They looked towards each other and said nothing. They had no words to share which the other would understand. They looked at each other again. This time they held the other's gaze and an overwhelming sense of emotion leapt from each of their stomachs into their chests. Heinrik leaned forward and kissed Anna gently on the lips in the sweetest, tenderest of touches.

Anna was surprised at the sensation. She had never been kissed by a man on the lips before. She responded by gently pressing her lips onto his and squeezing his hands in a spontaneous sign of encouragement. Anna's biggest fears were being extinguished. Heinrik might have been older than she was, but in her mind their relationship was one of equals. Now she'd had it confirmed. Heinrik did not think she was too young for him, and that made her feel good.

Chapter 70

The Woodman's Hut July 1944

OVER THE NEXT few nights and in the early hours of the morning Heinrik and Anna met on the Veranda of the Woodman's Hut where their relationship developed cautiously. They held hands, kissed and touched. Virtually nothing was said between them. They each acted as though the other were forbidden fruit. Just happy to be together.

It came to a point where Anna became an irresistible temptation for Heinrik. It was with great deliberation that he planned her seduction, for he just had to have her. To make her his own. Anna had thought about the same thing too, long and hard. She decided that she had to extinguish any intention she might have of giving herself to him. After all, Heinrik was German, the enemy. It made it quite impossible for them to have a future together. They would be friends; that was to be the limit. She had never been a supplicant, and her life wasn't going to be changed by this man to become one.

As Anna appeared on the veranda wrapped in a sheet in the form of a roman toga, Heinrik took her hand and led her down the steps to a small border of wildflowers near the woods edge. It was where he had earlier placed his two ground sheets. In the warmth of the night Heinrik unwrapped Anna until she stood naked in the starlight. He knelt down and as he did so his sheet fell to reveal his naked body. He looked up at her and with a smile and a gentle pull on her hand he encouraged Anna to join him.

What Anna didn't know was that, whilst Heinrik was still a novice lover, he had more experience than her and, in the world of the blind, the one-eyed man is king. This is not to suggest that there was anything cynical about Heinrik's behaviour. He had been totally captivated by the woman in front of him. He knew he had as strong and emotional bond with her as he'd ever had with anyone. Could he say he was in love? Yes, but was it an enduring love? He wasn't sure. How could he know when each could not express to the other what they were feeling or thinking?

Bit by bit, with each of Heinrik's touch, caress or kiss, Anna's resistance was lowered until she consciously decided that her world should change forever.

Chapter 71

The Woodman's Hut 20th August 1944

HEINRIK AND ANNA both woke with a startle. Wrapped in each other's bodies they did not move. Instead with their eyes wide open they looked enquiringly one of the other. The oasis of calm, which had surrounded the fields and forests of the Woodman's Hut since Heinrik had arrived was over. There were huge explosions in the air as Russian shell after shell pounded into the German defences.

Neither Heinrik nor Anna would have been able to tell you the date. Since they had become lovers, and shared laying on the groundsheet under the starlight, one day had merged into another in blissful happiness. They would have guessed that they were in August but that was all. In fact, it was 20 August 1944. The Red Army was on the march westward from Tiraspol. It had just broken out from the bridgeheads they held on the western side of the Dniester River and were now attacking towards Kishinev in what was to become known as the Jassy-Kishinev Offensive.[54]

Heinrik and Anna knew exactly where the Red Army bridgeheads over the Dniester River were for many a partisan had been injured trying to provide intelligence for the attacking Russian army. They were confident that they were safe from imminent attack as they were convinced that the Russians were facing one of the most powerful armoured formations ever established in the German army, and it was

---

[54] The Jassy-Kishinev Offensive is the name given to the series of battles the Russian Red Army fought against the German and Romanian Army Group South Ukraine which took place between 20th and 29th August 1944. It resulted in the encirclement and destruction of the German forces in the region with over 115,000 men taken prisoner. It allowed the Russian army to resume moving into the Balkans and westward through eastern Europe and towards Berlin.

well and truly dug in. This was true once. What they didn't know, but the Russians did, thanks not only to the local partisans, but to the fact that the British had broken the German's Enigma[55] code, was that most of the German's armour in the area had been moved to fight elsewhere on the Eastern Front, leaving their infantry very poorly protected.

Heinrik, Anna and Brigita dressed rapidly, as did many of the wounded men they were looking after. No one knew what to do for the best for the quantity of shells flying overhead was truly frightening.

Heinrik searched his bags to find his luger pistols. He had checked them every day when he first arrived at the Woodsman's Hut, but they were now gone.

"Where are they?" Heinrik shouted in Russian. "Where are my guns," he demanded. "We need them. You need them," he bellowed forcefully.

Brigita disappeared for a few seconds and then, with a smirk on her face, she returned with his two pistols, one in each hand dangling between her forefingers. She gave one of the guns to Anna, kept the other to herself and shared out the spare ammunition between them

"And the big guns?" asked Heinrik in Russian this time mimicking a rifle with his arms.

Brigita reached under her bed and produced a complete cache of weapons gathered, not only from Heinrik but from the injured men they had treated. Most of the guns were German which the partisans had been able to buy in Odessa from deserting soldiers.

"We need to go into the forest," said Brigita. "We will be safer there."

"And these?" said Anna pointing to their patients.

"Not now!" instructed Brigita. "We will be back, but we can't help anyone if we are dead!"

The two women rapidly threw things into bags as Heinrik looked on hopelessly. He had no idea what to do next. His dilemma was made

---

[55] The Enigma code machines were used to code German military communications in World War II. Their coded messages were broken by British codebreakers working at Bletchley Park.

worse by the most vicious row between mother and daughter which ended by Anna tugging on Heinrik's sleeve telling him to follow them; just as she had done when they left the Community Hall just eight weeks before

Heinrik joined the rush around the Woodman's Hut gathering his things which he threw into his two bags, taking time to fill his water bottles and the small camping stove with fuel from their oil lamps.

With Brigita leading, and Anna and Heinrik following, they travelled for about forty minutes deep into the forest. They took their time for many a careless hunter had left a trap which would hurt the unwary. Eventually, they came to a clearing. Although it might have appeared to have been an accidental find it was undoubtedly Brigita's subconscious which had bought them here. She had been before with her grandfather. It was the place he had made ready to keep his family safe should the Germans have invaded in 1914. There was one large shed surrounded by several smaller ones which fanned out going in to the forest in different directions and distances. The creator's hope was that an interloper might find one store but not all.

Instantly recognising the spot, Brigita ordered that this was where they would make camp. If it was good enough for Count Sacha Donici-Solokov then it was good enough for her. For five days they lazily followed the sun around their camp site and watched as wave after wave of Russian planes flew high above them destroying the German tanks and its army's defences below.

Later that afternoon, as Heinrik was lying down with Anna's head resting on his chest, Brigita asked: "I wonder how they're getting on in France? Do you think the British and American's will have so many planes?"

Heinrik immediately picked up on the word. "France?" What's happened in France?" he asked hurriedly.

"The British and Americans have invaded. We are now racing each other to get to Berlin" said Brigita confidently.

Heinrik thought about Victoria. How was she? How was his son? he wondered, always assuming she'd had a boy. He often thought about her, mostly in the bloom of his lovemaking with Anna. Sometimes he would compare them and sometimes he would contrast them. There were so many aspects of their lives which were similar. All of them were only children bought up by a single mother. The difference was that Heinrik and Victoria had spent their lives in permanent doubt. To both it was as though something was missing. Anna had none of that insecurity. She was a natural, confident leader, wiser than her years; wiser than Victoria and he put together. If he had to choose, then he knew he would, at that moment, choose Anna.

Chapter 72

Châteaux de Gressier August 1944

22ND AUGUST 1944 was a hot stifling night. In an effort to sleep, Juliette had the windows wide open to get some air into her bedroom, but it was making little difference. In her slumbers, she heard a huge, deep, heavy boom of an explosion, which appeared to have come from the centre of Bordeaux.

What Juliette heard was the work of Colonel Heinz Stahlschmidt, a German naval explosives expert. He had been ordered to destroy the port of Bordeaux so it could not be used to reinforce Allied forces. His means to this destruction were held in a German supply bunker at Rue Raze. It was a few hundred metres away from the submarine pens in the docks. This bunker was filled with thousands of pounds of ordnance. Using strips of dynamite laid inside the supply bunker, Stahlschmidt blew the store up. In the process, he saved the port from demolition, and became a hero of Bordeaux. The explosion shook the foundation of every house in Bordeaux and for miles around, including Château de Gressier.

Immediately after the boom, Juliette heard shouting in her house and saw lights flashing on to her ceiling. It was now obvious that something was happening. Juliette got out of bed and went to her bedroom window, which she forced open, even wider. Standing naked, she could see that, high on the hill and directly opposite, La Bête Blanche was in flames. It was well and truly alight and beyond saving. The Germans, who had been billeted there, had been evacuated an hour earlier. They had deliberately set fire to the place as they left, determined to destroy what they had turned into a cesspit.

It was a blaze too big to tackle, so La Bête Blanche was left to burn itself out as everyone watched on. By the end of the next day, all that was left standing were the two chimneys and a big steel crossbeam. It looked like a huge 'H' when viewed from a distance. All those at de Gressier who saw it told how the 'H' reminded them of Hitler. For Juliette, the 'H' secretly reminded her of Heinrik too, and thus her daughter. Without hesitation, she ordered that the whole of La Bête Blanche be razed to the ground and the site cleared.

Once the white ranch-style house was gone, Juliette missed it. Before, she had cursed every time she had seen it, because she knew how much Étienne hated it, but its absence created an emptiness in the skyline. One day, she told herself, she would put it back; but she never did.

Chapter 73

The Woodman's Hut August 1944

AFTER FIVE NIGHTS in the woods Brigita left early at daybreak to return to the Woodsman's Hut. She went on her own, telling the others to stay where they were. Brigita was certain she would travel there and back much faster without them.

With no curtain to give them the privacy they enjoyed in the Woodman's Hut, Heinrik and Anna's time in the forest camp with Brigita was noted by their celibacy. Now with Brigita on the trail, it was the first time the two lovers had been truly on their own. In this haven, they experimented in their lovemaking as only a young couple passionately in love know how.

Brigita arrived back at camp less than two hours after she had gone. Her return was forewarned by her shouts for Anna and Heinrik. They were needed back at the Woodman's Hut and urgently. The local partisans had joined the battle and were bringing in casualties from the Red Army for treatment.

When the three of them arrived back at the Woodman's Hut they were staggered to see the size of the problem. There were injured men everywhere; some on stretchers, some lying on the ground, others sitting dejectedly. Unlike Heinrik's first time of arrival at the Woodman's Hut, each injured man had field bandages roughly applied to their wounds. Further, there was little groaning from pain because morphine had been liberally used.

It was the kind of scene that Anna was born for. She tapped a medical orderly on the shoulder, easily identified by the two medical sacks carried by straps wrapped around his neck. Pointing to Heinrik, Anna ordered him to go with *the doctor* to set up an operating theatre in the Woodman's Hut.

If there was organised chaos outside in the field, it was total anarchy inside the Woodman's Hut. There were so many injured men it became hard to find any area of floor to step on. Brigita screamed and yelled for everyone to get out, but with their injuries very few could move. The fact was that no operation was going to take place in the Woodman's Hut until it had been emptied and cleaned.

Once again, it was a situation made for Anna's leadership. She called for two orderlies from the field, and firmly but politely asked them to move everyone outside. The first orderly started to protest. Anna explained why she wanted it done, but he protested some more. Suddenly Brigita lost her patience. She was taking none of his nonsense. Taking one of Heinrik's lugers she pointed it straight at his head. "Are you gonna do as you're told?" she said. The threat was obvious.

"Medic," called a voice from the corner. "Please do as the women say." It was the voice of an elderly, but junior officer leaning against the wall, dried blood covering his face. He spoke with such politeness that it calmed down what had become an explosive situation.

With the objective agreed, Heinrik, Brigita, Anna and the two orderlies moved everyone outside. It was then that they set out to scrub clean the inside of the hut ready to treat patients.

The outside stove was started so it could heat up the water in the wine barrel. It had now been lifted so there could be hot running water.

Heinrik unpacked his pathetic dissecting kit and put it in the boiling water along with the one syringe they had for administering morphine and anaesthetics.

"Is that it?" asked the orderly looking at the small number of implements placed in the boiling water.

Heinrik understood but nodded weakly in response. With his blonde hair much longer, and now in the clothes of partisans whose life Heinrik had been unable to save, he could have come from anywhere in Europe. However, to have spoken would immediately have identified him as German.

As the Woodman's Hut was being prepared, Anna, together with another orderly, was triaging every patient. Those who were going to die went in one group. These were usually the men with the worst stomach or chest injuries. Anna knew that Heinrik's success rate with this group of patients was poor; but the fact was that, without penicillin, the omens for these kinds of wounds were not good, irrespective of the surgeon you might have had.

Amongst those evacuated to the Woodman's Hut was a radio operator with a bad leg wound. He had made no transmission since he had arrived. No one had given him any instructions.

"Does that work?" asked Anna, as she was examining him during her assessment round.

"Yes."

"Can you radio for medical supplies?" she asked.

"Yes, if ordered."

"Then please do so," said Anna.

"But you are not an officer," protested the wireless operator. I can only transmit when I'm ordered by an officer.

"Please, I am ordering you to send a message asking for a medical team with supplies," said Anna. "It's that, or you get treated at the very, very end, if at all!"

The wireless operator looked at Anna bewildered. He did not know what his best option was. His dichotomy was ended by the elderly junior officer who had moved outside the hut and was now touring the injured men with her. "Do as she says," he ordered weakly. "The message: 50-60 serious casualties. More arriving. Request urgent medical support plus supplies." The officer stopped, looked at his map and read out the co-ordinates. Three times the wireless operator sent the message. On the last occasion he got an acknowledgement.

Heinrik, ready to start his first operation of the new batch, looked up. He found not the eyes of Anna whose support he was seeking as he had done at the start of every operation. Instead, before him, he saw the enquiring face of the medical orderly. Was this man really going to operate with brandy as a disinfectant, a schoolboy dissecting kit and the filed fishhook as needle he wondered. As Heinrik, with his cutthroat razor in hand, sliced into the patient's flesh, the orderly got his reply.

Chapter 74

The Woodman's Hut August 1944

LIEUTENANT-COLONEL RUSLAN BABACK had wondered about his orders. The coordinates he had been given to set up his field hospital appeared to be a long way from where he thought the main fighting was going on. But, even at his rank, he had learnt long ago not to question them. The imprisonment of his wife, daughter, and he in 1936 for even deigning to think, let alone express an opinion, in Stalin's Russia, gave a lesson no one would ever want repeated. For Baback the cost had already been far too high as he was never to see or hear of them again. Thus, it was with another surgeon and a compliment of women nurses and orderlies that his wagon train of five sets of horse and cart came off the main road and down what appeared to be miles of dirt track.

When he arrived at the Woodman's Hut, Baback had some understanding of his orders. For there he found a large number of injured men had been gathered away from the fighting and needed treatment.

Heinrik did not hear the Lieutenant-Colonel arrive. He was too busy concentrating on removing bullets from a man's lung and shoulder. It was only when his orderly stood rapidly to attention, did Heinrik notice his audience.

"Carry on," said Baback in a strong muscovite accent.

Heinrik did not understand what the man had said. He could see from his insignia that he was a high-ranking Russian officer. He nodded and chose to concentrate on the task in hand; saving a young man's life which might otherwise be lost.

Baback spoke again. Heinrik nodded again. He could do nothing else. He had not understood what had been said and certainly could not have replied without giving his nationality away. The Colonel watched absorbed by Heinrik's work. Almost immediately on his arrival he'd heard of the surgeon who was saving lives with a school dissecting kit. It was a rumour he was prepared to dismiss until that moment.

Baback moved to the veranda and shouted instructions. Within minutes, wrapped and presented for Heinrik's use was a full set of basic operating theatre equipment. It was just as he had seen in the operating theatre in Bamberg when he was growing up. He nodded his thanks and expertly applied the retractor around the open shoulder wound. He took out some of his patient's shattered scapula, but he had to find some way of holding it together. Heinrik held up the last round of steel wire knowing that his real need was for a metal plate, screws and a drill.

Once again Baback went to the door and shouted instructions. A few minutes later another bundle arrived with the equipment Heinrik needed. The Colonel watched as Heinrik drilled the collarbone and carefully plated it together. Heinrik had seen it done before, but this was the first time he'd actually done it.

When it came to sewing the patient up Heinrik picked up his old fishhook needle and showed it teasingly to Baback. The fact that he had been allowed to continue had given Heinrik a strange, almost outer body, feeling of confidence. After a few seconds, he put down the old fishhook and picked up a new surgical needle which he showed to Baback with another smile. Not a word was said between them.

Whilst Heinrik's crude operating technique was passing muster with the Colonel, his medical corps was doing exactly the opposite as far as Brigita was concerned. She was venting fury as hospital tents were erected and, in the process, were destroying her precious crops of wheat and maize. She became even more annoyed when they started to dig latrines in a position which would have contaminated the water in their drinking well.

Meanwhile, Anna was working with the other surgeon, a captain, taking him around the patient's she had triaged. They started with those she had assessed as were going to die even if they had been operated on. In the most part the Captain agreed with her, moving only a couple of men forward into the queue for an early operation. The rest would, as far as possible, be kept peaceful with morphine until they died.

Two operating tables were brought into the Woodman's Hut from one of the carts and within one hour of their arrival, the Colonel and the Captain were operating alongside Heinrik. All the time new patients were arriving, some on wheeled stretcher carts being pulled by dogs.

It was late into the night when Heinrik, Anna, Brigita, the Colonel, the Captain and three nurses sat down on the veranda to eat from the field hospital kitchen which had already served every wounded man. Brigita produced two bottles of Cricova wine which had come as presents from thankful families of partisans whom Heinrik had helped put back together.

The Colonel stood up and proposed a toast to Heinrik, Brigita and Anna. Heinrik understood exactly what was going on but had still not said a word.

The Colonel then presented Brigita with a chit. It was an IOU from the Red Army signed by him promising to pay her two bushels of wheat. It was in compensation for the crops that she had lost.

It was at that moment Brigita betrayed her daughters trust. "Heinrik's a German officer soldier," she said

Anna took a sharp intake of breath and stared at her mother wildly.

"I am a German pilot," said Heinrik in Russian, correcting her.

"And a doctor," added Anna

"I know," said Baback. "I have already been told by the partisans."

"He's a good doctor said Anna defensively

"He's a remarkable doctor," said Baback. "To have done so much with so little well..."

"I'm not a doctor," said Heinrik in Russian once again.

Baback looked at Heinrik carefully. "Of course not," he said. "Too young, but a very good trainee."

"Is he going to be arrested?" asked Anna anxiously.

"No, not while we're here," said Baback forcefully. He paused. "Here we work under the invisible flag. We take each man as we see him, friend or foe. We treat him according to his needs. The German surgeon, provided he continues to operate, stays with us until we're ordered on. Then I'll decide."

Heinrik understood exactly what had been said. He chose to say nothing more. He needed to plan his escape.

Chapter 75

The Woodman's Hut August 1944

THE WOODMAN'S HUT was quiet. Operations had stopped for the night. For the first time since Heinrik had arrived Brigita, Anna and he had the room to themselves as every patient had been moved into hospital tents outside. In exhaustion, each had gone to their own bed but only Brigita slept.

With the room empty of patients Heinrik had won back his old bed. It was a luxury to no longer sleep on a mattress thrown on the floor. Heinrik climbed out of his bed, reached underneath, and pulled out his bags. In the dark he felt around one, and then around the other, until he found what he was looking for. Very quietly he tiptoed across the room to Anna's bed where he squatted next to her.

"You have to look after something for me," said Heinrik in a whisper, as he handed Anna the cardboard box containing Victor's gold watch in its green velvet case.

"What is it?" whispered Anna in return.

"It's a watch," he said not knowing any other Russian word to describe it. "It belongs to a friend," he added. "It needs to be kept safe."

Anna propped herself up on her elbow and in the half-light took the case out of its cardboard sleeve and opened it. Heinrik lit the candle by the side of her bed so she could see it properly. Like everyone who had seen the watch before her, she had to take it out of its case and hold it, to caress it. Anna stroked the glass and ran her fingers over the engraving of Victor's name. As she moved the watch so the diamonds marking each hour twinkled in the candlelight.

"Who's Victor?" she asked.

"A friend's brother. I have to take it back to him," he said, deliberately changing Victoria's gender.

Anna leaned forward and kissed Heinrik on the lips. It was her way of saying yes. She laid her head back on her pillow with the box held tightly in her hand. She had already worked out that one day he would be taken as a prisoner of war, or would escape into the woods, and be gone. With this watch in her hand she knew that, whatever happened, he would come back to her. She just knew he would. With that thought a glow of happiness swept over her whole body as the baby, she did not yet know she had, continued to grow inside her.

Chapter 76

Moldova, Bucharest, and Bulgaria September – November 1944

LT. COL. BABACK'S orders to move his field hospital closer to Kishinev came at the end of September. It was an obvious order, far too late in coming, because the Woodman's Hut was a long way from anywhere. Its position had been an advantage to the partisans, but now it was a hindrance.

On the day Baback received his instructions, Heinrik was ordered to come to his tent. It was the one closest to the river which, with the flaps up, meant it was cooler than most of the others.

"Sit down," said Baback immediately Heinrik entered his tent. Heinrik did as he was told.

"What is your full name?" Baback asked officiously.

"Heinrik Klugman"

"What is your rank?" Baback asked in the same tone.

"Hauptmann."

Baback wrote down each of Heinrik's answers without looking at him.

"What was your Squadron?

"Atlantic Command."

Baback looked up. "You are a long way from the Atlantic," he observed.

"We were tasked to supply the front line, like everyone else," answered Heinrik.

"Even after the landings in France?" said Baback, not knowing whether to believe him or not.

"I was already serving on the Eastern Front" replied Heinrik assuredly.

"When did you crash?"

"I can't remember the date; the beginning of January 1944. The 6th or 7th something like that."

"Where did you crash?"

"I don't know exactly, somewhere near Suhokleya River."

"You've come along way. Who's helped you escape?"

The questions went on an on until one question caught Heinrik unawares.

"Have you ever been to Parata?"

"No, I don't think so. Where's that?" he replied innocently.

"It's not far from here," commented Baback lazily. "The NKVD has a report that a German soldier shot dead 11 Russian soldiers in an ambush." Baback's experience had taught him of the incompetence of the NKVD so he had already made up his mind that one German was unlikely to be able to kill so many Russians. He had decided it was more likely that the deaths had been at the hand of a group of partisans. Something it would be embarrassing for the NKVD to admit.

"I don't understand," said Heinrik, albeit he had understood perfectly.

"Do you speak English?" It was a strange question given that the two men had been working together for the last four weeks in broken Russian.

"Yes, it's my best foreign language," replied Heinrik in faltering Russian.

"Where did you learn, at medical school?" asked Baback in fluent English

Heinrik, confused by the change in language, nodded weakly.

"Where were you at medical school?".

"Nuremburg," said Heinrik.

"We'll be there shortly," said Baback, enjoying the schadenfreude moment. "On our way to Berlin," he added with a grin.

"What do you know about the killing of this group of Russian soldiers not far from here, at a place called Parata? It was a girls' dormitory," Baback asked more firmly.

Heinrik shook his head. "Nothing," he said. His heart thumped uncontrollably inside his chest and he worked hard to make sure there was no change either to his expression or demeanour.

"How did you get captured?

"Brigita captured me. She saw me walking over the fields, just here, near the river and she shot at me. Took me prisoner and then I started working. It's all. Look .." he said before showing Baback the scars of his flesh wound to prove his story. "She did that!"

"Anna lived in the dormitory where the soldiers were killed. Did you know that?"

Heinrik shook his head again. "What did she say?"

"She said she was here with you and you were captured by her mother before the soldiers were shot."

Apart from bringing forward the date, which was new to Heinrik, he knew their stories would tally. It was one of the few things that, at Anna's instance, Brigita, Heinrik and she had shared. Whether Brigita would keep to the story now, who knew?"

"We're leaving here," said Baback changing the subject. You're free to come with us or we can hand you over to the NKVD as a prisoner of war?"

Heinrik looked perplexed as he hadn't understood the two options he was being presented.

"Do you want to come with us?" demanded Baback, beginning to lose his patience.

"Brigita, Anna?" said Heinrik. "What are they doing?"

"Brigita's staying to look after the patients here. Anna has volunteered to come with us."

"Isn't she too young?" asked Heinrik.

"You should know," said Baback, his raised eyebrows gave an indication that he knew of their relationship.

Heinrik said nothing, for he thought his relationship with Anna was their secret. He was embarrassed to think that it had been shared with others.

"Come now," said Baback, recognising Heinrik's embarrassment. "We men, we need our little comforts, our little pleasures. He paused and then added, "She's volunteered. Nurse Anna has said she will come."

"And you?" asked Baback returning to his Russian language. "Are you coming with us?"

"Yes, I'll come," said Heinrik firmly in Russian. In reality he had no choice. To be taken prisoner by the NKVD was not an option worth contemplating.

"I need to make one thing clear," said Baback. "You try and escape and you'll be shot. Escape and be captured, you will be shot. We'll be in Berlin long before you. You'll have nowhere to hide. If you escape, I will make it my mission to find you, and you will be shot!" Never had Heinrik been so threatened.

"You might have saved Russian lives Hauptman Klugman," said Baback, "but remember you're the enemy. You caused all this." He waived his armsaround his tent in anger. "Not us. You're the enemy, and the enemy gets shot." It was as cold blooded a statement as Heinrik had ever heard.

Chapter 77

Kishinev, Bucharest, and Belgrade
September – November 1944

ANNA BITTERLY REGRETTED her decision to voluntarily stay with Baback's field hospital. She thought she was going with them just to Kishinev but once there, they were ordered on to Bucharest in Romania. She was persuaded to stay with them; after all Moldova and Romania had been cousin countries for nearly one thousand years.

No sooner had they set up the field hospital in Bucharest, and were settled in, than they were ordered on to Belgrade in Yugoslavia. The war was progressing very quickly in the Balkans and the Russian army swept through country after country with little resistance.

Anna's request to leave the field hospital in Bucharest to go home to Kishinev was rejected by the senior nurse, whose attitude was harsh and unforgiving. She had a bitter attitude, moulded by years of pre-war unhappiness from being treated by doctors as no better than a handmaiden, while working in facilities which were so downfallen that they gave her little chance to do her job properly.

The senior nurse told Anna that, since the Soviet Union had paid for her training as a nurse, she had to repay the cost of that training by staying at her post.

Anna knew it was a nonsense argument. She had received no training whatsoever. She appealed directly to Baback who had no interest. Long ago he had discovered the hell he suffered when he countermanded the orders of his senior nurse.

The journey from Bucharest to Belgrade was long, hard and arduous. Anna felt constantly tired and nauseous but nevertheless carried on without complaint. Once they were in Belgrade Heinrik and Anna saw little of each other, which added to her misery.

Anna worked in the tented wards, while Heinrik was assigned to the operating theatre, where there was much less work. The injuries from weapons of war had abated as the Germans, and their allies, started to give up the fight. Heinrik's tasks were primarily the odd dental extraction, the occasional need to stitch someone up, but mainly it was Baback and the Captain who did all the surgical work. It was a fact that Heinrik was ill-suited to serve the general medical needs of soldiers who arrived at their field hospital, for he had zero knowledge to help them. It was why his most common job was to carry out medical inspections after the soldiers had been through the delousing tent.

The only time that Anna and Heinrik could really meet was at mealtimes when they made a point of trying to sit together, albeit that Anna was horribly teased for being friends with the enemy.

It was while feeling sick and nibbling a small amount of bread for her breakfast, that Anna sat opposite Heinrik. "I'm pregnant," she said after they had said little other than the usual morning pleasantries.

"What?" asked Heinrik, as the Russian for pregnant was not a word he knew.

"I am pregnant," she said again. "With child." She tapped her tummy and then curved her hand over her belly in the universal sign of carrying a baby.

Heinrik would always look back at that moment and wish he had done something different; perhaps he could have smiled to show he was pleased or touched her hand in a sign of encouragement. Instead, the colour visibly drained from his face and a shocked expression took hold.

"How do you know?" he asked.

"I have been feeling sick in the morning and my breasts .... In any case, the captain has confirmed it," she said.

Heinrik could not think of a single thing to say. After a little while he asked: "will you go home?"

"I don't know; if they will let me."

"Will they let you?"

"When we were in Bucharest and I asked then, they said no. In any case, if they say yes, I've no idea how I'll get home."

"What can I do?" asked Heinrik.

There was a very long pause as Anna looked Heinrik squarely in the eyes. "Nothing," she said bitterly. "You know that, you can do nothing!" Every syllable in her voice oozed loathing.

Heinrik looked at the table, unable to look at Anna and her anger anymore.

"My mother managed without a man. I'll manage too," she spat out. "You men..." Anna paused as she sought the right words. "You're worthless. This mess, this war," she said angrily as she swung her arms around the tented dining room. "It's all the fault of men. On the farm we have just one boar, he serves all the sows, the rest get eaten. That's what we women should do. Keep just a few of you, but the rest, should be put down at birth. That way we'd be doing mankind a damn big favour!"

Anna got up from the table and looked at Heinrik. "You know what you can do?" she said. "You can damn well get lost."

Chapter 78

Belgrade November 1944

THE SENIOR NURSE'S solution to Anna's pregnancy was easy. She should have an abortion. The nurse even arranged for the captain to carry it out; just as he had done for many of the women travelling with the field hospital. When Anna rejected this, the nurse's next solution was for Anna to have her baby and to leave it in an orphanage in Belgrade.

"This way the baby will belong to the State from the start," she said. "It's the way it should be. No baby should belong to its mother. It should start its life, just as it will end up when it's an adult, with the State as its mother. Mother - child, State – child, whatever our age," she continued. "It's the new order. We all have an obligation to the State, to no one else, not even ourselves."

Anna had heard these Bolshevik lines from this nurse many times as they had travelled from Kishinev via Bucharest to Belgrade and, if she didn't before; she now knew it was thorough nonsense.

In the sea of inhumanity which permeated throughout the Russian army, there were millions of acts of love and kindness. One of those was the way Baback treated Anna, on learning she was pregnant and wanted to keep her baby. He'd had a daughter just a bit older than Anna when, for no reason, she was arrested in one of Stalin's Purges and killed in prison at the hands of the NKVD. He understood the love a parent has for their child, and in particular the needs of a daughter for their mother at the time of childbirth. He overruled his senior nurse, discharged Anna from the Russian Army, gave her permission to return to Kishinev and ordered her a travel warrant to get there.

At the same time Anna was getting her freedom, Baback gave

instructions for Heinrik to be arrested and held as a prisoner of war. His days as a faux doctor were over.

Chapter 79

Belgrade - November 1944

HEINRIK KNEW, LONG before Anna's reaction, that he had handled the news of Anna's baby and his pending fatherhood very badly. His one excuse; his eyes had told him, time and time again, what was in store for him as a prisoner of war.

As they travelled, they had passed field after field of abandoned and uncared for German soldiers without the basics of life: food, water or medical supplies.[56] He had heard how, during the previous winter, many German soldiers had slept in each other's arms only to find themselves, waking in the morning, clutching a corpse.

The first few days of Heinrik's arrest were very civilised. Baback had commandeered a school building in Belgrade as the billet for his field hospital, and his prison cell was a small room in the school. He was given a mattress, a table, and chair. He had his clothes, his Russian greatcoat and his German flying boots, but nothing else. Everything had gone. All he had to do was wait for the NKVD to decide where he should go.

While he waited Heinrik was fed a soldier's portion of food, albeit they were meagre. At his request, he was given paper and a pencil. He had to write to Anna before it was too late.

My Darling Anna. I am so sorry, so very sorry.

Heinrik wrote these first few words painstakingly in Russian, then he

---

[56] It is reported that, of the 115,000 German soldiers captured in the Jassy-Kishinev Offensive, only 500 made in back to Germany when, in 1958, the Russians repatriated all the prisoners of war they held.

wrote in German and with a poor translation in English on the back of his letter.

My reaction to the news that you are having my child was unforgivable. Please understand, my response was not at the news. It was not sadness, or disappointment, or disapproval, for I feel none of those things. I would like to be pleased, but my circumstances cannot make it so.

My behaviour was prompted only by my inability to help you, or our baby, in any way, as evidenced by my arrest. I face a frightening future. You only have to look around to know that.

God ordained that every child should have a mother and father, except our child. He has decreed that ours should have no father, and this hurts me more than I think you will ever begin to believe.

I have written a letter to our child. Would you be so kind as to make sure they get it when they are old enough. I would like them to know a little about me through these few words.

I love you and will always love you. If God permits, I will come and find you both.

With much love and affection.

Heinrik

Chapter 80

Belgrade February 1945

THE CAPTURE OF the Wolf's Lair on the 27th January 1945 by the Russian army had resulted in Hauptman Heinrik Klugman, decorated with the Iron Cross First Class, becoming a Person of Interest.

Although the German army had blown up and abandoned the Wolf's Lair just forty-eight hours before the Russians arrived, burning or taking all the important operational papers with them, Hans Baur's personnel records remained intact. The fire raged all around his wooden shed burning everything to the ground except the metal filing cabinet with its papers, and Heinrik's file, jammed tightly inside. They were just charred.

It was Baback's NKVD officer, now embedded with his military field hospital, who spotted Heinrik's name in the POI[57] list. Very unusually, Baback had avoided having anyone from the NKVD in his unit until they got to Belgrade. They were known to be highly disruptive because no one really knew who was in charge, for whilst they denied any operational responsibility, unquestionably everything was under their control. They held the power because no one wanted to be arrested, and taken away, by the secret police as so very often happened.

It was the head of the NKVD office in Belgrade who insisted Baback have someone seconded to his unit. It was a bad appointment from the outset. There was complete animosity between Baback and his NKVD officer who he thought ignorant, stupid and quite revolting. It was unsurprising as the NKVD officer was not a man noted for his personal hygiene.

It therefore took strong words by Baback to make sure that he

---

[57] Person of Interest

could attend the cross-examination of Heinrik, which the Belgrade office of the NKVD insisted be undertaken.

"You told me you flew in the Atlantic Command," said Baback to Heinrik. "I remember it very clearly," he said, as they sat down at a table in a room which had been set aside for the interview.

Heinrik nodded in the same amiable way that, until that moment, Baback and he had become accustomed to conducting their meetings.

"It is not true," yelled the NKVD officer. "You worked for Hitler. You flew in Hitler's flight." The man's diction was so poor that his words slid into each other as saliva poured out of his mouth and showered anyone who sat too close. "Yes, I was a pilot in the Führer's flight," replied Heinrik, as though it were no great surprise.

"You lied to me," said Baback accusingly, and with true astonishment in his voice.

"No," said Heinrik, "I just didn't tell you the whole truth. I flew for Hitler after I had flown with Atlantic Command."

"So what else was conveniently left out of your original statement?" asked the NKVD Officer as he stretched the word 'conveniently' so it carried all the sarcasm which he intended.

"Nothing," said Heinrik. His Russian was insufficient to understand the nuance of what was being said.

'Yes there is,' thought Baback. 'The deaths of the Russian soldiers at Parata.' He stared hard at Heinrik. You were involved in that, he thought. As Baback cast his mind back his view hardened. He was damn certain that Heinrik had been there.

The NKVD officer conducted the same kind of interrogation that Baback had carried out six months before, except it lacked the same finesse. The surgeon half-listened as he worked out whether he should tell of his suspicions. Then he heard the NKVD Officer ask: "So, when did you qualify as a doctor?"

"I didn't," said Heinrik.

"When did you start at medical school?"

"I didn't."

"But you've been operating on patients, Russian soldiers," said the NKVD officer, affronted that anyone other than a qualified doctor should carry out an operation.

"And saved many lives," added Baback. Whatever he was going to say about the soldiers killed at Parata, he was not going to say anything now.

The tone of the NKVD officer showed he was more than ready to question Baback's judgement.

"I got my training at Bamberg hospital," said Heinrik, suddenly deciding to go on the defensive. You can check, for academic purposes it was attached to Nuremberg University. I studied and worked in Bamberg Hospital's operating theatre."

Baback knew Heinrik had said something about Nuremberg, but he couldn't quite remember what. However, the questioning was enough to make him doubt his own judgement on Hauptmann Klugman, and thus gave him cause of concern for his own position; except, he kept saying to himself, this pilot knew how to operate and you couldn't get that kind of skill without training..

The questioning went on hour after hour. Baback kept leaving the interview and coming back again. On each return it appeared little progress had been made. The fact was that Heinrik was running rings around the man from the NKVD. Eventually the NKVD officer stopped and looked at Baback. "This man must go to Moscow immediately," he said, as he circled the word 'Doctor' on the top of his interview notes.

Chapter 81

Belgrade, Budapest, and Kiev February 1945

IT WAS BITTERLY cold when Heinrik, with two guards either side of him, set off on foot for Belgrade Railway Station; although, as Heinrik would admit; it was nothing like as cold as the Ukrainian Steppes.

His first task, on arriving in Belgrade, and before winter had truly set in, was to have his old pilot boots repaired. It was a decision he was benefitting from now because it was only his feet which felt passably warm. Apart from the clothes he stood up in, a purloined Russian army greatcoat was his only other possession. Without boots and a greatcoat, Heinrik knew he would not survive. He had no gloves and the shackles around his wrists, chained to another around his waist, made it difficult to put his hands in his coat pockets to stop them from freezing.

Heinrik's journey to Moscow was as long as it was complex. First there was a train to Budapest. There he and his guards changed trains to take them to Kiev where they changed, once again, onto a train bound for Moscow. Heinrik found the trains a complete shock. They were no more than animal carriages with straw laid around the floor, so very different from Germany or France. There was a wood burning stove in the corner to stop the occupants from freezing to death. They would spend hours in sidings going nowhere as another train had priority on the single track. They were so overcrowded it was impossible to find anywhere to lay down properly on a journey which took days.

Three times Heinrik thought he saw Anna on his journey. The first time was at Belgrade railway station. He did not call out for he was not sure it was her. The woman he saw had a scarf wrapped around her head to keep out the cold and the middle buttons of her winter coat was undone as her belly had expanded with the baby she was carrying. The doctors, nurses, and patients had organised a whip round to gather the money Anna needed to get home. Everyone had been very generous, which meant that she had a little more than her immediate needs.

Nor did Heinrik call out when he saw her at Budapest Station where they were waiting for the same train to Kiev. This time he was embarrassed. He did not want Anna to see him bound in chains. The last time Heinrik saw Anna was in the crowd going through the checkpoint at Kiev station. This time he was certain it was her. He called out in desperation. She didn't hear. He shouted again. There was now an urgency in his voice. He needed to hear her just one more time, see her smile, and tell her he loved her, but then he winced in pain as his guard yanked, with a twist, the chains on his wrists to stop him from shouting. When he opened his eyes, she was gone.

Chapter 82

Europe May 1945

FOR THE REST of their lives Col. Dovingdon, David, Juliette, Victoria, and Dominique would be able to tell you exactly where they were when, on 8th May 1945, they heard that the Second World War had ended in Europe. It was two days short of the fifth anniversary of the start of the Battle for France. None of them joined in any of the wild celebrations. They didn't rush onto the streets with everyone else. Instead, they each felt an overwhelming sense of loss, which gave rise to feelings of anger and despair. They all asked the same question: so much death and destruction to achieve what? Freedom was the only answer they had.

Over the five long years of war, the Estate of Château de Gressier had seen changes unlike any in its history. It was impoverished and broken, just as it was after the phylloxera aphid had destroyed its vines almost 100 years before. Nevertheless, that evening, Juliette went up to the Gallery, between the Cottage and the Cellar and started to turn on the lights. The de Gressier beacon, once again, shone bright over the valley, and beyond, telling everyone that: *it was safe to come home.*

Juliette did one other thing that evening. Throughout the war years she had been forced to wear socks, short or long. They had been darned many times. At great expense, she had been able to acquire some nylon stockings on the black market brought over by the US soldiers stationed in Bordeaux. She had never worn them before, and as she stretched them over her legs for the first time, she felt like a woman reborn. For others to see her wearing them in such impoverished times immediately re-established their Crazy Monkey as the Matriarch of Latoire village.

Sadly, Latoire Village had become a divided community as it learnt of those who had aided, and those who had resisted, the Germans during the occupation. It was fortunate for Juliette that the villagers ignored the succour she gave them at de Gressier. The scales of judgement landed in favour of her being a resistance worker, and a brave one at that, because all her work was done under the German's very noses. The reprisals against those who helped the Germans were as brutal and vicious as anything that happened at the end of the previous war. It proved to Juliette she had made the right decision in sending Victoria to England.

With no husband, and estranged from her father and daughter, Juliette felt desperately alone. She was beyond anger with Penrose who she thought should have been in touch. The length of time made her wonder whether he was dead.

Juliette yearned to go home to England to see her father and daughter, and her new grandchild; was it a boy or girl she would often wonder. But inexplicably, she dare not go. The reality was that Juliette was emotionally tied to de Gressier by the bodies of her husband and son, who were in its graveyard. It was for them that she decided she would do her duty. She would rebuild the Château de Gressier estate so, once again, it would be one of the Grand Cru houses of Bordeaux. Fortunately, the summer of 1945, and nature, immediately helped her with this task, for although the harvest was miniscule, Château de Gressier's wine production was incredibly rich in taste. In the opinion of many, the Bordeaux wines of that year were the best vintage of the twentieth century.

Immediately the war ended, Juliette started writing regularly to Victoria, reporting on events. She knew it was too early for Victoria to return safely to Château de Gressier. Nevertheless, she wrote of her wish that, one day, The Cottage would become Victoria's family home. Victoria refused to reply to her mother's letters. Whatever her justification, Victoria could not forgive her mother for 'throwing her out' when she was pregnant. Further, she thought it would be a betrayal to the man who had given her a home if she responded. As far as Victoria was concerned, Juliette had to make amends with her father, before there could be a rapprochement between her and her mother.

Col. Dovingdon and Victoria's lives settled down very quickly after Henry Bellanger was born. Victoria started to work every day at the Chicksands listening station, taking the bus out in the morning and back in the evening. As a mother with a young child, she was excused from working the night shift. Her job involved listening to an endless stream of dots and dashes of encoded German messages which she recorded as single letters, none of which made sense. It was a hard job as it required permanent concentration. You could not think about anything else for a second in case you missed a dot or a dash on a message vital to the war effort. Later, Victoria was transferred to a section which translated the decoded messages from German to English and with this she felt her sanity return. However, there was not a message she translated, which mentioned the Luftwaffe, or an aeroplane, when she did not wonder whether it involved Heinrik.

The Colonel, aided by his housekeeper, doted on Henry, his great-grandson, finding that his knees no longer creaked when he bent down on the floor to play with him and his back no longer hurt when he lifted him up. Having Victoria live with him gave him back the daughter he had once lost. Not a word was ever spoken between the Colonel and his granddaughter as to Henry's father. It was never relevant. As far as the Colonel was concerned, he was going to be as good a surrogate father as any child could ask for. As the Colonel played, taught and encouraged Henry, it was as though he was making up for the time he never gave his own children, and the grandson he never knew. There was one downfall: Henry was growing up to be a thoroughly spoiled child.

If Victoria or Henry were ever asked about Henry's father, they would simply say he was shot in the war. Apart from receiving the usual few words of condolence, it would never be mentioned again.

Dominique found life without Henri incredibly difficult as she missed him desperately. Henri's letter, read out at his funeral, was widely circulated after the war and was met with general approval. It brought Dominique some notoriety which she found embarrassing, for she felt guilty, and never forgave herself, for 'letting Henri down'.

As soon as the Germans were gone, Dominique left her house in Bordeaux with Pierre and returned to live in the Fisherman's Cottage with the intention of getting her old life back; teaching and running an orchestra. Her life had almost returned to as it was immediately after the First World War; a single woman bringing up a young son on her own, when the fishermen of Bordeaux formally acknowledged her heroic work with the resistance. It meant that she became an important local heroine in her own right.

Stephen's burial place was found. His resting place was in the churchyard at Saint Clothilde Church near Bruges on the outskirts of Bordeaux. Although his body had to be disinterred for identification purposes, Dominique decided it should not be moved to the church in Latoire village, but that his first resting place should be his last. There was a peace there which she found consoling. Juliette supported Dominique in her decision, provided she could keep Stephen's memorial plaque on the cemetery wall and the place she had reserved for him. Deep in Juliette's mind was that one day, when Dominique was buried with Henri, she might like to have her son lay alongside her.

Chapter 83

Bordeaux May 1945

JULIETTE HAD NO reason to think about Heinrik Klugman, or where he was until she had a phone call from a French Officer at Bergerac Airport, which had been under the command of the French army for many months.

"We have a German Eicher tractor here for you," said the Officer.

At first Juliette didn't know what he was talking about.

"It's been here some time," continued the Officer. "It's clearly labelled to be from a Hauptmann Heinrik Klugman in Bamberg, with instructions that it is to be delivered to Madame Juliette Guégan at Château de Gressier, Latoire Village – but the instructions are dated September 1942. Do you know anything about it?" he asked.

"Oh," said Juliette, now remembering her conversation with Heinrik about swapping Étienne's motorbike for a tractor.

"It's just the Commandant wants it off the base as soon as possible," said the Officer, trying to prompt Juliette into taking some action.

"Does it work?" she asked.

"I'm afraid I don't know," he answered, "but looking at it, I think it could be made to work."

"Yes, I know about it," acknowledged Juliette, after she had decided it was something she wanted. "I will arrange for it to be collected," she confirmed as for de Gressier Estate to have a working tractor, after so long without one, would be a godsend.

As soon as she put down the phone, Juliette started to cry, for she felt totally helpless and unable to deal with this, the smallest of issues. She missed Étienne, Penrose, and Stephen. None were there to help her, and she wanted their help now. It made her think of Jack Morris and she remembered the moment he walked across the lawn carrying

Victor and Victoria's gold pocket watches given to them by her father as their christening presents.

Juliette climbed the stairs to The Gallery and sat at Etienne's desk. She pulled out the bottom drawer where the watches were kept safe. Only one was there. It was Victoria's. Juliette searched and searched, only finding things which had long been lost. She was certain they had been together and now there was only one. It made no sense for she was certain that anyone stealing would have taken them both. It was as deep a niggle as there could possibly be. Victoria must have taken it with her she concluded, then made a mental note to write to her to ask. She never did.

Chapter 84

Kiev and Butyryka Prison, Moscow
March 1945 to January 1946

THE RUSSIAN PEOPLE have many attributes which make them quite remarkable, but even they would admit that 'organisational capital' was not one of their strong points. This was evidenced by the fact that it took nearly eight months to get Heinrik from the NKVD cells in Kiev to Butyrka Prison in Moscow. It was a simple problem, separate a man from his file and no one has any idea what should happen next. With the change of his guards at Budapest, Heinrik's file was lost and so he entered the timeless world of no-man's-land and his life went into suspension.

In Kiev Heinrik sat, lay, slept, and paced, as he spent his time in solitary confinement killing lice and bed bugs. He had no books to read. No one interviewed him and no one spoke to him. His only interaction was with a guard who, once a day, passed a bowl of watery, hardly warm cabbage soup with a thin slice of black bread, into his cell. From here Heinrik looked into the sky and watched the seasons move from spring, into summer and then autumn.

The only day Heinrik was to remember of that time was 9th May 1945 [58] - Victory Day. His guards celebrated by getting drunk and for the first time they beat him up badly; just for the fun of it. They vented all the anger they felt against Germany for starting the war, and ruining their lives, on this one German man. As he lay on his bed

---

[58] In Russia, Victory Day is on 9th May whereas it is on 8th May in Western Europe and referred to as Victory in Europe Day – VE Day, because the war with Japan was still continuing. This is because the end of operations against Germany, and its allies, was officially set as 23.01 Central Europe Time on 8th May, which was 00.01 on 9th May in Russia

in agony with his lip cut, nose broken, and ribs cracked he thought of his mother. Had she survived he wondered? Where was Victoria? What had happened to her and their child? He thought of Anna and wondered if she'd had her baby. As he lay still, for to move created a shooting pain in his back, he reflected on everything he had seen. It was a dreadful world to bring a child into he concluded, and with that he sunk into a depression which was as painful as his physical agony.

Eventually Heinrik's NKVD file caught up with its man and he was moved to Butyrkia Prison in Moscow. He did not know it then, but he was now caught up in the Russian Penal System. If the prison in Kiev had been bad, the conditions in Butyrkia were terrible. Alongside the Lubyanka, the word Butyrkia struck terror into every single Russian. So bad were the conditions, and so mindlessly cruel the guards, that the prison stairwell had nets across it to prevent suicides.

Day after day Heinrik was beaten through hour after hour of interview about being Hitler's physician. He was, after all, a doctor in the Führer's Flight so he must know about Hitler's health and, most importantly, his whereabouts. It was the arrival of Hans Baur at Butyrkia in November 1945 which probably saved Heinrik from being killed by the guards.

"Was Doctor Hauptman Heinrik Klugman one of Hitler's physicians?" Baur was asked, two or three days after his arrival at the same prison as Heinrik. Baur was also in a very bad way. One of his legs had been amputated and he had been subject to constant punishment beatings as Stalin, convinced that Hitler had escaped and was still alive, wanted to know where he was.

"No, certainly not. Theodor Morell was the Führer's doctor," said Baur emphatically.

"Who's Doctor Hauptman Klugman then? asked Baur's interrogator.

"He was only a pilot, a good one, but he was certainly not a doctor and definitely not the Führer's doctor," Baur volunteered quickly to stop another attack on his body.

"His file says he's a doctor," said the interrogator.

"He only met Hitler once," offered Baur. "No twice," he corrected himself, once in Bordeaux, just before he was appointed to the Fuhrer's Flight, and the other time when he got his iron cross.

"His file says he's a doctor, a surgeon, and there are reports of him doing operations on soldiers and saving their lives.

"Klugman's no more a doctor than me," said Baur. "Look at his age, he joined the Luftwaffe from school."

"But the file says he's a doctor," said the Interrogator.

"Then the file's wrong," insisted Baur.

But in Stalin's Russia nobody was going to argue with what was written in a file.

In January 1946 Heinrik was taken to a building in Moscow to face a trial. He did not know what was happening to him until he appeared in, what was obviously, a court room. He was not being treated as a prisoner of war but as a criminal, charged with crimes against the Soviet people. His trial was swift. He was given no legal representation, but he did have a translator. Heinrik was allowed to speak at which point the court was surprised to find that he could speak Russian, for no German had spoken Russian in their court before.

"Where did you learn your Russian?" asked the presiding Judge

During the war, in Moldova, Romania and Yugoslavia, when I was working with the Russian army as a medic," answered Heinrik

"As a spy more like," said the Judge.

"No," protested Heinrik loudly, but the point had been made and the court moved on.

Heinrik spoke in his defence saying he was no more than a pilot. He pointed out the work he had done for the Russian army since he was captured, but his guilt had already been determined. In a trial which lasted all of fifteen minutes, Heinrik was sentenced to fifteen years in prison. There was one saving grace. He was not categorised by the courts as a Katorga Prisoner. This meant that he would not serve his sentence in the specially designed Langpunkts prisons for the most hardened of war criminals.

Heinrik appealed against his conviction and sentence in writing, but it was quickly confirmed. He was to go to a Gulag [59]; a forced

---

[59] GULAG is the acronym for the Russian translation of 'Chief Administration of Corrective Labour Camps and Colonies.'

labour camp. This was tantamount to a death sentence for a Russian citizen[60]; for a German pilot it wasn't just a death sentence, but a lifetime in hell before death came.

---

[60] It is estimated that 14 million people moved through the Gulag system and nine out of every ten prisoners sent to a Gulag died there.

Chapter 85

Moscow January 1946

IVAN GYSONNOVICH SAT at his desk examining the signature. Although he had never seen the writing before he knew exactly who it was from. It wasn't that the letter had come in an envelope from the Kremlin which was causing him to worry, because he'd had these many times before. It was the signature at the bottom of the page which was causing his anxiety. It was from Stalin, and anyone who has a letter from Stalin has a problem.

Completely ruthless and totally without compassion, Stalin was weak when it came to mothers, not one or two, he would dismiss the petition of these as easily as he would swat a fly. However, when there was a petition signed by a large number of mothers his political antenna told him he needed to find a solution.

The petition to which Stalin had responded by writing to Ivan Gysonnovich, had demanded a doctor be appointed to Department 12 at River Camp Gulag (Special Camp 6) in Vorkuta, colloquially known as Vorkutlag. It was situated over 1,100 miles to the east of Moscow, just north of the Arctic Circle, on the Usa River. A doctor, they petitioned, would have been able to save their son's lives. It was not for their sakes that the mothers said they needed action but for the sakes of other mothers. It was too late for them, but they wanted to make sure that others did not suffer the same agonies of grief.

Known within the Russian penal system, but unknown to Stalin, for if he had known he would have ignored their demands, was that Department 12, within Special Camp 6, about which the mothers had petitioned, was where the NKVD imprisoned sex offenders. The inordinately high death rate, which the mothers had petitioned about, was for one group only, paedophiles.

The death penalty had been abolished in Russia for all crimes, other than treason, years before but, those who ran the penal system and Special Camp 6, had no such compunction in respect of sex offenders and particularly paedophiles who, supposedly, came into their care.

The man looking at Stalin's letter felt the same as all his colleagues. These prisoners were vermin and deserved to be treated as such. In his view the law and justice had failed society and only natural justice would see the matter put right. It was why there was an unwritten rule within the Gulag Administration Office which dictated that, anyone guilty of a sex offence, would end up at Department 12 of Special Camp 6.

On Stalin's orders, Ivan Gysonnovich had to find a doctor amongst the prison population to send to Vorkutlag and quickly. In the room next door to his, clerks were allocating those who had been sentenced by the courts to one of 53 Gulags and 423 Labour Camps throughout Russia. This was in response to a chaotic system where, those charged with delivering Stalin's industrial strategy, demanded more and more forced labour so they could meet their output targets.

Despite each person in the room having the same job, they each organised their work differently which created an ad hoc system with neither methodology nor logic. Gysonnovich walked into the room of clerks and demanded that he be brought the next file of any prisoner who had the magical word of Doctor in the title.

"I saw the file of a doctor yesterday" volunteered a woman whose skin, which had expanded when she was fat, but now hung in layers around her skinny body for the lack of food.. There was enthusiasm in her voice in the hope that this small amount of recognition would take her away from the boredom of her job.

"Get me the file," demanded Gysonnovich.

In an organised office to have found such a file would have been an easy task. However, in an office where everyone does everything without care and slightly differently, finding such a file involved everyone. Eventually it was found by a young handsome man blinded in one eye and with one leg amputated below the knee. He too was looking for preferment, so he held the file tightly, determined not to let anyone else get it before handing it directly to Gysonnovich, who hardly noticed from whom it came.

Gysonnovich read the file of a German doctor pilot who had performed operations on Russian soldiers and saved many lives during the Jassy-Kishinev Offensive. It was the same battle that the man who had handed him the file had lost his foot and eye.

Gysonnovich could not make out if he had qualified as a doctor or not, but it definitely said that the man had trained at Bamberg Hospital and at Nuremburg University. In any case, it said 'Doctor' on the front of the file and the file could not be wrong. But if he wasn't a doctor then so much the better, Gysonnovich was going to do nothing which would help a convicted paedophile.

"Send this man," Gysonnovich paused as he read the name. "Send Doctor Heinrik Klugman to Department 12 of Special Camp 6 straight away," he ordered, before he returned to his desk. He had to write back to Stalin and tell him that he had done as instructed.

Chapter 86

River Camp Gulag (Special Camp 6), Vorkuta February 1946

THE FIRST PRISONERS arrived in Vortuka Corrective Labour Camp in 1931 with nothing more than pickaxes, shovels, and basic carpentry tools. They managed to survive the winter and started to mine coal. By February 1946, when Heinrik marched up the frozen road towards Vorkutlag, as the gulag had become known, it had grown to 17 departments with 132 sub-camps and 62,700 inmates. It was one of the toughest forced labour camps throughout Russia.

The journey to Vortuka was the worst that Heinrik made, with many prisoners dying on the way; their bodies just thrown into the snow as the train travelled along. The train carriages were, once again, closed cattle trucks but this time with much less food, water, or heat and no sanitation. It was a relief to arrive at Vortuka and leave the filthy, vermin infested straw behind and breathe the freezing fresh air.

As Heinrik shuffled, with shackles around his wrists and ankles, through the Vorkutlag guardhouse he felt as fearful a foreboding as he had ever felt. He hobbled through one gate, into a space where he was searched, and then through a second gate, into the camp where he was told to wait. It was a process which was to happen every time he went in or out of the gulag

As befits a prison camp, there was a fence of barbed wire all-around, hung from telegraph poles which looked like rows of crucifixes, as the wooden struts hanging from the crossbars mirrored the arms of Jesus as he hung from the Cross. Fifteen metres outside the main fence, on the far side of no man's land, which was kept raked to look for escapers' footprints, there was another fence. This was lower but again dominated with spread out rolled barbed wire. All around there were high wooden watchtowers and inside the camp there was row upon row of wooden huts, set out exactly as prescribed by law.

As Heinrik stood in a row with other men, waiting to be searched, an Alsatian guard dog barked and snapped at his calves, making the hairs on the back of his neck bristle with fright. Most of the guards were former convicts who'd served their time and stayed in Vorkuta as they had no home to go to. The largest groups of inmates at Vorkutlag were German and Italian prisoners of war who, like Heinrik, had served on the Eastern front. But there was one difference between them and him. They had not been ordered to Vorkutlag by Stalin directly.

"Klugman, Klugman," shouted a voice.

Heinrik raised his hands tentatively.

"Follow me," instructed the voice. Whatever fear Heinrik felt from the dog was now heightened by being separated from the other men. Alone, he felt far more vulnerable.

Still shackled, Heinrik was ordered to the administration block and to the office of the Camp Chief, whose secret loathing of Stalin was as strong as his open loathing of the Germans.

"You've been ordered her by our Vozhd [61] said the Kommandant unable to bring himself to use Stalin's name. "He's ordered you to be attached to Department 12," he continued, looking at Heinrik's file. "Do you know why?"

Heinrik was shocked. How the hell does Stalin know my name he wondered. He didn't answer, something told him it was best to treat it as a rhetorical question.

The Kommandant kept reading. He expected to see that Heinrik was a sex offender, but there was nothing like that on his file.

"What were you charged with?" asked the Kommandant.

"Enemy of the Soviet people," replied Heinrik.

"You speak Russian" said the Commandant surprised.

Heinrik nodded. "A little," he said quietly.

"Only 15 years," commented the Kommandant, adding, "you can't have been a serious enemy," while thinking how easy it was to be one of those in Stalin's USSR.

_____

[61] Leader

The Kommandant looked up at Heinrik and frowned. "Do you know why you been ordered to Department 12? Do you know who they are?" he asked. He then looked at the guard who had brought him in and said: "make sure he sees everything, so he understands; really understands." As the Kommandant shut Heinrik's file he shouted to the guard: "Sentenced 24 hours SHIZO"[62].

---

[62] Acronym for Shtrafnye Izolyatory and means punishment isolation or solitary confinement

Chapter 87

Château de Gressier February 1946

SITTING AT HER writing table, Juliette looked at the envelope and the English stamp and postmark. She felt a degree of nervousness as she opened it as she did not recognise the handwriting. Two French bank notes fell from the sheet of thin airmail paper.

Dear Madame Guégan,
You and a colleague very kindly helped W.O. Stan Jacks and me to escape from France and get back home safely.

I am sorry to say that Stan did not survive the war. He was shot down over Germany in December 1944. He was a remarkable companion during those many weeks of travelling through France, when we were supported by the huge generosity of the French people.

One of the most generous moments was when you unhesitatingly gave Stan and me the little money you had in your purse. We could see in your face the financial burden to you of our whole expedition. We knew that someone, somewhere would be going without as a result of your kindness, and that person would probably be you.

As we waited in that small wood for our next guide, Stan and I resolved that we would do our very best not to spend that money and get it back to you as soon as we could. We saw that money as a token of our freedom, and now France is free it gives me great pleasure to return it to you. The twenty-franc note is the same one you gave me at the moment of our greatest need.

We both owe you, and your colleague, a debt of gratitude which we will never be able to repay. I have no hesitation in speaking for both Stan and me when I say you will always be in our hearts, wherever we are.

> *Yours sincerely,*
> *Donald Lea*

Juliette's tears fell onto the paper, smudging the ink as she tried to wipe it dry. She was stuck to the chair, unable to move, almost paralysed by a tight grip in her stomach, as she remembered those times and thought of Stephen and then of Victoria.

It was mid-morning when she went out to Penrose's[63] caravan. There she found the two airmen's wings which she had carefully hidden in the desk drawer. Returning to her desk, she pasted the letter from Donald into the de Gressier diary which she was now keeping, along with the twenty franc note and just one of the RAF wings. Then, taking very great care to choose her words, she wrote in the diary of her time as a *Passer* and Victoria's exodus to England. As she told herself many times, to have done so before would have been too dangerous.

Every other event of the war had been meticulously recorded, but not these, nor the work she did for the resistance. It was the only time she had broken Magdalena, Étienne's mother's rule of not telling the whole truth to her diary, and now it was time to make amends.

The events of those months crossing La Ligne flowed from her pen until it came to writing about the two nights she had spent with Stephen. How should she explain the passion between the two of them? He, a twenty-four-year-old man, who had never slept with any woman before, and she, who was the same age as his mother.

Juliette thought long and hard about what to write. She found it easy to explain to herself what had happened, but she worried if others would understand. She doubted whether anyone who hadn't shared such an intense experience would ever appreciate the circumstances which took them to the same bed. Stephen and she were living for

---

[63] Penrose Dovingdon changed his name to David Daunier in October 1920 just before leaving France, but it was as Penrose that Juliette always thought of her brother. During World War 1 Penrose had a caravan specially built from which he would command his Balloon Sections. Shortly after the end of the war Juliette retrieved Penrose's caravan from Célieux Ridge and brought it back to Château de Gressier for safe keeping. Read the Book – The Lands of de Gressier.

the day as, only a couple of hours before, they hadn't known if they would have a tomorrow. It was in the celebration of the now that they exhausted themselves in satisfying their most powerful of instincts, lusts.

Juliette decided to write of the intensity of her feelings each time the bedroom door closed, and they were alone. She described the moment when, in their love making, they transcended from being two persons into one. It was the most honest account she could write for Stephen deserved nothing less. Was the reason, she wondered, when they were so close to death, that they instinctively needed to try and make new life? After much thought, she concluded the reason was much simpler. At that moment, they both needed each other, and as she wrote in her diary, '*if you don't understand then you have not been there.*'

As Juliette closed the pages of her diary, emotionally charged after many hours of writing, she fingered the weaving of the remaining RAF badge on her desk. Then, with her hands shaking almost uncontrollably, tears falling down her cheeks, and the occasional sob stopping everything she was doing, she wrote back to Donald Lea.

She thanked him for the money and told of Stephen's execution for being a member of the resistance. She also told how their badges had been slipped into the fingers of her gloves, because she was never going to allow them to be shot as spies. She asked, very graciously, if she could keep one of the badges as a memorial to those moments. She returned the other.

Immediately Juliette had sealed the envelope to Donald Lea, she started to write to Victoria. She knew it might be in vain, for none of her previous letters had been answered, but she had to try. Still she did not know whether she had a grandson or a granddaughter, let alone their name.

Equally importantly, where was Victor's gold watch? It was missing and she couldn't find it anywhere. Did her daughter take it with her, she wondered. She wanted to ask, but it was far too delicate a question to ask in a letter, so once again, no mention was made of the missing watch.

Chapter 88

Punishment Block and Medical Block, Vorkutlag February 1946

THE PUNISHMENT CELLS were situated in their own wired off zone and were contained in the only brick building in the whole Vorkutlag camp. With steel bars at the windows it was as gloomy and foreboding a place as you could possibly imagine. Inside were normal prison cells which sometimes became so full of prisoners they had to take turns in sitting down. A little further away there were separate solitary confinement cells with just a bench. These rooms were so small that it was only possible to stand up or sit, but not lay down. Further along there were another two cells, each about one metre square where it was only possible to stand up.

"Strip," said the guard after he removed Heinrik's shackles. Other than releasing one wrist so he could eat, it was the first time they had come off since he had left Moscow nearly five weeks before.

Slowly Heinrik, undressed removing every item of clothing until he was standing in his bare feet and just his underwear. With three guards manhandling him he was vigorously thrown in to one of the one metre square cells. On the floor in the middle was a round concrete plinth, just the size of his feet below which was a moat ten centimetres deep, which was full of frozen water, urine and faeces, which also lined the walls.

"Don't touch the steel door," was the final shout of the guard as he slammed it behind Heinrik. "It will burn your skin off." Just then the light went out. It was suddenly pitch black.

Above Heinrik, beyond his reach was just one small window with no glass, just iron bars, which allowed the Arctic winter to drive straight through into the cell where he was standing.

No one could survive this, he told himself. I will be dead long before 24 hours is up he thought. He touched the wall cautiously with his finger. It was frozen but his skin didn't stick. He tapped his finger on to the steel door and, just as the guard said, a small part of the skin on his finger got stuck. It had to be yanked away. Heinrik knew that, to lean against the wall, would take his body heat and bring hypothermia and his death sooner. His survival, he concluded, was dependent upon standing still and upright all night unaided.

Within minutes he had no idea how long he had been there, as minutes seemed like hours, and hours a lifetime. He shivered uncontrollably as every part of his body hurt in the cold. Never had he felt like this even in the worse days of his trek through the Ukrainian Steppes. He tried leaning with his back against one wall and his knees against another but the cold penetrated so deeply into his kidneys that he had to stand up. Every now and then Heinrik had to suppress the most appalling panic attacks from claustrophobia as he worried about whether he would be in there for ever.

Heinrik's torpor was broken when the Judas hole in the steel door was opened and he was handed a bowl of lukewarm bean soup and a slice of bread made from unprocessed wheat. The warmth of the bowl relieved the ache in his hands from the cold which, until then, he had just about been able to deal with by placing them between his legs. Heinrik closed his eyes as he downed the salty soup in one go. The bread he ate more slowly and, as he chewed, he felt the first touch of frostbite dig deeply into his toes.

If the punishment had been as instructed, 24 hours, Heinrik would have died in that tiny room and the guards knew it. The last thing they wanted was the inconvenience of a dead body to deal with so time in the Centare Cells was adjusted informally to the time of year and the weather. Heinrik didn't know how long he had been in there when the door was unlocked, and he was instructed to get dressed. He knew he was close to the limit before he fell unconscious. As he put on his socks, he looked at the blackness of his toes which hurt like hell. Frostbite had already taken hold. His greatcoat was returned to him, but his airman's boots were gone; substituted for a pair of Russian boots, notorious for their ability to fall apart.

Heinrik was released from SHIZO just before 6.00am, just in time for the morning roll call. It was the first time he stood in row upon row with other prisoners as their number was counted. A routine which happened every morning before he went to work and every evening when he stopped.

Vortuka had a main hospital in the town for its 'free' citizens. No one from Vorkutlag went there other than the guards. The prisoners had their medical facility within the main administration area inside the camp. It was where Heinrik was marched on his first day.

"This man is to look after Department 12 prisoners," said the guard as he delivered Heinrik to the medical block. "On Stalin's orders," he added on his way out. These two words gave Heinrik a special status, but no one knew what that special status really meant.

As Heinrik arrived there was a queue, over one hundred metres long, of people waiting to see a doctor. He was placed at a small desk and his first patient was ordered in front of him. The man had a very bad gash to his head. He had been unable to get out of the way of the tree he was felling before it hit the ground. Heinrik examined the cut. It was long and deep and every now and then the clot in the wound would break loose and blood would pour down his face. It needed stitching together. Heinrik asked the nearest guard for surgical needle and thread in Russian for these were words he knew. The guard came forward looked at the wound and said simply: "yod."

"Yod?" repeated Heinrik.

"Da yod," said the guard crossly.

The doctor at the next desk handed Heinrik a bottle of iodine, and a used cloth, so he could apply it to the wound. He passed it over with a look which told him not to argue. Heinrik did as he was silently encouraged.

It took Heinrik a little while to understand the process. The queue was of men seeking a bol'naya nota, a sick note, not to go to work.

"Bol'naya Nota," said his next patient after he had sat down. He was an incredibly feeble man struggling to take a breath.

The doctor next to him, who had handed him iodine, now handed Heinrik a stethoscope without warning. Heinrik listened to the man's lungs. They didn't just crackle, they bubbled with the phelm of pneumonia. Heinrik had no idea of the Russian word for Lungenentzündung [64], which he whispered to the man next to him. "Pnevmoniya",[65] the doctor replied, also in a whisper, before adding, "don't ask for medicines we don't have any."

Heinrik picked up the stubbed pencil which had been placed on his desk and wrote the word 'Pnevmoniya' on a small square of paper which had the words Special Camp 6 - Bol'naya Nota crudely printed on the top. Heinrik handed it to the old man who looked at him without any expression, none at all. His fight for life had gone.

As soon as the old man stood up, the guard snatched the sick note from him, tore it into small pieces and threw it on to Heinrik's table. Heinrik seethed in anger but did nothing. There was no reaction from the old man. He would collapse and die on his way to work in the mine where he had worked for the last 12 years.

The queue was halted so that the doctors could, according to the law, have a five-minute break. Heinrik was offered a cigarette but he didn't smoke. In low voices they introduced themselves. In this small group was Dr Horst Rocholl who was captured during the battle for Stalingrad.

"We have it relatively easy here," said Rocholl. "We are the one small glimmer of humanity within this filth of inhumanity." He moved closer to Heinrik: "God only knows how he allowed this lot to win," he said not appreciating the hypocrisy. Although the German extermination camps were well broadcast, Rocholl, like every other German, dismissed the news as Russian propaganda. [66]

"Don't write any sick notes," Heinrik was told. They'll tear up everyone you issue today and perhaps for the next two or three days. You need to gain their confidence."

---

[64] Pneumonia

[65] Pneumonia

[66] Rocholl was released from the Vorkutlag in 1953 and very quickly learned the truth about the Nazi's extermination camps. He felt thoroughly ashamed for his own people. What he couldn't rationalise was the difference between the condemnation by the whole world of all Germans for the brazen act of genocide and why the same was not said about the cynical mass killings by Stalin of his own people; both comprised extermination on a gigantic scale.

"But that man was really very ill. If he's gone to work then he's probably dead by now, argued Heinrik."

"Don't fight the system. If you want to help people, work with it, don't fight it!" said one of the other doctors firmly. "We've all learnt it's for the best."

Those words 'don't fight the system' were to come in to Heinrik's head thousands of times over the remainder of his life.

Heinrik's living quarters were not in Department 12 as he had been told. They were with the others from the medical unit. His colleagues found him a bed and immediately Heinrik curled up into a small foetal ball. He enjoyed the first deep sleep he'd had for days.

Three days later, by candlelight and using a sharpened penknife, his colleagues amputated both Heinrik's big toes and his two smallest toes from his left foot. That one night in SHIZO was enough to ensure that he would never walk without a limp again.

Chapter 89

Punishment Block, Vorkutlag March 1946

"KLUGMAN," CAME A shout from the door of the medical unit as Heinrik was, once more, refusing to give a sick note to a man who clearly needed one. "A Department 12 prisoner has arrived"

Heinrik rose from his seat as the guard, who had yelled his name, snatched the only stethoscope from one of the doctors many desks away.

"Come, let's go," he was ordered.

It was with sheer terror that Heinrik was marched back to the punishment block into a cell where a very ordinary middle-aged man, of ordinary height and build, was standing naked.

"Examine him," said the senior guard immediately he saw Heinrik.

Heinrik did as he was told. He listened to the man's lungs and his heart. He examined the man's eyes and mouth, studied his hands, took his pulse and even checked his reflexes. There was only one thing to note and that was how hard and rapidly the man's heart thumped, but like Heinrik's, it was probably thumping out of sheer terror.

"Department 12 man," said the senior guard. Healthy?" he asked.

"Healthy," replied Heinrik.

"Sign the certificate of health," he was ordered. Heinrik could immediately see it was nothing of the sort. It had already been prepared recording intestine and kidney failure problems. Heinrik said nothing and signed.

"Drink this," said the senior guard as he handed the naked man a pint of water laced with vodka, then a second pint, and a third, a fourth and fifth. Then they handcuffed him behind his back and allowed him to sit down. Slowly, the alcohol was absorbed into the man's blood stream. He began to relax and started to talk to the guards, who responded with unusual banter. Every instinct told Heinrik that this man was being set up but for what, he did not know. Outside of the cell, in the corridor, a set of parallel bars had been brought in with compacted frozen snow deep along its handrails.

Heinrik was ordered to stay in his place while the naked man was walked to the back of the parallel bars. The door of the cell was locked with Heinrik inside. Suddenly six guards, two to each leg and one on each arm, picked up the naked man and spread eagled him, with his arms and legs yanked over each of the parallel bars. Then, using a heavy rope, the man's arms and legs were tied to the frame. Once tied, the man's torso was allowed to fall between the bars as his weight was taken by the ropes. It was then that Heinrik saw something which he never wanted to see again; except that he was to see it another twenty or even more times.

Taking a stick, the same diameter but half the length of a broom handle, the senior guard rammed it as hard as he could into the man's anus, time and time he pushed deliberately tearing his intestines, and puncturing his stomach. He forcefully wriggled the stick from side to side to rip the man's guts into shreds. The man's scream was so dreadful it instantly reminded Heinrik of the attack at the community hall near Parata, for it had the same mix of fear and intensity of pain.

Once the guard was certain of the damage done, another packed his bowel with cloth and paper to stop the blood flowing out of his bottom. Then, in the final acts of brutality, they yanked hard down on his testicles as they wrapped string around the top of his scrotum and tied it tightly to stop blood flow. His penis was next. They tied that very tightly with string too. Given the amount of water this man had drunk, he would need to urinate very soon but, with his penis in a tourniquet, there was no way he was going to be able to relieve his bladder.

The man was untied. He fell to the ground with a thump. "Get dressed, get dressed," yelled the guards to the semi-conscious man. He was hauled up, and with the help of the guards, he was dressed and put back in the cell where Heinrik was sitting. There was no need for handcuffs. This man was going nowhere, except later to the cemetery.

The man had, after some time, become fully conscious again. However, when Heinrik was released to join the pre-curfew parade he was still writhing on the floor choking on his own vomit of bile and blood.

"Paedophile," said one guard after another as Heinrik started to leave. It was the only word they spoke to him.

"Say nothing," said the senior guard and then added menacingly as he pointed to the parallel bars, "or the same will happen to you."

"I'll say nothing," said Heinrik, with panic in his voice.

"What does paedophile mean?" he asked Rocholl as soon as he saw him. "Does it have the same meaning as in German?"

"I think so," he replied. "I am told they kill them here straightaway."

In his head, Heinrik wanted to affirm what he knew, but his lips didn't move; not a sound came out of his mouth.

The next day after parade Heinrik was back in the prison block where his job was to watch over the Department 12 man who looked at him pleadingly as, in his conscious state, he groaned and moved to try and find some way of relieving the pain that consumed his whole body. Eventually the man's world fell into darkness as he became unconscious. It was to take the man 72 hours, after he'd been assaulted, to die. It was then that Heinrik understood. A cursory examination of this man, even naked, would show not a bruise on his body. His death was not the fault of the guards but from internal organ failure; all the same it was murder most foul.

Heinrik was perplexed for weeks by what he had seen. It haunted him as he thought it was possibly the worst death imaginable. Why didn't they just kill him, he wondered. But this was to fail to understand the Russians. The one thing they needed, to compensate for their miserable existence, was revenge. Revenge for the fact that they were here and a long way from their families. Revenge to make sure that, in their absence, their sons and daughters were protected from predators; like the man they had killed.

There was a strange form of justice in the camp. Slowly, over the course of months, and one at a time, those guards known to be involved in the torture of prisoners, and not just Department 12 prisoners, disappeared. It was assumed they had been murdered by one of their too many victims set on revenge. Nevertheless, it didn't stop a new man picking up the baton of torture, because someone had to do it. The discipline of the gulag required it.

Chapter 90

South Africa May 1948

IMMEDIATELY AFTER DESTINY and Newday had runaway from his home, David made some quick decisions. Satutu was to go to school in the morning for which he would pay. In the afternoon, she would be the housemaid responsible for the cleaning and washing. She would get her board and lodging for free and a weekly wage paid to her in cash.

It was a routine which suited them well. Satutu had not been in school before so she found the experience unsettling. Her mother had taught her to read and write well enough such that she was soon in a class of what she, and everyone else, guessed was the same age group. In the afternoon she attended to her chores taking more and more responsibility for the running of the house.

Although it was part of their initial bargain that David would cook for himself and she would wash up afterwards, she quickly took over cooking for the two of them. The first time she cooked for David she served him at the kitchen table where he liked to eat. In fact, there was little choice, for in all the years he had been living in the house, David had yet to buy any dining room furniture. Once David was served, Satutu took her plate to a small table in the scullery. This act of humility on Satutu's part caused David great anxiety. Although this was exactly as he had been brought up as a child, with a very clear distinction between upstairs and downstairs, the first world war years had forced officers and men in the trenches to eat, whatever food was available, together. The trenches were a leveller of men never known in history before. As a result, Satutu was invited to come and eat with him. It was a simple fact that David felt less uncomfortable with her sitting at his table with him; although at the start neither said anything.

Satutu started doing her school homework on the kitchen table, but each time there was a discussion between her and David on an essay to be written, they would end up in the library, and so it was here that she would retire to after she had cleared away the dinner things to study. David would go into his study to work and then later join her in the library where they would both sit and read until bedtime; Satutu with a cup of tea and David with a glass of port.

They both loved this room for if you were to compile a list of the top 100 most influential books of all times most, if not all, could be found there, along with hundreds more. Homer's 'Iliad', Plato's 'Republic', and Machiavelli's 'The Prince' adorned its shelves. It was because of David's memory of Drew, and her interest in the political sciences, that books by Thomas Paine, John Stuart Mills, Adam Smith and 'The Communist Manifesto' by Karl Marx and Friedrich Engels were among the first they read. They struggled with and abandoned the 'General Theory of Relativity' by Albert Einstein and, of course, there were also the complete works of Shakespeare, Chaucer, and Dickens to be studied. Over time they would read them all, neither of them learning how not to be a slave to a book, however painful they were to read.

When Satutu's school days were over, nothing really changed, she just took longer to do the household chores than she did before. In the evening, she read and studied whatever she wanted to. One of the subject matters which had taken her interest was the African American slave trade.

One night, as they sat in the library quietly reading, Satutu asked: "Do you know George Washington had a son called West Ford by a black slave girl called Venus when she was aged fifteen or sixteen?"

David looked up from his book and admitted he didn't.

"Apparently," she continued, "everyone recognised West Ford as George Washington's son, as he regularly picnicked and went to church with him. Uniquely, he was educated with the white children on Washington's plantation and was given his freedom when the President died."

David looked up again and pulled a face but Satutu had no idea what message that expression was supposed to convey.

"Did you know the children of slaves belong to their slave master?" asked Satutu.

"I did. It's where the expression 'born into slavery' comes from," replied David.

The next night, when David joined Satutu in the library, she immediately asked, "Did you know that Thomas Jefferson had seven children with Sally Hemings who was his daughter's black slave girl?"

David shook his head absent-mindedly, for he wasn't really listening.

"She was very young when she had his first child, probably much younger than I was when I came here," she continued.

David frowned, for when Satutu came to live with him she was hardly out of childhood.

"Its real hypocrisy," she added, "because he was against mixed marriages and interbreeding. He was convinced that blacks should not be assimilated into the American nation."

They spoke no more on the subject, but just when they were both ready to turn in Satutu looked up from her book and said, "Did you know President Tyler had two illegitimate children by his slaves and probably many more?"

"Who's President Tyler?" asked David.

"The tenth President of the United States," replied Satutu.

"Ah," said David, non-committedly.

At the bottom of the stairs, as they were climbing up to go to their separate beds, Satutu took David by the arm forcing him to turn and look at her.

"Would that have happened to me?" she asked.

David knew exactly what she was asking, but chose to feign ignorance by asking, "What do you mean?"

"If I had been bought by anyone else but you, and I'd been made pregnant by my slave master, would my children have belonged to him?" There was real anxiety in her voice.

"Possibly," then David paused, "but more likely you would have been sold into prostitution and your children would have been aborted to keep you working." His answer was given factually without any thought as to her feelings.

Satutu stopped halfway up the stairs and looked at him, her face visibly shocked by what he had said. "Seriously?" she asked.

"Yes, seriously, it was a good day for both of us when you came here." At this, David beamed a warm, loving smile at her. Satutu smiled back for David rarely smiled and when he did it was always a sign of approval. This one small gesture lifted her heart, for although she was going to bed a troubled woman, she was certain David meant this to be her home.

The next day David and Satutu travelled into Paarl as Satutu wanted to go to the civic library. Although she had been very many times before, it was obvious that, as a black person, she was not welcome, so she always asked David to accompany her. She wanted to read more about George Washington and Thomas Jefferson and their relationship with slaves. She selected the few books they had on their shelves, which David borrowed under his membership card, as she was not permitted one even though she had been going there regularly for nearly five years.

That afternoon, when her chores had been done, Satutu went into the library, settled down in a chair and started to flick aimlessly through the pages of the book on George Washington which she had borrowed. Her flicking stopped suddenly. Her eyes caught a picture of him sitting upright in bed with his housekeeper, a black woman. Although there was no caption, she studied it carefully. The woman was not naked. She was wearing a nightgown and, most importantly to Satutu, also a night cap. This wasn't a picture of a slave woman ravaged, as Satutu had assumed had happened, but of a man and woman in bed as though they were husband and wife. The hand drawing was very prim and proper for they sat upright, propped up by pillows with bedclothes up their chests. It never occurred to Satutu that the picture was part of the satire of the day, for she had not read all the accompanying words, just those underneath the picture which repeated one of Washington's quotations: "Be courteous to all, but intimate with few, and let those few be well tried before you give them your confidence."

To Satutu this picture showed that if the President of the United States could take a black woman to his bed, then so could David. She started to get uneasy and concerned. She wondered if, perhaps, it was her duty to go to him. Quickly she changed her mind, concluding that since he was the master it was his duty to take her to his bed and not the other way around.

Satutu began to think of marriage and the impossibility of it all, whether she was attractive enough, whether he didn't like the colour of her skin, even if he preferred men. Her mind was a confusion of thoughts and emotions. She could not get out of her mind why he had not taken her to his bed or come to hers.

If she had asked David, his answer would have been simple. When she had come into his house she was, in his eyes, just a child. Over the years she had blossomed into an incredibly attractive young woman: subtle and sexy, with joy and dance. But their relationship had a routine and stability about it which he didn't want to damage in any way. It could be said that he respected her too much. He knew she had the strength of character to rebuff any inappropriate remark or advance he might make, but he didn't want to risk it and embarrass them both. Although he would only ever admit to having a liking and fondness of Satutu, he was quietly in love with her. But for him the deciding factor was that he was 59 and she was forty years younger.

Chapter 91

South Africa May 1948

OVER DINNER THE next day, Satutu studied David like she had never studied him before. Just a few months earlier he had shaved off the moustache, which he had started to grow on the day he joined the army in 1915, saying he disliked the salt and pepper look which the grey hair gave him. As a result, he now looked much younger.

It was the steadiness of David's emotions which Satutu couldn't quite make out. In good times or bad, he had an evenness of temper which she found disconcerting. She could not work out whether that was the real him or whether he was working hard at keeping his emotions in check. Satutu had seen him angry only twice; once when a manager, whom he had trusted, had stolen from him, and another when an older man terrorized a younger one. It resulted in David knocking the bully out cold. David never admitted it, but that was the first time he had hit anyone in anger. Even in his days in the army boxing ring, when he was training for war, he had kept an even temper. Nevertheless, his reputation locally as a tough man was enhanced by the fracas. The fact was that Satutu, like everyone else, knew nothing about this man, except they guessed that, at some stage, he had served as an officer on the Western Front. It was part of his life which, everyone instinctively knew, David didn't want to be reminded about.

When David later joined Satutu in the Library, she was once again staring at the picture of the black woman in bed with George Washington. She had neither looked at nor read anything else since she had brought the book home. She quickly closed it when he came in. Unusually it was Satutu, rather than David, who poured his usual glass of port. Instead of making her usual pot of tea, Satutu excused herself, saying nothing more than she wanted an early night.

Instead of going immediately to bed, she bathed, brushed her hair which she wrapped under a new crocheted white cap and put on the same Victorian nightgown she had arrived in, unworn since that day all those years ago. It was loose then and now it fitted more tightly. She sat on her bed and waited, her ears straining for the sound of David climbing the stairs, but she heard nothing. The hands on the grandfather clock moved slowly. Satutu ventured onto the landing. All the lights downstairs were off. Only the landing nightlight was on. Satutu tiptoed to David's door. The squeaking floorboards made a sound much louder in her head than it was in reality. She put her ear next to the door and stopped breathing as she listened. There was not a sound. Satutu stopped herself knocking on the door as she would have normally done. Instead, she steeled herself, opened the door, and walked through.

David, who was lying on his back, turned his head to the door. Satutu's nakedness beneath her nightshirt was silhouetted against the light from the landing, which dimmed as she closed the door leaving it slightly ajar. There was just enough light for David to see Satutu undo the buttons on her nightgown which she allowed to slip over her shoulders and to the floor.

David said nothing as Satutu slipped between the sheets, he just opened his arm inviting her to slide in and lie on her side next to him. Not a word was spoken between them. Slowly, David started to explore the silkiness of her warm skin and the incredible softness of her hair. He had never felt anything like it before. Satutu's hand wandered over David's chest and his stomach, feeling the strength in his legs and arms, whilst deliberately avoiding his manhood. They each felt strengthened, encouraged, and most importantly comforted by the other's touch.

After a while, Satutu slid to lie on top of David as he wrapped his arms around her. It was David's turn to feel the strength in Satutu as his hands rode over the mountain of her proud tight small buttocks and then fell into the low land of her back and tiny waist. He ran his hands up and down, over and over her bottom, as he thought she was the sexiest thing he had ever touched. They both proceeded carefully, exploring, testing, and making sure that they did nothing which might upset the other, until they were slowly, unenergetically making love. At the end of their coupling, they kissed for the first time.

They made love twice more during the night, each time becoming better lovers, until they both fell into an exhausted sleep.

David woke before Satutu, and as the sun came into his bedroom, he found she was lying on her tummy her arms and legs outstretched. He was able to study her in a way that he had never done before. He loved the way the pinkness of the palms of her hands and soles of her feet blended into the dark mahogany of her skin, which was perfectly smooth with a silky shine and without a blemish. Her hair, released from its crocheted cap during the night, was jet black. Each strand, so fine and yet so densely packed on her head, fell about her in an unruly fashion. It was the softest smoothest thing that David had ever touched. Her bottom was covered with a corner of the sheet giving Satutu some modesty and, as he stared at what was in front of him, he wondered what it was in their genetics that gave African women such very sexy protruding buttocks.

Unable to resist the touch, David allowed his hand to run over Satutu's bottom, moving slowly from the back of her legs over her buttocks to the small of her back and then back again, as he did so she woke and turned over, without opening her eyes, where for the first time he studied the tautness of her breasts.

He moved his hand to stroke her breasts and once again his eyes enjoyed the change of colour of her nipples which became aroused as he caressed them gently with his fingers. She opened her eyes and smiled the happiest of smiles. David smiled back for not only was he happy, but he was looking at the most delicate and beautiful of faces. Long ago he had noticed how, when she stood still, she held her head high and erect, which on her thin eligant neck made her look like a model for some fine porcelain statue, and he was thinking exactly the same now.

David turned Satutu over to lie on her tummy and opening her legs just wide enough, and with the full weight of his body lying on top of her, he took her with all the energy and force which a slave master might have taken his concubine. As he collapsed, nuzzling kisses into Satutu's neck, she felt a deep sense of satisfaction that she had pleased her master, for she was certain that she would never leave his bed again.

The following morning, 27 May 1948, they woke to the news that the Reunited National Party, led by Daniel Malan, had defeated Prime Minister Jan Smuts in the General Election. Apartheid was coming to South Africa. David and Satutu were both stunned. Only two years before, George VI had travelled the whole country thanking the South Africans for their help in fighting World War II. Breaking all taboos, he had shaken the hands of black men and pinned well deserved medals on to their chests.

Chapter 92

South Africa November 1948

SATUTU HAD HEARD the saying 'a little learning is a very dangerous thing' and now she knew it was true. On learning she was pregnant, she had cursed herself for being so stupid, but then when you've been bought and sold as a slave, your views on freedom and life are very different from anyone else's. Although David had assured her she was free to leave at any time, even to the point of having written a contract between them, there always existed a debt of gratitude, an obligation, which in her head, could never be amortize.

Satutu, not for a moment, expected David to marry her. She simply thought that she and her children would live on the farm, just as slave families had in the past. Marriage wasn't even something for which she yearned, for she knew that their different skin colour made it impossible. It was with surprise, delight, and some embarrassment that, on learning she was pregnant, David had insisted she marry him. He knew the Government was working on legislation to make it illegal for most South African citizens to marry or pursue sexual relationships across racial lines. It was legislation which was a total anathema to him.

David wanted Satutu to have a French passport, and be a French citizen, just like him, in case their life as a mixed-race couple became intolerable and they had to flee. He thought the whole process of getting Satutu a French passport might be easier if they married in a former French colony, and so he chose Madagascar, and its capital city Antananarivo, as the place for their nuptials.

The first challenge came in getting a passport for Satutu as, having no birth certificate, she did not officially exist. To make matters worse, it was virtually impossible for a black person to get a South African passport, because the anti-black mood of the new government was permeating every office of state. With the help of a streetwise white lawyer, and a very dodgy and expensive private detective, a form of birth certificate was quickly produced from the Chief of the Mpondo tribe. It gave her mother's first name but in every other detail it was fictitious. She had never heard of the name given as her father nor her place or date of birth. There was only one other truth in the whole document: that Satutu was of Xhosa descent, as evidenced by her first language of Bantu. However, with this false document and lashings of buckshee paid by David's lawyer, a passport was procured.

David and Satutu travelled together by train from Cape Town to Johannesburg, always sitting separately. From there they flew to Antananarivo in a second-hand RAF Dakota converted into a very uncomfortable passenger plane. They found Antananarivo as racist as everywhere else, and even though they had reservations for two rooms, the hotel refused to give Satutu a room. A taxi driver took them to a bed and breakfast, made memorable by its stunning views over the city. No questions were asked, as it looked the kind of place where rooms could be rented by the hour. On arriving in their room, and finding it passably clean, they giggled like two school children on an adventure. After a shared shower they made love silently, as though they were two naughty teenagers, not wanting any problems should they be overheard.

Even though neither of them were Catholic, the next day they found a priest who, with few questions asked and a significant donation to his church, agreed to marry them. Nothing administratively, they discovered, was going to happen fast in Antananarivo, unless aided by buckshee. With the largesse of more US dollars to officials, and another 'gift' to the Church to help bring the power of God into the proceedings, the priest hastily organized a modest, but acceptably sized, vodiondry,[67] in which David thanked Satutu's absent parents for raising such a beautiful daughter. This was followed by the

---

[67] Vodiondry is a gift given by the groom to the bride's family. Vodiondry is a sign of respect and is offered by the groom as a consolation to the parents who are losing their cherished daughter.

shortest of Kabala ceremonies and then, as they shared a dish of rice, milk, and honey from the same black spoon, by local tradition, they became man and wife.

With these formalities completed, they could now register their marriage and get their marriage certificate. However, it was strangely important to David that they made their marriage vows in front of a God. He didn't know whether he believed in God or not but he did know that this was the most solemn act he was ever going to undertake, and so with two nuns acting as their witnesses, Satutu walked up the aisle in a simple long white dress, tailored perfectly to her curves, which she had packed for that moment. She wore the same crocheted white cap that she had worn when David had purchased her in the slave market. As David placed a gold wedding band on the ring finger of her left hand, she kissed the fingers of her right hand and placed them on her cap to acknowledge the good luck she thought it had brought her. Immediately they were declared married, they kissed the tenderest of kisses and David held her hand tightly, as though he never wanted to let it go.

Chapter 93

South Africa November 1948

THERE WAS NO honeymoon as David didn't like being away from his farm for too long. On their return there were several immediate changes. Firstly, he started calling Satutu Mrs. Daunier, making it clear to everyone that she was his wife and could speak on his behalf; although she rarely did. Secondly, there was an unspoken new division of labour with Mrs. Daunier taking full responsibility for the management of the house and the gardens. Finally, there was a change in strategy as events were soon to dictate.

Leon Tinnerman, hearing David was married and back at home, asked to see him. From the phone call it was clearly important. They met at the same tea shop on the waterfront where they had always met over the last 19 years. They had become good friends and talked about everything, except their families. Both being very private people, for quite different reasons, not once had they socialised together.

When David saw Leon he immediately thought he looked unwell. It was as though, in the last year, he had aged ten years and was now looking much older than his true age of fifty-eight.

"What's the matter?" asked David, starting the conversation.

"I want to sell our business," said Leon abruptly.

"Why?" David replied, shocked.

"I need to go home, David." There was pain in his voice as he spoke.

"Where? Moldova?" asked David, knowing that this was where Leon's family originated from before they had moved to Kraków, and he had subsequently come to Cape Town.

"No, Moldova's under Soviet control. They won't want an old Jew like me. They've learnt nothing from the holocaust. I am told that the USSR, or I should say Stalin's Russia, is just as nationalistic and anti-Jewish as they have always been. No, I need to go to Israel," Leon said firmly.

"Why there?"

"To find my family, whatever is left of it."

"Is this wise, Leon?" asked David sympathetically.

"You've been watching the news these last three years?" said Leon rhetorically, with an unusual element of sarcasm seeping into his soft voice.

David nodded.

"I don't think I have any family left," he said. His voice noticeably quivered as he spoke. "No brothers, sisters, cousins, nieces or nephews; all killed, David. The holocaust has not been kind to Polish Jews nor to my family. I think I am the only one left." Leon's eyes filled with water as the guilt of being the only survivor crushed his very being.

"I am so sorry Leon, so very sorry," said David, quietly shaking his head; but what else was there for him to say? Then he added in the hope that it provided some comfort, but it did not: "The war was not kind to the Jews in Bordeaux either. I recently read that, of the six thousand two hundred Jews deported from the city to the concentration camps, only twelve hundred were alive at the end of the war."

"It's the same story everywhere," said Leon, I really didn't know we were hated that much, or why, and I still don't. Someday, I hope someone will be able to explain it to me."

"It is not possible to explain the inexplicable," said David, perhaps a little too sharply.

"Perhaps, but we have a duty to ask ourselves whether we were responsible for creating an attitude of mind which enabled the holocaust to happen." Leon paused to gather his breath. "If we don't ask this question, find an answer, and then respond to it, history will only repeat itself time and time again.

David said nothing but nodded sympathetically.

"There was only forty years between my family being firebombed out of Moldova and all of them being killed. Wherever we have been, we have always been the minority, too easy to attack. I am sure that, by making Israel our Jewish home, we can unite in our homeland where we can be the majority, and this will make us strong. It is another reason why I have to go."

"Leon, I assure you the problem is not of Jewish making," said David, softening his voice in guilt at his earlier tone. "You are all better educated, and you all work hard. You have a strong sense of family and community. As a result, you are brighter and wealthier than most. The sad thing is that these factors make you different, and people are frightened by difference. It is too easy for us to blame our problems on those who are different to us, when the blame for our problems properly lie within us. You can ask the question any way you like Leon, but deep down the answer lies in envy and envy brings distrust. Why make yourself a lesser people to avoid envy."

"But there was never any distrust between us," said Leon.

"No," said David slowly shaking his head. "There was no distrust between us because we are so very much the same." Then he gently added, "If there is anything I can do to help, it is done."

"Please let me go home David, that's all I ask." His voice was soft, almost beyond despair, and there was a mournful pleading in his eyes.

"Of course," said David. It was not a matter for debate.

"I need to ask if you want to buy my share of our business?" said Leon, very directly.

David was stunned into silence. If there was one request he didn't expect, it was this one.

"Isn't your son going to take over the business?" he asked.

"No, we're all going as one family. We're going to build a new life there; where there will be strength in numbers," replied Leon, who now looking forward, was back in control of his voice.

David's mind went into overdrive as he considered the issues: what was the price, how was he going to pay for it, even more importantly, how was he going to manage it?

Leon watched as David's mind whirled. He knew exactly what he was thinking; he didn't want to say no and yet he didn't know how to say yes.

"If you don't want to buy it, I have someone who will," said Leon, in an effort to solve David's conundrum.

"Israel's not a country, is it?" asked David, changing the subject. He genuinely wondered why Leon saw this as going home.

"It is David. It became a state back in May."

"But it's not been recognised by the US, France, or Britain, has it?" asked David.

"The United Nations agreed last November that Palestine would be partitioned into two states."

"Yes, but those boarders haven't been fixed, have they? Most importantly there's the question of the international zone around Jerusalem to be resolved." David was perplexed as he knew the issues were complex.

"Palestine is ours," said Leon, so strongly that it was clear it was not a matter of debate.

"But you're going into a war zone," pleaded David. "The Arab-Israeli War is in full fight."

"I know. It's one of the reasons we're going. I didn't fight last time when we were being killed in our millions. I must fight this time to make sure that never happens again. It's my God given duty."

"Please Leon, isn't this all too risky?" asked David, out of genuine concern.

"No, President Truman declared his support for a Jewish State in Palestine when they voted for it at the UN. You don't think the US will allow Israel to lose, do you? No," said Leon again, this time answering his own question. "The Jewish lobby in the US will attach a huge amount of campaign funding so every President has to promise to make sure Israel is established and kept safe." Leon finished, confident in his prediction.

"But the British are against you, aren't they?" asked David.

"They're against Jerusalem being part of Israel, but that's not negotiable, it's ours, always has been. In any case, the British are irrelevant. They raised our hopes in 1917 with the Balfour Declaration, but only then because they needed our money to fight their war. After the war they kept our land for their own. They're only against it now because they have so many Arab interests, but Britain's bankrupt, so what they think doesn't matter," said Leon, presenting the arguments which were established and well-ordered in his head.

"Do you not feel safe here?" asked David.

"You, a white man married to a black woman, ask that question of a

Jew, when a rabid nationalist party has just been elected here? I think you know the answer."

David again nodded gracefully, recognising that Leon had thought long and hard about what he was doing.

"Leon," said David, then pausing. "I am sorry, but I don't want to buy the business. Not because it's not a good business. It's a great business, but because it's not my business. It's our business, but mainly it's your business, and I don't want it without you. So please feel free to sell it to whom you wish."

"But David, my buyer doesn't want it without you. It's your contacts which get the work."

"No, it's not Leon. You're being kind, but you produce a very good product at a good price. It's why you keep the work; all I've ever done is the paperwork."

"The buyer wants me for six months and you for one year after the sale."

"OK. Yes, I don't mind that, but they'll still buy my fruit. I don't want to work for nothing."

"David, they will pay us both a salary while we work during the handover period."

David nodded.

"What I propose is that we share the sale proceeds fifty-fifty, like we have always done," said Leon.

David quizzed Leon hard as to what was included in the sale price. Unsurprisingly, it included all the assets of both the fish and fruit tinning businesses, including both factories which were owned by Leon.

"Leon, I am sorry, but I can't accept your proposal," said David once he had worked through the detail.

Leon looked at first as though he was going to burst in anger, and then, without warning he deflated into his seat. Not once had they argued, and he didn't want to start now. He hadn't the energy. He thought his proposal was overly generous, and for David to have turned it down really hurt him. David got up, and went to the counter, where he got himself a pen and paper. Sitting down at the table, he wrote the numbers down as he spoke.

"Leon, this is what we are going to do. We take the agreed selling price. From it, we deduct the value of your factory net of any borrowings."

"There are no borrowings," said Leon, defensively.

"Ok, so we take the purchase price, deduct the depreciated cost of your factories, and then we share the balance fifty-fifty. It is not fair to you that I take half the value of the factories which you have paid for. I will not do it!" David was quite emphatic.

Leon smiled. David smiled back, as he saw his partners future life, which had momentarily been knocked from him, reawakened. They both knew it was the fairer deal. The two men shook hands in a prolonged handshake. It was the first time since they had ended their very first negotiations nearly twenty years before. It was an unusual thing for David to do as he did not shake hands with those he thought of as equal rank, but this was different. He knew he was saying goodbye to someone who was an incredibly special person.

That night, David shared what had happened with Satutu, who felt proud of him. She didn't want anything which wasn't truly theirs. David explained what he was going to do with the sale money. He was going to try and buy the two neighbouring farms. More importantly he was no longer going to sell his grapes into the local cooperative. Instead he was going to use the money to produce his own wine, with his own brand name, just as he had seen done at the de Gressier Estate. He was, he told her, going to rename the farm.

"From now on, I would like it to be called 'New Found Estate'," he said. "What do you think?"

Satutu sounded out the words "New Found Wines" several times. "It sounds very English, very modern," she said.

David puzzled at her response as his mind went back to days of the past.

Satutu got up and slowly walked round to sit on David's lap. Her lump was now beginning to show. As they cuddled their shortly to be born baby, they both agreed that New Found Estate wines sounded just perfect.

Chapter 94

South Africa 1949-1950

LIFE CHANGED DRAMATICALLY for both David and Satutu soon after David had agreed with Leon that the canning business would be sold. Their first baby, a son, was born in March 1949. David and Satutu were thrilled, but what should have been a moment of great joy for the community was also one of great anxiety. It was obvious for all to see that the baby was of mixed race and therefore conceived illegally.

David wanted to call his son Étienne Stoddart, or some derivation of those names, in recognition of Étienne Guégan, who had helped save his life, and his father. After much debate, it was agreed that he would be called Joseph Étienne Daunier.

The hours went into days and the days went into months as Satutu did little else but be a mother.

At the age of sixty, David found it hard to settle into fatherhood for the first time. Selling the tinning business was hugely time-consuming, made worse by the demands of the new owners who wanted their pound of flesh for the year after they bought the business. Not only did they want to make sure they kept the existing customers, but they expected him to source new contracts for them, even to the point of demanding he fly to England. He argued vehemently against going, telling them he had not been to England for over thirty years. It was only when he told them that he was a French national, with no position in British society, that the demand on his time by the new business owners abruptly stopped.

The end of selling the tinning business, and David's involvement in it, was marked by Leon making a surprise visit to see David in his home. He had never visited before. He had commissioned a sculpture as a good-bye present. David was immediately embarrassed as he had not thought about a gift for Leon. He became doubly so when Leon unwrapped a solid silver casting, standing about six inches tall and ten inches wide, of two hands shaking. On each silver wrist there was moulded the form of a 21-carat gold wristwatch. Instead of dials or hands, on the face of one watch was the Star of David, with each of its points marked by a large diamond, and on the other was the Cross of Jesus with a diamond at the centre, and at each of the ends of the cross. On side with the the Christian watch face David's name was inscribed and on the side with the Jewish watch face Leon's name was there. Across each of the gold watch straps, were engraved the words: "*A true partnership – where each is more generous to the other for then there is more than one hundred percent to share.*"

"I have one exactly the same," said Leon. "There are only two made, no more because I broke both the original sculpture and the mould."

David sat down and held the object in his hands, slowly stroking it as tears filled his eyes. Leon sat down as, seeing David's emotion, his eyes welled up too.

"Leon, I am so sorry, but I have bought you nothing. I didn't think...." said David, as he wiped his eyes and nose with the back of his hands.

"I should hope not," retorted Leon, firmly. You brought me something all those years ago; you brought this old Jew business."

David nodded.

"You know when you made your counter proposal for the way we shared the sale proceeds?"

David nodded again.

"Well, I decided then and there that I would buy you a present, a special present out of my extra bit. I wanted it to signify what we did. It took me a long time to decide, but I remembered that you, a Christian, and me, a Jew, did it all on just a handshake. Somehow, I think the world could learn a lot from the way you and I did business over all those years."

"It was a very trusting partnership," acknowledged David.

"I trust few people in this life David," said Leon, "but there was something, some instinct, which said I could trust you. Many times in the last few months I have wondered why. I concluded it was the way you paid upfront for the first sample tins of prunes. It was as though you were looking after my interests' right from the start."

"Leon, you will be the first person in South Africa I have ever told this to. I know you will respect my confidence, please," said David, his tone questioning as his voice fell quieter.

Leon nodded.

"I fought on the Western Front in the first war. There you had to trust the man next to you to do his job. Your life depended upon it and his life depended on you."

"Were you an officer?"

"Yes."

"Explains it," said Leon, knowingly.

"Explains what?" asked David.

"I am told that an English officer is trained to look after his horses first, his men second and only then himself. Is this true?"

"It is true, but then I'm French."

Leon looked puzzled at this remark. He knew it was not a lie because he'd seen David's passport, but he also knew it was not the whole truth for David's accent was too British for him to be anything else.

"It's why you paid for the samples. It was the way you were trained," he continued ignoring David's protest at his nationality. "You look after everyone else first, and only then do you look after yourself, but it's a very dangerous way of doing business, isn't it?" asked Leon.

"It was a strange time, Leon. You must remember that an officer fighting in the trenches had a life expectancy of only six to eight weeks. We were leading men who were generally much older than us. We felt under enormous pressure to work much harder than anyone else. All the young officers were always much tougher on themselves than on their men. In this way they led by example. Those officers who treated their men with kindness earned their respect and loyalty. It resulted in some enormous acts of bravery. It is very true; look after your troops and your troops will look after you."

"My grandfather was conscripted to fight in the Russo-Turkish war," said Leon. "I remember him telling me that soldiers don't go into a battle for a cause, they do so because they are ordered. But, once there, the soldier fights for the man to the left and right of him, for his fellow men, as he knows that they will fight for him too."

"We few, we happy few, we band of brothers," interrupted David."

"Shakespeare's Henry V?" asked Leon, standing up.

"Henry V," confirmed David getting up too. It was my father's most favourite saying. It was the way he saw his family."

The two men shook hands for the third and final time. They then did something they had never done before. They embraced each other, holding on longer than they might, for they both knew that they would never see the other again.

Chapter 95

South Africa 1949 - 1950

JUST FIFTEEN MONTHS after Joseph was born, David and Satutu had a daughter. Once again there was anxiety. It was obvious for all to see that the baby was of mixed race and therefore conceived illegally, but David and Satutu didn't care what others thought. To them she was both beautiful and magical. They nicknamed their little daughter Sunetta. It wasn't her real name. She was christened with the names Harriet Harmony, taking the name Harriet from her paternal grandmother and Harmony in recognition of her Xhosa background. Satutu never liked the names. She called her baby Sunshine the moment she was born, as sunny was exactly how she made her feel. It was David, recognising that he was never going to win the naming battle, who started calling her Sunetta, blending the name Sunshine with that of Juliette his sister; although not a word was ever mentioned of his sister's existence.

Although Satutu was much younger than her husband, it was apparent to all that she was the only person who was strangely unafraid of him. As David grew older, he garnered a greater commanding presence and became less tolerant; just as his own father had. Every outsider, looking in on their marriage, would comment on how it was a curious relationship of equals. Satutu's tactics were quite simple; she refused to argue with him. Instead, she would quietly and defiantly walk away, doing precisely what she thought best, for whilst he would occasionally hit out at his children for major misdemeanours, he never touched her in anger. In his own way, David needed her, and this brought their life into balance, each loving and in love with the other, knowing how far each could push the boundary without going too far. Each evening, whatever the tensions of the day, they would walk slowly around the farm, holding hands and saying little.

One of the early additions to the New Found Estate, paid for with the proceeds of selling the tinning business, was a swimming pool. While all the village children swam in the river, it was extremely dangerous. Now, with a son and a daughter who needed to learn to swim, David was able to convince himself, and others who needed convincing, namely Satutu, that it was not the luxury he had always yearned. He argued that the costs would be tax deductible, because when built, it could be classified as a water reservoir for the vineyard's irrigation system. It was a sweetness which caused David to splash out more on it than he otherwise might have done.

The pool he built was enclosed within in a walled garden; a suntrap with a summer house, changing room and patio. It was an enclave of privacy which David had originally treasured for himself. It was also one of the very few places in which apartheid was very subtly practised on the Estate; for Satutu had no desire to sit in the sun, get hot and then cold again. The pleasure completely escaped her. For David, as he swam up and down, it was a place where, for those few minutes, he could be carefree.

Very shortly after the pool had been built, Satutu noticed that it was hardly being used. On one of their evening walks she started to suggest that it should be shared with all those who worked on the Estate. David was adamantly against this. As Satutu questioned his reasoning, she became cross with him as she suspected he was being racially prejudiced. He became angry with her too, for with a black wife, the last thing that he would accept was that he was a racist. He would conveniently describe himself as being a culturalist, arguing that race, colour, or ethnicity had nothing to do with his feelings. He simply chose to mix with like-minded people, but a racist - never!

Once Satutu had an idea in her head she would goad, prod, and even nag until either she got her own way, or he provided her with a suitable explanation. On one of their walks, when Satutu raised the subject again, David exploded in shear exasperation.

"For Christ's sake Satutu," he yelled so loudly that he could easily be overheard. "They don't even wash their backsides. Do you want me swimming in their shit?!"

Satutu was livid. In fact, she was so furious with him she made a point of turning around and walking straight back to the house. There she would not see him. If he came into a room, she would walk out. In the evenings she refused to walk with him around the farm. At bedtime David would go up and Satutu would stay behind busying herself only going to sleep beside him when he was asleep. It wasn't the point he made, for he had made it well. She too had seen their workers defecate in the fields. It wasn't what he had said but the way he had said it. She felt insulted and embarrassed for anyone who might have heard them. Luckily, no-one did.

After three days of having placed David in solitary confinement, Satutu re-joined her husband on his evening walk around the farm, having refused each invitation before. It was, she concluded, time to bring their first serious argument to an end. The night was clear and the heavens sparkled. The heat of the earth meant that the evening was warm. David knew he had been scolded, and thought it unfair. At first, he bristled to have her next to him but, as she took hold of his hand, he was relieved to have her by his side again. On such a romantic night David was not in a mood to fight.

After they had walked arm in arm for about 10 minutes Satutu broke the silence.

"It's my fault too," she consoled him. "I didn't think about it, and I should have done."

"I think we were both wrong," he replied, diplomatically.

The sad fact was that the facilities on the farm for the field workers were non-existent. Satutu laid out her plans. They were to build a dormitory for the temporary workers, a refectory for eating and meeting, and an office so that the business could be taken away from the house and David's study could become just that. Most importantly, they were to provide shower rooms and toilets for the office staff and field hands. They were to put earth closets and water in the fields. Equally as importantly they were going to educate. As Satutu set out her plans to teach the men and women how to wash, David was taken back to his first day as a soldier.

In the army, it was a basic rule that you assumed nothing about the men under your command and you taught them everything. Even as an officer, he had been taught how to wash, shave and care for himself as though he had never had any education in these matters. It was agreed that David would teach the elder men and Satutu the elder women, who in turn would teach the rest.

It was a simple issue, which should have had no effect, but as she talked, David stopped listening for his mind was taking him back to horrendous earlier years. As they walked, and Satutu continued to talk, and as the evening got colder, David began to sweat and shake as his mind went back to times he thought he had left behind. He had an upsetting evening trying to get out of his mind the vision of standing there when, in very slow motion, he was told he was going to be shot.

That night, in their bedroom, David did something which he had never done before. Perhaps, he was later to wonder, it was because he was so agitated with her for bringing up something from his past which could still cause him pain. Whatever the reason, he thought her behaviour had been unacceptable. Suddenly and without warning, he pulled Satutu halfway across his knee. As she leant back in protest, he began to smack her bottom, still covered in the tight white jeans she was wearing; not too hard, but in a way which indicated who was in charge. Satutu wriggled and shouted out for him to stop as the spanking began to sting. Then she went completely silent as she remembered her position. She was a bought slave. She was his to command. When it started to hurt too much she didn't complain. She simply pushed herself up and moved to sit astride his lap where they started to kiss. Their lovemaking that night was long, intense and amorous as their third child was conceived.

As David slept the sleep of the exhausted, Satutu lay awake with a contented glow. If that was what love making was like after an argument, then perhaps they should argue more often, she thought. She also worried about the conflict which she now found within her. While she wanted to be an equal with David, there was something strangely comforting when he was being masterful and controlling; but it was also the tingling sensation which excited her. She wanted him to do it again. When he was holding her tight, with his warmth deep inside her, she delighted in being his supplicant, and yet she wanted to be treated as though they were one and the same. Why was it so confusing, she wondered?

As these thoughts went through her mind, she realised that, although he was much stronger than her and on occasions his lovemaking could be quite rough as he physically controlled her body, she never felt afraid. She was happy for David to be in charge. He made her feel safe, and the safest she ever felt was when she was in his arms; protected under his body with thoughts only about how good he was making her feel.

The task of teaching the female farmworkers how to wash was a giggle and a laugh for Satutu and all the elder women of the village. It was nature's way of helping them overcome the embarrassment they felt at showing their naked bodies. With the elder men of the village there was no community aspect. David gave his lessons in washing just as he had seen it done in the army. With them, the nightmares which had started days before, became more vivid and frightening. His dreams each night became the same. Running along a road, but only moving forward slowly as his feet felt so heavy, his boots clogged in mud. He would see the man in front of him shot and, as the man behind, he waited for his turn to be shot too; but the bullet never came. Instead, he would suddenly find himself under a pile of rubble, not being able to move, struggling, and fighting desperately to get out.

The power of David's nightmares would wake Satutu the moment they started. She would watch and get most anxious as he screamed out, perspiration oozing from every pore, soaking his hair and body. She would try to wake him, but he never responded. His mind was so gripped by the moment that he felt none of her prodding and shaking. Slowly, Satutu noticed that with each nightmare David started to become less confident and withdrawn. Neither David nor Satutu had heard anything of World War I shellshock, but as David told Satutu of his nightmares she learnt, for the first time, something of his life before South Africa.

David's response to his need for sleep without nightmares was to work on Satutu's building project with the same zealousness he had applied when he first came to South Africa. It was all finished just before their third child was born, a son they called Sidney Joseph Daunier. David chose his son's first name in recognition of the efforts made by Sidney Caprang during his Court Martial. For some inexplicable reason, Satutu nicknamed him Little Joe and naturally his elder brother became known as Big Joe.

Changes were also made to the swimming pool which was opened for use by all the estate workers. To comply with apartheid legislation, a formal timetable was instituted with swimming times depending upon ethnicity, white, black, or coloured. Under the apartheid laws David was classified as white, Satutu as black, and Big Joe, Sunetta, and Little Joe were coloured. It would have meant that David's family could not have swum together had it not been for the benefit of David and Satutu's marriage certificate. South Africa's racial categories caused practical problems for white Europeans, and so the law also designated the wife and children of a white man as honorary whites. As the wife and children of a Frenchman, Satutu, Big Joe, Sunetta and Little Joe were thus classified as honorary whites. It meant that, for four hours every day, David and his family had his precious swimming pool to themselves.

Chapter 96

Jerusalem February 1950

ON HIS THIRD day in Jerusalem, Leon Tinnerman, born the illegitimate son of Count Sacha Donici-Solokov and formerly known as Leon Tinicheaski, visited the Church of the Holy Sepulchre. He had to find the letters his father had ordered him, and his brothers and sisters, to write.

Leon carried with him a jam-jar with a tight glass and metal lid. For some inexplicable reason it had, at that moment, to be there with him. It had the name Donici-Solokov Glass and the year 1903 moulded on the outside. Inside there were three rouble coins of the Russian Empire, some smooth round stones and, placed around the edge, a series of sticks. It had been filled with soil gathered from the Donici-Solokov fields in Moldova. It was Leon's most precious object in the world. In monetary terms it was worthless. In emotional terms it was priceless.

Like everyone of Sacha Donici-Solokov's children, Leon would remember every single thing about the day the Count's two families met for the first and last time at the Community Hall near Parata,[68] in Moldova. It was 1st June 1903. The next day he, together with his maternal grandfather, his mother and all her children, would leave Moldova. They had been attacked, and their house and forge burned down in the Kishinev Pogrom only months before. They were fleeing to Kraków.

"You will write two letters which will be exactly the same,"

---

[68] Community Hall near Parata where the two wings of Count Sacha's family meet for the first time, is the same hall where, 41 years later, Mayanna (Anna) Solokov, Brigita Solokov's daughter, was rescued by Heinrik Klugman from an attack by Russian soldiers

instructed Leon's father to his gathered children. He went on: "You will send them to two Muslim families living in Jerusalem. You do not know them. I do not know them, and they do not know you. Their names are Joudeh and Nuseibeh. For over four hundred years these two Muslim families have held the key and unlocked the door to the Church of the Holy Sepulchre there. I choose them for two reasons. Firstly, it is the holiest site in Christianity but secondly, because of the Lord's covenant with Abraham. He told him to lead his people, the Jewish people, to the Promised Land where they were to build a great nation. Jerusalem is in the heart of that Promised Land. You will write, give your name, say you are a member of the great Donici-Solokov family and report on where you are, how you are and your status on this day every year. In these changing times, when the future has never been less certain, it is through two Muslim families, controlling a church for Christians, on lands promised to the Jews that we, the Donici-Solokov family, will have a way of keeping in touch. Whatever fortune brings us, this way we can always be sure that we can be there for each other."

After some confusion, Leon was able to track down the letters written by the count's children. They were in three large ring binder files with the words Donici-Solokov written on the outside. Each file was overflowing with letters, many duplicated as Leon's father had instructed.

Taking a seat offered to him at a table, Leon went to the back of the very first file. There was something satisfying about seeing twelve letters, and their duplicates, all dated 1st June 1904 and written as his father had instructed, precisely one year earlier. Leon shook his head as there was something very prescient about his father's orders. How did he know what was going to happen?

There was a letter from Aliza Tinicheaski, Leon's mother, and letters from each of his two brothers and two sisters. They all had Sacha as their father. There was a letter from Sacha's wife, Karina, and from each of his three half-brothers and two half-sisters. As Leon reflected, it was the most peculiar family arrangement and yet, at the time, it didn't seem odd at all.

The most recent file, number three, had the latest letter on top. It was from Leon, dated 1st June 1949. The next letter was his of the year before, and the next the year before that too, and so on. Leon started turning the pages, with urgency in his touch, until he came to June 1941. There were five letters from that year. One from him from Cape Town, and four from his brothers and sisters from the Podgórze District of Kraków.

He kept going back through the file. There was nothing after June 1932 from Karina, his father's legal wife and her five children. They had all stayed behind in Moldova when Leon and his family had been forced out by the Kishinev pogroms. Their last letters had a common theme. They all reported their hunger and the lack of food in the shops. Did they all die of starvation? he wondered.

With his heart in a panic, Leon started to turn the pages backwards and forwards, backwards and forwards, swapping between pages time and time again, not reading, just searching for what was not there. With each turn of a page he felt the void in his heart get bigger and bigger until he felt it might explode.

It was then that Leon saw it; a small card, yellowed with age and dirt, on which he recognised, Sophia, his eldest sister's small neat writing. On one side was the address of the Church of the Holy Sepulchre with a stamp and a date mark of December 1946. On the other was written:

10th July 1942 Podgórze,   District, Kraków

My Dear Brothers and Sisters. We have been given two hours to pack our things. We are being forcibly moved once again. Although only half of us were chosen, we have swapped with another family, so we are all going together to a work camp. Our hope is that the conditions there will be much better than here, where they are far less than adequate. We know nothing of Leon since he last wrote from Cape Town three years ago, when he was well. We send our affection and trust you are all well too. I will write to let you know where we are when we arrive there.

Jacob, Eva, Pavel, and Sophia.

Instinct and logic had already told Leon that his brothers and sisters had been killed in the holocaust but seeing Sophia's few words telling of them going to a work camp, confirmed his worst fears.

Something which had happened to others suddenly became very real and personal. Gradually, a mixture of emotions, anger, fear, despair, and guilt caused tears to well up in Leon's eyes. These soon yielded to sobs of uncontrollable crying. He felt so very, very lonely.

Leon looked for letters from his father. There were none. At first, he was surprised, and then he was not. After all, his father had abandoned them on the day his mother, his brothers and sisters and he had left Kishinev to go to Kraków.

It was just forty-seven years ago and yet from the files it was now clear that, of the thirteen people who had sat around the table on that 1st June 1903 date, everyone was dead apart from him.[69] He was the only survivor and he felt guilt and thankfulness in equal measure.

Leon thought more about the day he met his father's lawful wife and his half-brothers and sisters by her for the first time. The meeting was so tense at first, but ended up being good fun, with everyone so incredibly happy.

He remembered more of his father's words of that day and, in his head, he could hear his father's voice saying: *"Each of you is from my body, you are my family and this means that, forever more, you have a duty, a most solemn and sacred duty to look after each and every brother or sister. You are not a Christian or Jew first for I make no such distinction. Foremost you are from the line of Donici-Solokov, a line which prioritises it's belief in human love."* What a sensible philosophy thought Leon, prioritise human love. If others had done that, he would not now be sitting there alone.

Leon left the files open and walked out of the church's office into a

---

[69] Leon's father, Count Sacha Donici-Solokov, was also Brigita's grandfather, but neither Leon nor Brigita knew of the other's existence. Leon's half-brother, Simion Donici Solokov and his wife Anna were killed in 1919 during the Russian revolution. Simion and Anna were survived only by their eldest daughter Brigita Solokov, who was born in 1909. Of all of Count Sacha Donici-Solokov's ten children, by his legal and common law wives, only Leon was alive in 1950, and of his 7 grandchildren, only Brigita has survived to this date.

bright blue sky. There was a chill in the air which he found refreshing as it released him from the claustrophobic pressure which the news in the three files had created within him.

Deliberately, and in defiance of the teachings of the many Rabbis who had taught him, he walked into the Church of the Holy Sepulchre. He was taken by its breath-taking beauty of gold, silver, and lights. Leon sat in a pew and stared up at the ceiling for a long time. None of it made any sense to him. How could a God do all this harm and create all this hurt while making such a beautiful world?

Leon suddenly needed to pray. He realised he had never prayed for the souls of his mother and father, his brothers, and sisters before. Until a few moments ago he had lived in the hope they were still alive.

Leon blinked as he made his way out into the sunlight and walked the 500 metres to the Western Wall. There he placed his hand on the limestone and, as he did so, he felt his God bathe his whole body in peace.

Chapter 97

Hertfordshire June 1953

IT WAS COLONEL Dovingdon who insisted that Henry Bellanger should visit his grandmother during the summer holidays. He had been passionate about having his children, Juliette and Penrose, learn French fluently, and he was no less passionate about his great-grandson doing the same thing. It was the language of the diplomat, he would say.

It was Jack Morris, a long-standing friend of Juliette's, who would take Henry to stay at Château de Gressier at the start of the school summer holidays and bring him back at the end. There was something romantically sweet about the way Jack and Juliette would walk out together, around the vineyards, the farm, and the village hand-in-hand or arm-in-arm.

For years, Jack had struggled financially, but the need for Britain to build houses after the war suited his skills and temperament perfectly. In a world still desperately short of building materials, he had managed to become an independently wealthy housing developer. At last, he had the confidence to walk and talk alongside Juliette on equal terms, and Juliette felt so much more comfortable in her relationship with him as a result.

It was a phone call from Victoria to Henry, whilst he was staying at Château de Gressier, which eventually brought Juliette back to her childhood home. For a long time, Col. Dovingdon had been suffering from prostate cancer, but there was no telling whether he was going to die with it or from it. As it turned out it was the latter. Very suddenly his health deteriorated and, within a few weeks of announcing to his doctor he was in pain, it was obvious he was dying and did not have many days to live.

It was Victoria who was adamant that Henry should return home to see 'Bear', as he called his great-grandfather, and it was Henry who was even more resolute that Juliette should return with him. It was almost 35 years since Juliette had left England for the last time, and just over 11 years since she had said good-bye to her pregnant daughter. She had seen neither her father nor her daughter in all that time, and so it was therefore not surprising that her return to Imptice House, her childhood home, was coupled with some considerable anxiety.

Victoria was uncomfortably polite, but not gushing, when she opened the door to Juliette on her arrival. There was no embrace or cuddle as might have been expected between mother and daughter after so long; just between Victoria and her son, so pleased was she to have him home. It was obvious from her demeanour that Victoria remained angry and resentful. Whatever the rights and wrongs of the argument, as far as Victoria was concerned, she and her son had been abandoned by her mother in their hour of need, and that was unforgivable.

Juliette found it very strange walking back through the front door of the house in which she had grown from a baby to a woman who went to war. It was almost exactly as she had left it. The pictures on the walls, the ornaments, even the rugs on the floor had not changed. Victoria now had Juliette's bedroom and Henry had Penrose's; these were unrecognisable from Juliette's youth. As Juliette was shown to the guest room, she noticed one thing which was obviously different. The house was much quieter; for all the staff who had worked there in her youth, doing the daily chores, had all gone. It was a sign of the changing times.

Henry could not wait to see his Grandfather for these two had an incredibly strong, if sometimes fiery, bond. Although obviously frail, the determination of the old man to show his strength to his great-grandson meant any worries Henry might have had that the Colonel would not be there for him tomorrow were quickly abated.

Once Juliette had washed, and changed into a new set of clothes, the three of them gathered around the Colonel's bed. He acknowledged Juliette's presence by very slowly reaching out to her and smiling. She took his hand and gently wept. There was no immediate apology given or received by either of them. They were both too stubborn for that.

Juliette suddenly knew that, whilst he had been totally wrong, she had been damnably stupid to keep the feud up for so long, and the tears in her eyes told him she was sorry. After a little while, when it seemed to Juliette that they had never been apart, she leaned over and kissed him on the cheek. "Sorry Papa," she whispered in his ear. The Colonel's mouth moved as though in speech but no sound came out. His head and eyes were saying he was sorry too. It didn't have to be said, as he gently squeezed her hand. It was all she needed to receive, and with this, more silent tears fell from both their eyes.

As the Colonel peacefully drifted in and out of consciousness, Juliette sat and talked to her father about her mother and Penrose, remembering the good times they all had together, as Victoria and Henry quietly listened on. It was as though a whole dam of family history was being released.

In response to his question, Juliette told the Colonel how, with new identity papers, Penrose had walked out of Château de Gressier leaving everything behind, never to be seen or heard of again.

"I know he changed his name to David, Papa," she said, "but for the life of me, I can't remember what surname he chose. I only know it was not Downing but it was something like it. If I could, believe me, I'd go and look for him," she said. "He has to know that the army has reviewed his case and admitted that the decision of the Court Martial was flawed," she lied. "He was a hero, Papa," she said, "an unfairly treated hero!" What's wrong with telling half-a-lie, she thought. She was only telling her father what he needed to know in his dying hours.

The Colonel smiled without opening his eyes. It was the one thing he had been concerned about all his life, the good reputation of his family's name. It had driven him, perhaps more than anything else. It was why, for over thirty years, he had been virtually a recluse; welcoming people to see him, but rarely going out. The thought that anyone might speak badly about the Dovingdon name was one he preferred to avoid.

"The Dovingdon name ...," whispered the Colonel.

"Yes, Papa, it's safe. It's as good as it ever was." Juliette paused, as she wondered whether she should tell him. "You know, the one thing Penrose took when he left de Gressier?" she said, eventually.

The Colonel shook his head weakly.

"Your officer's cane."

The Colonel slowly opened his eyes wide. He needed to look into his daughter's face to know it was true.

"It meant a lot to him," she said, reassuringly.

The Colonel turned away from her, burying the side of his face into his pillow and he squeezed his eyes tight. His heart was breaking at the thought of his son treasuring something of his which was so worthless and yet so precious.

If there was one surprise for Juliette, it was to do with Victoria and the way she looked after the old man. There was a love, expressing itself in the tenderest and gentlest of actions as she nursed him. There was not a request she did not immediately attend to, nor a thought had by him, which she had not anticipated. It made Juliette immensely proud of the woman her daughter had become. She was a nurse too, a natural nurse.

Chapter 98

Hertfordshire June 1953

THE DAY FOLLOWING the Colonel and Juliette's rapprochement was highly auspicious. Ever since he had heard Princess Elizabeth speak on the radio from Cape Town on her twenty-first birthday, and as the Colonel would say: "make one of the best declarations ever made by a future monarch," [70] he had become a huge fan. Despite his frailty, the Colonel was determined to watch her being crowned Queen Elizabeth II on a huge television set with its tiny black and white screen. It had been installed in his bedroom specifically for the event.

On coronation day, with Juliette, Victoria, Henry, and his housekeeper by the Colonel's side, and with Jack and some of his family gathered around on chairs and his floor, this happy clan watched the crowning of their Queen on what was to be remembered as a magical day. It created such a positive mood throughout the land that it could be said that it was the day post war austerity came to an end in Britain.

Victoria confidently expected the Colonel to continue in his near-death state during the three hours of the television broadcast, but

---

[70] On 21 April 1947, Princess Elizabeth's twenty-first birthday, she was with her parents and younger sister on a tour of South Africa. In a speech broadcast on the radio, the Princess dedicated her life to the service of the Commonwealth. She said: "I declare before you all that my whole life, whether it be long or short, shall be devoted to your service and the service of our great imperial family to which we all belong. But I shall not have strength to carry out this resolution alone unless you join in it with me, as I now invite you to do. I know that your support will be unfailingly given. God help me to make good my vow, and God bless all of you who are willing to share in it."

the old campaigner, refusing to take his medication so he could stay awake, was having nothing of it. He studied every moment as though it was his last. After the service was over, the Colonel insisted on champagne being served to toast the Queen's health and her reign. Under the influence of the bubbles, he became proudly animated about the magnificence of the ceremony. "The best in the world," he exclaimed. "Nobody does it better."

Early the next morning, with Victoria sitting by his side, while the rest of the house slept, the Colonel took his last breath and slowly slipped away. It was as though, seeing the success of the Queen's coronation, Colonel Sir Stoddart Dovingdon could finally accept that the baton had been safely passed to a new generation. It was no longer his race to run. He missed his ninety-third birthday by just a few days.

The Colonel's Will was simple. He made ample provision for his housekeeper. He left Imptice House, with all its contents, to Victoria. The rest of his estate, which included Found House, his London home, he left to Henry to be held in trust until he was aged 25. This made his great-grandson an exceptionally wealthy young man.

The Colonel's funeral was a quiet, but sensitive affair, for most of his friends were dead and his business contacts had drifted away. Victoria painstakingly chose music and readings she knew he would have liked.

"It's time for you to come home," said Juliette to Victoria, as they walked alone back to Imptice House after the wake. To Victoria's relief, Henry had gone to a friend's house to play. It was a good distraction for an eleven-year old boy.

"Come and live at de Gressier," implored Juliette, as they strolled along. "There's the Cottage there already for you," she added, by way of encouragement.

"Our home is here, not in France," replied Victoria, firmly. "Henry starts his new school in September. I'm sorry, but things can't be changed now. I think we're going to move to Hertford so we are much nearer to his new school. I don't want him boarding and if we live there he won't have to."

"You're not going to stay here in Imptice House?" asked Juliette, surprised.

"No. I think I'm going to sell it, and buy somewhere in a village, more modern, easier to maintain. In any case, there's a new deputy head position starting at the beginning of January at a school in Hertford which I think is mine if I want it.

"Are you a teacher?" asked Juliette surprised. "In what?" she enquired, as she saw Victoria nod her head.

"Modern languages, French and German."

Juliette puckered her lips as she realised how much she didn't know about her daughter's life. She had been here for just over a week and they still hadn't talked properly.

"It makes so much sense to move," said Victoria, deliberately ignoring her mother's expression. As she said these words, Victoria made up her mind; that was exactly what she was going to do. The second chapter of her life had ended with the Colonel's death. She was about to start on a new third chapter.

They walked on in silence.

"Did you ever hear anything from ... ?" asked Victoria.

"No," answered Juliette promptly, instinctively knowing that she was thinking of Henry's father.

"He promised to come back to me. Did you know that?" said Victoria, with disappointment in her voice. "I always thought he would just turn up one day and say hello. In some ways I still do."

"Does he know about....?" Juliette asked.

"I wrote to tell him but...." There was no need to finish the sentence.

"What does Henry know?"

"His father was shot, that's all. What's said at de Gressier?" asked Victoria. "Does his surname not cause a problem?"

"No one knows it. When he's with me he's known as Henry Guégan that's all."

"Henry accepts this?"

"Yes, why not?" said Juliette puzzled, "after all, its his second to last name."

"I'll come home," Victoria paused, "back to France, back to de Gressier when I'm dead, so I can be with Victor. I need to be buried with him," she said earnestly. "Do you know, I have never felt truly whole since he died? I miss him every day, even today." She paused.

"Sometimes it hurts so much that I think, if I didn't have Henry, I'd give it all up."

Juliette took only half a pace in shock, as her daughter's message was frighteningly clear.

"The Colonel would have loved Victor," continued Victoria, a little wistfully. "I cannot tell you how well he got on with Henry."

"Did everyone call him 'Colonel'?" asked Juliette, deliberately changing the subject. Ever since Victor's drowning, she had a policy of never speaking about her son, and she wasn't going to change it now.

"It's what I've always called him, and so did everyone else. Henry always called him 'Bear.' It was a derivative from grand-père when he was learning to speak," Victoria explained.

"They all called him that when I lived here," reflected Juliette. "You know that name says everything. He was such a big man in our lives. Somehow you had to be just as big to deal with him; or fade into failure. It's what happened to my mother, she faded. She never had the strength needed to keep up. Me, I learnt to fight, and I've kept on fighting."

"It was your fight which kept you two apart, said Victoria, as they arrived at the front door of Imptice House. "Somehow I don't think it was worth it. Do you?"

Chapter 99

Hertfordshire June 1953

THERE WAS AN eerie emptiness in Imptice House as Juliette and Victoria walked back through its front door after the funeral. The grandfather clock in the hall had stopped and with that the heartbeat of the house had stopped too.

Juliette went upstairs to change and came down a few minutes later to find Victoria seated quietly in the Orangery, doing nothing but staring out of the window, a tray of tea and biscuits by her side. She was finding it strange that the house, in which she had always felt a guest, a lodger, was now her home.

Immediately Juliette saw Victoria, she handed over a package wrapped in brown paper and sealed with sticky tape. "This is yours," she said. "I think you should keep it. He would like you to have it."

Instinctively, Victoria knew what it was. It was the gold pocket watch that the Colonel had given her when she was born.

Juliette said nothing as she watched her daughter undo the wrapping, open the case, and look at the watch face. The time still showed ten minutes to two o'clock. The exact time set on the watch by the watchmaker all those years ago for it had never been wound. Victoria took the watch carefully out of its case and once again she was magnetically attracted to the strangely smooth, tactile feel of its glass and metal.

"Thank you," said Victoria looking up at her mother, smiling. "It's a good day to have it back, thank you."

"I can't find Victor's watch anywhere," said Juliette, almost as an aside. "I've searched the house high and low. Sometimes, I think I might have put it in his coffin, so he was buried with it, and other times I'm sure I didn't."

Victoria looked at her mother, scared, for she had never told her what she had done with Victor's watch.

"We had so much stolen in the war," Juliette continued quietly. "It makes me think it went with one of them; one of the Germans. But it's strange that only one watch was taken, just Victor's and not yours, particularly when they were always kept together."

Victoria listened to her mother's musings. She wasn't testing Victoria at all. From the way she spoke it was obvious that Juliette had no idea what she had done.

Victoria watched Juliette pour herself a cup of lukewarm tea from the pot, as she wondered what to do.

"I gave it to Heinrik," said Victoria, very matter-of-factly. "I gave it to him, no, I lent it to him so he'd come back to me."

Juliette said nothing. She looked at her daughter dumbfounded. There was total bewilderment in her eyes which said she needed an explanation, and fast.

"Victor didn't need it and I so wanted Heinrik to have it. I needed him to have it so he would come back to me. He promised he would," she pleaded. "I know he will when he can. I'm sure of it."

Juliette's mouth fell open and she raised her eyebrows in disbelief. She was about to speak in protest when she remembered the Eicher tractor, and the deal she had done with Heinrik over Étienne's motorbike when he had kept his word.

"There were so many of them captured by the Russians and taken as prisoners of war. I read everything there is about it. They say three million men," said Victoria.

"I thought most had been released."

"Yes, but a lot had to go to East Germany. They were needed for the reconstruction work, so many have not made it back to the West. Believe me, I'm an expert on this," said Victoria beginning to feel stronger in her defence.

"So Henry's father has got Victor's watch," said Juliette sternly.

Victoria nodded weakly.

"So you find Henry's father, and you find your brother's watch."

Victoria nodded again

"You find Victor's watch and you find Henry's father."

Victoria nodded for the third time.

"Well I think you know what you've got to do," said Juliette, calmly but very firmly. It was not a question. It was an unstated instruction.

There was silence and then Juliette started to speak again, more softly and in a more considered tone. "There's an old CS Lewis saying," she said. "You know, the man who wrote Narnia. He said: You can't go back and change the beginning. But you can start where you are and change the ending."

Victoria smiled at her mother for the message was clear.

That night, as Victoria lay in her bed, she looked at the face of the watch the Colonel had given her. The diamonds were sparkling in the faint light, and with the hands still set at ten minutes to two, she realised it was smiling at her. She wondered whether Victor's watch had been wound or if it was smiling too. Where on earth was it? How the hell was she going to find it? It was out there somewhere, and it had to come home to her. It just had to! All she had to do was make it happen.

Restlessly, Victoria rose from her bed and looked out of the window. There was a full moon, low in the sky. Was Heinrik looking at the moon, she wondered. Then she remembered the words of the poem the Colonel had taught her. They would always recite it on those special occasions when they stood together, looked at the moon, and thought of Juliette.

When the moon is high
and its beam shines bright.
Then think of me, for
I will think of you.

Chapter 100

Kishinev 30th March 1958

SUNDAY 30TH MARCH 1958 was Heidi Solokov's 13th birthday. Gathered around her, as she blew out the candles on her cake, were her mother Anna, her grandmother Brigita and Ruslan Baback. Not a thought was given by any of them to Heinrik Klugman, Heidi's father.

Anna returned to Kishinev in March 1945. She was tired, weary, and very pregnant, but nevertheless delighted to be back in the city she loved, although it had been completely destroyed.

Anna first went to the Woodman's Hut to find her mother, but she wasn't there. She started to panic, wondering whether Brigita might be dead. They were eventually reunited in the streets of Kishinev, still strewn with rubble from the bomb and shell damage. It was immediately obvious to Brigita she was going to be a grandmother.

"Heinrik's?" she asked, as the two cuddled tightly. They shook with relief at finding each other.

"Yes," said Anna as uncontrollable tears of joy poured down her cheeks.

"Where is he?" asked Brigita.

"I don't know, a prisoner of war somewhere."

"Oh," said Brigita. "I liked him. Well, ... for a German ... I liked him."

It was the last word that mother and daughter would ever have on the German pilot who shared their lives in the summer of 1944 at the Woodman's Hut.

As Brigita walked with Anna to take her to the one room she called home, Brigita was constantly acknowledged by the people she passed. She had become something of a local celebrity. Unknown to Anna at the time, but in response to her being taken into forced labour to work at the German boot factory near Parata, Brigita had joined the partisans. She was a fearless member of a group which was committed to harrying the German supply line wherever it was. She would help destroy their route ways and to blow up their convoys of lorries and supply trains. Brigita quickly discovered she had a particular skill; she was a marksman. From different strategic points, and well hidden, she would kill just one soldier, and then stay rock still for hours until it was safe to make her escape. It made the whole of the German occupation army nervous and slow to go about their work.

The problem with marksman killings was that the price through retribution was high; for every German soldier the partisan's killed the Germans killed between twenty and fifty Moldovan citizens depending on the rank of the soldier shot. It was why Brigita changed tactics. She became a temptress using her sexuality to encourage her German victims into a lair where she would kill them in a variety of ways in cold blood. She subsequently made sure the soldiers' bodies were never found. This way their absence was recorded as a desertion, which created the same problems with German morale, but had the advantage of bringing no reprisal killings on the very people Brigita was seeking to defend.

Brigita's war time activities, including those at the Woodman's Hut, meant that after the relief of Kishinev, and because of the needs of the Communist Party's public relations machinery, she had become a legend in her own lifetime. It had the disadvantage that many of the heroic stories ascribed to her were untrue. However, there were distinct advantages which accrued to Brigita as a result of her celebrity status. First she and Anna were amongst the first to be rehoused and so it was, in a two-room apartment, that Anna's daughter, Heidi was born. The second was that, in another major famine which Moldova suffered in 1946, Brigita was, once again, able to feed her daughter and granddaughter. In part this was thanks to the small quantity of crops she had been able to harvest in the fields of the Woodman's Hut. Unknown to Brigita or Heidi, they were a classic example of what George Orwell had written: "we are all equal, but some are more equal than others."[71]

---

[71] Animal Farm, published immediately after the end of the war, was George Orwell's commentary of the Communist system.

Brigita's local status was further enhanced when, after the war and he had been discharged from the medical corps, Lt. Col. Ruslan Baback came to find her. Ruslan's wife and only daughter had been killed in the Stalin purges long before the war had started. Baback's whole family had been of the intellectual class so feared by Stalin. Baback had only been released from his own cruel and punishing captivity, when the war started because his medical skills were needed. Baback's only son had been killed in the battle of Kursk in August 1943. It meant he had no one in the world.

Brigita was incredibly surprised when Ruslan Baback turned up. Although they had worked all day together in the Woodman's Hut not an atom of romance had ever been shared between them. However, from the moment he left to take his medical unit into Kishinev he was determined to come back and be with her for there was no woman he admired more. In Brigita, Ruslan had found a kinship which he had not found with anyone since his wife died. Why did Brigita not see this? She had built such a hard shell around her that she was impervious to the emotion that any man showed towards her.

It was on a day when Brigita was being totally impossible and had exploded in one of her renowned rages that, very silently, Ruslan took control. He squeezed Brigita's arms, thrust them into her side and lifted her off the ground to physically place her in a chair. In that moment everything changed in their relationship. Ruslan had held her in exactly the same way that her grandfather had lifted her out of the bushes after the fire at Valikey House in which she had seen her mother, brother and baby sister burn to their deaths. For the first time since Sasha Donici-Solokov had died Brigita felt safe. Her outer shell melted, and the downturn of her lips started to slowly rise again so that her natural look became a smile.

On the day of Heidi's birthday, Brigita held a senior job in the Communist Party. Ruslan had a senior surgical position in the Kishinev hospital and Anna had a job working as an administrator on rebuilding the city's hot water factory and distribution system which had been so badly destroyed.

That night, cocooned in the safety of their apartment with the curtains closed and their room transformed from a sitting room into a bedroom, Anna went to the bottom drawer of her wardrobe and lifted out a wooden box.

"I think this is something you should see," she said to Heidi as she reached inside. "I thought I would save it for your sixteenth birthday, but I think it's something we could share today. I have a letter for you." Anna paused and looked into Heidi's eyes to make sure she had her attention. "Its from your father," she said.

Anna reached into the wooden box and took out Victor's watch, still in its velvet case which was still in its cardboard sleeve. Carefully she opened the velvet box and then took out the letter which Heinrik had written to his unborn child. Very carefully Anna unfolded the letter and passed it to Heidi who started to read.

"I can't make out all the words," said Heidi after she had studied the letter for a little while

"It is written in a mixture of Russian and German. I have a translation," said Anna. She handed another page to her daughter.

"So my father was German," said Heidi as she got halfway down the page. There was no surprise in her voice. "Why didn't you say?" she asked

"You didn't need the burden," said Anna. "To be a child of a German, a child of the enemy, it was not a good thing to be."

"It's still not good, is it?" said Heidi, as the Cold War, which now existed between East and West, was a feature of everyday news.

"No, but it's less bad than it was," said Anna encouragingly, before adding, "still, we need to keep it to ourselves."

"Does Babushka[72] know?" asked Heidi.

Anna nodded.

"And Uncle Ruslan?" Heidi asked as she turned to the letter again. She read quietly until she got to the end.

"My name, Heidi," she said. You named me after him; Heinrik, Heidi. I never knew."

"Do you mind? asked Anna.

Heidi paused for a moment and thought. "No, I like the name," she said. "It's different."

---

[72] Grandmother

Anna took Victor's watch out of its case and handed it to Heidi.

"Your father gave this to me for safekeeping," she said. "He said it belonged to his best friend. I imagine his name was Victor as that is the name engraved on the back. I understand there's another one identical with the name Victoria on it."

Heidi stroked the gold pocket watch carefully. She felt its smoothness and looked carefully at the diamonds which twinkled on the watch face. She ran her fingers over the Dovingdon crest engraved on the back. She closed her eyes and, as tears started to develop, she squeezed them tight. The emotion of holding something her father had touched was overwhelming.

Heidi returned to the letter and started to study the translation which Anna had given her.

"Here, in his letter he says I was born out of love. Was that true?" asked Heidi, as she choked in her tears.

Anna held her daughter tight and cried too. "Oh yes," she said firmly. "When he gave me the watch, he said he would come back and collect it. I think it was his way of proving he would come back to me, to us."

"But he never did," said Heidi.

"No," said Anna quietly, with regret in her voice.

"What happened to him, Mama? asked Heidi.

"I don't know. Sent to some Gulag somewhere." Anna paused. He probably died there, many did."

"What was he like?"

Anna paused again as she thought. "He was a very nice man. Not handsome but quite good looking. He always stood upright, very tall, just like you. There was something very strange about him which gave him an appeal. He denied ever having trained as a doctor, but he had the skill of knowing exactly what to do in an operation as though he had been a surgeon all his life."

Anna took back the watch from Heidi. She needed to hold it just has she had done many times in the last thirteen years.

"I stood opposite him as he did his very first operation to amputate a man's leg. He did it perfectly, as though he had done it a thousand times before .... Do you know what was nice about it?"

"No," said Heidi as she looked carefully at her mother's face, which in turn was studying the watch.

"He needed me." Anna didn't look up. Her faced looked down at the watch which was resting on her lap. "I was only seventeen. He was twenty-three," she continued. "At each of those moments, when he was about to operate, he would look into my face and silently seek my consent. I would smile and nod back, only then would he start. Not once, not twice but every time." The memory was all too much, causing Anna to burst into sobs. "He needed me. He really, really needed me," she cried realising once again that she bore the pain of a broken heart.

As Anna and Heidi were packing away Victor's watch, in the other room Brigita was stroking a jam-jar with the name Donici-Solokov moulded into the glass. It was filled with exactly the same mix of wood, stones, soil, and coins as the jam-jar valued so highly by Leon Tinnerman. Like him, it was her only possession from her grandfather's time. The Donici part of her surname, formerly used by Anna and her, had been dropped as they reluctantly accepted the obvious, the russification of Moldova and the obliteration of Romania from its history.

As she did every Sunday evening, Brigita thought of her huge family; now all gone. Why was she the only one chosen to survive, she would ask herself. It made no sense to her. She would think back to Pechea House and Valikey House, both belonging to her grandfather and destroyed in the revolution. Then there was the bridge her family had built across the Dniester River, and the steam engine, both blown up and destroyed, first in the revolution and then the war. The loss of their farmlands, and the shortages of food which followed, as those who did not know how to farm took control of the farms. It was the fact that Stalin's days were well and truly over that gave Brigita hope.

Had it all been worth it she would ask herself. Was it better back then she wondered. For very many, it was probably not. Was it better now for everyone, certainly not. Could a better future for Moldova be built? She was certain of it. In memory of her mother, father, and grandparents, she would make it so, but most of all she would make sure it was better for Anna and Heidi's sake. It was these thoughts which gave her a renewed sense of destiny, of purpose which would drive her through the week ahead.

Above all, Brigita wanted a free Moldova. A country independent of Russia or Romania or Turkey, just as her Grandfather had wanted but she knew it couldn't come, not yet. One day it would; she was sure of it, and when that time came, she would be the first to hoist the Moldovan flag and fly it high above their parliament building.

Chapter 101

Vorkutlag to Plauen, East Germany
January 1957 - July 1958

HEINRIK KLUGMAN'S LIFE in Vorkutlag continued with unending monotony. He froze in winter and boiled in summer, when he was eaten alive by the mosquitoes and flies. The only time his routine changed was when there was a flurry of activity because someone was trapped. A man or woman caught in a mine fall, a rail truck accident or a tree collapsing on its feller and an amputation was needed to free them. Long ago Heinrik's colleagues recognised that he was the most experienced in this kind of work and sent him. It was true, he gave the victim the best hope for survival. But it was also out of his colleagues' desire for their self-preservation that they volunteered him because the scene of most accidents was highly dangerous.

By the spring of 1953, Heinrik's teeth had fallen out, his skin was permanently festered with sores, his eyesight was failing, and his legs were beginning to swell. These were all the signs that he was slowly starving to death. Another year, and if nothing changed, Heinrik would have gone insane with hunger after which he would have died.

The death of Stalin in March 1953 changed the mood in Vorkutlag significantly. The sense of hopelessness was replaced with a hint of optimism that there might soon be change. However, it was the arrest of Lavrentiy Beria, head of the NKVD under Stalin, in June 1953, which was to bring the most immediate change as 18,000 camp workers went on strike. It was a bloodless battle until, on 1st August 1953, Vorkutlag Camp Chief Derevyanko ordered his guards to fire directly into the peaceful mob of striking workers; sixty-six were killed and 135 wounded, many of whom were deprived of medical attention. The strike was over, but it shocked the authorities and slowly conditions started to improve with food rations increased. Heinrik was reprieved from his death sentence by starvation, but only just.

When Dr Rocholl, his fellow German medic, was released, and sent home to West Germany, in 1953, Heinrik's mental disposition was adversely affected, and badly so. The one person he could identify with, was friends with, was gone. Then, in October 1955, when Heinrik heard that Baur and all the German General prisoners of war, held at the Woikova Camp, had been released, he fell into a deep depression. He could not understand why he had been ignored. He feared never getting home.

The next big change came in February 1956 when, in a secret speech, Nikita Khrushchev [73], criticised Stalin and listed his crimes. It was the beginning of the end of the Gulag regime. The ruthlessness and cruelty in the camps immediately lightened.

In January 1957, exactly eleven years after he was sentenced to fifteen years in prison, Heinrik was marched, without any warning, to the gates of Vorkutlag and released. He was a free man. He had 5,000 grams of bread in his hand, 500 grams for each of the ten days he was expected to travel. He was given a new set of second-hand clothes. He possessed 10 roubles as the rest of the money he had carefully accumulated in the camp was confiscated during a thorough exit search. He was given no train ticket. Nevertheless, he had a permit to go to the German Democratic Republic (East Germany).[74]

As Heinrik stood outside the gates of Vorkutlag there was no euphoria, no exhilaration, no joy, no happiness, or sense of uplift. He was bewildered and completely and utterly exhausted. No man or woman could go through the gulag system without their perspective on life being changed for ever, and Heinrik was no different.

He just wanted to go home. It was eighteen years since he left Bamberg and he had only seen his mother once in all that time – at the parade ceremony at which he became a pilot officer. He didn't even know if she was alive. His only wish was to sit in his old garden and watch the water in the stream rush by.

---

[73] First Secretary of the Communist Party of the Soviet Union,

[74] The final German prisoners of war were released a year later in 1958

Heinrik could not remember how, in the spring of 1957, he got to Plauen. He knew exactly why he had chosen to go there. He had been told that he could catch a train there which would take him to Hoff, and from there he could cross the border into the Federal Republic of Germany (West Germany). Once in Hoff, Heinrik knew he could easily make it to Bamberg and home.

The things Heinrik remembered about his journey were the long tedious train rides, and even longer walks; not easy for a man hobbling because of amputated toes. He also knew he only survived because of the soup kitchens in every town and the generosity of the Russian people. When he spoke Russian, he no longer spoke it with a German accent and, because of that, the word Vorkutlag was a passport to kindness.

In Plauen, Heinrik learnt, for the first time, of a special border built by East Germany in 1952 to stop its citizens leaving to work in the more prosperous West Germany. He also found that, if he was to get back to his hometown of Bamberg, he needed an exit visa and, in a country full of '*hemorrhagic citizens* [75]', it was virtually impossible to get a permit.

To get from Vorkuta to Plauen, Heinrik had travelled over 5,400 km and Bamberg was only 135 km further on. His destination was so close physically, but as far as East German bureaucracy was concerned, it could have been the end of the world. He was not going home without a West German sponsor. He didn't have one of those and with no response to his letters from his mother, or her lover Herr Schmidt, or anyone else at Bamberg Hospital who might have known him, and been able to help, he was stuck.

Heinrik enquired about getting a visa to go to France to be with Victoria but that was even more difficult than getting a visa to Bamberg. The price the authorities charged for an exit visa to go to a country like France, the United Kingdom or the United States was prohibitively expensive. He thought he had no chance of raising that kind of money. If only Victoria had known she would have gladly paid the fee very many times over, but she did not.

---

[75] The name given to those who were seeking to travel from East to West after the iron curtain had been erected.

Heinrik thought of going to Kishinev to be with Anna hoping that, as it was also part of the USSR, he could more easily get a travel permit, but that was denied too. Like Vorkutlag, Heinrik was once again in a place he didn't want to be.

Very quickly Heinrik found work, washing up in the kitchens of Plauen's hospital, but he could find nowhere to sleep. Week after week, when he finished work and at weekends, he carried his few possessions aimlessly around the town until he found a place to doss down, in the hope that he would not be disturbed by the occupying Russian Red Army or the GDR police. The saving grace of working in the hospital kitchen was that he was fed every day, and with surreptitious use of the hospital bathrooms, he was able to keep himself clean.

Every week Heinrik talked to the council officials about getting his own apartment but a scruffy single old looking man was low down in their priorities. Eventually, he was found a bed in a single room in a hostel. It was sheer luxury when compared to Vorkutlag but he was only allowed to use it between 7pm at night and 7am in the morning, irrespective of the weather. The mention of being a Luftwaffe pilot and winner of the Iron Cross carried no favours; in fact, it made things worse. Those were the old days. They were not the present. No one in Plauen wanted to be reminded of the war they had lost.

One early summer Sunday morning, desperate in his loneliness, Heinrik took the bus out of Plauen and travelled north-east to see Göltzschtalbrücke. He had been told it was the largest brick railway viaduct anywhere in the world with a reputation as a place where people committed suicide. He went because he intended to jump and take his own life too. He felt so very depressed. He could no longer bear to look back on what had happened to him and, with the feeling of ill-health which permanently racked his body, he was certain he had no future; just a lifetime of further pain to look forward to. It had all gone so desperately wrong. What was the point of it all he wondered?

As he climbed the hill, which took him seventy-eight metres to the top, Heinrik noticed how the views became more and more impressive. The world was a truly beautiful place he thought. It was just the people in it who were so horrible. Keep away from people, find and visit the beauty spots of the world and life might be worth living, he decided.

As he climbed down, Heinrik did not feel a sense of failure in not taking his own life, as others who contemplate suicide often feel when they don't complete their mission. Instead, he felt pleased with himself. He had given himself a reason to live. Every weekend, whatever the weather he would go in search of the local beauty spots. These trips brought him a solace he found nowhere else.

In July 1958 Heinrik was evicted from his hostel. He had done nothing wrong. He had been there a year, the maximum time permissible, and he had found no other accommodation which he was required to have done. This was because there was no accommodation to be had if Heinrik were to have a room to himself. In Plauen, every single man was expected to share, and after Vorkutlag, Heinrik could not contemplate the thought of sharing a room with anyone again. He would prefer to sleep outside than have someone, whom he did not trust and could never trust, sleep next to him.

On the last Sunday in July, late in the evening, and after carrying his bags all day, Heinrik settled down close to some trees by the grassy banks of the White Elster River. He was 37 years old and looked twice that age. He watched the river flow by. He thought of the stream flowing at the bottom of his garden home near Bamberg. Once again, Heinrik realised he had nothing to live for. He tried to read his book, but it was too much effort. He needed to die he thought, as he laid down to rest. The ground and air were still warm from the summer sun. He closed his eyes, relaxed, and fell asleep. He was never to wake up again. His sub-conscious had granted him his wish. To the authorities of Plauen another bag man with no name had just died.

Amongst Heinrik's modest possessions were two letters. They had been written months before but never posted. They were to Victoria and Anna. They were virtually identical, save for their names at the start. These letters told his story from his arrest as a Prisoner of War, where he was now and how he could not get home. Why they weren't posted no one knew, because Heinrik had written religiously to his mother in Bamberg every month from the day of his release without receiving a single reply.

The letters were read several times by the municipal official whose job it was to deal with the affairs of those who died without a known family. He read the exact same words of love in each of Heinrik's two letters. He had used identical phrases to describe his yearning to see each of them, and their child. They gave him something to live for during his worst days in Vorkutlag, he wrote.

From the style of the handwriting and the words on the page the official tried to work out who Heinrik Klugman had been. He was obviously well educated; he could tell that. But were his propositions of love real, he asked himself, almost too cynically. Two women, two children, two countries, no one has a life like that, except perhaps in war time.

The letters remained on the official's desk for several days as he wondered what to do. It was the addresses on the envelope which crystallised his thinking. The letter to Anna Solokov in Kishinev was posted. After all, Moldova was part of the USSR and an ally. The letter to Victoria Guégan was placed in Heinrik Klugman's file where it was to remain until reopened nearly half a century later. After all, France was an enemy, and it would be far too risky for the official to post a letter to a person in an enemy state, for the Stasi[76] had their eyes and ears everywhere.

---

[76] East Germany's secret police

Chapter 102

Imptice House, Hertfordshire July 1958

ALL THAT WAS left of the great man's life was one pathetic, but lovingly hand-painted lead soldier given to Colonel Sir Stoddart Dovingdon by Henry. Every other of his possessions, including the rest of his toy soldier collection, had been dissipated on the winds, just as a dandelion sheds it seeds.

Victoria knew she had to move on and leave Imptice House, but it had taken her much longer than she liked to find a place she wanted to call home. Eventually she chose a brand new four bedroomed house at the end of a cul-de-sac on a small estate in a beautiful village just outside Hertford. It was far too large for her and Henry's needs but, having spent her childhood and youth at Château de Gressier, and latterly in the spacious surroundings of Imptice House, Victoria could not contemplate living anywhere smaller. Nevertheless, the move meant downsizing by giant proportions.

On her return to Château de Gressier, Juliette had taken a few possessions, mainly pictures, photographs and small items which reminded her of her mother, but otherwise Imptice House had remained unchanged from the day the Colonel had died until a few days ago when the furniture, paintings, silver, and porcelain, everything which made Imptice House grand, other than that which Victoria prized, had gone to auction, and with them went a lifetime of memories.

In two generations, the old campaigner would be completely forgotten. The Colonel, once a colossus in Henry Bellanger's life, now seemed as though he had never been: transient, irrelevant – his very being now represented by the toy soldier which Henry had given him for his eighty-fifth birthday and which he now held preciously in his hand.

Henry didn't want to leave Imptice House. It had been the only home he had known. It was different for his mother. Victoria had always felt as though she was a lodger there, trapped by her circumstances. Firstly, with the Colonel looking after her and Henry, and then with her looking after him, they became co-dependents in a changing world. Now she felt free, ready to move on. It was time for Victoria and Henry to say their final goodbye.

Mother and son toured their old home. As they did so they knew that this was their past and their future lay elsewhere. There was only one thing left to do before they closed the door for the last time. It was to empty the safe. Its contents were few. There were some exquisite pieces of jewellery which had belonged to Lady Primrose, Victoria's grandmother, whom she had never met. They were too old-fashioned to be worn but contained some outstanding gemstones which, one day, she intended to re-fashion into something more modern which she would wear.

Nestled deep inside the safe was probably one of the lesser valuable items in monetary terms, but to Victoria it was, other than her son, the most precious thing in her life. She reached inside and took out a cardboard box covering a velvet green case which she handed carefully to Henry before putting her hand back inside the safe to take out the other jewellery boxes.

"It was given to me by Bear," said Victoria, referring to the Colonel by the nickname given to him by Henry when he was just learning to talk. "It was a christening present." Then, in a quietened voice, she added, "It's one of a pair."

Henry took the box, removed the green case, and opened the lid. For the first time he looked upon a full hunter 18 carat gold pocket watch with each hour marked with a large sparkling diamond. The back was beautifully and very delicately engraved with the Dovingdon family crest and below that the name 'Victoria'.

Henry took the watch out of its case. Like the few people who had touched it before him, he caressed the gold and glass object for it was smooth and tactile, warm and gentle, inviting to touch. There was one other thing about it which impressed Henry that no one else, other than his great-grandfather, had noticed. It was very slim, and this made it an item of outstanding skill and great beauty.

Henry looked at the watch face and noticed it had stopped. Automatically, and without thinking, he moved the bevels of the winder between his fingers and for the first time in thirty-three years the watch began to tick. Time had stopped standing still.

"Where's the other one?" asked Henry, innocently as he set the correct time.

"The other one's engraved Victor," answered Victoria. "It was given away during the war to ..." Victoria paused. Should she say she wondered. Instead, she continued: "a very special member of our family, on the promise that one day it would be returned."

Oh, Uncle Ba-Ba, the black sheep of the family, thought Henry, assuming his mother was talking about her estranged Uncle Penrose.

Victoria put her arms around her son. "I'm sure it will come home one day because ....", but her words petered out for, once again, in the emotion of the moment, she found that she could not tell Henry the truth. It was her secret and it would have to remain just hers for a little while longer.

Thank you for reading The Vines of de Gressier. I do hope you enjoyed it.

If you liked this book, it would be helpful if you would post a positive review on Amazon at www.amazon.com

If you would like to know more about the lives of Juliette Guégan, David Daunier and Victoria and Henry Bellanger then this is told in the next book,

The Soul of de Gressier.

If you would like to know when other two books in the de Gressier series will be published, then please follow us on social media at:

Facebook Page: @DeGressier

Twitter: @deGressier

Website: www.de.gressier.com

About the Author

Charles Bunker was an international corporate financier and entrepreneurial businessman before retiring to become an essayist, pamphlet writer and author. He uses his experiences in business and politics, his interest in history and international affairs, and his observation of people as the bedrock of his writing. Widely travelled, Charles is the proprietor of the famous Orchard Tea Rooms in Grantchester renowned for its connection with Rupert Brooke, Virginia Woolf, E.M Forster and many other literary, philosophical and scientific talents over the last 120 years.

Printed in Great Britain
by Amazon